The Reluctant Wizard

Volume One of the Lokins Legacy Series

by

Robert Wilkins

ISBN-13: 978-1-944662-84-4

Cover Design by Diana Henderson

Dedication

This is for my wife, Debra, without whose patience, support, encouragement, and ability to get my butt into action, this book would not be possible.

Acknowledgements

I would like to thank Bernie Ashman whose belief in this manuscript and continued encouragement were instrumental in bringing this book to fruition. I would also like to thank my editor, Diana Henderson, who took my unruly words and wrestled them into what you are about to read. Finally, I extend my gratitude to Realization Press and to Drew Becker whose expert and inspired work we now hold in our hands.

Table of Contents

Chapter One

J ake was riding high after receiving his acceptance letter into the agricultural program at NC State University. This was the next step in his plan to return this land to a working farm. It seemed appropriate that he should plant his garden today.

By the afternoon, he was feeling the effects of both the sun and the hard work. The rows had been furrowed, the seeds dropped, and the seedlings from his hot house transplanted. Now he walked each row with a five-gallon bucket of water and a dipper, making sure that each seed and seedling received its initial watering. Sweat rolled from under his hat into his eyes and soaked his clothes. Without thinking, he wiped his forearm across his face, making it worse. As he struggled to clear his eyes, Jake thought he detected movement in the distance. When he could see again, he looked toward the road. Through the heat waves rising from the gravel, he saw an old man walking. He thought that unusual as there were only three farms on this road. Besides, nobody came to visit on a weekday. Jake continued to watch the man with his peripheral vision as he watered. He turned to finish the last row, his back to the road. The tractor waited at the end of the row. Climbing into the seat, he looked back to the road but didn't see anyone. He started the tractor and drove it and the trailer back to the barn.

He was pleased with himself as he walked toward the house. A crow flew over and voiced a loud call. Jake followed the crow's flight, tracking him until he disappeared beyond a stand of trees. When his line of sight returned to ground level, Jake spotted the man standing at the farther end of the garden. He wore bib overalls and a worn brown fedora. His hat was pulled down so that most of his face was in shadow. The old man gave a nod but said nothing.

"Afternoon," Jake said, returning the man's gesture. "Can I help you with something?"

The old man turned, walked to the porch, took a chair, and began to rock.

Jake felt his ire rise. He was hot, tired, and in no mood to be disrespected. "Look here, Mister..."

The stranger raised his head and turned his eyes to Jake. Two milky orbs replaced his pupils, but he still looked directly into Jake's face. His vacant stare created an emotion Jake could not fully identify. The blind man brought one hand up to scratch his whiskered chin. When he removed his hat, thick white hair fell below his shoulders. A bead of sweat crawled down Jake's neck. A closer look revealed that the man and his clothes were completely dry although he had walked in the heat and humidity.

"Are you Jake Lokins, the son of Lonnie Lokins Jr. and grandson of Lonnie Sr.?"

"I'm Jake Lokins and Lonnie was my daddy and grandaddy's name, but I don't know much about them. They both passed away before I was old enough to know them."

"Uh huh," the man said with a grunt. "My name's Randolph Meekins and I knew them both. They told me to come to you when it was time."

Jake heard the crow again and turned to see him perched on the barn. Jake almost smiled. He had never heard of Randolph Meekins, but he thought he knew the sound of a con man when he heard one.

"My daddy and grandaddy told you to come see me? I don't see how that could be true since neither of them got to know me before they died. Maybe you should be moving along, Mr. Meekins."

Nothing changed in the old man's countenance. "Your daddy and Lonnie Senior might be dead, or they might not. We served together and they couldn't get back...."

That statement got Jake's attention. Not even the best con man would try to pull that one. Before Jake could reply, Meekins continued.

"Now it's your turn to serve. That's why I'm here. It's time you learned the truth."

Jake tried to hold on to his anger, but it was being replaced by bewilderment. "I don't know what you're talking about, but I don't like what I'm hearing."

Meekins stood and walked past Jake. Without turning around, he said, "Your mama's coming. I'll be back tomorrow, and we'll get started."

Jake watched as the old man walked down the dirt path. He was as surefooted as anyone with two functioning eyes. Jake heard a vehicle turn off the main road and his mother's car appeared. She slowed and stopped the car beside Randolph Meekins. They talked for a few minutes before she accelerated, throwing a cloud of dust that seemed to hang suspended for several moments in the humid air. When she came to a stop, Jake looked up and the old man was gone. His mother looked like she had seen a ghost. She put her head against the steering wheel and started to cry.

Chapter Two

"**M**ama, what's wrong?   What did that old man say to you?"

Without replying, she got out of the car and went inside. Again, Jake heard the crow. When he turned, his eyes fell on the garden. How could a day that started out with so much promise turn bad so fast? Without spotting the crow, Jake we inside.

By the time he stepped into the living room, his mother had gone into her bedroom and closed the door. He stood in the middle of the room, immobilized. His emotions moved from feelings of doubt and anger to frustration and bewilderment. His mother was the type of person who always remained positive. She took any challenge in stride. Through the years he watched as she faced one situation after another. Nothing broke her spirit. Jake did not consider himself a violent person, but if he could have gotten his hands on Randolph Meekins, he would make him pay for his mother's suffering.

Dinnertime came and passed. Jake made himself a sandwich. Now he really knew that something was wrong. His mother always insisted that they have dinner together unless something important should interfere. Nothing was ever deemed that vital when they were home together. Not knowing what to do, he did nothing.

₨   ⁃

Nan felt foolish. She had known this day would come. She had chosen to raise Jake like a normal child. Keeping the family history a secret seemed the prudent thing to do, but now she second-guessed herself. She looked around the room and wondered what the future would hold for both Jake and her. Would he be able to handle what was ahead?

Walking into the bathroom, she looked in the mirror. She dabbed her eyes with a cloth, hoping the red would disappear. Of course, he would handle it, she thought. He was his father's son.

Next, she went to her closet. She closed her eyes, whispered the words, and ran her hand along the left wall. A compartment appeared. Reaching inside, she found what she was looking for. Another pass of her hand and the wall was solid. She took a few deep breaths to calm herself.

"Time to face the music," she said.

ဆာ ဆ

At 7:00 p.m., she opened the bedroom door and came out. She was carrying a book Jake had never seen. She took a seat on the couch and opened it.

"Come sit with me, son. I've got some things to show you."

Jake wanted to question her but decided against it. He settled on the couch and looked at the open book.

On the first page was a picture of his father, his grandfather, and Randolph Meekins. They stood side by side in an open field. Behind them, a mountain covered the entire backdrop. The mountain was an odd shade of purple and appeared a little out of focus. The three men wore identical suits, a white shirt, and a tie of the same color as the suit. Each man wore a small apron with a folded cloth draped from its center. Jake's father was holding a baby, wrapped in one of the aprons. In the picture, his father looked young and happy, and his grandfather looked proud. Mr. Meekins gazed straight ahead, his fully functional eyes fixed on something in the distance.

Jake took the book and placed it in his lap. As he turned the pages, his mother said nothing. Each time he tried to question her, she would shush him, reach over, and turn another page.

As he looked on, he felt his pulse quicken. All the photos were from the same period, and many were of the three men. There were a few photos of other people, but his mother would not answer his inquiries into their identity. There was even a picture of his mother, sitting on a blanket with the baby.

There was something strange about the book, but he couldn't decide what. When he tried to turn the next page, he realized that a section of the book appeared to be sealed with wax. When Jake tried to pull the pages apart, his mother put her hand over his and said, "Not yet, Jake."

The last page of the book was free. It held a picture of nineteen men standing in three rows. In front of them, a blanket held six babies and three toddlers playing together. To the right of the group stood Randolph Meekins.

It was then that Jake saw it. Although the men were of varying ages, Randolph Meekins looked almost exactly as he had while standing at the garden. The only difference was his restored eyesight. He turned to his mother and was about to speak when she said, "Jake, I love you and I know you have lots of questions. There is a lot about our family that you need to learn, but I'm not the one to teach you. When Randolph comes tomorrow, you need to go with him."

She didn't give him time to reply. She got up, kissed him on his forehead, went into her bedroom, and closed the door.

Chapter Three

Jake could never remember his dreams although he sensed that they were vivid. Sometime when he would wake, it was almost like he was still in the dream, but they would quickly melt away.

Last night, after his mother left the room, he tried to sort things out. In one afternoon and evening, his whole sense of reality had shifted. He finally fell asleep on the couch.

In his dream he heard a tractor, his tractor. When he opened his eyes, the sound persisted. He shook his head to clear it, but the hum of the tractor was still there. Then, he heard voices. He threw the covers aside and went to investigate.

The front door was open. When he pushed through the screen door and onto the porch, he found his mother and Randolph Meekins rocking their chairs and having a conversation. None of the tension of the previous day was apparent. When his mother saw him, she rose from the chair, walked over, and kissed his cheek.

"Honey, I've got some things packed for you. You take care and do exactly as Randolph tells you. I love you, Jake." They embraced and she went into the house.

"Good morning," said Meekins. "Are you ready to go?"

Meekins faced straight ahead, his blind eyes vacant. A wooden walking stick rested across the arms of the chair. Jake noticed the ornate carvings covering it but did not recognize any of the symbols. Meekins rested his hands upon it. His fingers flexed as if his patience was forced.

"No, sir, I need to change clothes and get ready."

"You'll need to hurry," Meekins said.

"What do I need to bring with me?"

"Only what your mother has packed for you."

Not knowing what to do or say, he went back inside. He brushed his teeth, showered, and got dressed. He found the small bag on the couch. In addition to a few items of clothing, Jake found the picture of Meekins with his mother and father. He still had the white apron wrapped around him.

With his bag strapped across his shoulder, Jake tapped on his mother's door. There was no answer.

"Bye, Mama," he said through the door. "I love you."

Back on the porch, Mr. Meekins was talking with two young men. They looked as if they could have been twins. Upon further inspection, one appeared to be a year or two older than the other.

"Jake, this is Michael and Micah McAfee."

As Meekins spoke, first one and then the other presented his hand for Jake to shake.

"Pleased to meet you, Mr. Lokins," said the one introduced as Micah. "We'll take good care of her for you."

Jake didn't know if they were talking about the farm or his mother, and they did not elaborate. Sensing Jake's unease, Meekins said, "This is what they are trained to do. They know all about farming, and I can assure you that your mama couldn't be safer. We'll be looking in from time to time, and you'll be home some."

"Will I be home in time to attend college in the fall?" Jake had a feeling in the pit of his stomach that he already knew the answer.

The McAfee brothers exchanged a look and returned to work.

"Jake, I can't answer your question now," said Meekins. "Let me just say that your future will be in your own hands."

Jake didn't know whether to feel better or worse. He turned to the yard and saw that the McAfee brothers were both busy. It was as if they had read his mind as to what needed doing.

Randolph Meekins stood and tapped his cane on the porch floor. "Let's go," he said.

"Do you want to take my truck, Mr. Meekins?"

"No, Jake, we can walk from here."

Without another word, he began walking. Jake shouldered his bag and followed. His mind had been in turmoil for almost a day and now was no different. He felt like a fool, a lost child, or a pawn in someone else's chess game. When they were halfway the path, Jake took one more look at his home. The brothers had stopped what they were doing and stared down the path. His mother had stepped outside and stood on the edge of the porch. He raised his hand to wave goodbye. She threw him a kiss and her hands ended in a prayerful clasp just below her chin.

As they walked along, Meekins tapped a steady rhythm with his walking stick. Jake wanted to ask more questions but remained silent. He looked over his shoulder but could no longer see his home. Meekins came to a stop and Jake almost walked past him. The old man walked a short way into the woods across from the Clyde Atkins farm. Jake thought that Meekins might need to relieve himself and was unsure if he should follow. The old man stopped, turned around, and motioned Jake to come ahead. Jake walked up to him and began to speak. Meekins raised his cane into a horizontal position and pulled it into his chest.

Everything changed.

Chapter Four

They were standing on the outskirts of a small town. In the distance, Jake could see storefronts with what looked like living quarters above them. The few signs he could read displayed names, none of which he recognized. Sidewalks were wide but not many pedestrians were present. A few vehicles were parked along the street, but they were too far away to discern the make and model. He could not see any structures over two stories. The air was warm but not hot and a slight breeze stirred. When he looked, the whole scene seemed to shimmer.

To say that he was disoriented would be a gross understatement. One minute, he's standing in a forest in rural North Carolina and the next he is God knows where. He looked at Randolph Meekins and asked, "Where are we?"

When Meekins turned, Jake took a step back. His eyes were blue and clear and looked directly into Jake's. From under his fedora, hair cascaded onto his shoulders and his beard fell to mid-chest.

"Let's not get into that now. If you will be patient, I'll see to it that everything will be explained once we get to The Farm."

Jake wanted to protest but was stopped short by the realization that he was no longer dressed in his own clothes. Instead of his shirt and jeans, he now wore black slacks held in place by a belt. He had on a pressed, white shirt and a tie to match his pants. He was normally uncomfortable is such clothes, but these wore so well that he had not noticed the difference. The sneakers he had left home in were gone, replaced by black lace-up shoes. Jake was so taken by Meekins' functioning eyes that he had not noticed that he, too, was dressed differently. They were clothed alike. Jake ran his fingers through his hair and discovered that it had grown. In addition to all of this, he now had the beginnings of a thick beard. Somehow, this was the strangest thing of all because he had never been able to grow a beard.

He didn't have much time to contemplate it because Meekins said, "Here comes our ride."

Jake investigated the distance and didn't see anything. The road they stood beside was completely devoid of traffic. He saw movement at the edge of the town. A vehicle akin to a pickup truck with three full sets of doors came out of one of the streets and turned toward them. The large brown truck appeared to be well used and rode low to the ground. It came to a stop in front of them. In the bed were several large bags that looked like food for livestock. Meekins opened the second door on the driver's side and got in.

The front passenger door swung open, and a voice from inside said, "Get in, Jake. We've got a way to go and it's best we get started."

The voice was definitely female. Jake climbed into the truck and settled down. The truck must have been equipped with a hydraulic system because, as they started forward, the body of the vehicle started to rise and stabilized at least three feet above the pavement.

Jake looked at the driver's profile. She was in her early twenties. Her brown hair held lots of blonde highlights and fell below her shoulders. She must have sensed him looking because she reached to push it back. Her fingers were long and slender. The ear that she pushed the hair behind was large and pointed at its crest. When she turned to face him, he saw that her eyes were almond shaped and larger than he was used to seeing. Her eyebrows were long and formed into an antennae-like structure. Her nose was pert, and her lips were small but full. The effect on Jake was one of wonder, but he also found her features quite striking.

"What's the matter? Haven't you ever seen a faerie before?"

"No. I mean, I'm sorry. I didn't mean to stare."

From the back seat came a chuckle. "Take it easy on him, Gwynn," said Meekins. "We've just arrived and he doesn't understand us yet."

"I'm just jerking you around, Jake," said Gwynn with a smile. "Welcome to The Farm."

She fell silent and Jake looked straight ahead. He was filled with questions. Why was he here? If his mother knew all this, how could she have kept it from him? How was any of this possible? Was it all a hallucination induced by yesterday's heat and, if so, would he recover? It felt real, but so many dreams do.

His attention waned as he contemplated all this. When he again looked out the window, he could see a purple mountain range in the distance. These looked to be the same mountains from the picture his mother had shown him. Of all the things he had seen since coming to this strange land, the mountain had the greatest impact. This must all be real. If so, this was the place of his birth and early childhood. This morning he had left what he considered to be his home. Now, as strange as it might be, he was home once more.

Chapter Five

Gwynn applied the brakes and turned into a single-track driveway that opened between two runs of fencing. As they followed the path, a lone small farmhouse came into view. She slowed to a stop and Meekins got out.

"This is where we get started, Jake," he said before turning to Gwynn. "Gwynn, put the truck away and meet us inside."

Gwynn looked at Jake with a devilish grin. He was still trying to wrap his head around the faerie thing. She let out the clutch, rolled forward, and disappeared. She, the truck, and everything in it just blinked out of sight. Jake's knees went weak as he stared at the place where the truck had been.

"Don't worry, Jake," said Meekins putting his hand on Jake's shoulder. "You'll understand everything soon. Let's go inside."

They stepped onto the porch and approached an old door built from rough-hewn lumber and joined in a way that was simple but showed a high level of craftsmanship. The doorknob appeared to be made of stone and was smooth and polished. Meekins reached for the knob. Before he could touch it, the door swung inward in an effortless way. Jake was just about to comment when his eyes were drawn inside.

Once again, he felt disoriented. From the outside, it seemed like a rustic farmhouse, but from the door the interior looked like the lobby of a Metropolitan train station. The main hall appeared to be the length of a football field and twice as wide. Multiple corridors ran from each side. At the back of the room, a staircase rose to a catwalk, which encircled the second floor.

The lobby area was busy. Bodies moved in all directions. Some were human, both male and female. Some were humanlike, and others didn't resemble anything that Jake had ever seen. Jake looked at Mr. Meekins, who smiled and patted him on the shoulder.

"I know," said Jake. "I'll understand it all soon."

Jake stepped through the door and saw Gwynn walking toward him. It was good to see a familiar face even if it belonged to a faerie.

"Gwynn will show you to your room," said Meekins. "Get some rest and I'll send for you in a while."

Jake's head was spinning and filled with questions, but it was obvious that no answers would be immediately forthcoming.

Gwynn touched his arm and said, "Let's go before your jaw drops any further. Don't concern yourself with the differences; we are all together as one."

He followed her up the stairs, around the catwalk, and down a corridor. They came to a door with his name on it and a sign that read "off limits."

"Everything you need is inside. Get cleaned up and rest, but don't touch anything. Someone will come for you in a while."

With that, she put her hand on the door. He heard the click of the lock as it disengaged.

Gwynn left him at the door. Opening it, he found a small cubicle furnished with a single bed and a table with two drawers. There was a lamp on the table, and the covers had been turned down on the bed. Just inside the left wall, another door led to a bathroom equipped with a shower, a toilet, and a lavatory. Next to the bathroom was a walk-in closet. Rods ran down both sides of the closet, and there was a shelf across the back. On one side hung a normal wardrobe. On the other, the rod was full of what he had come to think of as the uniform. The rear shelf held underwear, socks, and a few white aprons like those in the picture. Shoes lined the floor under the shelf. There were drawers under each row of clothes but when he attempted to open them, he could not. He remembered Gwynn's admonition to touch nothing.

He went into the bathroom, relieved himself, and looked inside the cabinet. It held the standard toiletries of a brand he didn't recognize. Although he had attended to his hygiene before leaving this morning, he felt dirty and unkempt. When he looked in the mirror, he appeared to have been traveling for several days. He decided to shower but to not shave. He had always wanted a beard.

When he stepped out of the shower, he felt like a new man. There were fresh clothes laid out on the bed. He didn't remember them being there and hadn't heard anyone enter the room. A walking stick much like the one used by Mr. Meekins stood in the corner of the room. He didn't recall seeing it when he came in. He reached for it but, as his hand neared it, what felt like an electrical shock ran up his arm. He snatched his hand back and decided that the stick was one of the things he was not supposed to touch.

As he sat on the edge of the bed, he felt as if he could not hold his eyes open any longer. He reclined and drifted into a peaceful sleep. He awoke one time and turned on his side to face the open room. The walking stick was now beside the bed. He was not surprised.

Chapter Six

A knock awakened Jake. He didn't know how long he had slept. He had not seen a clock or any type of timekeeping device since his arrival. Expecting Gwynn, he opened the door and looked over his visitor's head. Adjusting his view, he saw a being approximately four feet tall and almost as wide. His hair was long, thick, and unruly. His beard fell to mid-chest and was the thickest Jake had ever seen, his mustache obscuring his upper lip. His eyebrows were long and bushy. The only features of his face that were visible were a bulbous nose, large ears, and piercing eyes. Although short, there was nothing small about him, and massive muscles revealed his likely strength. His clothing was made from skins but fit him well except that his shirt did not meet his pants. An ample amount of belly protruded from under his shirt. The man stood patiently while Jake scanned him from head to toe. Jake knew he was being rude, but in fairness he was being hit by wave after wave of sensory overload.

"Hello, Mr. Jake. My name is Raj and I'm one of your allies," he said with a voice that was deep but soothing. "The master wants to see you now. I'll show you to his quarters. I'm happy to be working with you. Don't forget your staff."

All of this was said without a breath or pause. Jake could not reply until Raj fell silent. He didn't really know what to say, so he only replied, "It's nice to meet you too."

Jake turned to retrieve the walking stick and almost tripped over it. He bent to pick it up and felt a tingle like static electricity. Raj was halfway down the hall, so Jake hurried to catch him. As Jake drew abreast, Raj looked over and made a few quick steps, which put him back out front. Jake got the message and followed Raj down the steps and through the lobby. They turned down a corridor and walked for what felt like a quarter mile. Jake wondered just how big this place could be. Raj stopped to face a door, which reached from floor to ceiling. It opened and the staff pulled him inside.

"See you in a while," said Raj as the door was closing.

The room was cavernous. Proportion had no meaning in this place. There was no relationship between what was and how it should have been. Leather-bound volumes lined one wall. Some looked ancient and the rest really old. The shelves on the other wall held jars containing items that were foreign to Jake's understanding. A large, slowly-spinning globe on a floor stand marked the center of the room. Jake did not see any recognizable land masses. A massive table was placed in front of a window, which comprised one entire wall. Heavy drapes, running floor to ceiling, were drawn aside.

Standing behind the table was Randolph Meekins. Over his suit, he wore a robe, the hem almost touching the floor. His hair was pulled into a ponytail. His eyes were clear, and a smile played upon his lips.

"Well, Jake, what do you think about 'The Farm'?"

"It's amazing, although I don't understand most things and can't even comprehend others. Most of all, I don't know why I'm here."

"You belong here. It's your birthright. You should have been here long ago but, with your Daddy gone, we chose to have you and your mother remain in the world we left this morning. There were other reasons too. I came for you because we can no longer deny what you are."

"You will have to excuse me, but I don't know anything about what you are saying. I'm only here because my mama said I should come with you. Now I'm in a strange place where humans make up only a portion of the population. I have so many questions and don't know how to ask them. You say we can no longer deny what I am. Well, what *am* I?"

"First, let me explain who we are," said Meekins. "Then I will explain why you are here. The Society of Builders is a group made up of beings from many origins. We are charged with maintaining the balance on this and many other worlds. Most times, all we do is observe. Sometimes, we have to nudge things in the proper direction. From time to time, we have to intervene in a more forceful manner. All major actions are documented. You will be able to review some of the major events as they concern the world you called home. This will help you better understand how our mission is executed. As a builder, you must take the appropriate action."

Jake felt both confused and intrigued. "How do you know what the appropriate action is and when to take it?"

"The Society is made up of many levels. There are individuals who take care of maintenance. They keep us running smoothly. There are service people like the McAfee brothers who handle many duties such as running your farm in your absence. There are soldiers, who are ready to fight and die if need be, to protect us or to further our mission. Allies like Raj and Gwynn are very intelligent, and most have some gift or ability that sets them apart. It also allows them to serve with one special individual, a wizard. You are one of those wizards. Wizards are not recruited, found, or accepted through application. Wizards are born. Most are born from parents who were also wizards, either male or female. In your case, both your mother and father were wizards."

"To answer your question," he went on, "you already know the appropriate actions and when to take them. You were born knowing. All we must teach you is how to get out of your own way and trust the flow. Although you will have allies to help you execute those decisions, the decisions and their consequences will be yours and yours alone. The way flows through you. You only have to let it guide you."

Jake wanted answers but now that they were coming they only created more questions. "That sounds like magic," Jake said.

"Magic is real. Everything that you have ever imagined or dreaded is real. There has never been a myth or monster that is not based on fact. There are those whose sole purpose is to oppose us and foster chaos. You will be a direct threat to them. Remember, our way is just and must be rendered. Your allies will serve you unto death. If death comes, it is very real. I know that you have more questions, especially now, and all will be answered. Now, take some time to digest what I have told you. Get to know this place. Raj and Gwynn will help you get acquainted with everything. Please don't quiz them. Tomorrow, we will talk about what will happen next."

When Meekins was finished speaking, the staff in Jake's hand came alive. Of its own volition, it pulled him toward the door. The door opened and Raj was waiting.

"What do you want to do now, boss?"

Jake was deep in thought. When he did not answer right away, Raj began to walk. Jake followed. They walked the total circumference of the catwalk. Raj explained that this side was the administration section of the building. The other side, where Jake's room was located, was made up of temporary living quarters. He was the only one using these rooms now. As they continued, Jake was able to investigate some of the offices. The people inside—at least he had come to think of them as people—were all busy and appeared to work in harmony. The actions of the workers resembled that of any busy office in any city in the world. The different species reminded him of a scene from a science-fiction movie in which aliens from different planets were gathered in a bar.

Raj led him down the stairs and into the busy lobby. Jake still had a tough time wrapping his head around all this. This feeling was only exacerbated when Raj opened the door to go outside and once again he stood in front of the seemingly little farmhouse. Jake was so disoriented that he lost his grip on the walking stick. Instead of falling to the ground, it hovered and glided back into his palm. Raj, who was walking ahead, had not noticed. They strolled the grounds, which were much like a working farm. There were fields, most planted and being worked, livestock pastures, and barns.

There was activity everywhere. All manner of beings completed the tasks at hand.

"We are completely self-sufficient," said Raj.

Something about being in this farming environment helped Jake relax. He almost felt at home. As they progressed, Jake saw fields that were cleared and manicured but nothing planted. Raj explained that they were for logistical purposes, and many were the location of gates. Jake could see no gates.

They walked through a group of trees and out into a training area. The exercises looked strenuous and dangerous. Trainees grunted and weapons clashed. Again, Jake was startled by the diversity of the inhabitants of The Farm.

"I think I'd like to go back to my room," said Jake.

"Right, boss," replied Raj.

On the way back, they passed close to some of the workers. All seemed friendly, and some even addressed him by name. Jake tried not to display his wonder. Besides, he felt he was getting used to the sensory overload.

Back in his room, Jake placed the staff in the corner and flopped onto the bed. He had taken in a lot of information and had started to accept some things, which he had never entertained as being possible. He tried to remain calm but found it hard to maintain balance after having his life turned upside down. Yesterday he had been a young man trying to enjoy his summer before starting college in the fall. Today he was in a world whose inhabitants were straight out of his imagination and storybooks. In addition to that, he was supposed to be some kind of "wizard" in a secret society, and his only job was to save worlds. How many worlds were there anyway?

He heard a faint noise. Suspended in mid-air, the staff hovered at the foot of the bed as if waiting for him like an old hound. He held out his hand and the staff moved into it. He felt no reason to be surprised. He took the staff in both hands and tested the weight of it. Tossing it into the air, he watched as it floated back into his hands. He tossed it higher and, while it was on the way down, he pulled his hands back. It hovered waiting for him. As he moved his hands, the staff would follow their direction. He decided to see how responsive it was. Grabbing the staff with both hands, he pivoted his body toward the door, pushing his hands forward to maintain balance. The staff jerked to the right and pointed itself at the door. Suddenly, a blinding light manifest itself from the tip of the staff. The door to his room was ripped from its hinges and hurled into the hall. Before Jake realized what had happened, Raj was standing in the doorway with a medieval looking axe at the ready. The staff turned its point toward Raj and zeroed in on him. He had to dive for the floor to avoid the next blast. Jake realized he was still pointing and lowered his arms. The staff came to rest at his side and seemed like an ordinary walking stick.

Raj looked up from the floor. Sweat covered his face and a hint of smoke rose from his hair. "I'll get somebody to fix the door, boss. In the meantime, let's get you to another room. It's almost time to meet your other allies."

With that, Raj turned and came through the hole where the door had been. "We'll have to get you a new room," Raj said.

They walked two doors down and Raj opened the door for him.

"I'll give you a few minutes," said Raj.

Jake sat on the edge of the bed in the new room and lowered his head into his hands. The staff came to rest across his legs.

Chapter Seven

His things were transferred to his new space. When the last of it was done, he left the door open, took a seat at the small desk, and tried to make sense of all he had seen and been told. He heard someone clear his throat. At the door stood an extremely tall man. He was lanky and thin. His eyes were so green that they didn't look natural. His narrow nose ended in a sharp point. He had a wisp of a beard and hair that was cut close on the sides, but a thick shock of curls topped his head. His hair, beard, and eyebrows were the color of a peeled carrot. Jake noticed that his hands were so large as to be out of proportion. His clothes looked out of place on his frame. His shirt, which was worn outside of his pants, was full and billowed at the shoulders and sleeves. His pants resembled jeans but were made from a material with no seams.

"Top o' the day to you, Captain. It's time to get going and be about your tasks. My name is Seamus O'Donnegan and I'm one of yours. Now, make fast and let's go."

The staff began to vibrate as if urging him to go. Since arriving, he had followed one person after another and still didn't have a firm grasp of what was happening to him. He rose, picked up the staff, making sure not to point it toward Seamus, and walked through the door.

Seamus and Jake walked down the stairs and into one of the corridors. They came to a door and Seamus opened it, using the conventional method. Stepping aside, he let Jake enter first.

An oversized wooden table stood in the center of the large room. Around the table were large, leather-clad chairs, eight on each side, and an even bigger chair at each end. On the far side of the table sat Gwynn and Raj. Seamus walked to the near side and took a seat next to the head of the table. Next to him, a black cat lay upon a garment of some description.

"Take your seat at the head of the table," said a voice from the chair Jake was standing behind.

Jake walked to the head of the table and sat. He felt small in the huge chair. Facing him was the oldest person he had ever seen. The old man's body looked frail, his back bent, and a hump deformed his right shoulder. His wrinkled skin had a yellow pallor. His fingers were drawn like talons, and his joints threatened to protrude from the skin. When he raised his head, his eyes were crystal-clear, and there was no question as to the intelligence behind them.

"Good afternoon, Jake," said the man. "My name is Alphonse. I'll be your guide for the next few days as you learn more about both us and you. The others at the table are your allies. Together you will carry out the work of the Society. You've already met Raj, Gwynn, and Seamus. This is Kathryn," he said and gestured toward the black cat.

"Hello, Jake," said the cat, who spoke in English with a pronounced southern accent. "I'm very happy to meet you."

Jake looked at the cat and didn't know what to say. So far, everyone he had met as allies could in some way pass for human. He was having enough trouble trying to comprehend everything, but a talking cat was past his ability to adapt. "Hello," he finally stammered and looked toward Alphonse.

"Kathryn, that's enough," said Alphonse.

The feline flinched like any cat that had been scolded. It then cowered and crawled under the garment, which covered the seat of the chair. In an instant, the robe shot upward. Standing in the chair was a beautiful young woman. She pulled the robe around herself and secured its cloth belt. "Like I said, hello, Jake."

She was what his mama would have called slight. She could not have weighed a hundred pounds. Her hair was jet black and her eyes a greenish yellow; her skin was so pale as to look translucent. Beneath her finely-chiseled nose, full, deep red lips smiled alluringly. Overall, she was hauntingly beautiful, and he had trouble pulling his eyes away from her.

Alphonse spoke, "This is your team except for one member. He is on assignment but will be back soon." Alphonse turned to the others and said, "I need some time alone with Jake. The rest of you are excused."

Except for Kathryn, they all stood and one by one offered Jake their hand. As she came by, she leaned over and touched her nose to the side of his face. Then they were gone.

"Jake, I know you are confused and rightfully so. You must have seen a lot since you've been here that appears fantastical and would seem to go counter to everything you have learned up to now. It's my job to acclimate you to your new life and guide you as you prepare to serve."

"Mr. Alphonse, I came here because my mother said I should. I don't know how much she knows about where I am or what I may do, but I know she would never send me anywhere bad. That's why I'm here and why I try to remain calm and open minded. I just hope I'm not crazy."

Alphonse laughed and clapped his hands. The skin on the back of his hands seemed to sag away from the bones. The sound of his hands slapping together was barely audible, but Jake thought he felt the chair shake.

"Your mother knows this place quite well. She has been a part of it since she was a child just as your father and his father before him. Generations of your family on both sides were born and raised here. You were the first not to be raised here, the reason for which you will soon learn. The union of your mother and father produced you. This is how we know you are one of us. Now it is time for you to take your rightful place and fulfill your destiny. Let me show you something."

He stood on shaky legs and walked to Jake's end of the table. Jake started to stand but was motioned back into his seat. As he came even with Jake's chair, he stopped and placed his left hand on Jake's shoulder. With a swiftness that did not seem possible for a man of his age, he slapped his right hand to Jake's forehead. Jake felt himself falling into a deep void. His body became weightless.

Chapter Eight

It was like one of those dreams where you are falling but don't know from where or how far it is to the ground. They say if you ever see yourself hit the ground, you will never wake up. Jake always woke before the crash. He was not afraid as he fell; he knew he would not collide with whatever lay below. He didn't. What happened next was so bizarre that he had a hard time thinking about it rationally.

As he fell, he began to decelerate and finally stopped descending altogether. His feet couldn't find anything solid beneath him. He was suspended—supported without any effort on his part. Lights flashed all around him. No, they were more than flickers of light; they were images. He couldn't keep any of them in his mind; they moved too fast. He thought he glimpsed his mother as a younger woman, but he couldn't be sure. He had the unmistakable feeling that he was being filled with information, much like you would download a file into a computer.

The space around him crackled with energy. Once he stopped trying to focus, he could see all around him. The combined energy around him must have sensed the change because the flashing stopped. The images froze and began to organize into a huge collection. They began to drop one by one like the old drawings used to produce animation in the time before computer-generated images. He still could not or was not allowed to clearly see the images. Even so, on some level, he knew what they meant.

This went on for what seemed like an eternity. He felt himself growing tired and wanted to sleep. He was so weary. A tremendous need to yawn overcame him. He stretched his arms over his head, leaned back, and opened his mouth. His yawn was so wide that his eyes almost squinted shut. Out of the slit that remained, he saw all the images vaporize. The vapor rolled and swirled and then found his open mouth. He could feel it enter his mouth and pass through his throat, but there was nothing he could do. The vapor had no physical substance, so he had no trouble taking it all in. As the last bit came into his mouth, something tickled his nose and he had to sneeze.

When he sneezed, he woke up. He was back in his room. He sat up and sneezed two more times. He couldn't remember coming back to his room or preparing for bed. What he did recall was a vastly different personal history from the one he had held as true only a short while ago. There would be no more thoughts of attending college. He had already abandoned his goal of making their land a working farm. He knew he was where he belonged and was eager to set about his task.

He arose, went into the bathroom, showered, and brushed his teeth. There was so much to think about that he found himself unable to focus on a single thing. He dressed in one of the black suits, a white shirt, and a black tie. They fit as if tailored for him. A pair of cap-toe black shoes, which rose to cover his ankles, and socks that felt like they were caressing his feet, completed the outfit.

After getting dressed, he walked toward the door. As a reflex, he extended his right arm with his palm facing outward. The staff crossed the room of its own volition and settled into his hand. He opened the door with his left hand and turned toward Randolph Meekins' office. He knew that was where he was meant to go.

When he reached the door, the staff vibrated in his hand and the door swung inward. Randolph Meekins sat behind his large desk. His hands were folded in front of him, and his eyes locked onto Jake as he crossed the room. As he drew closer to the desk, Jake noticed that Mr. Alphonse was seated in one of the wingback chairs.

"Good morning, Jake," said Meekins. "I hope you rested well."

"Yes, sir, I did. Good morning, Mr. Alphonse," Jake said, turning to face him. Alphonse nodded but said nothing.

Jake became aware that the globe was spinning faster than when last he saw it. The staff was urging him toward the open chair. He didn't know what to say, so he remained silent.

Meekins looked at Jake, nodded his head, and smiled. "Jake, I know that you have been through a lot these last few days, and I appreciate the way you have handled it. You may have more questions now and in the days to come. Rest assured they too will be answered. You will soon be sent out to take care of Society business. You probably think you are not ready, but let me assure you, you are. You now have all the knowledge and ability you will need, and more will become available to you as necessary. Your allies will be invaluable to you, but above all listen to your head and your heart and follow your instincts."

"But, sir, I've only been here for a short while."

"Jake, due to circumstances, you were not afforded the luxury of growing up on 'The Farm,' but that doesn't make you any less a wizard. You were born a wizard. We believe, if anything, your upbringing on the other side will make you stronger. You will have a unique perspective not available to those who have lived here exclusively. Trust yourself, Jake. The staff you carry will be a great help as you make your way."

"Is the staff a weapon?" Jake asked, remembering what happened in his first room.

Alphonse answered. "The staff must and will be your constant companion. It is a warrior rather than a weapon. It is a guide, a mentor, and a support both physically and emotionally. It will serve as your moral compass and, as you learn to listen, it will tell you many things. It will protect you from harm and assist you as you conduct the affairs of The Society. With your staff and your allies, you will be able to face many great challenges."

"Now," said Mr. Meekins. "For the final act of your training and your first assignment, I'm sending you back home. You will have to find the way and make the transition by yourself. I know that you have the desire to speak with your mother about these things. You will have fifteen days to get there, settle things with your mother, and return here. You will spend the rest of the day here and may leave, at your will, tomorrow. You must always keep your staff with you. Your final ally will visit you in that world. Now go."

Jake stood and offered his hand to Meekins. Meekins gripped it and, with his free hand, made subtle adjustments to Jake's fingers.

"This is the grip by which we recognize one and another of us. You will meet others in the most unlikely places. Remember the grip and use it. Our brothers and sisters will know you immediately, and normal beings will not recognize the difference."

Jake paused, turned to Mr. Alphonse, and took his hand, using the grip.

Alphonse nodded his head in the affirmative and almost smiled. "Well done, wizard."

Chapter Nine

The little man made his way along the rock wall. Water seeped from the rocks and gathered on the floor. Bare lights hung from the ceiling and cast long, ominous shadows. The man tried not to splash as he hurried along but found it impossible. His shoes, socks, and cuffs were soaked. The squishing sound, combined with the slap of his shoes, created a rhythm that he found disquieting.

He had only returned to the keep a short while ago, but there was no time for rest. The news he bore was too important. His dread increased as he worked his way deeper into the mountain. He thought his heart would burst from his chest.

The lights became brighter as he neared the inner chambers. He knew he was being observed but dared not seek to discover who or what was watching. He would not make any move that could be construed as suspicious.

Normally, he would have taken his information to his regent, and the regent would pass it on, but this was too important. The regent of the third province had told him that any delay could cause disastrous consequences. He wondered if the consequences would befall the kingdom or the one bearing the news.

Ahead, he could see the guards posted beside the door of the inner chamber. As he approached, the guards came to attention and made ready their spears. The man knew all of this was for show because the door was protected by a powerful spell and could not be breached.

"Greetings. Alain Bulwark to see the Lord High Determiner," the man said with more conviction than he felt. "I have news concerning the Society of Builders that must be communicated immediately."

The guards did not move aside. Their eyes bored into him as if the only decision to be made was where to dispose of his body. He tried to swallow but his mouth was too dry. He wanted to turn and run but knew that death would come immediately if he did. He was finding it difficult to breathe and felt he might lose consciousness. The door began to open. The guards moved aside, and Alain Bulwark stepped into the inner chamber.

The lighting was still dim inside the door but became brighter as he approached the raised dais. Upon it was a large throne made of leather and wood. Its arms were carved to resemble the leg and foot of the great bear. Sitting on the throne was the Lord High Determiner. Standing at his side was the Sorcerer Jamal.

The Determiner was a giant of a man, although rumor had it that he was not a man at all. Looking up at him, Alain felt tiny and insignificant. The Determiner's hands were as big as the carved bear paws. His face was broad with sharp features and framed by his flowing hair and thick beard. From Bulwark's perspective, the Determiner's eyes seemed to be of two different colors, although he could not make out the hue of either. The Determiner was indeed an imposing figure.

The Lord High Determiner slid forward in his seat and gazed down at Alain Bulwark. He seemed both amused and annoyed that an untitled individual had requested an audience.

"And who might you be?" asked the Determiner in a deep and loud voice.

"I am your servant, Alain Bulwark. I am a courier in your messaging service. The message I bring was given to me by our senior operative stationed in the inner world. I was directed to deliver it to you without delay. Thus I stand before you."

"Make haste with the message for howling's sake!"

"The message is that the Lokins boy has been summoned to The Farm. The Master of the Society retrieved him personally. It is said that the boy is already functioning as a wizard and is making ready to do the bidding of the Society."

The Sorcerer Jamal said something, but his words did not reach Alain Bulwark. The Determiner leaned back in his seat and slammed his fist against the arm of the chair. All motion stopped in the chamber except that a soldier came to stand behind Bulwark.

"How can it be that this is the first I should hear of this?" Looking at the man standing behind Bulwark, he said, "We cannot allow this to come to fruition. Notify our people in all the lands and demand that the Lokins boy be killed. This should have been taken care of in times before."

Bulwark thought he detected a hint of dread in the Determiner's voice.

The Lord High Determiner shifted his gaze back to Bulwark but said nothing. He waved his hand in a dismissive gesture. As Bulwark began to bow, he felt a sting and the head of a spear protruded from his chest, a stream of blood falling from it to the floor.

Chapter Ten

J ake awoke early and looked outside. It was a fine day for his trip home. After showering, he found his old clothes hanging in the closet. He didn't remember having them; his attire had changed as they crossed over. He packed a few items, thinking that he wouldn't need much since he was going home. He was excited but had some apprehension concerning the talk he would have with his mother. Taking the staff in hand, he left his room.

Upon passing through the front door, he again stood on the porch of an old farmhouse. Gwynn was rocking in one of the chairs. He took the other.

"Good morning, Gwynn," he said. "I'm ready to go. Where is the truck?"

"Good morning, Jake," she said. "There is no truck for you. You must make your own way. We're not allowed to help. Good luck be with you."

Her words hit him like a punch in the stomach. He realized he was on his own. The staff tugged in his hand, so, with only a nod, he set off on his journey.

He turned to look back a few times just in case Gwynn was joking. He hoped that after a few laughs she would come along in the truck. By the time The Farm was out of sight, he had given up on that notion. He was trying to remember the ride in and equating that with how far he would have to walk.

The road was straight but made up of hill after hill. Jake hadn't noticed them on the way in but became acutely aware after a few miles. He set a steady but forgiving pace.

The temperature was comfortable with mild humidity. The sky was a deep blue with not a cloud in sight. As he walked, he realized he had not seen any dwellings or cultivated land. He couldn't remember ever traveling so far without seeing any sign of man's intrusion upon the earth.

He felt he should soon reach the town where Gwynn had picked them up, but after several more hours it was still not in sight. No signage or remembered landmarks by which he could gauge his progress were anywhere in view.

As dusk approached, he grew tired and decided to find a place to rest. He stepped into the edge of the woods. A short distance into the trees, he found a large boulder protruding from the ground. It was rounder on top but had a flat place on its side that was formed like the back of a chair. A bed of leaves lay around the rock. Jake looked back toward the road and thought that he still had not seen a single *being* since leaving The Farm. Normally he would have thought human, but, after the events of the past week, he found that description too limiting. He was still contemplating this as he sat down on the leaves and leaned back against the rock. He rested the staff beside him, closed his eyes, and fell asleep.

He was awakened by a buzzing noise that sounded like a swarm of angry bees. He opened his eyes but saw nothing. The darkness that surrounded him was complete. There appeared to be neither a single star in the sky nor any moonlight. The buzzing became more intense. He reached in the darkness for the staff and his wrist banged against it. The staff was standing upright and vibrating wildly. He wrapped his fingers around it and it began to calm down. The staff pulled his arm across his body, forcing him to turn in that direction. Three lights approached through the woods on a direct trajectory to his location. He did not feel afraid but was on edge because of the actions of the staff. He wanted to hide until he could observe those approaching but knew that any movement on the leaves would betray his position. He slipped his body downward so his head would be below the crown of the boulder and pulled the staff close, willing it to silence. Each breath sounded like an explosion, and his heartbeat felt like a bass drum. Surely, he thought, if there was any danger he was lost.

With his back to the rock, he could no longer see the lights. He turned his head to better hear whatever was approaching. He discerned nothing. He waited. Unless the lantern carriers sensed his presence and stopped, they should have already been upon him. He held his position for what seemed like a long time. Still not perceiving anything, he decided to venture a look. He pivoted on his left hip and leaned over as quietly as possible. He turned his head and sighted down the side of the boulder. He saw nothing. It was like the whole thing had been a play of his imagination. Jake was about to breathe a sigh of relief when the staff began vibrating, and he was pulled back around. What he saw made him lose his breath.

Three men sat opposite him. They formed a loose semi-circle. A pile of twigs separated Jake from the men. The man in the middle leaned in and touched a flame to the kindling. There was no smoldering or smoke. At his touch, the fire was fully realized. The staff moved into a horizontal position. It moved left to right as if monitoring the strangers. Six eyes followed the staff's every move.

"Greetings, wizard," said the fire starter. "May we pass the time with you and enjoy your fire?"

The speaker sat on a log which Jake could not remember being there. The stranger was an extremely tall man, and his knees almost rose to his chin. He could not have been comfortable. His manner of dress was not readily definable. He may have been a manual laborer but could just as well have been a traveling merchant. Jake could not make out his features, but his eyes glowed from the fire. The other two men were dressed identically to the stranger but did not show any expression as they stared across the flame.

The hair on Jake's arm began to tingle as if charged with electricity. Something wasn't right with this situation; Jake didn't need the vibrating staff to alert him to that fact.

"Who are you and what do you want?" Jake tried to sound firm. "You act as if you know me. You come here uninvited, and you will remain uninvited until I understand who you are."

Jake was trying to gather his legs so as not to be in such a vulnerable position. He tightened the grip on the staff and pulled it to his side, the tip pointing directly at the man who had spoken. "State your business or be on your way."

"We only mean to help. This forest is unusual and many fall under its influence. We can offer guidance."

Jake tried to look directly at the man but still found it impossible to define his face. "That's kind of you, but I'm not under the influence of anything and only mean to continue my journey."

The stranger stood and looked down at Jake. The other two rose and appeared to be awaiting instructions.

"Well, we'll be on our way. Gentlemen, it seems we are not welcome to share the wizard's fire."

They turned as if to walk back into the forest. Jake got to his feet, trying not to show his discomfort. As the men walked away, each took a different path into the trees. Jake was about to extinguish the fire when, without warning, it blazed up and started to burn a phosphorous glow. Jake was momentarily blinded. The staff vibrated in his hand, so he turned away from the light and dove for the protection of the rock. He felt a movement in the wind as if something had passed over his head. The rock shaded him from the light, so his vision began to clear. Jake was frightened but was not frozen by his fear. He detected movement to his left. One of the men who had seemed inanimate a short while ago ran at him, brandishing a short sword. The man raised his arm, making his intentions clear. Jake took a step back and brought the tip of the staff to bear on him, center mass. Jake wasn't sure how to make it work but prayed that it would. He was not disappointed.

The staff bucked in his hand and a force leapt from its tip. The attacker was disintegrated. He was there and then he wasn't. Jake gasped and must have loosened his grip because he dropped the staff when something slapped across both of his arms. A pair of arms wrapped around him and began dragging him away, pulling him into the woods. He could not get enough of a hold to fight back. The fire was just a speck of light through the trees. Jake's arms were pinned to his side so he could not summon the staff, and his chest was being squeezed with increasing pressure. He tried to thrash about, but nothing seemed to ease his predicament. The man who had done all the talking stepped from behind a tree. He extended his arms and opened his hands. It was as if a light had been turned on in the middle of the forest. A ball of light was suspended above each palm. He lowered his arms and the lights continued to hover and illuminate the forest.

"Wizard, you have made this more difficult than it needed to be. It would have been much better if you had shown some hospitality. We could have taken care of our business during the night and your passing would have been painless. Now, you have forced me to handle things in a less civilized manner."

Jake continued to struggle against the vice-like grip that trapped him. What he had taken for a small group of robbers had turned out to be assassins. He was about to be killed and didn't have any idea why. He looked through the trees and tried to summon the staff.

"It cannot help you now," said the stranger, realizing what Jake was trying to do. "You cannot overcome my power. It's just another useless stick lying on the forest floor. Don't worry; I'll gather it when we are finished here. It'll make a great souvenir." The man's eyes sparkled with satisfaction.

Suddenly the man's face changed. It was as if all the light went out of his eyes. They turned black and, in the shadows cast by the spheres, disappeared. He raised his hands to a level just under the light and regained a hold on them. He cocked his right arm as if he were going to throw a baseball.

Jake resigned himself to his fate but decided to go out as defiantly as possible. He straightened himself and stared directly into the black orbs. Jake was determined not to flinch. As Jake stared ahead, the man's eyes began to glow a bright red. Jake saw the cocked arm begin to move forward.

Something else caught Jake's eye and his gaze shifted. At first, he thought a moth drawn by the light had landed on the man's shirt, but then the shirt began to change color. It was blood and what he had thought to be a moth was instead an arrowhead protruding from the man's chest. The iron grip, which had rendered him immobile, loosened and fell away. The two glowing balls of light began to flicker. The assassin fell to his knees, and the forest was immersed in darkness.

Jake didn't know what had happened to the man who was holding him. When he was released, he fell to the side and scampered away. He oriented himself to the campsite. Seeing the briefest flicker of light from the fire, he crawled toward it. When he reached the edge of the clearing, he paused to listen and observe. He was acting on pure instinct. He summoned the staff. Once it was in his hand, he felt safe to enter the clearing. He found his bag and retrieved his flashlight. With the light in one hand and his staff at the ready in the other, he returned to the woods. It took a while to find the body. It was lying face down and was quite dead. Jake was still on guard because he didn't know the whereabouts of the third man. The light soon found him or what was left of him. The clothes he had worn were shriveled up into an untidy rumple. The creature inside the clothes was wasting away at an alarming rate. There was only a skeleton with some skin stretched across it. As Jake watched, the skin wrinkled and became dust. Next, the bones began to deteriorate.

When Jake turned away from the bodies, a giant of a man dressed like a character from a medieval movie stepped out of the woods with his hand extended over his head. His clothing was made from coarse cloth, and his shoes were a rough suede sewn together with rawhide strips. Jake had the tip of the staff aimed at the man's midsection. Jake lowered it but remained vigilant. He would not be taken unaware again.

"May I retrieve my arrow from the back of the necromancer?" he asked while slowly walking to the corpse. "I think we put him in direct communion with his minions. I would like to have my arrow back."

What could Jake say? If not for that arrow, he would be the corpse lying on the forest floor. "Go ahead, archer, and thank you."

The archer walked to the body, placed his right foot on its back, and pulled the arrow out, tearing more flesh as he did. "He won't mind a bit," he said when he saw Jake's expression. "You are most welcome, young wizard. Would ye name be Jake Lokins?"

"How did you know?"

"I heard ye was taking a wee trip home, and I thought I might see you on the road, but I didn't think I'd have to kill a man to meet you. Oh well, anytime we can free the worlds of a necromancer is a good day. They're a nasty lot. They'll use the dead to do their bidding and then drop them wherever they stand when they are of no more use. True evil, I say."

"Is that what happened to him?" Jake asked, pointing to the heap of dust.

"Aye. Once the necromancer was dead, his hold on the dead man was finished."

The giant spoke as if these things were normal, and Jake guessed they were. He still had a hard time reconciling it.

Returning his attention to the giant, Jake said, "I'm lucky you came along when you did. I got one with the staff, but it must have been another zombie."

"There is not much luck to it. You called me from the road. If our wizard is in trouble, all his allies can feel it even if they can't easily get to him. Now, all your allies know you are safe."

"Are you one of my allies?"

"Aye, Thom Thomas at your service," he said with a bow. "I was trying to get back to The Farm before you left but was delayed. Why have ye not made it home?"

"I was on my way but grew tired."

"The necromancer in all probably conjured your fatigue in order to do his business." Thom pointed to the dust pile and said, "Don't mistake that for a zombie. Zombies are a different evil. Don't worry. You'll learn all that when you get back."

Jake thought he had a lot to learn but only said, "I guess I'll make it home tomorrow."

"Tomorrow it is then. Might I share your camp for the evening?"

"Yes, I'd like that very much."

They returned to the clearing. The fire was waning, so Thom scavenged some wood to build it back. Jake returned to his position against the boulder while Thom sat on the log vacated by the necromancer. It felt odd to Jake that they would act so normal while a corpse and a twice-dead pile of ashes lay a short distance away. They ate cheese and jerky from Thom's pack. Jake could think of nothing to say. He began to feel uneasy about the silence, but Thom didn't seem to mind. After a while, Thom pushed the log back from the fire, gathered some leaves into a bed, and lay back, using the log as a pillow. He began to hum a tune that Jake found soothing. Jake fell asleep listening to it.

When Jake awoke, Thom Thomas was gone. The fire had been refreshed, and a piece of parchment lay beside his hand. He picked it up and read: "Wizard, keep your staff as close as your heart, and it will protect you. Wield it and it becomes a mighty weapon. Follow it and it will guide you through many worlds. It can find a gate and see you safely through. Be safe and I will await your return."

Jake made ready and returned to the road, still not knowing his way. He set a pace and walked through mid-day. The staff began to vibrate. He thought he must be getting close to town. He took a few more steps and the vibration ceased. He stepped back and it resumed. He sensed a tug to his left. He turned and proceeded slowly. The vibration became stronger with each step. He was now off the road and standing in tall grass. After a few more steps, the vibrations stopped, and the staff pulled itself into a horizontal orientation. Jake stopped and looked across the field. Tall grass swayed in the breeze and clouds slowly drifted overhead. He felt the tension go out of his arms. He straightened his body and pulled the staff back into his chest. When it touched him, he was home.

Chapter Eleven

The news of the Lokins boy being summoned to The Farm enraged the Lord High Determiner. By extension, the entire keep was in a turmoil. It was only a matter of time until the effect of the Determiner's mood would be felt throughout the land. He and his subjects had believed that the child and his mother's departure from The Farm meant they would not have to deal with another Lokins. As time passed the potential of the Lokins boy taking his place among wizards had receded in probability. Now, not only was it probable but it was an actuality.

At the Determiner's command, Jamal, the sorcerer, had set a course of action into motion to prevent the true power of this wizard from coming to fruition. Jamal could not be content to sit by and wait for the result, so he was on the move.

He left his chambers and, keeping to the shadows, went to the rear stairway. He climbed down to the main hall of the keep. On the surface, it looked like business as usual, but Jamal knew better. He descended two more levels to the dungeon. The smell of sweat and urine permeated the air. The space was always damp and cold. No one could survive these conditions for long. Someone must have sensed his presence because a murmur started and grew in intensity.

The men chosen as dungeon guards were a slovenly group, but they would not disregard their duties altogether. Jamal did not want to be seen.

He slid along the wall, letting the shadows conceal him, until he found his destination. He turned, placed his palm against the wall, and whispered his incantation. A door opened where there had been solid rock. He stepped through and proceeded down another steep flight of steps.

When he reached the bottom, he spread his arms with his palms up. He brought them together at the top of their arc and torches came aflame. In contrast to the dungeon, this chamber was dry and warm. Only he, the minister of defense, and the Lord High Determiner knew of its existence and could access it. Everyone involved in building and readying this chamber had been executed upon its completion.

The chamber was lined on both sides with vaults, all invisible to the naked eye. If anyone were to stumble upon this room, they would see only blank walls.

Jamal knew that most of the vaults were empty. This was a special place. He walked the full length of the room. When he reached the corner, he faced left. Laying both palms against the wall, he gently pushed. Two vaults became visible and separated from the wall so that he could gain access. He pulled both vaults at the same time, and they glided outward as if on a bed of air.

He took a deep breath and was surprised that he had his eyes closed. He lifted his eyelid and looked into the vaults. There in peaceful repose were two bodies. Jamal knew their names: Lonnie Lokins Sr. and Lonnie Lokins Jr.

Chapter Twelve

Jake stood in the edge of the woods across from the field where he and Randolph Meekins had transitioned into the world of The Farm. The field had been cut and large bales of hay dotted the landscape, waiting to be gathered. The leaves on the trees were starting to turn the colors of autumn.

Again, Jake felt disoriented. Months appeared to have passed in this world while less than a week had elapsed in the other. A breeze stirred and the gust felt cool against his skin. He looked up the road and saw a puff of smoke lift over the horizon. Jake thought that his mother must already be using the fireplace. This thought pleased him. As he walked toward the crest of the hill, smoke began to bellow. He knew something was wrong and started to run. As he topped the hill, he saw the barn engulfed in flames. The roof had collapsed. He knew it was lost. Where were the McAfee brothers, and why weren't they fighting the fire? Jake ran for the barn, but the heat was too intense. The staff vibrated and physically pushed him back from the flames. He knew nothing could be saved. He leveled the staff, pointed it toward the barn, and pushed the tip forward. A blast of light and energy erupted from the staff and the barn disappeared. All that remained was scorched earth.

He ran to the cabin and threw open the door. "Mama," he yelled but got no response. The staff pushed against his chest and forced him to slow. There was no way to describe the panic and dread he was feeling. He knew he needed to act rationally. He searched each room of the house but found no signs of life. All was in order, but everyone was gone.

He walked back outside and out of habit glanced at the garden. It looked as it always had at the end of the season. Green was giving way to brown and more than the allowable number of weeds were present. Suddenly, Jake realized that nobody had responded to the fire. In the country, neighbors depended on each other. If there was a need or an emergency, people gave a hand, yet nobody was there. He decided to go to the Atkins farm for some answers.

His truck was missing. He grabbed the key to the old Ford tractor, fired it up, and set off across the pasture that separated the farms. The staff lay across his legs and emitted a low buzzing sound. As he approached the top of the hill, the staff created a downward force on his legs. He knew he had to stop the tractor and proceed on foot. He walked to the top of the hill but was not prepared for what he saw.

He had stood on this hill many times, looking down at Mr. Atkins's farm. Jake aspired to model their farm on the Atkins house, barn, and the layout of his pastures and fields. Mr. Atkins was always there to answer questions and provide guidance about farming. He was flattered that Jake wanted to implement his ideas. Jake always thought Mr. Atkins "had it all," but now he looked down on a scene of devastation. Everything was gone and the ground where the farm had stood still smoldered. Smoke rose in wisps and drifted on the wind. The only thing recognizable was Jake's truck, which was turned on its side. His legs gave way, and he fell to his knees. Never had he felt such a sense of loss.

The staff urged him down the hill. As he got closer, he saw legs extended beyond the bed of the truck. With no thought of caution, he rounded the truck. Lying on the ground and obviously dead was Micah McAfee. He was burned almost beyond recognition, and a hole the size of a softball was blown through his midsection.

Jake had been so eager to get home. He wanted to talk with his mother about what he had learned. Instead, since leaving The Farm, he had been attacked and everything he held dear destroyed. The rage that had been building in him burst forth. He stabbed the end of the staff into the ground, and a boom like a clap of thunder blasted from it. The force caused the truck to shift and expose more of Micah's body. Jake saw that Micah held something in his hand. He knelt, rested the staff against his knee, and pulled Micah's fingers apart. At first glance it could have been mistaken for a piece of skin, which had detached from his palm. It fell from Micah's grip and Jake could see that it was a scrap of parchment. On it was written: "They have come for you, but she is safe."

Jake collapsed to the ground but was careful not to lose his grip on the staff. A rush of relief ran through his body. The question at the forefront of his mind had been answered. His mother was safe; at least she had been at the time of Micah's death. The question remained: where was she? What had caused all this destruction and what should he do now? He had to assess his situation and formulate a course of action.

Jake felt as if a switch had been thrown inside him. His mind settled and his pulse slowed. He knew what must be done. The realization he was experiencing could only be a by-product of his radical experience with Mr. Alphonse. Along with the personal history he had ingested, an equal amount of training and understanding must have been downloaded into his mind. All he had to do was avail himself of it. Realizing he had an iron grip on the staff, he loosened his fingers. He would have sworn that it purred.

Micah's body was in no condition to be moved, and there weren't any implements to dig a grave, but Jake didn't want to leave him as carrion for the animals and birds. He did the only thing he could. He pointed the staff at Micah's remains and vaporized them.

"I'm sorry, Micah," he said with a sigh.

Chapter Thirteen

Back at the cabin, Jake collapsed on the couch. Although he was calm and had faith in what he had learned, there was a side of him that wanted to erase the last week. He longed to go back to being the farm boy, living with his mother and waiting to start college. That could never be. He was on an irreversible path. He wanted answers. He decided to find out all that he could and return to The Farm.

Meticulously, he searched each room for any indication of what had taken place. There were no signs of struggle or of the panic that would precede a fight or flight situation. The only thing that seemed strange was the absence of the scrapbook that his mother had shown him. Since he had never seen it before, he didn't know if it was missing or well concealed. There was also the possibility that it was invisible to him. After his visit to The Farm, he couldn't discount anything.

Throughout the search, he kept the staff in his hand. He didn't want a replay of what had happened in the forest. It began emitting a low pulsing hum. This was a new communication, which was how he had come to think of the various emanations. He pulled the staff into the weapon orientation and moved along the wall into the living room. As he entered, he saw a shadow slide past the window. Micah's note came to mind: "They have come for you." He didn't have a clue who "they" were, but he knew how to put up a fight. He heard feet moving along the porch. He aimed the staff at the door. Should he wait for the door to come down or preempt that with a blast and keep blasting until everything was gone? He thought he must be fatigued because the staff was becoming difficult to hold on target. He saw the doorknob turn. He watched it rotate a quarter turn and hesitate. He readied himself. The door swung inward. *Now!*

The staff bucked in his hands but didn't emit the blast of energy that pulverized everything in its path. He was bewildered because at the last second, he had pulled it back and pointed it at the ceiling.

"Don't shoot, boss," someone yelled. It was Raj.

Jake stood there with pieces of his ceiling raining down on him as his allies assembled in the living room.

As each one walked through the door, their transformation became apparent to Jake. They appeared as if they might live down the road. Their clothes looked like they could belong to any person of this world. Gwynn's face had softened, and her features were no longer fairylike. Seamus didn't appear as tall as Jake remembered and his hands were normal in size. Thom Thomas was still large but not the giant of a man he had been in the woods. Kathryn looked like she might have just left her job at city hall. The only person who was consistent with his memory was Raj.

"We got here as quick as we could," Raj said. "Can you bring us up to speed? Everything is happening so fast. Thomas told us about what happened with the necromancer. I thought we would have a few more days together at The Farm, but that doesn't seem possible. We're here to help."

"Thank you all," said Jake. He told them what he had found after getting home. "Micah McAfee is dead, and Michael and my mother are gone. I found a note saying she was all right. Whoever or whatever did this was after me, but I don't know why. I've got to find her!" After pausing for a breath, Jake asked, "How did you know to come, and what happened to everyone's appearance?"

Gwynn spoke up. "As a team we're bound both physically and mentally. When something threatens one of us, we all feel it. When the wizard is in danger, the sensing is the strongest. We were not chosen at random to be your allies. We have always been your allies; we just couldn't make ourselves known until you joined us.

"As far as our appearance goes, that's both simple and complicated. When we travel, we take on the appearance of the inhabitants of the world in which we operate. The only time we appear as ourselves is on our home world, at The Farm, or if the wizard wills it. Even Kathryn changes when she shifts. She morphs into a feline equivalent for that world. Raj only maintained his appearance so that you would not blast us into oblivion before we could explain."

With that, Raj transformed into a rugged young man with long hair and a beard. He was dressed in a plaid shirt, jeans, and laced boots.

"We need to find out where Michael and my mother went. We also need to look around to assess our situation."

"I'll take care of that," said Kathryn. The dress she was wearing fell in a heap on the floor. From underneath, a black cat appeared and ran out the door.

Jake looked from one ally to another and realized how little he knew about them beyond their names. He determined to learn more but realized that would be better one on one.

"What's the plan, boss?" Raj asked.

Jake paused. The plan? What was the plan? He recognized it was up to him to make the plan, but he sure could use some help. He knew they were vulnerable as they stood together. "We need to set up some kind of perimeter in case whatever did this comes back."

"That would be you and me, Thom," said Raj. "I'll take the front and you the back."

"Aye," said Thomas and stood to leave. He walked to the open door, reached outside, and retrieved a long bow and a quiver of arrows. Reaching out again, he pulled back a double-edged battle ax and tossed it to Raj. "Keep a keen eye, little man, and yell if ye need any help."

Raj caught the ax in one hand, emitted a low growl, closed one eye, and drew a bead on Thomas with the other. He was still mumbling as he strode past Thomas and out the front door. Thomas roared with laughter and walked through the kitchen and out the back door.

Seamus stood and said, "I think I'll take a walk around as well. Perhaps I can get a feel for what happened." He too walked outside.

Only Gwynn remained with Jake. "Gwynn, can you tell me about our team? How did we come to be chosen for each other?"

"In time, you will remember all these things. We are all children of 'Society' members. We are chosen when we are very young. Most teams are raised together. In our case, you were not raised on The Farm, so we didn't know if or when we would be a team. We each received temporary assignments and filled in as needed until you arrived. Everyone is very happy to be with you. It would have been nice if we had more time to get to know each other, but there is something about you that has upset our opposition enough to take direct action."

"Why me and who is the opposition?"

"Nobody's sure why they suddenly should come after one wizard. The opposition is chaos, evil, and it is whoever or whatever stands to gain from disorder. Its leader is a ruler known as The Lord High Determiner and his Sorcerer Jamal. They can direct and control chaos. They and all the horrible creatures and manifestations you have ever heard about or imagined. Good cannot exist without evil."

My God, Jake thought. *What am I doing here?*

This was not going the way Jake thought it would. Just as he began to try to clarify the situation, all hell broke loose.

He heard Thomas shout and, without thinking, was at the door. Seamus was running toward the house with three large dogs on his heels. There had always been stray dogs around but nothing like these. They were extremely large, their heads reaching well above Seamus' waist. One was slightly ahead of the others and was gaining on Seamus. Thomas knocked an arrow and pulled his bow full draw. He let go the arrow, and it sailed past Seamus, just missing him, and impaled the lead dog. Thomas was trying to ready another arrow but there wasn't time. He tossed the bow aside, withdrew a knife, and assumed a defensive posture. Jake realized that once again he had moved without the staff. He was powerless and, worst of all, unable to help his allies.

Jake turned to retrieve the staff but froze when he saw a Bengal tiger charging across his yard. It took the second dog by surprise and brought it down. There was a yelp and pained barks but the dog, or was it a wolf, was no match for the big cat. It soon whimpered and became still. The tiger didn't relent but continued to tear at the wolf's flesh. The wolf was being meticulously dismembered.

Seamus was fifty feet from the cabin door with the third wolf tight on his heels. The wolf changed direction and Jake realized it was coming for him. It leapt and wrapped its paws over Jake's shoulders. Jake knew that death was at hand. He felt something hot and wet on his neck and anticipated the sharpness of fangs. At the same time, he heard a thud and felt the wolf's grip loosen. The weight of it dragged him to the ground. When he hit the porch, his head twisted to the right. He found himself staring into the vacant eyes of a dismembered human head. Jake's breath left him. He rolled onto his back and saw Raj, covered in blood, with his ax swinging from his right hand.

"That was too close, boss," he said and reached his hand to help Jake up. Across the yard lay piles of human remains. Only the one with Thomas's arrow sticking from his chest could be called a body. The next one was a mass of parts, and standing over it was a nude Kathryn. She wiped her arm across her mouth, it came away smeared with blood. She looked at Jake and smiled. The third one was beheaded and lay at Jake's feet.

"Damned werewolves," said Seamus. "I always have trouble sensing them."

Jake turned to go inside. Gwynn was standing in the doorway. She had the staff in one hand and a short sword in the other.

"You may be needing this," she said as she passed the staff to him.

He felt everyone's eyes on him as he took possession of it. In that moment he felt as if he had let them all down. Gwynn smiled and he felt the hands of all his allies upon his shoulders. Together they went inside.

Chapter Fourteen

While everyone was cleaning up, Jake took the staff outside and did some cleaning of his own. The trick of blasting bodies into oblivion was coming in handy. Having just learned it, he had already used it on five dead and two undead bodies. As he wielded the staff, he thought of how much easier it would have been if he had remembered to keep the staff with him and resolved to do so from now on.

Back inside, Jake and his allies assembled in the living room, and everyone was clearly exhausted. Seamus was especially downcast because he saw the closeness of the werewolf attack as his fault.

"I don't know what it is with the wolves," said Seamus. "I can't seem to sense them until they are on me. I'm sorry, Jake. I let you down."

"Don't concern yourself with it," said Jake. He walked over and put his hand on Seamus' shoulder.

"Whoever is after me is certainly determined. If anyone here is a weak link, it's me." Turning to the others he said, "I still don't know what I'm doing or why I'm doing it. I'm trying to trust my instincts like Mr. Alphonse said, but there's so much coming so fast."

Jake looked from face to face and each of the allies met his gaze. He could detect no doubt. He sensed what must be done. He reached for the staff. When he gripped it, there was electricity in the air and bolt-like sparks danced from the tip. He had everyone's attention.

"There will be no more waiting to be attacked. From this moment forward, we will control the situation. We will find my mother and Michael McAfee, and we will eliminate any further threat to them or us."

Jake knew this was a bold statement but daring was what the situation called for.

Each of his allies stood and walked past him. Each in turn took his hand, using the grip he had been shown. The staff began to hum, vibrate, and emit power.

Seamus said, "I don't think your mother will stay in this world. I feel she will try to get back to The Farm. I also fear they can't take the most direct route. Until she reaches The Farm, she remains in real danger. I don't think they will kill her, but they will try to capture her and use her to get to you. Michael, on the other hand, is of no use to them; he will die."

"How will they cross?" asked Jake.

"There is a spell that can be used by someone as powerful as your mother, but it takes time to execute and doesn't always put the spellbinder precisely where they intend, so there are risks involved," answered Seamus.

Gwynn stood and held her arms out, bent at the elbows and slightly away from her body. She mumbled a word Jake couldn't understand and turned her hands palms up. When she straightened her fingers, a tablet-like devise materialized. She moved her fingers across the screen and continued to speak in low tones as she tapped and made swiping motions.

Nobody was surprised but Jake. Gwynn was totally immersed. Jake watched the reflection of the screen dance across her eyes. She pushed her hair behind her ear. Remembering her pointed ears and elongated finger, Jake thought how beautiful she was. As the thought came to him, she looked up at him ever so briefly and smiled. Then she was back to her task.

Jake felt a gentle pressure against his leg. He looked to find a black cat weaving between his legs. A few head butts later, the cat rolled on its back and stretched its legs to full extension. Without thinking, he reached to pet the cat. When his hand was only inches away, it bolted to the bedroom.

Moments later, Kathryn came back through the door. She was dressed in jeans, a cable knit sweater, and flat-heeled boots worn outside the jeans. She smiled mischievously and butted her head against Jake's shoulder as she passed him. Jake heard an audible groan from all the others, which caused Kathryn to smile. She made a hand gesture with her middle finger that was neither feline nor ladylike.

Gwynn turned her head from the screen and nodded in the affirmative. She moved toward Jake and the others gathered around. The device was much like a standard tablet computer, but the screen was filled with symbols, the like of which Jake had never seen. There was a depth to the display that made Jake feel he could reach into it but never find the bottom. Upon looking at the screen, Jake knew this was not some strange computer language or form of mathematics he had failed to study. This was a different reality from the one he was used to.

Gwynn touched a crescent, which was pulsating an amber glow. "This is our location," she said and looked at Jake. He must have had a blank expression because she began to explain.

"Each of the flashing lights is the position of a wizard. Your light is brightest as another wizard's would be to his allies. The stationary lights are the position of a 'gate.' We pass through the gates from one world to another. They are stationary, but where they take you can be manipulated. The lights can be laid over a grid to give us directions to the gate. This device is known as a posit. It will only show itself to you or me. We are the only ones who can call it into being. If something happens to both of us, it ceases to exist. I'll teach you how to call it."

After thirty minutes of instructions and at least fifty unsuccessful attempts, Jake finally summoned the Posit. He saw their position but seemed to be the only wizard in the vicinity. The locations of the gates were scattered, but two were within walking distance. One was the gate that he traversed to get back home. They would take the second one as that was probably the one used by his mother.

Everyone awaited his instructions. He wished he had more time to get used to his role as leader, but he was a wizard and lead he must.

"Seamus says my mother cannot take the direct path back to The Farm, so we will take the second gate," he said and pointed to the light on the Posit. "Maybe we'll find Michael and my mother. If not, maybe we can pick up their trail. Thom, you and Raj have one more look around to be sure it is safe to move. Seamus, you and Kathryn pack everything from here that may be useful. Let's be ready to go in thirty minutes."

The team set about its tasks as Gwynn and Jake regarded the Posit. In only a short time, everyone reassembled ready to move out.

As they walked away, Jake was struck with thoughts of how his life could never be the same. He wondered if he or his mother could ever return to the only place he had ever known as home. He was filled with a sense of loss. He took one last look, turned, and walked away.

The trip to the second gate was longer, but nobody complained. They walked in a loose formation, but each was vigilant. When they finally reached the gate, they formed as a group to be transported. After checking that they were ready, Jake brought the staff to his chest.

The field disappeared.

Chapter Fifteen

The Lord High Determiner paced back and forth across his private chambers. Soon he would have to take his place upon the throne and make hundreds of decisions, which nobody else could seem to make. Everyone came to him for answers. Sometimes he would issue a simple edict and that would do until the next sheep was rushed into his audience to plead his pitiful existence. Sometimes if the plea was too mundane or the question especially asinine, the poor fool would get more than his answer. A flogging was the price for wasting the Determiner's time. In extreme cases, the loss of a head would ensure that no more problems were forthcoming. Such was the price of leadership.

He walked to the mirror and regarded his image. Most days, the Determiner gazed back at him, but from time to time that mutinous rogue Salvatore Vaccaro would stare back with a gleam in his eye. When that happened, he knew it was going to be a glorious day.

The knock was almost imperceptible. It had to be Jamal. The Determiner signaled to the guard and Jamal was admitted. With a wave of his hand, the Determiner dismissed the Supreme Protectorate to wait in the corridor. By the look on Jamal's face, the news was not good. He felt his anger begin to rise. He could not let it get out of control. He needed the sorcerer.

"My Lord," began Jamal, "I regret to tell you that the wolves failed in eliminating the Lokins boy. They thought they had more time, but the allies had already assembled with the wizard. They have already transitioned. We are trying to locate them now. We have word that they did not return to The Society Farm. I will discover the destination soon." When he finished speaking, Jamal took a step back, waiting for the explosion that he knew was coming.

Without saying a word, the Determiner walked past Jamal and into the corridor. Jamal followed. Together they strode to the royal chambers. When the guards opened the door, the Determiner went inside and signaled for everyone but Jamal to leave. He climbed onto the dais and sat upon his throne. Before Jamal could take his place next to the Determiner, he was stopped by the slamming of a fist against the arm of the throne.

"The fools!" he shouted. "It seems all we deal with is fools. The necromancer fails first and now the werewolves. They dare to go after a wizard in twos and threes. Did they not know that this wizard is a Lokins?"

"They were told, my Lord."

"Well, at least he saved me the trouble of having to kill them. We are through with these idiots. If I must send an army after them, I will have my bidding done. We cannot afford to let Lokins mature into his role as wizard."

After the rage, the silence in the chambers was complete. The Determiner raised his head and stared past Jamal, then lowered his gaze to meet the sorcerer's.

"Summon Major Bannar!"

Chapter Sixteen

Jake expected they would be moved through the gate as a unit and then assemble in a discreet place to assess their situation. He had hoped to find his mother and Michael McAfee and be back at The Farm by day's end. None of that happened.

Jake was in the edge of a forest. The land rose in front of him, and he could see the crest of a hill. The land was barren between his position and the hilltop. He had been standing as he traversed the gate, but now he was down on one knee with the staff resting under his right hand. He was alone.

His surroundings looked nothing like the world in which he had spent twenty years. Colors were subdued and there was no luster. Leaves were olive drab with no differentiation in hue among the different species. The ground and flora appeared dull and uninteresting. He looked up at a sky that reminded him of the most dismal morning in his world when rain was a foregone conclusion. What could have been a sun was cast behind the veil of gray, so not much heat or light could penetrate. Beside the first sphere, which he thought of as the sun, was another body, oval in shape. It looked as if it were spinning in a counterclockwise direction. He knew he was far from home.

Jake tried to stand and abruptly fell onto his side. He rolled onto his back and assumed a sitting position. Encased in calf-high boots, his feet looked three times their normal size. The boots were made of a rough material that did not resemble a natural substance. A skintight garment that reminded him of tights covered his legs and continued up to his waist. They too were constructed of an unrecognizable fabric. A pullover jersey fell to his upper thigh and obscured his view. The lightness of the clothes contrasted directly to the heaviness of the boots. The best description of the shade was neutral or an absence of color.

He was shocked at first but then remembered the changes that took place with his allies as they joined him at his house. He wondered what changes had taken place in his facial structure. He stood and walked around a bit to acclimate himself to the weight of the footwear. He soon became comfortable in them. The ground under him felt spongy and indented when stepped on but sprang back when he lifted his weight. The oversized boots acted much like snowshoes. Was this whole world of this nature or only the portion in which he found himself? It was time to explore and try to reconnect with the others.

He opened his hand, palm down, and the staff rose to meet him. He walked to the last row of trees and paused to observe his surroundings. He needed to decide which direction to take. He was about to emerge from the trees when he heard an anguished scream coming from over the hill. Gripping the staff in both hands, he stepped back into the trees.

A movement caught his eye. A creature, feline in nature, topped the hill so fast it became airborne. Jake could not determine its shape as it rolled, head over heels, before hitting the ground. When it regained its feet, Jake could see the animal was no taller than a house cat but over twice as wide. Long whiskers covering the face blew back as the animal ran. From the neck back, its fur was close to the skin, and its tail was short but covered with long hair. The cat's feet were not out of proportion to its body. Jake had the thought the cat's weight was such that it would not have trouble traversing the spongy ground. He also thought it might be Kathryn.

The cause of the cat's discomfort became clear as two birds flew over the hill. As they flew, they would take turns diving at the cat. Their long, pointed beaks clearly meant to inflict as much damage as possible. Jake stepped from the woods and the cat changed direction and came straight at him. He leaned the staff against his body and began frantically waving his hand over his head. The birds saw him and, after one more dive, peeled away and began gaining altitude. The cat ran past him and nestled behind a tree.

"Kathryn, is that you?" he asked, turning toward the cat, which was still cowered down.

"Yes, it is Jake. Those birds came out of nowhere. I was trying to have a look around and must have gotten too close to their nest. Where are the others?"

"I don't know. You're the first I've seen since passing through. Would you mind changing back? I still have trouble carrying on a two-way conversation with a cat."

"You'd love that, wouldn't you? I don't have any clothes. They're over the hill. You'll have to help me retrieve them—in case the birds are waiting." She stood as a cat and walked between his shoes as cats are prone to do. Jake found it awkward.

"Kathryn, stop, please! Where are we? Have you been here before today?"

"I don't think so. This is a soft terrain world. I've only experienced one other like it, and I hope this is not that world again."

Jake secured the staff and said, "Let's go get your clothes and try to find the others. Nice figure, by the way."

She hissed and followed him out of the forest and back up the hill.

The terrain continued to compress beneath their feet as they traversed the open area. Walking took more effort here, much like trudging through loose sand, and Jake's legs were becoming tired. The size of his boots made it possible without sinking too far, but their weight only added to his dilemma. In her feline form, Kathryn was light enough and strong enough to proceed without any obvious discomfort.

A set of structures appeared ahead but turned out to be large boulders as they neared. They were surrounded by flat, barren land.

The massive stones appeared as if they had bubbled up from the center of the planet. The largest was the size of a two-story building and the smallest as big as a compact car. Jake found a place where he hoped he couldn't be seen from the plain and slumped down to rest. Kathryn continued slinking behind one of the larger rocks. After a few minutes, she reappeared in human form. She was dressed much like Jake, but the form fitting clothes looked better on her. She caught him staring.

"Oh, Jake, you make me feel like a kitten again," she said with a sly smile.

Jake felt himself blush. Why did she have such an effect on him? He looked away.

He didn't have long to feel embarrassed because they heard voices. He and Kathryn slipped back into the shadow of the rock and turned their attention to the sound. The procession was just visible on the horizon. The flatness of the terrain and a steady breeze must have allowed the voices to reach them. Jake watched as they grew closer.

At the head of the procession was a vehicle that, with the right amount of imagination, could be a cross between a jeep and a troop carrier. It was open-topped, and the body rode well above the ground. What could only be thought of as tires looked to be about three feet wide with two-thirds of each extending toward the center of the vehicle. Until he had seen the procession, Jake had not realized there was a road. Instead of tread, paddles that must have been used to traverse the open ground protruded from the tires. This was confirmed when one of the vehicles left the road. The treads dug into the ground and propelled the vehicle forward. As it moved, it didn't tear the ground but rolled it up, creating little wakes that soon smoothed back out as the vehicle progressed.

There were two enormous "people" in the cab of the truck and six more on benches in the back.

Behind the jeep were two lines of what Jake at first took for horses but turned out to be mechanized vehicles. Atop each was another large individual. Jake could see no contact point between the vehicle and the ground. They seemed to hover. Ten of these vehicles formed each column.

Jake debated whether to make himself known and had almost decided to chance it when a platform came into view. It was pulled along by two of the motorcycles. Besides the rider, each bike had a passenger equipped with a weapon held upright, facing toward the rear.

Jake must have moved away from the boulder because at that instant Kathryn grabbed his shirttail and pulled him back. When he snapped his head around to look at her, she was pointing back to the caravan. What he saw froze his heart.

On the platform were Seamus, Thomas, and Raj. They were smaller than the others and dressed like him and Kathryn, but it was definitely them. There were four others on the wagon as well—all bound and obviously prisoners.

The staff vibrating by his side brought his attention into focus. There were ten more riders behind the platform. The lead carrier was close enough for Jake to see that this army was not human. They were a species which he would not have imagined before his visit to The Farm. The soldiers' heads looked like drawings of Neanderthals that he had studied in school. Their skin was gray and seemed thick, almost elephantine. The armor each appeared to wear turned out to be their own naked body. They had no genitalia that Jake could see. His inspection was cut short by movement beside him.

As he turned, Kathryn was slipping off her tights, having already shed her tunic and boots. She had on no underwear. She ignored his surprise and gawking and leaned into his ear, whispering, "I've got to let them know we've seen them."

Before he could reply, her body transformed into the feline form she had appeared in earlier. She moved through the rock formation and perched herself on the last one. At first, nobody noticed her; then one of the motorcycle riders saw her. He pulled a weapon from the front of the cycle and took aim. Kathryn didn't move. As the soldier started to fire, Thomas tried to stand and caused the wagon to rock. The movement must have distracted the shooter because, when he fired, the projectile went high over Kathryn's head. She leapt from the boulder and ran for the wooded area. One guard jumped from the cycle to the wagon and slapped Thomas across the face. Thomas slumped into a seated position. He must have said something to the others because, one by one, they looked toward the rocks.

Jake knew he could not confront the caravan and demand the release of his allies. He would probably join them. The staff was slowly pulsing in his hand. It was warning him to be patient. He didn't know how he knew that, but he did with a certainty beyond question. He leaned against the rock and closed his eyes.

Chapter Seventeen

Jake must have dozed because a sharp vibration of the staff brought him to attention. When his eyes snapped open, he found Kathryn across from him in human form and dressed. She too was on guard. Something was coming through the rocks to the left. An opening appeared in one of the boulders and Gwynn stepped through. The final member of the team was accounted for. She was not attired like the rest of them. Her appearance was still fae. Jake didn't understand that but was elated nonetheless. He rose, ran to her, and hugged her to him. He heard Kathryn grunt her disapproval. Gwynn didn't know what to do. Behind Gwynn, four others, all fae, stepped through the opening. Gwynn introduced them as Elic, Simon, Arac, and Celine. Once they had acknowledged each other, Gwynn motioned Jake to the side. The fae and Kathryn moved away and sat opposite of each other.

"Have you seen the others?" asked Gwynn without preamble.

"Yes, they're being held captive, but they know that we're here and that we are aware of their predicament. How did you find us, and how did you find your people?"

"They found me. They are fae but not my people. We all look alike to you."

Now it was Jake's turn to groan. Gwynn moved her hand and the posit came into view.

"This is how I found you." She opened the posit, and he saw the blinking red light. Jake saw the location of the gate they had come through. He also noted two more gates. Their options out of this world were but three. Before they could think about that, they had to find and rescue Seamus, Thomas, and Raj.

As if reading Jake's mind, Gwynn said, "The fae can lead us to where the others are being held, but we must prepare ourselves and plan. They have offered us food and shelter. If you agree, we can go with them now."

"Do you trust them?"

"They've already saved me once and led me here. I have never met a fae who was deceitful, but this is a different world."

"We'll go with them but remain cautious and not allow ourselves to be separated. What do they know of us?"

"They know you are a wizard and our leader, but they don't know how much power you have."

Jake didn't know how much power he had.

Gwynn turned to the fae. "We are ready."

Elic and Arac took the lead, then Gwynn and Jake, followed by Simon and Celine. Kathryn lagged behind. Jake was becoming annoyed by Kathryn's lax behavior. Gwynn placed a hand on his arm, and he understood that Kathryn was not being slack. Kathryn was taking a defensive position to keep them from being sandwiched between the fae. Jake made a mental note not to be so fast to judge the behavior of his allies. Elic and Arac laid their hands on the boulder from which they appeared, and a door opened.

Jake was prepared to step into a dark corridor and proceed through a series of tunnels to reach their destination. Instead, he found himself in a whole different world. They were walking along a path that had been cleared through some trees. The ground was solid, and the sky was a pale green. The explosion of colors came as a stark contrast to where they had been only moments earlier. He looked at Gwynn.

"A layered world," she said with the same degree of concern she would exhibit if telling a child that fire was hot. Jake knew he would need further explanation when time and opportunity availed itself.

After walking through the forest for a short while, they came upon a grassy plain that extended as far as the eye could see. From there, they walked for what felt like hours. No one was the least bit concerned that they were open and exposed. The staff hung loosely in his right hand and didn't vibrate or communicate in any way. Jake took that as a positive sign. He realized that since they had entered this world they had not seen another living creature, be it human, fae, or animal. He filed another question for Gwynn.

The weather was neither cold nor hot. The path was like a nature trail back in Jake's home world. It was made of perfectly level, compacted soil and showed no signs of vehicular use. Manicured grass formed the borders of the path with a line so flawless that it looked like a seamstress had laid a straight edge and cut along it. All trees appeared to be of the same variety and did not vary in height or shape more than a few inches. Small shrubs and flowers were the only things that grew as individual entities. The sky above was vast and of one color.

Distance was difficult to discern. Jake wondered if their surroundings were some type of illusion. That he had arrived in a different place that seemed to occupy the same space only added to Jake's confusion. Again, he found himself reasoning out an environment and circumstances that, until a short while ago, he would have dismissed as absurd.

Something changed. The best way to describe the transformation would be an increase in atmospheric pressure. Jake felt a closeness as if he were in a confined space. Gwynn sensed it too. She touched his arm and applied a downward force. Jake nodded his head in acknowledgment. He looked back at Kathryn; she had dropped further back and was moving from side to side of the procession. He repositioned the staff so that he was holding it with two hands. It emitted a low vibration that did not feel like a warning. Gwynn removed her hand from his arm and moved a short distance away so that he would have a whole range of motion. She had seen enough to know that he would not hesitate to unleash the force of the staff in defense of the team. There was no change in the demeanor of the fae. Elic and Arac stopped and turned to face them.

"We are almost there," said Elic. "We must stop and acclimate ourselves to the atmosphere of our village." He recognized Jake's new posture and smiled. "You are in no danger, wizard. My ancestors and your ancestors traveled many paths together and fought many battles at each other's sides before the worlds were splintered."

With that, the fae took a seat. Gwynn and Jake followed suit, but Kathryn took a place a distance behind them.

After a short while, Jake's breathing became steady, and the feeling of pressure dissipated. The fae stood as did Jake, Gwynn, and Kathryn. Instead of continuing their journey, Celine took a few steps and reached her hand out. An opening appeared but what was on the other side was not visible. Celine, Elic, and Arac moved through and disappeared. Simon stepped up and motioned them through. Jake signaled Kathryn to come ahead, and she and Gwynn went through.

"Come," he said. "The door will close when the last fae traverses."

Jake took the step and Simon followed.

Chapter Eighteen

Thomas slumped back into a seated position. His face burned and there was a ringing in his ear. He had been in many hand-to-hand combat situations but could not remember being slapped so hard with an open hand. No matter; it was worth it. Kathryn had been brave, holding her position until he had noticed her. His head began to clear.

"Kathryn was just up the hill, so the others will be notified," he said in a quiet voice. He was pleased that both Raj and Seamus had heard him. Neither of the three knew what lay ahead, but each was assured that everything possible would be done to free them.

It was a boost to each man's confidence and was the first positive since they transitioned.

After Jake performed the transition, Raj had found himself in a vast open area. He landed flat on his back, and the weight of his body compressed the surface below him. Looking around, he saw both Thomas and Seamus. They were all separated by about a hundred yards. The other two were upright and walking toward each other with an awkward, unsteady gait.

"Here," yelled Raj, although it appeared that Seamus had already spotted him.

"Hello, little man," Thomas said when they were all together. "Have you seen Jake or the ladies?"

Raj bristled at being called "little man" but was secretly pleased to be reunited with the other two.

"No sign of anyone until I saw your ugly face."

Thomas slapped Raj on the shoulder. What was meant to be an act of comradery knocked Raj off his feet. He bounced back up as if he had landed on a trampoline.

Before anything could go any further, Seamus said, "I don't sense that they are close. I hope they are all right."

"You worry too much, leprechaun," Thomas boomed. "How did you get so tall anyway?"

"Why can't you just call us by our names?" said Seamus, although he knew that any protest was useless.

Raj thought all the banter was a substitute for saying how happy they were to be together. Without another word, they turned to the task of finding the others.

For as far as they could see, the land appeared desolate. It was Thomas who saw the road. Normally, they would look for cover until they could assess their new situation. Since there was no cover, they thought there was no reason to avoid the road.

The convoy descended upon them before they realized. Upon seeing it, they slowed their pace. They were unsure what to do until two motorcycle-like vehicles broke away from the procession and raced toward them.

"Run," yelled Seamus.

They did but there was nowhere to run to or to hide. The big shoes that were native to this world were not made for a swift escape. They left the road and set off across the open terrain. Raj and Thomas were having the hardest time because of their weight. Seamus, who was thin and had longer legs, pulled ahead. Thinking in conventional terms, Raj reasoned that the motorcycles might have a hard time traversing the spongy surface. They did not.

The cycles, each with a driver and a rider on the back, glided *above* the terrain. One pulled alongside Thomas and another beside Raj. The passengers of each stood and with practiced precision leapt from the bike and onto Thomas and Raj. Thomas was ready to fight but found himself pinned beneath the body of a gigantic creature. Raj did not fare any better. Seamus might have gotten away but could not bring himself to abandon his allies. He turned and charged headlong into the creature atop Raj. His hit hardly registered. The driver of the first motorcycle pulled alongside, stopped the bike, dismounted, and in short order subdued Seamus.

Soon all three were shackled, hand and foot, and marched back to the waiting convoy. They were loaded onto a platform-like wagon with several other unfortunate souls.

Chapter Nineteen

here was no slamming of the door; it just disappeared. They were in a courtyard with fae of all ages. In the short time that the existence of fae was made known to him, Jake had not considered the existence of elderly fae or newborns. He must have thought they came into being fully realized.

Everyone was scurrying about and those who noticed them at all smiled and continued. Shops and storefronts stood all around the square. All services were available, just as they would have been in any town in America. No modes of transportation were apparent but, after seeing the convoy topside, Jake felt that some must exist.

They crossed the courtyard and stopped in front of a building with a formidable metal door. There were no windows in the building. Elic turned to face them. Jake had not noticed the departure of Arac, Simon, and Celine.

"Will you please come with me? This is the office of the Gohrn. We must see him for your accommodations and to speak of those held above."

Without awaiting comment, he turned and motioned with his hand. The door opened inward. As they stepped through, they found themselves at the bottom of a stone stairway. The space was only big enough to accommodate those assembled. There were no other doors or windows. A solid wall surrounded them. The door had disappeared and so had Kathryn. He started to inquire but an almost imperceptible movement of Gwynn's head made him hold his question. They began to climb. When they reached the first landing, another flight of steps rose before them. They repeated this three more times until they arrived at the fifth level. Jake only remembered it being a two-story building. Again Elic motioned a door into existence.

They faced a room that was three times the width of the building they had entered. This entire world seemed to be full of physical and spatial contradictions. Jake didn't know why he should be surprised after his visit to The Farm. The ceiling was at least twelve feet high with a pattern that reminded Jake of some of the old office buildings back home. It was covered with panels that had been stamped out of thin metal. No two panels were alike. The walls were lined with small cubes with openings about the size of a deck of cards. In each cube was a scroll. Rows of tables lined up across the floor with fae standing on each side of them. All appeared busy working on scrolls.

As one, they stopped what they were doing and turned their scrolls face down. They looked to one end of the room. Jake's eyes followed.

There, in a raised area with an enormous desk and a high-backed chair, sat a small fae man. Jake found himself wondering if the man's feet touched the floor. The man did not act surprised by their intrusion. He raised a small hand and motioned them forward.

"The Gohrn will see you now," said Elic. He turned and left the room.

Jake and Gwynn walked to the platform but, as he started to step up, Gwynn grabbed his arm. She addressed the Gohrn in a language that Jake could not understand.

"Please come forward," he said. Gwynn and Jake both approached the desk. Jake had no idea what to say, how to explain their presence, or what to ask for in order to rescue their allies.

"Welcome to you and your companions, wizard. You must excuse any reluctance that you may sense in my manner or speech. Throughout our history, we have pledged our allegiance to the Society of Builders and stood ready to help in any way we can. But the truth is this is the first time our pledge has been tested."

"Sir," replied Jake. "I can assure you that I don't want to cause you or your people any discomfort. However, I find myself in a situation that must be dealt with in an expeditious manner. The well-being of some of my colleagues is at stake, and I must secure their freedom. Any help you can offer is deeply appreciated."

"Our relationship with the world above is an uneasy peace. We coexist with the knowledge that we inhabit two very different portions of the same world. Ours is an intellectual society while theirs is a more physical existence. While we value order, planning, basic rights, and freedom, they favor brute strength and control. Any outsider is treated with distrust, and most are conscripted into involuntary servitude."

"You mean slavery," Jake said before he could help himself. Gwynn shifted uneasily beside him, but the thought of his companions as indentured labor was unbearable to Jake. He squeezed the staff tightly. If he could blast the entire upper world into oblivion to save his allies, he would.

"Their ways are not our ways," said the Gohrn. "We mean to help you, but I will have to confer with our Council of Regents to determine how best to do it. Please be our guest for the night. We will speak again tomorrow."

"Sir, would you happen to have maps of the land above so that I may familiarize myself?" he pressed to Gwynn's discomfort.

"I believe I can arrange that," said the Gohrn flatly. He looked down at his desk, and Elic appeared just behind them.

"I'll show you to your quarters now," Elic said.

Chapter Twenty

Their lodgings consisted of a suite of rooms with a large common area with several short hallways, each leading to a bathroom and sleeping quarters. Jake was relieved that the fae did not separate him from Gwynn. Although the furniture was sized a bit smaller than that back home, Jake found it quite comfortable. There was food laid out on a table, but Jake didn't recognize any of the offerings. He kept waiting for Gwynn to scold him for his lack of decorum, but instead she brought him bits of food to taste. She explained what each dish was and shared its closest equivalent that he would know. Being from a small rural town, he had never tried or even heard of some of the food she described from his world. Still, he found several offerings quite good and ate them with relish. He had not realized how famished he was.

A knock came at the door. Gwynn went to answer it but called Jake. He arrived to find a slight female with eyes as large and blue as robin's eggs. They each took a second to appraise each other. Her eyes locked onto Jake's for a beat or two longer than Jake deemed necessary. Next, her hand shot from behind her back. Jake jumped back and the staff flew into his hand. His stance relaxed when he saw she held only two scrolls. She slowly moved back a step, clearly trying not to show her terror at seeing the staff move of its own volition.

"Please give the Gohrn my sincere thanks," he said, gently taking the scrolls from her. Without saying anything, she turned and hurried down the hall.

Jake closed the door and started back to the common area. There was another bump at the door. He thought the girl must have forgotten to relay some message. When Jake again opened the door, he found an empty corridor but felt something brush past his leg. When he turned, there was a cat-like creature already curled up in his chair. Kathryn was home.

A surge of relief flowed through Jake, which he found surprising. So much so that he almost forgot the scrolls. He went to the chair and forced his way beside the cat. He reached out and stroked its head much like he would do to a normal cat.

"Oh, Jake, I didn't know you cared," came Kathryn's voice from the mouth of the cat. His hand recoiled and his breath caught so fast that he became choked and went into a coughing fit.

The laughter coming from both females so embarrassed him that he felt a rush of heat as his face reddened.

"Touchy, touchy," said Kathryn continuing to laugh. "I'd like to reconfigure now. Do you want me to do it with or without something to cover me?"

Jake stammered furthering his discomfort but was rescued when Gwynn dropped a robe over Kathryn. The cat made two complete circles under the robe before it started to rise as Kathryn resumed her human form. She did not hurry in closing the robe. Jake stared on and Gwynn shook her head.

While Kathryn took a bath and ate, Jake unrolled the scrolls. There was a map of the above world and one of the lands of the fae. Gwynn came over and pointed to the area where she had found him. A series of marks led Jake's eyes to the location of the boulder field. The path on which the caravan traveled was shown by a serpentine line. It ran from what must be some type of agricultural or industrial complex on one end to a compound on the other. The map offered no more than an overview.

"Did you see this area before you were picked up by the fae?" Jake asked.

"No, I took for granted that they just found me by happenstance although, in after thought, they were in a hurry to move on. I wonder why they were there in the first place?" Gwynn walked to the chair and sat. She thought for a minute and said, "I think they were sent to fetch me and, in turn, you."

Jake began to feel uncomfortable, but reason prevented him from seeing malice in the actions of the fae. They could have left him and his friends on the surface, and their existence would have never been known. No, there had to be more to it than was apparent.

Turning his attention back to the map, his thoughts turned to the compound. "They are being held there," he said, pointing to the map. "And we know nothing about it."

"I can help with that," said Kathryn emerging from the bath and toweling her hair. "The common belief among the fae is that the compound is impenetrable. I overheard Arac and Celine talking about it while I was a cat. They knew we were here and how many we were. They failed to reach Raj, Seamus, and Thomas in time. I believe that presents as big a problem for them as it does for us. Tomorrow should prove interesting."

Gwynn rose and called up the posit, then walked to the table and held it over the scroll. The map became superimposed on the screen. Jake saw that his light was blinking but weak. He looked at Gwynn.

"Don't worry, Jake, it only means that you are not on the surface that we are observing. These two gates will be available to us," she said, pointing to two beacons, both near the work complex.

"That means if we retrieve them from the compound, we will have to travel almost the entire area before we can escape," said Jake, stating the obvious. "We need to know more."

Jake exchanged scrolls and once again Gwynn held the posit above it. Jake's light became brighter. He felt much better. The only thing showing on the map was the area in which they currently resided. No indication of any routes of travel to or from the city appeared, and no passages were shown. Either this was an extremely compact land, or the map had been edited. Jake found both options troubling. Looking up, he noticed that both Gwynn and Kathryn appeared perplexed.

"You two get some rest. I'm going to see what I can find out," said Kathryn as the robe slumped to the floor. "Jake, if you please," she said, walking to the door. He opened the door, and she slipped outside.

"What do you make of this?" Jake asked Gwynn.

"I don't know, Jake. Perhaps this world *is* that small, but I suspect it more likely the map is false. I don't know why they would wish to limit our knowledge. Let Kathryn do what she does best—snoop around."

Jake rolled both scrolls and placed them on the table. Gwynn retook her chair, but the posit was nowhere in sight. Jake paced about the room, trying to formulate a plan with the limited knowledge available. Gwynn followed him with her eyes but said nothing. They both jumped when they hear a bump at the door. Jake opened it and Kathryn sauntered in. She nosed her way under the crumpled robe and transformed. "I can't get out of the building," she said. "The doors are all locked and we seem to be the only ones here."

Once again, Jake had more questions than answers. Not knowing what to say, he took the staff and walked down the hallway to his sleeping quarters, leaving Gwynn and Kathryn quietly talking on the couch.

Chapter Twenty-One

J ake awoke early. He spent the time pacing, trying to come up with a plan. He knew he had to act quickly and decisively. He thought of his allies in captivity. He anguished over the conditions they must have to contend with. The idea of them being forced to work created a mental picture that was almost unbearable. He determined that, with or without the help of the fae, he would act soon.

Gwynn walked into the room just as a knock sounded. Jake turned his palm down and the staff came to him. When Gwynn opened the door, Elic appeared accompanied by the girl who had delivered the maps, bearing a new tray of food. She looked past Gwynn and directly at Jake. With only a slight hesitation, she stepped into the room. Removing the old tray, she replaced it with the new and made a hasty retreat.

"Good morning, wizard," Elic said with a smile. "I trust you found everything satisfactory and had a good night's sleep?"

"Yes," Jake answered. "It was good but I must confess that I am becoming very anxious about the well-being of those in captivity. When will I be able to begin securing my allies' freedom?"

"You will begin soon, wizard. The council will convene later this morning. I will come for you at that time."

He turned to leave but his eyes settled on Gwynn.

"Some of our sisters will celebrate the 'Rite of Noa' this morning, and you are welcome to join them."

Gwynn bowed and said, "Thank you."

Laying the staff aside, Jake walked to the tray and began to eat. "What is this rite of Noa?"

Gwynn took a deep breath and explained, "Noa was the daughter of Zelle and Wynoor, the king and queen of the fae. Noa convinced her father, Zelle, to call a council meeting of all faeries, sprites, wood nymphs, and pixies. The goal would be to unite all for the good and continuation of our species. Until that time, all courts lived independently, each making their own rules and mores of behavior. Each had to, in turn, defend itself, which was not an easy task. Most fae lived in fear, hiding from the world at large.

"Zelle led the council and eventually all were united. Noa then persuaded her father to make the existence of all known and to form an alliance with humans and other peaceful beings. Again, he was successful. This is how we became allied with the Society of Builders. Thus began generations of peace and harmony among all beings so inclined. Upon the death of Zelle, Noa was called to become queen. Noa was the first female fae to reign as true queen, not just the wife of a king. Of course, there were those who clung to the old ways, most of which banded together to form the Unseelie Court. The rites of Noa is a celebration performed by female fae on a regular basis to honor the accomplishments of Noa. It is to give thanks for the life that we have and to keep the legend alive."

Even after all Jake had seen and done, he still found it hard to accept that there were so many worlds with so much life and history in each. "This sounds like something you would want to take part in," he said.

"I would love to if I were in my native court and we did not have allies in danger."

Jake looked into her eyes and nodded his approval. A bump sounded at the door.

"Kathryn must be back," Gwynn said. "She left this morning as soon as she could find a way out."

When Jake opened the door, Kathryn came in and ran to her bedroom without a word. In a moment she returned wrapped in a robe. Her face, hands, and feet were dirty, and she looked as if she was exhausted. She sat on the couch and pulled her feet up under her.

Without preamble, Jake asked, "Well, what did you find?"

"I'm doing fine. Thank you so much for asking."

Admonished, Jake plopped down in a nearby chair and threw up his hands.

"Give him a break, Kat," said Gwynn. "We are going to the council in a few hours."

"Here in the city, everything appears to be fine, but I don't think things are actually as they appear. The further I traveled away from the city, the more anxious the people became. Also, the population began to lessen until, only about an hour out of town, it became nonexistent. It's not that the land is barren or forbidding. It's anything but. There are farms, homes, and services, but everything is abandoned and grown over. I didn't sense anything toxic, but I don't know how things work here. It's like someone or something either drew the population in or forced them to move."

Jake thought what Kathryn had described was what the map depicted but why?

"Thanks, Kathryn. Good work," said Jake. He turned to Gwynn and said, "Maybe you should go to the ceremony and see what you can pick up without creating suspicion. If they call me to council before you get back, I'll try to represent us. If there is anything I don't understand, I'll either seek clarification or ask that you be sent for."

"Whatever you think best, Jake," Gwynn replied. She tried to hide it, but Jake thought he detected a trace of elation in her voice. "The ceremony starts soon, so I should get ready." She left the living room.

"What do you think, Kathryn?"

"The fae have been very kind to us so far. They proclaim a willingness to help us, but I sense some hesitation. I don't think we are in any danger while we are here, but you should probably develop different scenarios to take into account varying degrees of help."

Jake felt ashamed. For whatever reason, he had never considered Kathryn's intellect. He had thought only of her ability to take on feline form, but in a few sentences she had summed up their entire situation. She had also confirmed a feeling he had but could not put his finger on. He would never underestimate her again.

"Thank you, Kathryn. I believe your assessment is spot on. We will need to proceed cautiously."

Jake heard the door to Gwynn's bedroom open. When she appeared, he had his second revelation of the morning. Gwynn wore a dress, the first he'd ever seen her wear. The bodice was form fitting. It tied around her neck and was joined to the front of the skirt. It was a shade of blue that Jake could not remember ever seeing. As she moved, the hue appeared to change almost like it was adapting to nearby colors. The skirt fell to mid-calf and appeared to be made up of hundreds of scarves in varying colors. When she took a step, her leg would find its way through the scarves. Her deep brown footwear was a cross between a sandal and a boot with one thin strap running between her toes and a boot top. The boot top covered the area between her ankle and mid-calf with only an inch of skin bare beneath the bottom of the skirt. The wafer-thin soles contoured to her feet. She had pulled her hair back and braided it with a band of small flowers, greenery, and twigs woven in.

She was beautiful. The most striking thing, what surprised Jake most, was a set of gossamer wings that showed behind her. Small and shaped like a butterfly's wings, they were made of a transparent, silklike substance woven over the most delicate framework. He thought at first that they might be attached to the dress, but when she walked past he saw they grew from her back and would shift position as her muscles moved.

Kathryn must have registered his surprise because she had a big smile on her face as she said, "Isn't she beautiful, Jake?" Turning to Gwynn before Jake could reply, she said, "You are truly beautiful, sweetie. It has been a long time since I've seen you reveal."

"It's been a long time since there has been an occasion to reveal. Jake, are you sure I should go?"

"Yes, I'm sure," said Jake. "And you are beautiful. Don't worry; Kathryn and I can take care of things here. Find out what you can."

Jake thought he saw her blush as she opened the door. In the hallway he saw Celine dressed much like Gwynn, wings and all. He had no idea how Celine had known to come for Gwynn.

As soon as the door closed, another knock came. It was Elic. "Come, wizard, the council awaits."

Jake turned to Kathryn, but she was nowhere in sight.

Chapter Twenty-Two

Seamus had tossed and turned all night. Now he was awake but didn't have any concept of time. There were no windows, so day and night looked the same. It must be morning because some of the other prisoners were beginning to stir.

He tried to remain observant after their capture and hoped that by doing so he could plan a route of escape. For the most part, the land was flat and desolate. There were some forested areas but no large plains of vegetation. Two groups of large rocks were the only other protrusions from the landscape. He had to wonder if this entire world was as barren as what he had so far experienced.

When the compound came into sight, Seamus was dazzled by the size of it. A moat, which surrounded the compound, was the first water he had seen. From bank to bank, the moat appeared to be approximately two hundred feet wide. The depth was hard to estimate. Two security vessels patrolled the waters. Seamus could not tell if the vessels floated or hovered above the moat. Each boat was manned by the same creatures that made up the convoy. Seamus wondered if they were the dominant species here. He knew they were not the only species since he shared the wagon with other human-like prisoners.

As the convoy approached the bridge, the enormity of the compound became apparent. Seamus had to lean back so his eyes could see the top of the wall. Even with its immense height, the structure inside dwarfed the surrounding barricade.

When they were midway across the bridge, the doors to the compound opened. It was an onslaught to the senses. The contrast between what he had seen and what he now viewed was mind numbing. People, most humanoid, scurried to and fro in the courtyard. The creatures that had captured Seamus and his allies were present but imposed no restrictions on the citizenry. If anything, they appeared to lay back and be as unobtrusive as possible.

The courtyard seemed to go on into infinity. There were green areas just beyond the courtyard and trees in the distance. Seamus wondered if all the inhabitants of the world resided in this one area.

As the convoy rolled into the courtyard, people took little to no notice. Seamus looked at both Thomas and Raj. Raj appeared to be struck by the same wonder as Seamus. Thomas, on the other hand, looked as if his only thought was of destroying the whole thing and killing anyone who got in his way. Seamus found this oddly assuring.

The convoy stopped outside the castle-like structure, which dominated the square. One of the creatures leapt upon the wagon and motioned for them to disembark. When Seamus stepped off the wagon, he found the ground under his feet solid. He took a quick glance around and saw that solid terrain filled the courtyard.

Guards formed a loose perimeter around them and marched them into the palace. It was spacious and well-appointed, but they had little time to observe it. They were marched down several flights of steps into what was obviously a dungeon and placed into individual cells. As soon as the doors were locked, a human went cell to cell offering a ladle of water to each prisoner. When he had served each man, he returned to his own cell and pulled the door closed behind him. Seamus thought the man must be a trustee and made note to be aware and beware of him.

Seamus, Thomas, and Raj were placed in adjacent cells, so they were able to communicate until Raj noticed the trustee trying to eavesdrop.

When food came, it was flavorful and nutritious. They were each given their fill.

The cells were relatively comfortable, considering that the entire area was cool and damp.

Now, in the morning, activity was in full swing. The trustee pushed a cart down the aisle between rows of cells. He served each prisoner a ladle of water and left each one with a steaming mug of beverage. Another man followed with a tray of food for each inmate. On the tray was this world's equivalent of an English breakfast. There were eggs, sausages, bacon, beans, tomatoes, mushrooms, and a baguette.

Seamus thought for prisoners they were certainly fed well. He would soon find out why.

Chapter Twenty-Three

Gwynn followed Celine down the stairs and out of the building. They turned east and continued to walk. In her Court of Origin, the Rite of Noa was always held outside, and it appeared to be so here. They walked to the edge of town and down a path that led to an area of forest. Gwynn could hear the drums beating in a slow rhythm.

Celine said little during their walk, but as they approached the sound of drumming and chatting, she turned to Gwynn, and said, "Thank you for attending our rite. This is a ceremony that all fae women are welcome to celebrate. Though we are from different courts, we share a common history and hold common lore to be true. I know that you now dwell among the Society of Builders, but as sisters we will celebrate together. May the wisdom and compassion of our greater Queen Noa be with you."

"And also with you, sister," returned Gwynn.

They entered a clearing and Gwynn was filled with joy by what she saw. There were hundreds of female fae present. They had formed circles, the first of which lined the outer circumference of the clearing. Two feet inside the first loop another formed and so on until, in the center, there was but one fae, the Nan. As Gwynn and Celine came forward, the outer circle broke, and they were absorbed into it. They began circling in a counterclockwise direction while the next circle in rotated clockwise. The drummers formed the last loop before the Nan. They maintained a rhythmic beat that dictated the rate of rotation. Gwynn knew that the speed would vary as the rite progressed.

They all chanted in a low voice, "Tha gaol agamort, Noa. Taped lead, Noa." (I love you, Noa. Thank you, Noa.)

Only the Nan was stationary. Being the oldest of the female fae, she was designated to lead the rites. The Nan extended her arms above her head and spread her fingers. Her wings began to flutter, and she lifted from the forest floor and hovered. Seconds later, each circle from center to back also used their wings to rise and hover. Gwynn felt a rush of freedom and joy. It had been a long while since she had loosened her wings, let alone used them to fly.

The Nan began the invocation, "Noa, our beloved queen and inspiration, we bring thanks for all the freedom you have made possible for us. We treasure your wisdom and pledge that we will follow your example in all our undertakings. We further affirm that we will use our resources to help all those of the inner court who may for any reason require support and encouragement to fulfill any needs be they physical, mental, or spiritual."

Gwynn was following the ceremony with practiced ease. These words were spoken in every celebration of the Rites of Noa no matter where the courts of fae chose to dwell. The next words were not of the ceremony and took complete control of her attention.

"Noa, we beseech you to help us find a solution to the troubles of our outlying territories. We have lost so many of our brothers and sisters and have been made to scamper like frightened rabbits. While we would not presume to enter into conflict, we must have the wisdom to move forward and the strength to perform as necessary to reach a cessation of the hostilities visited upon us."

Gwynn had heard Kathryn telling Jake about the territory beyond the city. Now she had confirmation of the nature of the exodus of fae from their homes to the safety of the city. But would the city continue to be safe? The implications of what she had learned led her to consider that this situation might require the attention of the Society of Builders.

The rest of the ceremony passed without her being mentally present. At its conclusion, she asked Celine to lead her to council chambers once she changed clothes. She had to find some way to tell Jake what she had heard. Gwynn tried not to betray the hurry she was in.

"Thank you, Celine, for accompanying me to the rites and letting me take part. It has been quite a while since I have been able to attend."

"You are very welcome, Gwynn."

It was all Gwynn could do to refrain from breaking into a run or taking wing to get back to the city proper.

After changing, Celine led her to the council chambers and left her on the steps. Once inside, a member of the guard stopped her.

"I'm sorry, but you cannot go in until a recess is called. Please wait here," he said and pointed to a bench on the opposite wall.

Gwynn knew that no amount of pleading or cajoling would gain her entrance.

"Thank you," she said with as much of a smile as she could muster and took a seat.

Chapter Twenty-Four

Elic also left Jake on the steps of the council chamber. He promised to return at the conclusion of Jake's meeting. Once inside, Jake was also asked to wait but was soon called.

The chamber was more amphitheater than courtroom. Seats formed a semicircle and descended for twenty rows. At the bottom was a raised platform with a desk that measured twenty feet from end to end. Behind the center area of the desk sat five of the oldest men Jake had ever seen. Outward from them and separated by several feet were four more people, two men and two women. These fae were quite a bit younger but still old. Jake recognized the Gohrn as one of the younger people.

Several fae were in the seating area. Jake wondered if they were here in an official capacity or were just observers. He was shown to a seat directly opposite the man at the center of the desk. Jake felt uncertain and somewhat threatened, although there was no justification for either. The fae in the center looked at Jake and tried what could be described as a smile. Before the old fae could speak, the door at the back opened and one of the guards walked down the outer aisle. He stepped onto the platform and whispered in the ear of the man that Jake thought of as the chairman. After delivering his message, the guard moved back and the chairman once again turned to Jake.

"Wizard, on behalf of the council and the court, let me extend our welcome. We hope that you have found our hospitality pleasing to you and your company. Before we begin, I have been informed that the fae Gwendolyn is outside and requesting entry. The council was going to provide an advocate to offer clarification concerning anything we speak of today. The fae Gwendolyn can act in that capacity if you wish."

"Concerning the hospitality, we could not ask for any better, thank you. I would very much like Gwynn to act as my advocate."

With that, the guard returned to the door, and Gwynn was escorted to the seat beside Jake. He was deeply relieved to have her with him.

"Greetings, Gwendolyn," said the chairman.

"Greetings. I am honored to be in the presence of this esteemed council. Please accept my deepest apologies for any delay I may have caused."

The chairman nodded his approval and then turned his attention to Jake. "Again, let me extend greetings to you, wizard. I am Selonk, Chief Convener of the Council of Regents for Alon Court. I know that you already recognize Seemik, the Gohrn of our court. The other members of the court will introduce themselves as necessary."

The Chief Convener went on to explain the history of the relationship between the fae community at large and the Society of Builders. Jake felt himself becoming anxious as he waited for the Chief Convener to come back to the current situation. Gwynn sensed his unease and placed a hand on his arm.

Finally, the convener finished his oration, paused, and said to Jake, "While your presence here is most welcome, although unexpected, the situation in which we find ourselves in is not without challenges. Throughout our time, we have endured an uneasy peace with those above. Over time, they have become covetous of some of our resources. Some of their factions would have us become subservient to them. We are determined to remain a free and independent people. Any provocation may give them all the reason they need to accelerate their aggressions."

Jake stood and said, "Sir, I'm sorry for any inconvenience our being here may have caused you. We certainly don't wish to interfere with your security or wellbeing, but I plan to do everything in my power to secure the freedom of my colleagues. While any help you give us would be appreciated, if you feel that helping us would be detrimental to you and your court, we are willing to proceed alone, but proceed we will." With that, he returned to his seat.

The members of the council glanced at one another and shared a few whispered exchanges. Gwynn's hand once more found Jake's arm. She leaned into him and whispered, "Tread carefully. I need to speak with you as soon as possible."

Once again, Jake stood. "Sir, I mean no disrespect, but I find myself in a very difficult position. May I have a minute to confer with my advocate?"

"Rest assured, we mean to help you, but we have to find the best course of action. We will adjourn for you to speak with Gwendolyn and reconvene in fifteen minutes." The members of the council stood and exited through a door in the rear wall.

Gwynn spent most of the time telling Jake what she had learned through the Nan. She asked Jake not to reveal what she had heard. She also impressed upon him the stature of the Council of Regents and the importance of proceeding delicately. He gave her his assurance that he would do his best.

The council returned and the session reconvened.

"Wizard, let me give you the plan which we, the council of regents, have discussed and agreed upon. The plan is not without risks, both on your part and ours. There are also contingencies which we must explore. I'm sure that some of the contingencies will be distasteful to us all."

He paused, took a deep breath, opened a book that had been placed before him, and proceeded. "We propose that your best chance for success would be realized in trying to rescue your allies on the road between the compound and the work area. We further believe that the best time would be during the waning hours of the day as they make their way from the work area to compound. The window for escape would be wider and the guards more fatigued.

While we prefer that no fae be involved in the attack, we know that is an impossibility since Gwendolyn is a member of the Society and will already be involved. We will also allow Elic, Arac, Simon, and Celine to accompany you. I can assure you that they are very capable and more than willing to engage those from above. We also have keys to the shackles that your colleagues will be bound with. Perhaps your shifter can find a way to get them into the hands of the captives. You may use our doorways to get to the surface and during your escape if necessary, although we would prefer that they not be needed.

"Now, we must discuss some of the unpleasantries. We will have more soldiers available to help you if things become dire. They will only be deployed upon the order of my representative, Captain Sellue."

He pointed to the fae soldier who had been at the door and had escorted Gwynn into the chamber. The Chief Convener once again paused. With a deep breath, he continued, "It is imperative that should any fae, including Gwendolyn, be killed during your rescue attempt that no body be left to be found."

Jake had body disposal down but couldn't fathom blasting Gwynn.

"All fae dress as those above. If we feel we have been compromised, Captain Sellue will have orders to attack and kill everyone in the convoy except your three colleagues and any fae, including any remaining prisoners."

Jake was shocked by this last condition. He looked to Gwynn, who seemed equally disturbed. Immediately, through some knowledge given him during the session with Mr. Alphonse, Jake knew how wrong the final condition was.

He rose and said, "I must protest the last condition. It is not in the mandate of the Society of Builders to take the life of innocents."

"Wizard, there are no innocents among the guards and overseers escorting the prisoners. They are ruthless and without principle. We cannot let any evidence of our involvement become the knowledge of those in power above. We will not ask you to violate the mandates of the Society, but you cannot ask us to endanger every fae in this court. If there is a need for any killing of those you term innocent, Captain Sellue and his men will carry it out. The only alternative would be for you to take them into your group and let them escape with you. What we laid out are our terms. Now you must decide if they are acceptable to you. In either case, I will send the key, which you will need to free your allies, to your quarters tonight. Elic will accompany you back now. He will return tomorrow to make further plans if you wish to go ahead. We wish you good luck. Would you like to add anything before we adjourn?"

"Thank you for your hospitality and the offer of your help. I will consider carefully how best to proceed. I believe that the situation in which the fae of this court find themselves would be of interest to the Society of Builders, and I plan to address it."

Without replying, the Chief Convener rapped his desk with a gavel and all the members of the Council of Regents rose and departed. Jake found Captain Sellue waiting to escort him and Gwynn from the chambers. Elic was at the inner door ready to take them back to their quarters.

When they arrived, Elic turned to Jake and said, "Wizard, Jake, do not worry. We are capable and have managed to live through many encounters with those above. I look forward to seeing you tomorrow morning."

With that, he reached out his hand to shake. Jake took the hand and was quite surprised when Elic assumed the grip taught him by Randolph Meekins. He saw the shadow of a smile cross Gwynn's face.

Jake released Elic's hand and said, "Until tomorrow."

Back in the suite, Jake asked, "How long have you known that Elic was one of us?"

"Only as long as you have," replied Gwynn. "I must say I was quite surprised. I wonder why he did not reveal himself earlier?"

Kathryn walked in and said, "A good question. I'm sorry but I overheard. Do you think this could be a deception?"

"I don't think so," said Gwynn. "As I said earlier, the fae are not a deceptive species, and they certainly don't skirt around difficult issues as we just saw first-hand."

"Nonetheless, we must be mindful of our circumstance," said Jake.

Jake spent the next hour filling Kathryn in on the terms of their prospective help. When he finished and had acknowledged the fine work done by both Kathryn and Gwynn, he asked for their input. They both agreed that some of the terms offered by the fae went counter to Society beliefs. They also agreed that the chance of rescuing Thomas, Raj, and Seamus increased exponentially with the help of the fae. The most important thing was the freedom of their allies. They decided to accept the terms as laid out by the Council of Regents. They also concurred that they would do everything possible to avoid the death of anyone who was not a combatant.

They did not need to worry.

Chapter Twenty-Five

Raj never had trouble sleeping. Thomas had joked about it on previous missions together. Raj was thankful for his ability. It was his contention that a well-rested body was more valuable in a fight than one wracked with worry and restlessness.

His cell was directly across from the trustee. Raj woke from a sound sleep as the trustee began his day. When the food was served, Raj looked at it in disbelief. Although Raj was not a worrier, he was a realist. He knew that food this flavorful and this plentiful was not given to prisoners without a reason. He was right.

Soon, a contingent of the guard creatures came down the steps. The trustee went from cell to cell, unlocking and opening the doors, and then motioned the prisoners forward. They were marched up the stairs and into the courtyard. There was no way to tell the hour, but the courtyard was all but deserted. Raj worked himself into a position between Thomas and Seamus. They were loaded onto the wagon and shackled into place along with almost thirty other prisoners. The convoy formed and began to move. Once underway, the creatures paid little attention to the prisoners.

"What do you make of all of this?" Thomas asked.

Before answering, Seamus looked around at the other prisoners to see if anyone was paying undue attention to them. A few others carried on conversations, but none of the prisoners seemed especially interested in the three of them.

"This is not a typical imprisonment," said Seamus, looking from prisoner to prisoner. "Everyone looks healthy."

"Where do you think they are taking us?" asked Raj. "There are so many of us this morning. There were only a few when they picked us up yesterday."

"Should we try to make a break for it?" asked Thomas, seeming to forget the shackles binding his hands and feet.

"Jake will do everything he can to get us out," said Seamus.

"We need to see what a full day holds," said Raj. "There may be a time when we are not shackled. When we work, they will at least have to give us our hands."

They fell into silence as each man contemplated his own scenario of capture and escape.

The convoy rolled past the boulders where they had seen Kathryn, but there were no signs of life.

A large industrial complex came into view. Several buildings looked to be warehouse size but none over two stories. No windows were visible, but there were several doors spaced across the front of each building. Each door was a normal size, so the idea of a warehouse was diminished. The ground surrounding the complex seemed solid. Seamus wondered if this was a natural phenomenon or a feat of engineering.

As they stepped off the wagon, they were divided into two groups, one composed of twenty men and the other of ten. Seamus, Thomas, and Raj were among the ten. The guards led them into one of the smaller buildings, where they were each given a locker and a pair of white coveralls. After changing, they were escorted into a larger area.

The first thing Raj noticed was the temperature. It must have been close to a hundred degrees Fahrenheit. He saw a glassed-in area atop a platform at the rear of the building. It looked to be air-conditioned and was manned by humanoids.

Creatures were posted at each door leading out of the building, and two stood at the bottom of the stairs.

Across the floor, flames rose beneath several covered vats.

Some of the prisoners must have worked in this building before because they instructed the new men as to what was expected. Each man was responsible for the loading of three vats. They were told to go to the area under the rear platform where blocks of material were being fed from above. Because of his size, Thomas was chosen to stack the blocks as they fell from above. Seamus and Raj fell into a routine of carrying blocks from vat to vat to vat, lifting the top and dropping their burden into an already viscous bubbling mixture. There always seemed to be room for the new addition. Raj reasoned that there must be some type of draining system, probably piping the resultant product to one of the other buildings.

There were no breaks, no lunch, nor any interruptions to the production routine. By the end of the day, they were exhausted and hungry. It was all the three allies could do to drag themselves onto the wagon.

No one spoke on the trip back to the compound. Each man was trying to solve the puzzle as to what they were manufacturing. The most troubling thing was that only the ten men from the vat room were on the wagon.

Chapter Twenty-Six

The same female fae made the delivery. In a single package was a key, which looked forged, and a map showing some doors to the world above. The girl stepped right inside the entry and said, "I also have a note for you, wizard. I was asked to bring your answer to the Chief Convener."

Jake opened the note and read:

Enclosed you will find the key that will open the shackles binding your allies. There is also a map with passages through which you can access the world above. You will not be able to transfer through these doors without help, so help will be provided.

The compound is sealed each evening at 2200 hours and reopened at 0600 the next morning. The front gate is heavily guarded but, if your shifter can gain access, she will only encounter light resistance if any at all. It is imperative that she carry out her mission in as stealthy a manner as possible. If she is detected, or worse, detained, the rescue of your comrades will be almost impossible.

We are ready to assist you according to the terms discussed earlier. If you are prepared to proceed, please make it known to the courier. If so, Celine will be ready to assist the shifter at 1900 hours and will wait above to facilitate their return. If for any reason the shifter is not back at the rendezvous area shortly after 2200, Celine will return alone, and we will assume the mission has failed.

The courier also has a map of what we know about the layout of the compound and keep. The map is compiled from the memories of the few of us who have been inside the keep and allowed to return.

If you feel you need more time to plan, we will delay until tomorrow evening. Remember the 2200 closing and the need for stealth.

Please give the courier your answer.

Jake folded the letter and looked at Kathryn. She nodded. To the courier he said, "Please tell the Chief Convener that we understand and are ready to proceed."

Without a word, the courier stepped through the door and closed it behind her.

"How will we proceed?" asked Gwynn.

"I think the next step is up to me," said Kathryn. "I have to get the key into the hands of either Thomas, Raj, or Seamus."

Jake looked at the key and then at Kathryn. "How will you carry it?"

"In the feline form of this world, I have long hair. Gwynn can weave it so it can't be seen." She shifted into her feline form.

Gwynn slipped from the couch onto the floor, took the key, and went to work. It took her about fifteen minutes to secure the key in a way that allowed it to be completely hidden. Kathryn shook herself, ran about the room, jumping and rolling. When they were both satisfied that the key was secure and well concealed, Gwynn returned to the couch, and Kathryn, in true feline fashion, curled up on the rug and went to sleep.

Jake felt as if he had a brick in his stomach. Neither he nor Gwynn was inclined to talk. Each feared that if they were to say too much they would reveal their apprehension about the task ahead for Kathryn.

Chapter Twenty-Seven

The knock came just before 1900. Jake opened the door. He almost didn't recognize Celine. She was dressed in an all-black outfit of a material that looked like it had been poured over her body. Her hair was secured beneath a close-fitting cap. Streaks of grease paint covered her face and the back of her hands. A sword hung from one side of her belt and a holster with a weapon on the other. The holster was secured at the bottom by a band around her thigh. A dagger hung upside down in a scabbard between her breasts.

Jake stepped back involuntarily and motioned her to come in, hoping to disguise his retreat. It didn't work. Celine smiled and moved into the room.

"Don't be concerned with my weaponry. I'm under strict instructions not to use them except to save my own life. If I had to use them, it would only delay the inevitable."

Before Jake could reply, Kathryn slipped between his feet and into the hall. "Shall we get started?" she said.

Celine looked down at Kathryn, a surprised expression on her face. It was Jake's turn to smile.

"Good luck and please be careful," he said as they walked away. He thought he saw a slight nod of Celine's head, and the cat's tail swished back and forth. It had begun.

ℝ ℞

Kathryn took a position behind Celine. She had no idea as to the direction they should take, plus she liked to travel behind someone so heavily armed.

After exiting the building, they turned left and walked until they were out of sight of the city. They approached a stand of trees, but instead of entering they stopped. Celine placed her hand on a small tree and a door opened. Celine stepped aside for Kathryn to go through. She did so and turned back to face the opening. As Celine walked through, the door disappeared.

They were in a narrow corridor. The lighting was dim but they had no trouble seeing. Kathryn felt her pupils fully dilate and her visibility was improved. They continued for a short while until Celine stopped and turned to Kathryn.

"This is the door to the world above. When I open it, we will both step through so it will close as quickly as possible. We seldom make passage at night. There will be trees present and I will wait for you among the trees. As you continue onward, you will come to a steep incline. When you top the hill, you will be able to see the compound. Take care as you approach and perhaps you can enter without being seen. Once inside the keep proper, the dungeon is located two levels below. Cells line both sides of the wall and are somewhat open. Finding your allies should not be a problem unless you are detected. Remember, all areas are secured at 2200 hours, and there is no way out after that. I will open the door at precisely 2215. If you are not here, we will consider the mission lost."

"I'll be here," Kathryn said with a confidence she did not feel.

Celine turned and disappeared among the trees.

Kathryn took a minute to let her eyes adjust. After that, she set off in the direction Celine had indicated. The ground was soft, but her lack of weight and the size of her paws kept the going from being difficult. She saw the steep incline Celine had spoken of and headed toward it. Nearing the top of the hill, she slowed and moved forward in a crouch.

The compound was, she estimated, a quarter mile away. Two boats sailed in opposite directions in the moat. She could see two guards, one on each side of the gate. They appeared to be attentive without being rigid. Each guard in turn scanned the horizon before falling back into conversation. From their demeanor and limited field of interest, Kathryn surmised that there must be other guards stationed about to protect other sectors. She had the feeling that it had been quite a while since anyone had attempted unlawful access.

She slipped down the hill and moved farther to the left to take advantage of the shadows cast by the bridge railings. She assumed a hunting posture and moved forward with care. Every few yards, she would stop and smell the air for any sign of hidden guards. Her feline vision was a great help in all of this. She saw the first of the other guards as she was coming off the bridge. He was heavily armed and more vigilant than the gate guards. Kathryn was sure he had a counterpart on the other side of the compound. If things went right, they would not present a problem for her.

Now was the moment of truth. She stepped from the shadows and walked toward the left side of the gate. Neither guard appeared to notice her approach. Could it be this easy? The answer was yes and no. She had hoped to pass behind the guard and through the gate, but his position was too close to the wall. She would have to go in front of him.

As she stepped forward, the voice of an unseen guard said, "Hey, Joomoe, it looks like that damn lynxine is out again."

Now, all eyes were on her. Fortune favors the bold, so she kept moving forward but gave a wider birth.

"See if you can catch him," came the voice again.

The guard who had been addressed as Joomoe leaned his weapon against the wall and assumed a crouch. Kathryn jumped straight up as if she had been surprised and ran a short distance away. Joomoe murmured something under his breath and readied for a second try. Kathryn didn't want to be caught for fear of him finding the key. She decided to take an all or nothing approach. She let him get almost close enough to grab her. She feigned a move to run away but instead made a full circle and ran between his legs. He made a grab for her and lost his balance. He let go a string of expletives that didn't need a translation. As he fell, she made for the gate. She could hear laughter from at least five different sources. The other gate guard was laughing also but made a half-hearted kick in her direction. She was inside the compound.

That could have gone worse, she thought. She had lost track of time and was unsure of how long she had to complete the mission. She felt as if an hour had passed but hoped it was less. She looked about but didn't see anybody. As the note had stated, once inside the compound, she met no resistance. She easily slipped into the keep. She hurried to the back corner and found the stairs leading down. She systematically used all her senses to scan the area but didn't detect anyone. She wanted to descend at full speed but knew that to do so would be foolish. She made her way down the steps, stopping on each landing to listen before moving on. After two flights of steps, she found herself in the dungeon. She peered around the stairwell to get her bearings before proceeding. There were ten cells on each wall. There was no sign of a jailer. As she walked by the first few cells, she found that some contained a single prisoner and some housed two. All prisoners were asleep. She reasoned that her best chance of recognizing her allies fell between Thomas for his size and Raj for his unique shape. She continued working her way down the cells. She stopped at each one and feigned cleaning herself until she could eliminate the possibility of the occupants being either Thomas or Raj. As she approached the last few cells, she heard voices coming from down the passageway. It must have been the location of the dungeon keeper. She surmised from the conversation that three men were present in the room. Knowing their whereabouts made her feel better. At the seventh cell, she found her quarry. Each of the final three cells on the left contained one prisoner. She was assured by the shapes that she had found her allies.

Kathryn slipped between the bars and in seconds confirmed that her suspicions had been correct. She awakened Seamus as he was the least likely to rouse in full combat mode, thus ruining her plan to silently complete her task and escape. The easiest way would be to morph into human form and use one hand to cover his mouth as she woke him. She rejected that idea because she didn't know how that would affect the key. It was woven into an area where she, in human form, had no hair.

She jumped onto the cot, moved to his head, and whispered, "Seamus, wake up."

He didn't move. She repeated her action and this time got a stir. She backed off so as not to startle him as he came awake. Luck was again on her side. He opened his eyes, turned over, and didn't seem at all surprised to see her. She moved to his ear and informed him of their intention to free them. She told him about the key and, as he reached out, moved to show him its whereabouts. Seamus began working to loosen the braid but was not having much luck. When the sound of chairs scraping against the floor came from the guard's room, he became impatient. Without preamble, he gave the key a jerk, dislodging not only the key but a good amount of cat fur as well.

The auditory expression of feline pain slipped from her lips before she could prevent it. She had to escape. She jumped from the cot, shot through the bars, and raced down the hall as the sounds of the guards emerging from their room signaled behind her.

"It's just the lynxine," came the shout as something landed behind her with a clank.

When she topped the first flight of stairs, she paused to listen for anyone pursuing her. There was no sound.

Mission accomplished, she thought. *Just got to make it back.*

She felt pretty good about herself until she reached the top of the second flight of stairs. There, just outside the door, was a creature of the same species as that which she had assumed, only much bigger and not happy with her presence. It arched its back and stepped sideways, making a noise that was unmistakably a challenge. Kathryn didn't want to fight another feline for fear of drawing someone's attention. That choice was taken away from her. The lynxine leapt and dug its claws into her back. She tried to roll away, but he was too quick. Pain shot through her shoulder as his momentum pushed them back through the doorway and they both tumbled down the stairs. His claws were ripping her flesh. *To hell with this*, she thought. She assumed human form.

If the opposing feline was surprised, he didn't show it. He was still trying to gain further purchase when Kathryn reached over her shoulder, grabbed a handful of fur, and yanked. When he came loose, it ripped her flesh where he had been dug in. She held him at arm's length as he continued to rip at her body. She changed tack. Reaching with her right hand, she gripped the animal by its hind legs. In one motion, she slammed his head into the wall and flung him down the stairs. He lay motionless on the landing. She hoped he was not dead, but the successful completion of the mission came first.

She was bleeding from several wounds and, when she re-assumed feline form, found her fur wet with blood and saliva. Where she had been injured on her arm translated to an injured front leg and paw. She could delay no longer. She ran toward the gate as quickly as her injuries would allow. To her relief, the gate was still open. She had completely lost track of time. Gathering all her strength, she sprinted for the opening. Just as she got to the opening, the guard Joomoe looked inside. When Kathryn saw him, she launched herself into the air, trying to look like she was pouncing on him. He quickly pulled back and barked another string of expletives. Kathryn sailed past him, landed badly, regained her feet, and ran for the bridge. To her surprise, nobody followed.

Working through the pain, Kathryn hurried up and over the hill and into the wooded area. Ahead of her, Celine stepped from the cover of the trees. Kathryn saw her extend her hand and the door to the land of the fae open. She didn't know if Celine had opened the door because she had seen her approach or if time had run out and she was going to be left behind. Mustering all her energy, Kathryn accelerated. She ran through the door and lost consciousness.

Chapter Twenty-Eight

Seamus lay awake on his cot, the key and a tuft of fur still clasped in his hand. He was trying to remember everything she told him. He wished he had used the time they were together to get more details, but his pulling the key and her screech had called for an expeditious escape. He had the key to open their shackles but had no idea when or where he was to use it.

He had two problems to solve. First, he had to secure the key on his person in a manner that would be easy to access but difficult to detect. His first thought was to put it in his boot, but he soon rejected the idea because he would have to remove the boot to get it. They had not been searched since the first day of their imprisonment. Could he take a chance and just put it in his pocket? No, he decided.

The solution to his first dilemma came with breakfast. Along with the tray of food was a utensil much like a fork. He used it to create a small rip in the quilted lining of his boot. He worked the key into the rip and tested it. Now it would ride within easy reach on the inside of his left ankle, he hoped.

The second problem was how and what to tell Thomas and Raj. When he finished eating, he slid his empty tray through the slot beneath the door. Instead of returning to his bed, he moved closer to the left of his cell. Thomas saw him and moved discreetly into earshot.

"Kathryn came last night," Seamus whispered. "She brought a key to our shackles, but I did not find out when or where we are to use it. She had to leave suddenly."

"Not to worry, leprechaun," Thomas returned with a light chuckle. "You will know when the time is right. Your sensitivities will guide you. Have faith."

"Can you tell Raj?"

"I had best wait until we are on the wagon. The trustee is back in his cell, and we still can't trust him."

Seamus returned to his bunk. He was restless but tried to conceal it. A few times he got up and walked at different paces and performed simulated tasks to assure himself that the key would be safe and remain accessible.

The morning crept by at a snail's pace. They were finally gathered and loaded onto the wagon. As they began their journey to the work site, Seamus watched as Thomas relayed the news to Raj. When they had finished talking, Raj looked straight ahead. Finally, a movement caught Seamus' eye. He looked toward Raj. The elfin man gave him a nod and a thumbs up.

Seamus felt better knowing that both Thomas and Raj were informed. The key, although well hidden, felt like an anvil against his ankle. Everything was as set as it could be. The chance of a successful escape depended on his ability to feel when the rescue was to take place. He had to have faith in his sensitivity; he just hoped no werewolves would be present.

Chapter Twenty-Nine

A bright light penetrated Kathryn's eyelids as she regained consciousness. She opened her eyes and turned her head away from the large overhead light. When she tried to wipe her eyes, she saw the bandage on her arm. She paused to give herself a mental body check. Her leg was stiff and bandaged. Both her arm and leg ached, but a much worse pain shot through her when she tried to roll onto her back.

"Damn you, Seamus O'Donnegan," she said.

A laugh came from the other side of the bed. Without thinking, she turned to that side and the pain came again. When her eyes cleared, she saw it was Jake in the chair beside her bed. She became aware that she was naked beneath the sheets.

"I would ask you how you feel, but I think I know," he said with a smile. "I'm happy that you got back, but I have to ask if the rescue has been compromised."

"No, all my problems were caused by another feline. Visitors are not welcome in his kingdom. I had to shift to keep from getting mauled worse than I did. I hope I didn't kill the poor creature."

"Did you find them?"

"Yes, and I was relaying the plan when Seamus took it upon himself to rip my fur out by the roots. I didn't get to finish because of the guards, but he knows enough and understands what the key is for. Where am I?"

"You're in the infirmary. When Celine carried you in, you appeared to be badly hurt. There was a lot of blood. You were still in feline form, but you shifted during the night. The doctor had to bandage everything again. It didn't seem to be an unpleasant task for him."

Again, she noticed her nakedness and pulled her blanket up.

"The fae went into high alert, even though Celine told them she didn't think the authorities above had been alerted. The doctors think you will be out of here by tomorrow evening."

"I'll be out of here in fifteen minutes. We've got a job to do." She sat up in bed, but the look on her face told the story. She didn't have to be told to settle back down.

"I've already spoken with the Chief Convener, and we've postponed the mission until you have recovered enough to travel. If we are successful in our mission, we will make our way to a gate and leave this world. If we are not successful, we will probably never leave the world above. In either case, we will not return to the world of the fae. They will have fulfilled their obligation to the Society. I'm sure they will be relieved to see us go."

Jake stood, approached the bed, and touched her cheek. "You gave us quite a scare. I'm happy things were not as bad as they first appeared. Get some rest and I'll see you tomorrow."

He turned and walked toward the door but paused at the chair. He tossed her one of the robes that had been supplied to their room.

"Oh, yeah, you might need this," he said with a look of mischief on his face.

She growled as he left the room.

Chapter Thirty

Jake returned to their quarters to find it empty. He wondered where Gwynn had gone but was happy to have some time to himself. Since Kathryn's return, his mind had been in turmoil. He tried to tell himself it was anxiety over having to leave Thomas, Raj, and Seamus in captivity for another day. He could also blame it on his concern for Kathryn's recovery and ability to take part in the rescue and subsequent escape. He was concerned with those things, but in his heart he knew the true cause for his unrest. This was the first time he would lead his team into confrontation. Until now, every battle, every casualty, and every action had been in reaction to someone else's aggression. Now he would be the one to initiate the fight. In the short time he had been a wizard, he had grown to trust the knowledge that was imparted through the actions of Mr. Alphonse. He also knew the power wielded through the staff. He had an underlying belief that he also possessed powers and abilities of which he could not avail himself yet. These would reveal themselves when they were needed. Finally, he had seen and trusted the skills of his allies, but now three were in chains and one was hospitalized.

He closed his eyes and tried to visualize the procession that transported the prisoners. He was not totally surprised when the scene began to replay itself like a movie. As he counted the guards and their escorts, a knot started forming in his stomach. The lead vehicle had a driver, a passenger, and six guards in the bed. Twenty men on motorcycles came next. Two more motorcycle-like vehicles pulled the prison wagon, each with a driver and a rear-facing guard.

Ten more riders followed the wagon. Forty-two enemy combatants made up the procession.

The six men in the back of lead vehicle and the two rear-facing guards would have the fastest access to their weapons. The two rear-facing guards would present the greatest danger to the prisoners. Every other member of the convoy would have to make some adjustment to their situation before being able to fully engage in battle. He would formulate his plan and confer with Gwynn and Kathryn. Later, he would ask for a meeting with Elic, Arac, Simon, Celine, and Captain Sellue.

Jake was concentrating on his plan when something bumped against the door. He tensed and his heart rate accelerated as adrenalin rushed into his system. He jumped to his feet, and all his notes were strewn across the floor. The bump came again.

He summoned the staff and opened the door. It was Gwynn and Celine. Each had their arms full of what could only be weapons. They walked to the table and Jake helped to unburden them. Once their arms were free, Jake asked Celine if she could arrange a meeting with the other fae. She answered in the affirmative and asked if she could be of further assistance.

"I think I understand how everything works and can explain it to Jake," said Gwynn. "Thank you for everything."

After a slight bow to each other, Celine departed.

Jake turned back to the table and lifted a futuristic-looking weapon. It appeared to be a type of rifle.

"It looks more complicated than it is," said Gwynn. "At its heart it's just a very powerful, cylinder-operated air rifle."

She lifted one and ejected the magazine. The magazine was filled with elongated projectiles. Each projectile appeared to be the radius of a pencil and was covered front to back with barbs. Next, she opened a compartment in the weapon's stock and removed a small cylinder.

"There are forty projectiles in each magazine. I have five magazines for each weapon. They are propelled by gas emitted from the cylinder. They shoot at a range and velocity of the AR-15 rifle in your world. The projectiles make this a gruesome weapon. They are weighted more to one end so that, once they leave the weapon, they tend to tumble end over end. The survival rate of someone hit center mass is almost nil."

Jake knew little about military weaponry, having done all of his hunting with a shotgun, but he recognized how deadly this weapon could be.

Gwynn continued, "On the positive side, these weapons are almost silent in their operation, making them perfect for our rescue. We should have a few seconds before they know they are being attacked. On the negative side, these are the same weapons that will be used against us."

Jake considered all of this and looked back to the table. There was a pistol variation of the rifle. He lifted it to feel the weight and balance of it. All the remaining items on the table were some variations of weapons he was familiar with. There were knives like that worn by Celine on Kathryn's mission and some canisters that Jake took to be grenades. Gwynn confirmed this and explained how they were used. The last items on the table were a crossbow, a war ax, and a traditional long bow with a quiver of arrows. Jake looked at Gwynn, questioning the last two items.

"Those were recovered from the site of Thomas and Raj's capture. If we can carry them along, I know they would like to have them back."

After a moment, Jake turned from the table and walked to the sitting area. "Gwynn, you know that I have never planned an assault. I must trust that somehow I will come up with a workable solution, one with a high probability of success. Any help you could give me would be appreciated."

"Jake, you are a wizard. I know you learned this later than most due to the uniqueness of your situation."

Jake wondered what his situation was and how it came about.

Gwynn continued, "Although you are young at being a wizard, you come from a line of the most wise and powerful leaders of the Society of Builders. Your ancestry can be traced back to the beginning. Your mother's line is also ancient and revered. Your genealogy made it possible to accelerate your training. Don't feel that the short time you spent at The Farm in any way hampers your abilities to perform as a wizard. Mr. Meekins and Mr. Alphonse would have never given you the title and released you from The Farm if they didn't think you were ready. Jake, I and all your allies trust you. We have waited a long time for you to join us, and we have enough confidence to follow you into battle. While you plan the rescue, I will pull up the posit and plot our escape."

Before he could reply, she summoned the posit and walked down the hall. Jake retrieved his notes, seated himself on the couch, pulled up a small table, and took out his notebook. With his right hand, he brushed back his hair.

"God help us all," he said to himself and began to plan.

Chapter Thirty-One

Kathryn had drifted in and out of sleep all afternoon. She was thankful she had gotten the key into Seamus's hands and managed to escape but felt she had failed on several levels. She should never have cried out when he pulled the key free. She should have been more careful so as not to have a confrontation with the alpha male feline. Now she was injured and in the infirmary. What would that do to the mission?

They had given her something to help her rest, and she was just coming out of a deep sleep. At the edge of consciousness, she felt warm and relaxed. She also felt damp. That too was comforting. She didn't want to wake up yet. Just a few more minutes, she thought, and turned onto her side. As she rolled over, she took in a mouthful of liquid and came fully awake. Her eyes opened wide, and she expelled the liquid from her mouth.

No longer in her bed, she was now suspended in a tank filled with a viscous liquid. Her head had been on a small pillow-like pedestal, and her body floated just beneath the surface in a gelatinous substance. Her first thought was to escape the tank, but this was the first time she had been pain free since her return. Still, she wanted to know where she was.

"Hello, child. How are you feeling?" said a voice from behind her.

"Fine, I think," said Kathryn.

The voice behind her began a low humming sound. Kathryn wanted to turn to the voice but was so relaxed she couldn't move. She hovered on the verge of sleep.

"You relax, honey. Give me a few more hours and you will be as good as new."

"As good as new?"

"The colloughon you are floating in is from a special place known only to chosen members of my tribe. We are charged with its care and use. When administered by a chosen one, it has great restorative powers. So together we are going to make you well."

Kathryn didn't know how to reply but she didn't need to. The voice returned to humming. The sound began to intensify and move around. Finally, a small female fae came around the side of the tank.

The fae shaman, for that is how Kathryn had begun to think of her, seemed to float instead of walk. When she came in full view, Kathryn could see that she, in fact, was floating. Her wings were exposed and fluttering so fast that it allowed her to hover over the floor. She was no taller than four feet. Her body was perfectly proportioned and free of clothing. Her hair was pure white, which when considered with the sound of her voice, made Kathryn think she was of an advanced age, but her face and body looked like a young girl. Kathryn was mesmerized. She wanted to ask some questions, but she was immobilized and unable to speak. Her condition should be cause for alarm, but she was at peace.

When the shaman had circled the tank twice, the humming became a chant. She spread her arms and the movement of her wings intensified. She rose above the tank and began to spin. Her hands were clasped above her head. She spun faster and faster. She brought her hands down by her side. Without any effort she stopped mid-spin and hovered. Her arms came up to shoulder level and extended out to the side. She was silent for a while but then said a series of words spoken in a perfect rhythm. The last of the words lingered on her lips. When the sound had almost dissipated, she began spinning in a counterclockwise direction and opened her hands. From each hand came a cloud of dust. At first, it lingered in the air but then drifted down to the tank and into the colloughon.

Kathryn fell into a deep sleep.

Chapter Thirty-Two

As instructed, Jamal had gone to summon Major Bannar. He didn't understand why someone of his importance would be given such a menial task. What were runners and junior soldiers for anyway? This was not the first time he had been treated as such. "Things will be different one day soon," he repeated like a mantra, as he stomped about in search of the Determiner's golden boy.

When he at last found someone with intelligence enough to know, he was told that the major was out on maneuvers. At least this was something going his way, he thought, and allowed himself a deep breath. Jamal left word for Bannar to report to his quarters. He would send him on to see the Determiner. Now he had some time to formulate a plan. He sent a messenger to inform the Determiner of the major's circumstances.

The last thing that Jamal desired was the Lokins boy dead. Jamal wanted the opportunity to place the young wizard at the side of his father and grandfather. That's why he had arranged to have the ineptest of his minions pursue the boy. This was his chance to play the gambit he had boldly undertaken so many years ago.

He had been a young sorcerer given in service to the Lord High Determiner by his Uncle Warell, his mentor. He had been led to believe this was a prestigious position. In some courts, it would have been prestigious, but the Determiner valued only himself and held everyone else in contempt. Jamal prided himself on having, over time, worked himself into the Determiner's confidence. Beneath his cloak of loyalty, Jamal wore a desire to usurp the Determiner and take the kingdom for himself.

The first step in his plan took place when Lonnie Lokins Sr. and Lonnie Lokins Jr. were captured at a time when the Determiner was away from the palace.

⅘◇   ⅙

Jamal was more than an apt student. He studied and mastered all the works, spells, and conjures Warell put before him. In addition, he spent countless hours poring over obscure volumes. Some of the things he read in the old tomes were laughable, having been disproved or passed off as lore. In addition, magic in some of the spells had been improved upon. Jamal gave each spell the same credence as any other.

When the Lokins men were brought before him, opportunity intersected with preparation. These two wizards were legendary among the Society of Builders and all who opposed them. As first and second-generation wizards, they wielded tremendous power. The condition and circumstances of their capture was never clear, but that didn't matter to Jamal. There was a standing order that any of the leadership of the Society of Builders, especially the Lokins father and son, Randolph Meekins, or Anson Alphonse, immediately be put to death upon their capture. In the Determiner's absence, the task fell to Jamal. Two things came together to make this a perfect storm.

First, the execution order had to be carried out immediately, before the Society could mount a rescue. It could not be delayed until the Determiner's return. Second, Jamal's disillusionment with the reign of the Determiner and his knowledge of the spell of temporal stasis led to his decisive action.

A quick spell of immobility rendered the Lokins men helpless while he reviewed his books and acquainted himself with the spell. He would need the powder of a diamond, emerald, ruby, and sapphire. Not all standard sorcerer's stock but easy enough to come by in a rich palace. After gathering his supplies and reciting his incantation several times, the moment of truth arrived.

It was not a total surprise when the spell worked. Jamal was beset by both a feeling of accomplishment and anxiety.

The spell of temporal stasis essentially put the two Lokins men in a permanent state of suspended animation. To them, time would cease to pass. They would not grow older, and no bodily function would be present. If the spell worked as promised, no harm would come to them. If it didn't, they would die without gaining consciousness. The incantation could only be reversed by Jamal or another sorcerer who was familiar with the spell.

Thus began his plan to take over the kingdom. It would also be the greatest ruse within his knowledge. The Determiner would believe his enemies to be dead and their bodies held in the crypt below the dungeon, and Jamal only had to wait for Jake to join his father and grandfather.

Ever the curious student, Jamal had read years earlier of a series of spells where, if he controlled the entire lineage of wizards, he could transfer their knowledge and power to himself. He had waited patiently for the last male Lokins to be proclaimed a wizard. Now he only had to find a way to keep him alive.

Chapter Thirty-Three

Jake had the rough outline of his plan mapped out. As he thought it through, he came to two decisions. First, the rescue could not take place tomorrow. He felt the need to go above and reconnoiter the terrain. He needed to look for cover and for him, Gwynn, and Kathryn if possible to walk the spongy surface before being forced to fight on it. He also wanted to practice with the air powered rifles. It would be a fool's game to fight on such a foreign surface with unfamiliar weapons. He hoped one more day would not be crucial to Thomas, Seamus, or Raj.

His second realization troubled him deeply, but he could not hide from the truth. They would have to eliminate the entire enemy force. The prospect of killing the guard and escorts went against his basic nature and the tenets of the Society. He would have to remember what the Chef Convener said, "There are no innocents among the guards." Jake didn't know what he was hoping for when he began his plan. It was naïve to think that such a rescue could be accomplished without bloodshed. His purpose was to see that his allies were rescued and returned to safety. He wanted to maximize the damage to the opposing forces while limiting the harm to his comrades. He had to come to grips with the reality of having to dispose of the body of any of his troops killed in action. He could leave no indication that he had received any help from the fae. As he considered the various scenarios, he found himself able to visualize each. This made it possible to eliminate some portions of each scenario and keep the best parts. Slowly, his plan took shape. He was surprised so many hours had passed as he strategized.

Soon the fae girl brought the evening meal. When she placed it on the table, she also had an envelope for Jake. Celine would escort them to the Hall of the Chief Convener for a meeting in one hour.

Before Jake could get to the table to uncover the food, another knock came. When he opened the door, there stood Kathryn looking fit and healthy. Without thinking, he grabbed her and swung her about.

"Go easy, big fellow," she said. "I just got over being mauled by one big lug."

He put her down and called for Gwynn. When she entered the room, she didn't seem at all surprised to see Kathryn. When the food was uncovered, there were three servings of everything. Jake seemed to be the only one who didn't know that Kathryn would be there.

They ate, discussed some of the rescue plan, and Gwynn spoke of the route of escape. They were just finishing when Celine arrived.

Chapter Thirty-Four

They were led through the vast Hall of the Chief Convener into a room outfitted with a large conference table. The Chief Convener sat at the head of the table. Captain Sellue and another soldier stood to his right. Arac, Elic, and Simon occupied the next three chairs. Everyone rose as Jake and his companions entered the room. The Chief Convener greeted them and motioned them to the chairs on his left. Jake took the first, Gwynn the next, Kathryn the third, and Celine settled into the fourth. When they were all seated, the door opened and the fae girl who had made all the deliveries came in and took the seat at the other end of the table.

The Chief Convener stood and said, "Welcome, wizard; welcome Gwendolyn." He looked at Kathryn and added, "Welcome, shifter. I am glad that you are well." After a brief pause, he continued, "You know Captain Sellue. This is Master Mark Quall. He is Captain Sellue's second and will assume command if need be."

The soldier rose and bowed to those across the table. His bow was deepest to Jake and the woman on the end.

"This is Melanay," continued the Chief Convener. "She is the faerie queen of our court and the leader of our people."

Through his shock, Jake stood and bowed deeply.

She stood and said, "Welcome, wizard. I hope you have found a way to enjoy your stay here. I'm sorry for any subterfuge I may have employed these past few days, but I wanted to know you without the pressure of protocol. You appear to be a wise and compassionate leader who feels deeply for his allies. This is good since now you hold not only their wellbeing in your hands but ours as well. I am sure that you have devised a plan that is mindful of all your responsibilities. The Chief Convener and Captain Sellue are also very capable. They will hear your plan and offer suggestions as they deem fit. In the end, it will be your plan, and we will support you as much as we can. I wish you well." She turned and walked back through the door.

"Let us begin," said the Chief Convener.

Over the next three hours, Jake presented his plan. There was not much debate and only a few suggestions from Captain Sellue. The rescue would take place in two days, and they would spend tomorrow above. By the time they adjourned, Jake felt completely exhausted.

Chapter Thirty-Five

The convoy was ready to leave the courtyard. For the third day, Thomas, Seamus, and Raj were shackled to the wagon. The key to the shackles rode safely in Seamus's boot.

Each day they kept watch as they moved along the route for any sign of Jake and a rescue effort. So far, nothing was forthcoming. They each knew that a rescue was inevitable, but some happenings at the workplace were a cause for concern. There were always more prisoners on the wagon to the work area than back to the compound. So far, the three allies had been among those returning. What would they do if one or all of them were selected to stay? They made a pact to not allow themselves to be separated, even at the peril of death.

Again, when they arrived at the work site, they were assigned to the vat room. Being the biggest and strongest, Thomas was given the job to catch and stack the blocks of material coming from above.

A human supervisor worked the floor to see that all the vats were properly cared for. When not checking the vats, he took station at the bottom of the stairs. Early on the second day, the man said something and was surprised when Thomas understood and answered. This led Thomas to believe that most prisoners were foreign and didn't know their captor's native language. Once started, the man engaged in snippets of conversation throughout the day.

Once the day's work got underway, the supervisor, as Thomas had come to think of him, made his rounds. When he was convinced that things were operating smoothly, he took up his place at the staircase. After a few minutes, he said, "You are obviously not from this area, neither above nor below. How did you come to be imprisoned here? What is your offense?"

Thomas knew he had to tread lightly with his answers. He also saw the opportunity to gather some information.

"I'm not sure of my offense or that of my colleagues," he said, indicating Raj and Seamus. "We were only passing through when we were picked up by the beings that manned the convoy.

"You were a victim of circumstances," said the man with an expression of irony. "While entering our land is not an offense, any traveler detected will be detained. You and your comrades are strong and work well. I will keep you in this building as long as I can." Before Thomas could say anything, the man walked off to perform another round.

Thomas continued his task. He reasoned that unaware travelers were the source of an endless supply of prisoners. He wondered if, after so many hours of indentured service, they were set free to resume their travels.

As Raj and Seamus came to get the blocks to replenish the vats, Thomas told them about what he had learned. He was determined to discover all that he could.

During the course of the day, the creature guards were replaced one by one. They appeared to be identical. Thomas tried to think of even one of the creatures with a different look, build, or set of actions. He could not.

When the supervisor came back, after a few verbal exchanges, Thomas said, "I know we are only one step in a process, and I'm an inquisitive soul, so may I ask what we are manufacturing?"

The supervisor looked at Thomas for a long time and then walked off for another set of rounds. Thomas realized that as a member of prison labor he had probably breached protocol with his question, but he had to try. When the supervisor returned to the stairs, he stood silently.

After about ten minutes, two of the front doors opened. In walked five of the creature guards. They moved robotically around

126

the walls, each taking the place of one of their like that had been there since morning.

The supervisor watched as the change of guard took place. When the change was complete and the original creatures had exited the building, the supervisor audibly cleared his throat. When Thomas looked at him, he turned and said, "There's the answer to your question."

"The guards and soldiers are made from the material that is made here?" asked Thomas.

The supervisor held Thomas's eye for what seemed an eternity before saying, "Yes, and the remains of the unfortunate ones."

Chapter Thirty-Six

As agreed, Jake, Gwynn, and Kathryn met with Elic, Arac, Simon, and Celine after the morning meal to spend the greater part of the day above. Before leaving, they pulled on the oversized boots. Although they looked ungainly, Jake found they fit well and were easy to maneuver in. He was relieved.

Once above, the ground was just as he remembered it. Although spongy, the surface provided a bounce that proved to be energizing after Jake became accustomed to it. They entered the world above in a grove of trees. The plants and foliage felt solid. Jake considered this paradox. Solid objects growing and living in a yielding ground. In addition to this wonder, he found that when he stepped close to one of the smaller plants, instead of leaning with the compressed surface, it righted itself to stay erect. He asked Elic if the same were true of larger objects such as trees, boulders, and bodies of water? Elic replied in the affirmative as if it were a given. Jake decided they should run on the surface and discovered that the bodies of his companions reacted in the same way. Nobody made a misstep.

After they became acclimated to the terrain and felt comfortable with movement, Jake asked to be shown the road used to transport the prisoners. Because of the lack of cover, they decided that only Jake and Elic would go.

The road was covered in a substance much like hard rubber. It was flexible enough to move under the weight of the vehicles but rigid enough to allow the passage of the vehicles without extreme undulations. It was only wide enough for one truck or two motorcycles to pass at a time.

"The only traffic we have observed here is the prisoner transport."

Jake nodded and turned to walk along the road. He found it more difficult to traverse than the natural terrain. When asked if the guards wore the large footwear, Elic told him that the guards wore one-piece molded uniforms. The boots were normal size to allow them to better operate the vehicles. This pleased Jake. If he could derail the convoy and move the fight to the natural terrain, their chance for success would improve greatly. Jake had seen all he needed, so he and Elic rejoined the others.

Next, Jake wanted to see the area where the prisoners were taken every day. Going far in the world above presented too much danger, so they returned below to travel and use another door closer to their destination.

Upon emerging, Elic told Jake they had traveled the equivalent of twelve miles. This amazed Jake as he felt they had only been traveling for thirty minutes. With that and what he had learned before, he gauged the distance between the compound and the work area to be twenty miles. With the speed at which he observed the convoy moving, he estimated it would take seventy-five minutes to get from place to place. That was a short window of time to initiate a rescue, clean up the scene, and manage an escape.

With no cover at the point where they again emerged from below, Elic and Jake belly crawled to a place where they could see the work area. Jake observed the buildings but didn't detect any signs of work taking place. The only sign of life was a group of the guards standing against the fence that enclosed the area. They did not appear to do anything but stand there. The vehicles of the convoy were staged by the main gate.

"Do the same guards that man the fence and buildings also manage the transportation?" Jake asked.

"For the most part, they do. There is a small contingent that stays behind to guard the facilities."

Jake found that reassuring. The main body of those who would be sent to pursue them would be dispatched from the compound.

Their escape route would lead them back toward the work area, but any resistance would be limited. He further refined his plan. The closer to this point he could launch the attack, the better their chances of escape.

"I would like to walk along the road to find the best place to attack."

"It will not be safe to do that until after the prisoners are transported. We will need to use another access point so as not to be observed from here."

"Very well," said Jake. "Do we have time to practice using the weapons?"

"Yes, but we will go below for that. When the time is right, we will walk the road."

Chapter Thirty-Seven

The practice range was in an area formed from dirt and loam. This was ideal as it would absorb the projectiles instead of just stopping them. Any other material might allow for a ricochet, which could be deadly for anyone in the area. Jake would carry a rifle and use it. Although he had the staff, it left traces that would signify a force foreign to the world above. Jake hoped he would not need to employ the staff. His plan called for it only in the case of a death among the fae. The body should be eliminated so no connection could be made between the attack and the fae.

Since Gwynn had already become familiar with the weapons, only Kathryn and Jake needed to practice shooting them.

Several life-sized manikins stood at the far end of the range. Kathryn stepped to the line and took the weapon, testing its weight. She moved it from carrying to firing position several times. After looking it over once more, she jacked a projectile into the chamber and slammed the bolt closed. The firing selector was set to single shot. Once on the mission, it could be moved to either fire a burst of three projectiles or to fully automatic where it would continue to fire if the trigger was depressed or until the magazine was empty. Kathryn assumed a stance that had her left foot in front of her right. Her right foot was perpendicular to her left and directly under her body. She brought the rifle to her shoulder sighted down the barrel and squeezed the trigger. The sound of the rifle was like someone breaking the seal on a pressurized container. A puff of air blew through her hair. Down range a mannikin's arm fell off. She muttered something under her breath and shook her hair back.

When she brought the rifle to her shoulder, she hit the next four center mass, tearing a large hole through each of them. She placed the rifle on the table and turned to Jake.

"Your turn," she said.

Jake tried to remember everything Kathryn had done. Being from the South and hunting most of his life, he was no stranger to firearms. His mother had taught him to shoot when he was ten years old and presented him with a shotgun on his eleventh birthday. Last year he had purchased a Winchester Arms 30-30 lever action and practiced when he could. Even so, he completely missed his first shot. It took him three more before he hit a target and six more to find center mass. When he put the rifle on the table, he felt pretty good. With the damage done by each projectile, the success of the mission would not depend on hitting center mass. The fae in attendance were pleased with the results.

"There's still a little time before we can return above. Let's have our meal and rest until then," said Celine. She led them to a room where food was waiting for them.

They each went through a serving line and chose what they wanted to eat. Jake had become fond of fae cuisine and had no problem making several selections. When he entered the adjoining room, which was set up with tables, he noticed Elic sitting alone at a table for two. Since Elic had performed the handshake to signify that he was a member of the Society of Builders, Jake wondered how this was possible. He took the other chair. Elic looked up from his food and smiled. Jake reached out his hand and once again Elic assumed the grip.

"Hello, wizard, you have a good plan, and I believe we will free your allies. I hope you will not suffer any losses."

Jake thought that was a strange thing to say, although in his heart he had hoped the same. Jake looked at Elic and asked, "How did you come to be here and away from the Society?"

"I'm an orphan, and it was my choice to leave."

"An orphan?"

"Yes, the only surviving member of my team. Rather than be taken in by another wizard, I returned home. I was at such a loss at that time that I believed I would not function well with another team."

"Will you tell me about it?"

Chapter Thirty-Eight

Elic's Story

"I was born on The Farm. My father is Aaron Emit and my mother was Anise Tabon Emit. They were also born on The Farm. My grandfather and grandmother were the first of our line to serve the Society. They were recruited and moved to The Farm at the behest of Randolph Meekins."

Jake looked at Elic and guessed that he must be close to thirty years old. If he and his parents were born on The Farm and his grandparents were recruited by Randolph Meekins, you were probably looking at a period of at least sixty years. How old was Randolph Meekins? Jake broke from his thoughts and returned his attention to Elic.

"There were many of us, children I mean, and we were encouraged to interact. My best friend and constant companion was Eamon Flarrity, the son of one of the most famous wizards in the Society. He was only eclipsed by your father. By the time we were teens, we understood that Eamon was a wizard and that I would be with him. My family were sensitives. Our ability to discern truth from lies, right from wrong, and wise from unwise, made us valuable in dealing with people and situations. We could sense if going into a situation was advantageous or troubling. At least, my parents and grandparents could."

At that point, Elic's eyes fell away from Jake's. His shoulder slumped and his face twisted. Jake felt the urge to reach out and touch him, but his better judgment told him it was not the time. He waited.

"Eamon's team of allies had been chosen almost at birth. As with all teams, there were five of us. We were told we were like the fingers of a hand; we must work together to be our best."

At this, Elic smiled and then broke into a laugh. Jake cocked his head as if to inquire.

"Our best warrior was Tarok; his species only had three fingers and a large thumb. The analogy was lost on Tarok. Lenour was our posit master and fixer, and Landor was another brave soul and fierce fighter. Great things were expected of us. We fulfilled the promise—until the day we didn't."

Jake sensed Elic had reached the crux of the story. When he looked at Elic, he saw a man in deep emotional stress. His eyes were averted, and he had a hard time swallowing the drink he took before continuing.

"We gated to a world much like our own, The Farm, I mean. It was supposed to be a routine interaction and an opportunity to reaffirm our relationship. There shouldn't have been any trouble. The town where our liaison was to take place could only be reached through a pass in the hills that surrounded the town. As we approached the entrance to the pass, Eamon paused and looked at me. I swear, I didn't feel any danger or ill will. I signaled him to proceed. Just as we were reaching the end of the pass, we were met by two individuals. I still sensed no malevolence. At this time, Eamon's staff began vibrating violently. Rocks and boulders began to rain down on us. The last thing I remembered was the look in Eamon's eyes as he turned to me.

"I awoke back at The Farm," he continued. "When Eamon died, his staff became useless except for emitting a signal that could be traced to find us. I was told that I was the only survivor. Evidently, I had been caught by a glancing blow, knocked unconscious, and mistaken for dead. It was only then that I was told of the Determiner."

"The Determiner?" Jake asked.

Elic looked up from his meal and met Jake's eyes for the first time since they had begun the conversation. He wore a haunted look, and Jake recoiled when he recognized the pain that relaying this story was causing Elic. The man took a deep breath, and his demeanor intensified.

"Oh, Jake," Elic said. "You are just as naïve as I was. I, too, believed that the Society of Builders was a unique entity. I believed that we were the only group that had an interest in the wellbeing and harmony of the many worlds. In a way, I was right. There are other groups who would wish to impose their will upon the many worlds and bend them to servitude with only one purpose: to promote and implement some nefarious agenda. The Determiner is the leader of such a group. Why we are not made aware of them and how best to prepare for their actions is a question I posed to Randolph Meekins from my recovery bed."

"And how did he respond?"

"He said that the very nature of our mission brought with it an inherent danger, whether it be from different surroundings or from some faction with an opposing ideology. He said that it was important not to focus on one certain threat but to be aware of our surroundings at all times and to constantly assess our situation."

Elic paused, pushed his plate away, and continued, "Mr. Meekins then pulled a chair to my bedside and took a seat. I could tell he had more to say but was evaluating the merits of sharing it. After a while, he told me that every team had two ways of assessing danger. The staff, carried by the wizard, was the first. The wood of the staff was from an ancient type of tree. Only certain members of the Society who were born with the ability to commune with the tree could harvest the wood that would be formed into the staff. The wood is energized with what he called 'a knowing,' which could be communicated to the wizard. In the hands of a wizard, that staff becomes active, but in other hands it's just a piece of wood. When held by a wizard, the staff will warn of danger. The other warning system is the adept or sensitive. He or she is assigned to each team for the express purpose of constant evaluation of the team's situation. I was the sensitive for our team, and I didn't sense the danger. I failed in my purpose and all who were with me died. Realizing that my abilities as a sensitive were inadequate, I had no desire to put another team in danger. I asked to be released and have spent my life since here."

"How did you come to this place? Weren't you born on The Farm?"

"This is my mother's coven. They accepted me after a request from Randolph Meekins."

Jake had not noticed the passage of time and was surprised when Celine appeared at the table. She told them it was safe to go above. Jake and Elic would return to reconnoiter the route and choose a site for the rescue.

Chapter Thirty-Nine

They entered the world above in the midst of a small group of trees. Elic explained that this was the first area of cover. The location was a little less than halfway between the compound and the work area. They stayed as close to the woodlands as possible and kept the road always in sight. After traveling approximately three miles, they found themselves at the edge of forest. To go forward they would have to do so without cover. Jake's eyes followed the road as it led away from the forest. In the distance he saw large boulders rising from the ground. Before proceeding, Jake consulted Elic.

"Do you sense it's safe to proceed?"

It was apparent Elic had not expected the question. When his eyes found Jake's, they seemed filled with doubt.

"Elic, you were and are a sensitive," Jake said. "I trust your judgment. Now, can we safely go ahead?"

Elic felt his pulse quicken. The moisture forming in the palms of his hands was unsettling. He wanted to avoid the question but knew he could not.

"I feel no impending danger," he said at last.

"Good," said Jake. The staff did not give notice of anything either. "Let's go to that group of boulders; they may be just what we need. Are these the same rocks where you found us?"

"No, we found you closer to the compound."

Upon reaching the first boulder, Jake could see that the road took an abrupt turn to avoid the rocks.

"It is said that these were peaks of some very high mountains," said Elic. "They could not be excavated when the road was being built."

"Do they extend into your world?" asked Jake.

"No, although it would seem logical that they would. Our worlds exist independent from each other. It is said that you could completely uncover these formations and never become aware of the world of the fae."

Jake knew this was the place to launch the rescue. The turn in the road was severe enough to cause the vehicles to slow in order to negotiate it. Furthermore, if he could damage the road a short distance past the turn, he might be able to stop them completely. The effect would be to have part of the procession facing one way and the other portion facing the other. This would make their coordinating a defense more difficult. He shared his thought with Elic, paying close attention to his reaction.

"What do you think, Elic?"

"This is probably the best point. As we go farther along the road, cover becomes scarce. Captain Sellue can conceal his troops in the woods. There is a door just beyond the copse. The return to our world should be easy. It is not unusual for the road to be damaged from time to time due to the nature of the surrounding ground. I'm not aware of a total breech ever taking place."

"I think I've seen enough," Jake said. "When I return below, I will finalize my plan. Can we communicate later today?"

"Yes, I will make Captain Sellue and the others aware of what has been decided. I will let you know when we all can meet."

"If nobody has any objection, we will attempt the rescue tomorrow."

Elic turned to lead the way to the door and passage below.

As they were returning to their quarters, Jake told Gwynn and Kathryn of the plan. They both pulled abreast of him in an act of solidarity.

Chapter Forty

Seeing and choosing the site of the rescue created an explosion of emotions in Jake. First, it made the whole situation real. The prospect of freeing his allies was both resolute and affirming. Still, a sense of dread kept invading his thinking. He knew it would be unrealistic to think that an act such as they were planning could be without consequences both immediate and long term. To engage in such actions would carry a cost in lives. As the wizard, the leader, all of this rested upon his shoulders.

His thoughts ran back to the days before he met Randolph Meekins when his most pressing problems were enough rain for his crops, crop prices at market time, and how he was going to attend college and keep his place going. When he compared the difficulties of that life to the burden of life and death, he had to wonder if he were man enough to bear the burden. If only he had as much faith in himself as others seemed to feel. On some deep subconscious level, he knew he would prevail. Having only practiced his wizardry for a short time, he had already navigated situations he previously would not have believed could exist.

The meeting with Captain Sellue, Elic, Arac, Celine, and Simon had been swift and positive. In the interest of time and efficiency, they agreed Jake should use the power of the staff to interrupt the road. Captain Sellue asked that the rescue be swift and decisive, thus limiting the exposure of the fae. The captain also stated what Jake had come to comprehend. No enemy combatants could remain alive. With that stated and affirmed, Captain Sellue and his troops could take a more aggressive role in the rescue. This should bring the mission to a quick conclusion. It would still be up to Jake and the power of the staff to dispose of any bodies.

After the meeting, Jake expressed his uncertainty as to whether this severe an action would be sanctioned by the Society of Builders. Both Gwynn and Kathryn assured him that, given the circumstances, they had little choice.

While he continued to debate the moral and ethical questions raised by the proposed action, Gwynn used the posit to plan their escape. She identified three gates they could use. The closest one, which they had employed to get to this world, should take them back. The second would send them further into another world unfamiliar to them. The most distant gate should take them to The Farm.

All gates were subject to a change of position. Both their origin and proposed destination depended on the shifting situations of the many known worlds. Jake had learned of the flux of the gates the hard way when the same gate that should have taken him back to The Farm instead brought him here. The results of the rescue effort, the resulting aftermath, and the extent of pursuit would dictate their choice of gate when the time came.

Later that night as Jake tried to go to sleep, he thought of his mother. He had come here hoping to find her and Michael McAfee but had neither seen nor heard from her. Could she still be here? Had she only passed through this world and transitioned to another one? Was it possible she was safe back at The Farm?

All these things played about in Jake's head. Several times he started to give up on sleep and get up, but he would need the rest in order to be his best for the task ahead. His mind began to wander, as it was prone to do, on the edge of sleep. With the image of his mother fading in and out of his thoughts, he fell into a fitful sleep.

Chapter Forty-One

The realization that some prisoners were being sacrificed to become the core for these creatures deeply troubled Thomas. He tried not to reveal the effect the answer to his question had on him, but he began to pay closer attention to the guard assigned to this building. He tried not to be obvious to either the guards or the supervisor. Clad from head to toe in body armor, the guards' gear seemed to be overkill in this setting. Now, with his newfound understanding and closer observation, Thomas realized it was not body armor at all. There were no break points or overlaps, which would be present with conventional armor. The creature's entire body was, in all probability, encased in the material he was handling. They were processing the material and piping it into another building where encasement was taking place.

Thomas realized the ten prisoners assigned to the room where he and his friends worked were the only safe ones. But for how long? What happened to the consciousness of those who were chosen to become guards? Were they reprogrammed or through some technique replaced? The motor functions of the creatures appeared normal, but he had never heard one speak.

He mulled over these thoughts for the rest of the workday. As they were loaded into the wagon, he made sure to sit between Raj and Seamus.

After hearing what Thomas had learned, Seamus said, "I feel sure that Jake will come for us soon."

"We can't let either of us become one of those monsters," replied Raj.

Thomas grunted and slapped his hand on his leg with enough force to draw the attention of the other prisoners. "I would rather die in a fight than be put into a situation as I would imagine it to be."

"I serve the Society and I serve my wizard. I will not let myself become such as that," said Raj, looking at the guard facing the wagon from the back of a motorcycle.

"We may not be able to wait on Jake," said Thomas.

"How can he, Gwynn, and Kathryn rescue us?"

"Listen to me!" said Seamus after hearing his two allies rant. "I meant that the part of me that serves the Society as a sensitive feels sure that the rescue attempt is *imminent*. We can't initiate any kind of action until there is no alternative."

Seamus's statement brought reassurance and calm and led them to scan the countryside for any signs of their rescuers.

Upon their arrival at the compound, as they were being unloaded, Raj leaned into Thomas and said, "Don't underestimate Jake, you big lug. Remember his linage. A wizard with his staff, a fae, and a wild cat sound pretty formidable to me."

He's right, Thomas thought. That Raj was returning to his verbal banter made him feel encouraged.

They were all tired, hungry, and sleepy and tomorrow was another day.

Chapter Forty-Two

Jamal returned to his quarters with a smile on his face. He had
spent so much time trying to formulate the perfect presentation
to achieve his goal of keeping Jake Lokins alive. In the end, almost
anything would have worked.

He had been called to the Determiner's formal chamber. When
he arrived, he was surprised to be alone with the Determiner. The
Royal Guards who were normally stationed on the inside of the
chamber door had been asked to wait outside. On any other day,
the Determiner would be conducting business, seeing one subject
or dignitary after another.

"Is Major Bannar available yet?" asked the Determiner as soon as
Jamal was within earshot.

"He should be available within the next two hours, my lord,"
replied Jamal as he reached the dais.

The Determiner nodded his head and paused. Jamal was getting
ready to try what he considered his reasoning with the best chance
of success.

Before Jamal could speak, the Determiner said, "Maybe I've
been too hasty. The ineptitude of the fools sent to kill the Lokins
boy may turn out to be fortuitous."

"How so, my lord?" asked Jamal, trying to buy time.

"The Lokins boy has been left alone for all these years, and now suddenly he is activated, made a wizard in short order, and sent out with a team of allies."

The boy was sent out alone, Jamal thought. *It was only after you sent your assassins that he was joined by his allies.* He said nothing.

The Determiner continued, "I have come to suspect that there is more here than meets the eye. There must be some plan or crisis behind his activation. I want to know what Meekins and Alphonse are up to. We know where Lokins is, which is troubling."

"Yes, my lord," said Jamal. "Our consolation is that he is in the land of one of our staunchest allies."

"Allies be damned!" roared the Determiner. "If anything should happen to Lokins, the plan will be shifted to another wizard, and we would have to go through the trouble of locating *that* one. I want Lokins under surveillance until we uncover this plot. I also want him kept safe. Once we know their plan, we can eliminate Lokins and his allies."

Jamal could not believe what he was hearing. He decided to still play his gambit.

"My lord, there might be a chance to capture or kill the mother also. Now that the boy has been made wizard, she will almost certainly resume her duties on the council. She wields a lot of power."

The Determiner again nodded his head.

"Yes, capturing them both is an interesting option. Have Major Bannar sent to me as quickly as he becomes available."

Jamal knew he had been dismissed. He could not believe his good fortune.

ॐ   ॐ

Jamal was interrupted from his reflections by a knock at his door. It was Bannar.

"Lord Jamal, I was told to come directly to your chambers," said Bannar with a salute.

"Ah, Major, it is good to see you back from your maneuvers. There has been a change of plans. You should go to the formal chamber of the Lord High Determiner."

Bannar did not ask any questions. With another salute, he turned and walked away.

Jamal closed his door.

Chapter Forty-Three

They awoke to the first gray, overcast day they had experienced since being brought to the land of the fae. Jake wondered if the brooding sky was a harbinger of what lay ahead. He tried not to let his uncertainty show after Gwynn and Kathryn joined him.

The mood of the whole morning was one of silence and contemplation. Not having any experience in battle, Jake had no way of knowing how normal their behavior was.

After a forced lunch, they began to prepare for the task ahead. They each packed the essential tools for the rescue and their escape. Jake noticed his pack was much smaller than those carried by Gwynn and Kathryn. When he questioned them about it, they explained that he needed to be able to maneuver more freely than either of them. Besides, once they were in position, all packs would be stored until after the rescue. He didn't like the idea of carrying less but saw the wisdom in it. He threw his pack over his shoulders and settled it onto his back. Next, he slung his rifle over one shoulder and reached for the staff. He felt much better once it was in his grip. He sensed a weak but persistent vibration emanating from its length. Gwynn was equipped with a rifle, a bandoleer with extra magazines, and a pistol with additional cartridges. She also had two knives, one the length of a short sword, the other a dagger. Each woman checked the fit and position of the Gwynn's equipment and then both checked Jake's. Once that was done, Kathryn opened the door and they both stood aside so Jake could go through. Watching their preparation and the professional way they carried themselves was both assuring and disquieting.

As they exited the building, they saw Celine, Elic, Simon, and Arac waiting on the street. They were similarly appointed. Together they made their way to the door that led above.

Chapter Forty-Four

The sky was even darker when they transitioned above. No rain was falling but, from the look of the clouds, it was imminent. Captain Sellue was waiting for them, but his troops were nowhere to be seen.

"It looks like we may face some challenges from the weather as well as the guards," he said. "In any case, it will be a fine day for a fight."

Spoken like a true warrior, Jake thought. But he said only, "I hope the rain holds off."

"To the contrary, wizard, a good storm would be to our advantage."

"How so?"

"We won't be counting on mechanized vehicles. Vehicles are not an advantage on this terrain when the rains come."

Jake considered this and hoped Captain Sellue's confidence would carry through to his troops.

"Where are your men, Captain Sellue?"

"They are already deployed and under cover."

Jake would have asked where but didn't want to appear to doubt the captain's judgment.

Elic stepped up and said, "Let's go take care of the road."

Jake nodded and said, "First, I have to speak with Kathryn."

He and Kathryn reaffirmed their plan for letting the men know the rescue was about to take place.

Her clothes then fell in a heap, and she stood in feline form. Gwynn picked up the discarded clothing and stuffed it into the backpack Kathryn had worn. Without anything further, Kathryn loped off in the direction of the work area. Jake motioned to Elic, and they headed for the road.

As they left the forest and neared the road, Jake felt a chill in the air, and the breeze, which had been prevalent since they had emerged from below, began to stiffen.

"Looks like the rain is on its way," said Elic.

Jake thought he detected a bit of dread in Elic's voice.

"Does it rain much here?" Jake asked.

"Not at this time of year. When it does it tends to be a storm with lots of thunder and lightning."

"It picked a good day to come," said Jake, trying to make his voice sound light with just a touch of sarcasm. Instead, the words came out clipped and strained. He wanted to ask Elic if he intuited that anything was wrong. He didn't have to ask.

"I don't feel that we are in any danger at this time or that we should delay the rescue, but remember what I told you about my gift."

"I trust your intuition, Elic."

Elic looked at Jake, lowered his head, and they both walked into the wind.

By the time they reached the bend in the road, the chill had settled into their bones. They stepped onto the hard surface and walked ahead to a point which they felt was half the length of the convoy.

"Let's do this thing," Jake said more to himself than to Elic. He stepped forward and found the center of the road. Placing his feet shoulder width apart, he brought the staff to the center of his body with the tip resting just above the pavement. He grasped it with both hands and concentrated all his attention to the point below the staff. The vibration intensified. He touched the staff to the surface of the road and felt an electrical shock run through his body. A small fissure appeared and extended from the staff in both directions. It spanned the entire width of the road but would not be enough to affect the convoy.

"What now?" Elic asked, looking from the road to Jake.

"More of the same, I guess," replied Jake. He stepped across the tear and paced out, approximately eight feet. Again, he assumed his previous posture and repeated his action. Once again, a crack formed and ran the width of the road. He had created two distinct grooves in the road but didn't know if they would do anything to stop the convoy. He couldn't take a chance. He walked back to the other side of the rift and stood beside Elic. When he gripped the staff as if he were parrying with an adversary, Elic stepped back. Jake pointed the tip of the staff at the midpoint between the two cuts and pushed it forward. A bolt of light shot from the staff and struck the pavement. The hard surface disappeared along with a foot of terrain below it. He turned away and started walking back to the forest.

Before they had taken twelve steps, another flash of light caught them, this time from the heavens. A clap of thunder sounded that shook the ground under their feet. Rain began to pelt them. It felt like pins pricking their skin. They ran toward the forest. By the time they reached the shelter of the trees, they were both soaked. Gwynn stepped forward and held out a cloak for each of them.

Captain Sellue asked, "Did you take care of it?"

"I'll say he did!" said Elic.

Chapter Forty-Five

Seamus was relieved when the supervisor called a stop for the day. He had toiled hard to keep up with his workload, but it was becoming more difficult each day. Despite the abundance of food they were offered, Seamus knew he was losing weight, which was diminishing his strength and his ability to keep up. More than once today he had found the supervisor looking his way. He feared that within the next few days he would not be chosen to work in the vat room. He knew what that could mean.

As they exited the building, they were met by a heavy downpour, the first they had encountered since arriving. Again, they arranged themselves into a configuration that allowed them to all sit together on the wagon. Once the guard had shackled and checked the prisoners, he returned to the back of a motorcycle, and the convoy began to move. Some of the prisoners were murmuring as the rain pelted them. No provisions had been made to keep them dry. Each guard had been issued a poncho-like garment. As they moved along, all the prisoners could do was lower their heads and endure.

If she had not cried out, they would have missed her. The cry was almost like a human baby in need of its mother. When the prisoners looked up, they saw the rain-soaked cat walking toward cover. Seamus, Raj, and Thomas realized what this meant. Freedom was almost at hand. Some of the other prisoners laughed at the misfortune of the feline caught out in the rain. That they were in as bad if not worse shape did not seem to register.

The key felt like an anchor attached to Seamus's boot. He had been careful in its concealment. Now the time was at hand to get ready to use it. The three of them had decided to let the rescue effort demand the guard's attention before unlocking the shackles. Seamus had been designated to sit between Thomas and Raj to better conceal his movements as he freed the key. Before making a move, Seamus looked at both Thomas and Raj to be sure that they had seen Kathryn. They both nodded.

Next to Thomas sat the prisoner by the name of Aron. He worked with them in the vat room. Now he seemed to be overly interested in the nonverbal communication that passed among the allies. Seamus made a note to keep an eye on him. Thomas also noticed Aron's inquiring look.

Seamus had no idea where the rescue attempt would take place and didn't want to reveal the key too early. He closed his eyes and let his chin fall upon his chest as if trying to sleep. After letting a few minutes pass, Seamus looked toward Aron through slitted eyelids. He was engaged in conversation with the prisoner beside him. Seamus slipped his long finger into the cuff of his boots. He felt the key riding there. Pulling it from the boot, he secured it in his fist. Looking back at Aron and around the wagon, he didn't think his action had been observed.

Now, all they could do was wait.

Chapter Forty-Six

Kathryn had hoped to communicate with Seamus without being seen by others. Realizing that would be impossible, she had let out a cry and tried to act as if she was distressed by being caught in the rain. It wasn't too much of an act as she was distressed. Like most other felines, she abhorred being wet. Once she was sure she had been seen, she darted toward the staging area.

As she ran, she thought about her part in the coming fight. She had originally thought she might be of greater value in her feline form, but now she hoped to fight as a human. She hated the rain, but it was much worse as a feline.

The first thing she did upon arriving at the encampment was to find Gwynn. She wanted her dry clothes and a towel. Next, she found Jake. He was standing with Celine, Elic, Simon, and Arac. Captain Sellue and two soldiers stood a few feet away.

"The convoy is on the move," she said.

Jake felt a pang of apprehension, knowing the fight would begin in only minutes.

"Was there anything unusual happening?" asked Jake.

"Nothing unusual but all the guards are in cloaks against the rain, so they may be hampered in responding."

Jake turned to Captain Sellue and asked, "Are you ready, captain?"

"Ready, wizard," he said and turned to the others. "Take your positions!"

Celine and Arac ran from the woods and took a position behind the largest boulder. Simon and Elic fell into a prone position and sighted down their rifles. Gwynn and Kathryn chambered a round of ammunition and moved to the far end of the forest. They hoped to attack the rear of the convoy. Captain Sellue and the two soldiers had moved out of sight without Jake seeing their position. That left Jake, armed with a rifle and his staff, at the center of the attack. Even though they had discussed and planned everything, when he saw the reality of it, he felt fear rising in him.

The rain continued to pound and had now turned into a full-blown storm. Lightning flashes struck the ground, and claps of thunder shook the land beneath his feet. Before Jake could decide if he should be assured or distressed by the violent turn in the weather, the convoy came into view. It moved at a faster pace than he had expected, probably trying to hurry out of the storm. Jake watched the approach.

When they came to the bend in the road, the lead vehicle slowed to negotiate the turn. The troops riding in the bed of the truck huddled against the rain. Jake felt encouraged. Once the turn was made, the driver accelerated. The motorcycles had no trouble with the turn. They slowed only because the truck had. The driver of the lead vehicle had almost regained his speed when he came to the breach in the road. The rain must have prevented him from seeing it because he didn't brake. The front axle dropped into the crevasse. The metal along the underside of the truck made a screaming noise as it jolted to a halt.

What happened next both surprised and amazed Jake.

Chapter Forty-Seven

Seamus' muscles felt taut with anticipation as he rode alongside his allies in the convoy. After freeing the key, he pulled his hands close to his body as if seeking protection from the rain. After a while, he felt like it was time to act. With slow, deliberate movements, he fitted the key into his shackles and freed himself. He couldn't pass the key because his shackles would fall to the floor if he moved, alerting the guards. He looked about and noticed the prisoner Aron staring at him. A flash of lightning bright enough to temporarily blind them gave Thomas enough reason to act surprised and lean into Seamus. He took the key without Seamus having to move. Thomas had just begun to unshackle himself when the sound of screeching metal came, and he dropped the key. He had one hand free and moved to retrieve it. When he did, Aron stood suddenly. He was not shackled and held a knife in his hand. Aron shouted to the guard and was going for Thomas with the knife. Seamus intercepted him and they both fell to the floor of the wagon.

Thomas dove for the key. Upon retrieving it, he loosened his other shackle. The guard in the motorcycle and facing them was aiming his weapon at Thomas when his head disappeared in a cloud of blood. Thomas gave the key to Raj and went to help Seamus.

The two men were locked in a death grip. They looked like two animals rolling about. Thomas reached into the fray and snatched the man off Seamus. Thomas wrenched Aron's neck without hesitation and dropped the body over the side. When he looked back, Seamus was still on the floor, the knife protruding from his body. The blade had entered just under his ribcage and was thrust upward through Seamus's heart. Nothing could be done for him.

Raj had passed the key to the other prisoners, and they were busy freeing themselves. Thomas lifted Seamus's body and he and Raj dropped over the side and took cover behind a wheel. Raj retrieved the weapon that had been used by the headless guard. All hell was breaking loose above them.

Chapter Forty-Eight

When the battle began, everything around Jake went into slow motion. The torrential rain become individual drops. He could almost see his reflection in each one as they passed his field of vision. His first thought was of how beautiful they were. He forced himself to look through them to the convoy and what was taking place. He watched as Simon sighted his rifle on the man guarding the prisoners. The man's head was completely vaporized—all in slow motion.

He saw Thomas and Raj go over the side of the wagon and assumed that Seamus had preceded them. Hearing shouts from farther back in the procession, he realized that Gwynn and Kathryn had entered the fray. They were charging the motorcycle riders who rode behind the wagon. The riders had been intent upon what was happening on the wagon. Five of them perished before they realized they were under attack. Once they comprehended their predicament, they returned fire, and the two women took to the ground. The undulations of the ground provided some cover, but they could no longer able wield their rifles without peril.

Their situation broke the spell and sent Jake into action. He ran for the rear of the convoy. He could find no way to use the rifle without relinquishing control of the staff. Still, he charged. A rifle round silently flew over his head, and he realized how vulnerable he was. In his peripheral vision, he saw Gwynn rising from cover to draw fire. Without having to make a conscious decision, he brought the staff to bear on the motorcycles and their riders. He pushed it forward and a blinding light emerged from its tip. This was a greater force than Jake had seen until this time. The power of the discharge toppled him. As he rolled, he tried to gain control of his body. Upon doing so, he rose to his knees and swung the staff in the direction of the convoy. The motorcycles and their riders were gone. He had wiped the entire rear guard out and disintegrated their bodies and vehicles. Gwynn had changed her direction after the blast and was now under the wagon with the freed prisoners. Kathryn was nowhere to be seen.

Jake looked to the front of the wagon. The riders and guards had organized and taken cover behind their vehicles. Two distinct battles were underway. Those caught on the road before the curve were firing on Jake's position. Those closer to the breech were fighting the fae who had attacked from behind the boulder. One of the fae was lying motionless beside the rocks. Everyone was pinned down and could only fire their weapons at great risk. How had he thought that seven people could defeat forty-two seasoned troops? Adding to his distress, he watched as the convoy took advantage of their superior position. A single rider had been dispatched in the direction of the keep. He was on his motorcycle and already out of range of their weapons. It would be only a short while before reinforcements were sent.

Had all this been for nothing? Trying to mount any kind of attack would be suicide. He could not rise to use the staff. He could no longer concern himself with any deception that would shield the fae from blame. If the rider returned with others, there would be no hiding the fae's involvement. All the toplander troops had to do was keep them pinned down until help arrived. Jake could not just lie on the ground while forces were being summoned to slay his allies and confederates. He readied himself and closed his eyes in prayer.

Chapter Forty-Nine

Before he could spring into action, the sky darkened. A cloud so thick it diverted the rain passed overhead. Jake rolled onto his back, looked up, and thought he was hallucinating. Fae troops filled the sky. Jake could not make out any individuals, but they were all dressed in some lightweight uniform consisting of form-fitting tights that covered their legs to mid-calf. A quiver for arrows to feed their bows was attached along the leg of half the troops. The other half of the fae carried spears. All, both male and female, were naked from the waist up. A head covering completed the uniform.

They had reached the convoy. The archers hovered and rained arrows down on the enemy troops while the lancers swooped down and made parrying attacks, more to keep the enemy's heads down than to directly engage. Some of the enemy troops diverted their attention from Jake and began to fire on the airborne fae. He watched as several fell from the sky. As each tumbled, they tried to crash into a toplander. Jake had never imagined such as what he was witnessing. He sprang up but could not bring the staff into action for fear of damaging the fae onslaught. Gwynn evidently had made a like decision as they both ran to the wagon, diving underneath to avoid an errant arrow.

Safely under the wagon, he turned to find only Thomas and Raj. Their expression was all he needed to realize the fate of Seamus. Gwynn emitted an audible groan. Jake's first emotion was rage. He rolled and used the staff to vaporize a motorcycle and the soldier behind it. Gwynn put her hand on his shoulder, and with her touch he slumped to the ground. He had not contemplated the loss of one of his own. Thomas and Raj joined Gwynn in comforting him. The cacophony of battle ceased, and a silence came over the area.

Jake slipped from the cover of the wagon. As he stepped free, he saw bodies scattered about the terrain. There were fae soldiers, topside troops, and what must have been the other prisoners, most of which had joined the battle with weapons retrieved from the dead. Celine, Elic, and Simon walked toward him. It was Arac who had fallen at the beginning of the battle. They each bore wounds and were covered with mud and blood, but they seemed well enough. Jake looked at the wagon and saw Seamus with the knife still protruding from his body.

"A traitor was planted among us," Thomas said without being asked. "Seamus engaged him before he could alarm the guards—a heroic act for which we owe him our lives. The traitor meant to get the key before we could free ourselves."

Jake acknowledged Seamus's sacrifice, then asked, "Where is Kathryn?"

Before anyone could reply, Jake heard a noise coming from above him. He brought the staff about but recognized Captain Sellue before activating it. Captain Sellue settled to the ground.

"We have accomplished our task," said the captain looking from Thomas to Raj and then to Jake.

"Not without cost," replied Jake.

"There are always costs, wizard."

Jake couldn't believe that Captain Sellue could be so accepting of the death of his troops but realized that the captain had seen much more fighting than he.

"I fear we have exceeded the purview of the council as far as our involvement in your rescue, but you were in peril. I also saw the rider escape and ride for the keep, so I thought time was of the essence."

"Thank you, Captain," was all Jake could say.

"It looks as if we have a mess to clean up if we are to have any deniability at all," said the captain. "I just hope we have time to accomplish it."

"I can take care of that if you and the others would like to return below. Thank the Chief Convener for me and assure him of the gratitude of the Society."

The captain offered his hand, which Jake took. He lifted into the air and moved toward the wooded area. Celine, Elic, and Simon remained stationary.

After the captain was out of sight, Celine and Simon began gathering any weapons that could be traced to the fae and placing them in a pile for Jake to dispose of. Jake began the process of removing the bodies of the fallen fae. From body to body, he moved and in turn brought the staff to life to erase any sign of fae involvement. All the while, he kept his eye on the horizon for signs of topland reinforcements. The last fae to remove was Arac. His fellow fighters were there with him. They each said some words in a language Jake could not understand then stepped back as Jake completed his task. That left only Seamus.

Chapter Fifty

Gwynn, Thomas, and Raj had taken Seamus's body from the wagon and removed the knife. They arranged the body to resemble one who was only asleep. Jake joined the gathering, looked from face to face, and knelt beside the body. He reached out, touched Seamus's cheek, and felt the staff vibrate several times then quiet itself. Jake rose and not knowing where it came from said, "Nah moam arthic. Neh joam articam. Mehhan shoa, Seamus O'Donnegan, mehan shoa abot."

"Mehhan shoa abot," said the others in unison.

Jake stood and made ready to dispose of the body. Just as he raised the staff, he heard a gasp behind him. Gwynn, Thomas, and Raj were staring over his shoulder. The gasp came from Celine, and as she made it she stumbled into Jake's arm. He stopped to look, expecting to see enemy reinforcements charging toward their position. Instead, he saw a Bengal tiger walking toward them. In its jaws it carried the dead body of one of the toplanders. It was obvious that Celine and her mates had never seen this type of animal before. They moved closer behind Jake, waiting for a sign as to how to handle this situation. At the edge of the gathering, the cat dropped the carcass, walked to where Gwynn stood, took up the bag and went behind a boulder. Jake waited.

Kathryn stepped from behind the boulder with the bag in her hand. The fighters from below looked one to the other as if more questions had been raised than answered.

Pointing to the body, she said, "That's the rider from the convoy. I almost didn't catch him. I did the best I could to hide the motorcycle before I returned, but it will be found." Then she saw Seamus and said quietly, "Mehhan shoa abot."

Everyone but Jake took a step back, and with a flash Seamus was gone. After a moment of respect, Jake said, "I guess we should move out."

"We will accompany you for a distance," Celine said.

Before they began their journey, Jake took time to welcome Raj and Thomas and inquire about their wellbeing. Both attested to being well and thankful to be out of captivity.

"When we reach a place of safety, there is a matter I need to make you aware of," said Thomas.

"We will speak further after we travel a while," said Jake. Turning to Celine, Jake said, "I know this was not how we planned it, but I hope no blame will fall on the people of your world."

"Thank you for your concern. However, after examining the scene, I fear they will surmise our involvement."

Jake feared that Celine spoke the truth. He moved to the back of the convoy and without a word raised the staff. Fire leapt from the tip. Jake made a sweeping motion. As he did so, it was like an eraser rubbing out a misspelled word. Everything disappeared.

"They will have no evidence," he said and began his journey westward.

Chapter Fifty-One

The group moved to the cover of the trees. Jake knew it would not be possible to cover the distance required without being exposed on open ground. He thought it prudent to seek cover for as long as possible. As they walked, everyone in turn sought out Thomas and Raj and welcomed them back. Soon there were groups traveling together as if all cares were laid aside.

Jake caught up to Elic. They exchanged a glance and walked on together.

"Elic, the death of Seamus was a deep loss to me and to the team. He was also our sensitive, so without him we are vulnerable. I want you to join our team and become our ally."

Elic looked at Jake and slowed, falling behind him by several paces. Jake stopped and waited for him to come abreast.

"Jake, you know what I told you about my last team. I don't think I could face that type of failure again."

"I don't think you should be so hard on yourself. With the forces you spoke of, it is a real possibility that the danger was masked in some way. The fact that you alone survived was a fortunate accumulation of circumstances. When I have asked for your evaluation of a situation, you have been accurate beyond question."

"I just don't know if I want to risk it."

Jake didn't know how to respond so they walked in silence. They soon came to the place of parting.

"We will not forget the hospitality of the fae. The rescue of our allies would never have been possible without your help. The Society of Builders will know of your gallantry."

As everyone said their individual goodbyes, Jake again approached Elic. "I hope you will think about what I asked you."

Before Elic could reply, Jake called for Gwynn. "Gwynn, would you show Elic our destination?"

Gwynn looked from Jake to Elic and then raised her hands to summon the posit. She pointed to the two positions she and Jake had discussed.

"It will take us a day to reach the first and a while longer for the second. If you wish to join us, you can meet us there. We plan to use the second one but have the first if need be."

Elic looked at Gwynn and Jake before saying, "I will consider it. I must talk with the Grohn and assess any impact that joining you would have on our community. In any case, thank you for your confidence."

He reached out his hand. Jake took it and they formed the grip of The Society. As their hands touched, a shadow appeared to run across his countenance. He leaned in to Jake's shoulder and whispered, "Be careful, Jake. I feel there could be danger ahead. Be vigilant and move with as much stealth as possible."

As a group, the fae disappeared through a door that had opened in the trunk of a large tree.

Jake turned and relayed Elic's words. In turn, each of the allies acknowledged the warning. Without instruction or preamble, Kathryn's clothes fell to the ground, and she set off in the appropriate direction in feline form.

Jake looked back in the direction of the battle. "Goodbye, Seamus," he said with a sigh of regret. He turned and they continued their journey.

Chapter Fifty-Two

During the battle the rain had slowed, becoming only a drizzle by the time Kathryn returned with the rider. The sky appeared to be clearing as they began their journey but now was darkening and bolts of lightning were visible on the horizon. They stayed in the trees until they had no choice but to travel over open ground.

They had traveled only a short distance when the rain returned in earnest. The drops pelted them like tiny stones thrown from above. Without protective clothing, their only choice was to lower their heads and continue. Jake felt the decrease in visibility could be both an asset and a liability. He thought of Kathryn somewhere out ahead in feline form. She must be more miserable than they were.

Claps of thunder and flashes of lightning became more prevalent. Somewhere between outbursts, Jake thought he heard a squawk from above. He looked up but could see nothing. The force of the rain made him look away.

As the day wore on, they became almost numb to the downpour. Once you are soaked to the skin, it doesn't feel like additional rainfall makes a difference. There was no sign of the storm easing in intensity, so by late afternoon they started looking for shelter. Jake felt as if they had put enough distance between themselves and the rescue site to enjoy at least a modicum of safety. He had just relayed his thoughts to the others when he saw Kathryn approaching. When she joined them, she made no move to transition into human form.

"I am so sick of this damn rain. It's bad enough if you're not a cat, but..." Her voice trailed off. "Anyway, there's a wooded area just about a mile ahead. It's the last one for about five more miles, so we may want to take shelter there for the night."

Jake still couldn't get used to a cat talking although he knew it was Kathryn.

"I think we are all ready to get out of this," Jake said. Everyone nodded in acquiescence.

Now that they had a reachable goal, they moved with purpose. Kathryn ran ahead, proposing to find the best place to set up camp. Jake suspected it was also to get out of the downpour.

Once they arrived, they found themselves in a thick forest with a dense canopy. The rain only penetrated the foliage in a few areas. It had the effect of being inside of a tent. They settled among the trees and passed food around. Jake was famished. After they ate and drank, they became so drowsy they could hardly remain awake. The staff was still, so Jake assumed they were safe enough.

Rising to his feet, Jake said, "Why don't you all get some sleep. I can stay awake for a while and keep watch." He nestled the staff in his arms and moved to the edge of the forest. He took care to stay far enough back to avoid both the rain and possible detection. He settled his back against a tree and sat facing the open area they had just traversed. He was thinking about the events of the day when he fell asleep.

In a dream, he was back on his land. The feeling of happiness and contentment felt so intense. Even while sleeping, he subconsciously knew there had to be a counterpoint. No matter, he was happy and looking forward to the day's work. He was determined to make a living from the meager acreage. He didn't want to leave it. His mother was cooking breakfast. When he came out of his room, he greeted her as they did every morning.

"Do you want a cup of coffee to take on the porch with you?" she asked as he passed behind her.

"No, thanks. I'll be right back in."

He opened the door and stepped outside. He almost lost his breath. The air was thick with smoke. He began to cough and then he felt the heat. It came from the side of the house. He feared that his skin would be blistered, but he had to find the source of the smoke. When he got to the edge of the porch, the barn was ablaze. The fire was working its way across the yard toward the house. He turned to run back inside to warn his mother. Before he could get to the door, he walked through a giant spider web. He fought through it and ran into the living room. His mother was nowhere to be found. Flames shot through the windows and the back door, trapping him. Then he remembered his reality and jerked awake. Kathryn was beside him.

"I think someone is out there," she whispered.

Chapter Fifty-Three

J ake was instantly alert. He wondered how long he had slept and how long Kathryn had been with him. These were fleeting thoughts as he keyed in on what she had said. He picked up the staff and felt a low vibration. It didn't feel like a warning, more of an alert.

"I heard it only a few minutes ago. Whatever is out there is not too worried about stealth. It was walking with no attempt to hide its presence. I can check it out if you want me to."

After a moment, Jake said, "Let's just hold tight and see what happens. If it's an animal, it may pass on. If it's a human, any attempt to find it could alert it to our presence. I'll stay here. Why don't you go back to the camp and warn the others?"

Without a sound, she slipped away. Jake tried to concentrate on his surroundings. He strained to hear any movement but could discern nothing. The vibration of the staff remained constant. He wished Seamus was alive and here to warn him of impending danger. He remained in a state of alert until the sky began to lighten. From his vantage point, he could see well into the surrounding area. There was no sign of movement in the open. As the sun broke the horizon, he stood and did a 360-degree scan. He saw nothing. Remembering the efficiency of Captain Sellue's attack yesterday, he turned his attention to the sky. The devastation that rained down on the convoy had made a deep impression on him, and he didn't want his team subjected to such an attack. Everything looked clear, but the staff continued to vibrate. He couldn't wait much longer. Any delay getting to the gate leading from this world was a chance to be detected and captured. That would mean they might never be able to get home.

He had almost decided to join the others and get underway when he heard a twig snap to his left. He moved to face the noise and pointed the tip of the staff in that direction. He heard something moving in the bush, but it sounded as if it were moving away. He decided to investigate because any further delay would be just as dangerous as whatever was out there. He moved into the woods to his left, keeping the staff at the ready. He had traveled about two hundred feet when he heard something between a snort and a growl. Another fifteen feet and he was looking at the rear end of an animal. Its head seemed to be ensnared in bramble. It shook its head violently from side to side, trying to back out of the tangle. Jake was weighing the possibility of helping the creature when it broke free and turned to face him. It looked like a cross between a wild boar and a large dog. The body was slender but looked powerful. The legs were long and roped with muscle. A tail was almost nonexistent. Its ears were large and stood erect. Specks of blood dotted its head where thorns had made small lacerations as it had struggled to free itself. Its huge, squarely-shaped head held black eyes that appeared to be both blank and piercing. This paradox momentarily startled Jake. Its snout was elongated and porcine in appearance. The most frightening features were the tusks that protruded from each side of its mouth. They were over ten inches long, pure white, curved outward, and obviously sharp. Wire-like hair stood away from the body. The hair was so erect that Jake could not decide if it was for protection or some kind of weapon.

While Jake had studied the animal, it had been studying him. Its eyes did not leave him. Jake couldn't decide what to do. Should he turn away and return to the others? Would it attack if he turned his back? Would it eventually leave of its own volition? As he contemplated all these things, time was passing. Jake heard another sound off to his right. He glanced toward the noise just as another animal stepped through the trees. The second animal assumed the same posture as the first. Jake at once reassessed his situation. While neither animal acted aggressively, the thought of having to deal with two riveted him in place. He could feel time passing but could not summon the wherewithal to move. A bead of sweat began at his hairline and trickled to the crease between his eyes and down his nose. It was maddening but he could not move. He heard another sound from the woods on his left. His apprehension increased as he imagined a third beast. He shifted his vision to the left but could see nothing. He heard another shift, and a voice came from his left.

"These creatures are part of the search effort. They will not attack until commanded to do so. The one who can give the command is certainly nearby and closing on their signal. They will track you or try to contain you until he arrives. The only way to survive is to destroy them. I have my sights trained on the one directly in front of you. When I shoot, you must destroy the other one before he escapes. Be mindful because there may be more unseen."

The voice had spoken calmly and at a low volume. Whether the creatures heard or understood was uncertain, but, as Jake oriented himself to the right, both creatures adjusted their position. From his left came the sound of a puff of air. The creature in front of him came apart. Instead of flesh and blood, only a pile of mechanical parts remained. It so surprised Jake that he almost let the second animal escape. Just before it disappeared into the woods, Jake aimed the staff and vaporized it. When he turned, he found Elic standing in front of him.

"We must move as quickly as possible before the hunters arrive."

Jake had questions but trusted that what Elic said was true. Halfway to the camp, they were met by the others, already packed and prepared to move. Everyone saw Elic and acknowledged him before continuing.

Moving into a position beside of Jake, Gwynn said, "We have another mile of cover, and then it's all open ground. As of this morning, both gates are still available. Which will you choose?"

"I feel the prudent thing will be to return to The Farm. Perhaps my mother is already there. If not, I can at least get counseling as to how to proceed. I have invited Elic to join us as our sensitive and must get the approval of Mister Meekins. We also must make everyone aware of Seamus's death. Unless we are deterred, we will return to The Farm."

Gwynn voiced her approval and moved to inform the others.

Thomas was next to seek Jake out. He came alongside and walked a short while in silence. "I think Elic will make a good fit."

"I appreciate your approval. I feel that the whole team will agree. At least I hope so."

Next, Thomas told Jake about what was going on in the work area. This troubled Jake on several levels. He wondered if that were why the fae had all moved into the safety of the city. He would ask Elic. Jake did not know how to confront the problem. They were on the run, being pursued, and their only chance of survival was to reach the gate. If he took time to address the problem, it could mean the death of them all. He also wondered how the Society would have them handle it.

"Thomas, let me think. I will consider what, if anything, we can do," said Jake, although he knew in his heart that this situation would probably be addressed later and with guidance from the Society.

Chapter Fifty-Four

The group moved through the wooded area with ease. Elic took up a position at the rear of the procession to sense if the pursuit was closing in. Jake could see that the forest was coming to an end. Beyond, only barren land awaited them. He decided they should pause for nourishment and water before proceeding.

As they rested, Elic took a seat next to Jake and said, "I don't think we are being followed. That doesn't mean there is no danger. They obviously know we are here. The Findalhounds are proof of that. Our presence was transmitted to the hunters, and they will continue pursuit even though the beasts were destroyed. I sense we will have contact before reaching our destination."

"I can only ask that you keep me apprised of our situation. We have no alternative to continuing on open ground."

Turning away from Elic, Jake summoned Gwynn. When she arrived, he motioned her to sit. "Gwynn, how far will we have to travel in the open?"

Without comment, she brought up the posit. She made some gestures on the screen and said, "We are nine miles from the first gate."

Jake thought for a minute and then called for the others. They took positions around him and waited in silence.

"I want to let you all know what I understand about our situation. First, if you are not already aware, I have asked Elic to join us. He has been and still is a member of the Society. He is a sensitive and, with the loss of Seamus, I think he will be a good fit for us. If anyone has questions about my decision, I will be happy to speak with you as soon as we are safe. Next, we are most certainly being pursued. We have no way of knowing how large the party is or how well equipped they are. We also have nine miles of open ground ahead of us. I am not comfortable with this situation. What I propose is that we double back, using the trees for cover. Our goal will be to meet those coming for us on our terms and, if possible, eliminate the danger. I propose that Elic and Gwynn go ahead toward the gate for two reasons. First, we need those who pursue us to believe we are moving ahead in that direction. My second reason is that they are both fae. If captured or killed, it could trigger retribution toward those who have helped us. I am open to suggestions, so feel free to offer them."

Raj stood. He appeared to have lost some weight during his captivity but still struck a fearsome image. He nodded his head in approval toward Elic, turned to Jake and said, "Boss, I think the plan is a good one. We'll be much better off to meet our pursuers head on and with some cover. The only thing that concerns me is splitting up again. Who is to say that there is no danger ahead? If any of us are captured, we will be no better off than we were yesterday. With all respect, I think we should live or die as a complete unit. We are not as good as individuals as we are as a team."

Jake looked from person to person. Although no one spoke, he could see that what Raj had said was valid in everyone's mind. He weighed the merits of staying together against the danger that could be imposed upon the fae community. In the end, he realized the best way to protect the fae was to do everything in his power to avoid capture.

"Thank you, Raj. We'll stay together as a team," he said. "Now, let's backtrack and see what we're up against. We'll form two groups and separate just enough to keep from being taken by surprise but stay close enough together to maintain visual contact."

Elic and Gwynn lined up beside Jake while Kathryn, Raj, and Thomas moved a little deeper into the forest. Each group moved quietly back across ground they had already covered. After about a half mile, Elic reached out and touched Jake's arm. Elic had raised a clenched fist, signaling the others to stop. Both groups came to a halt. Elic's hand went to his nose. Only then did Jake smell the difference in the air. The breeze was tinged with a metallic scent. Upon recognizing the odor, a sense of dread permeated Jake's being. He signaled everyone down. Weapons were brought to the ready. He motioned for Elic to accompany him as he slowly crept forward. Jake had the staff at the ready. Kneeling, they both crawled along the forest floor. As they moved to the edge of the cover, Jake could see them—fifteen of the troopers in full battle gear and three more Findalhounds. They were all dead. The pools of blood surrounding the troopers were still fresh and wet. The Findalhounds looked as if they had been disassembled and laid out like some diagram.

Jake felt Elic slump beside of him and feared the worst. When he turned, he saw that Elic had just sat flatly on the ground. He did not look well. His complexion had gone pale, and his skin was glossed with a sheen of sweat. With a cross between a whimper and a whisper, Elic said, "The Determiner."

Chapter Fifty-Five

Jake could not believe the change in Elic. The man who had taken part in yesterday's battle had been brave, even daring. The voice that had spoken to him from the wooded area with instructions concerning the Findalhounds had been cool, confident, and direct. Now, that same man was visibly trembling. He was frozen in place as if he could no longer move of his own volition. Jake had read about post-traumatic stress and something called the thousand-yard stare, but now he saw it firsthand.

When Jake put his hand on Elic's shoulder, he pulled away violently and turned toward Jake as if to attack. The others had joined them, so at Elic's sudden move Thomas wrapped his huge arms around him and pulled him away from the rest of the group. Elic slumped in Thomas's arms. Thomas lowered the unconscious Elic to the ground but took up a guarding position where his head rested.

"He'll be fine," was all Jake could think to say, but the others were not so sure. Jake moved to the edge of the woods to further survey the carnage. There could be no survivors. He looked about the area but could see no sign of the attacking force. He was about to decide to proceed with their journey when he heard Elic's voice calling his name. Jake walked back to Elic's position and asked Thomas to give them some time. Thomas nodded agreement but only moved away enough to give them some privacy. He stayed well within range if Jake needed him.

"Jake, I'm sorry," said Elic. "I hoped to never have to think about the Determiner again, but I know this is his work. He is probably not here himself, but this has his brand all over it. I don't feel any danger, but you know what I told you about my previous experience. I don't know if I can trust how I feel."

Jake recognized the doubt in Elic's eyes. He knew his reaction to Elic's uncertainty would mean the difference between Elic becoming a member of his team or returning to the fae and living out his time in fear and shame. Jake quickly weighed his responsibility to Elic against his responsibility for the others. He felt he could depend on Elic and his abilities.

"I trust you, Elic. Should we go on to the gates or develop another plan?"

Elic sat up and rested his back against a nearby tree. Jake waved the others over. Thomas moved closer but remained standing, looking over Elic and the group at the battlefield beyond.

Jake spoke. "Elic sees this as the works of a group that is diametrically opposed to the ideals of the Society and its members. He has encountered them before with disastrous results. He doesn't feel that we are in imminent danger from them. The other thing we can be sure of is that the victims of this attack were also after us. They will soon be missed. When they are found, we likely will be credited with this massacre also. They will probably redouble their efforts to find us. We must reach the gateway out of this world as quickly as possible. From this point forward, speed is more important than stealth."

"Jake, take a look," Thomas said. Jake followed Thomas's pointed finger and saw what looked like a truck sitting just beyond the killing field. Thomas continued, "I haven't seen any movement around the truck. Perhaps we could use it to speed up our journey. Do you mind if I look?"

Jake gave him the go ahead and watched as Thomas moved clear of the trees. Unconsciously, Jake had brought the staff to bear across the open area and was ready to blast away anything that moved. Everyone's eyes were on the scene of mass destruction. They all breathed a sigh of relief when Thomas reached the truck.

He walked around it, opened the doors, and looked into the storage area. After a brief pause, he stepped clear of the truck and waved them forward.

"Let's go," said Jake. "Pick up any spare ammunition that will fit our weapons and anything else we can use."

Together, they made their way across the open area. By the time they reached the truck, they each had several clips of projectiles. Somewhere Raj had found a sword. They stashed everything in the back of the truck. Thomas and Raj jumped into the bed of the truck, each taking a position with weapons ready. Kathryn and Gwynn got into the back compartment of the truck cab. Gwynn summoned the posit. Jake went to the driver's side door, but after looking inside he hesitated. He didn't recognize any of the controls.

Seeing Jake's hesitation, Elic said, "Better let me take care of driving. I've handled one of these before."

Jake moved to the passenger side. Elic fired up the truck and drove toward the gates. Gwynn checked the posit to ascertain that both gates were still available. Kathryn surveyed one side of the terrain while Jake took the other. Nobody observed the large bird that was drifting on the warm currents high above the ground. Nor did they notice when it took wing and flew off ahead of them.

Chapter Fifty-Six

The bird appeared on the horizon. Major Bannar knew that the wizard and his companions were on the move. The bird approached Bannar's position, making sure it had been seen. The major raised his right fist and opened his hand. Seeing the open palm, the bird silently reversed his course. The next sighting of the bird would indicate the group was near. Now there was nothing to do but wait.

This was the strangest mission Bannar had ever undertaken. When the Lord Determiner had requested his presence, he had felt the excitement of an upcoming assignment. As one of the most highly decorated officers in service to the Determiner, he was only chosen for the most difficult and important missions. That most of his undertakings included violent confrontation was not lost on him nor any of the other officers. Most of his fellow officers envied Bannar for his closeness with the Determiner. Some were so jealous they would probably kill him if given the opportunity without fear of detection. One such man, Othan, had been assigned as his second in command. Othan had led the attack and massacre of the local forces. As he awaited Othan's return, he thought again about the assignment.

When he had entered the Determiner's chamber, he found him seated on his high back throne. What was not normal was that they were alone. The Determiner was always accompanied by several Supreme Protectors and his Sorcerer Jamal. Bannar stepped to the edge of the dais and knelt until summoned forward.

"Major Bannar, I have called you here because I need you to handle a very delicate situation for me."

Bannar was now at full attention. Most of his work would never be considered "delicate."

"Jake Lokins has been located. It seems that he and his team mistakenly entered a world for no known purpose. Circumstances drew him into confrontation, and now he is trying to leave that world. His becoming an active wizard within the Society of Builders could be problematic but to what extent is not clear at this time. What I want you to do is take a group and make certain he escapes. I don't want any harm to come to him at this time."

Bannar could not believe what he was hearing. He had been charged with the safety of a member of the Society.

"When they make a safe transition, I want you to send the regular troops back here and both you and Captain Othan follow and monitor their activities. You will carry a communiq and will be in direct communication with me. You leave within the hour."

As soon as Bannar, Othan, and the others transitioned, they found chaos. The Scoutwing they brought with them alerted Bannar to a military pursuit. Soldiers and hounds were closing in on Lokins. Othan and the troops were dispatched to initiate action against this force. They did so with extreme prejudice.

The return of Captain Othan and his men interrupted Bannar's thoughts. It was obvious they were all worn out. Three men were injured and had to be carried by others. Bannar cursed. His troops almost never suffered injuries when they executed one of his plans. There had been no time for planning, so a spontaneous response was mounted. He motioned for Othan.

"Yes, Major?" he said upon his approach.

"Captain Othan, we must transport these men away from here before the wizard arrives. Tell all the men to prepare for transport. You and I will remain behind."

"But, Major, what if there is more trouble?"

"We'll have to hope there isn't anymore. With injured troops, there is a greater chance of detection. Make the men ready for transport."

With a salute, Othan turned and called out orders. The injured were carried on the backs of other soldiers as they gathered at the point of transport. When all was ready, Bannar summoned his communiq and made the transfer. Othan turned and looked him in the eye. He snapped a salute, which betrayed his displeasure with the situation. Bannar believed he had done the right thing by sending the troops back but could not deny the empty feeling in the pit of his stomach. He had gone somewhat counter to the Determiner's instructions, which was not usually a healthy thing to do.

"Let's conceal ourselves before they arrive," said Bannar.

Together, Bannar and Othan ran to a group of large boulders where they could hide.

Chapter Fifty-Seven

Elic did indeed know how to handle the vehicle. Soon he had it speeding along at a breakneck pace. There was not much conversation as everyone was about their duties. Jake surveyed the terrain from the passenger side window. Everything seemed fine. A shadow thrown across the sandy ground drew his attention. By itself it was no cause for alarm, but Jake felt certain he had seen the shadow several times. Everyone looked toward him as he slid his torso through the open window and rotated onto his back. As a reflex, Elic grabbed Jake's belt. His action caused him to pull the steering wheel and the truck to swerve across the road. He then overcompensated and sent the truck shooting back across the road. The rocking of the truck became exaggerated, and Jake wondered if they would overturn. Elic wisely took his foot from the accelerator and let the truck coast to a halt. Thomas slapped his enormous hand against the petition between the bed and the cab. Jake checked that everyone was safe and breathed a sigh of relief.

Jake opened the door and stepped to the ground. Everyone joined him. Above them a large bird hovered. It reminded him of a bird of prey. Jake wondered if it was a real bird or a mechanical device such as the Findalhounds. The bird broke its circle and flew off toward the horizon as if it realized it had been spotted.

"That's peculiar," Jake said to no one. "I kept seeing a shadow pass over us and thought I'd take a look. I'm sorry if I startled anyone."

All eyes went toward Elic. Instead of acknowledging his erratic driving, he said, "Something about this doesn't feel right."

Jake saw that everyone agreed with Elic and said, "We may be driving into a trap. I think it's time to ditch the truck and proceed on foot."

Gwynn stepped forward and extended the posit for Jake to see. "The gate that I believe will take us back to The Farm is approximately one mile ahead directly over the horizon," she said, pointing toward a blinking light on the display. "The other is about half that distance, due east."

Without being asked, Elic said, "Jake, I feel strongly that we should not attempt to go directly back to The Farm."

"I agree," said Gwynn.

Jake looked around and everyone appeared to be of the same opinion.

"Due east it is. We'll use that gate and then try to find another one to get back to The Farm. We don't need to leave the truck here. It will aid anyone pursuing us by showing them the point at which we took foot."

"I can take care of the truck," volunteered Elic.

Kathryn stepped forward and said, "I think I can drive this thing. I'll take it back a ways and abandon it. I can catch up faster than anyone else by transitioning. I can rejoin you before you reach the gate. Just have my clothes ready."

Jake took only a few seconds to agree with Kathryn. "She's right. She can travel faster than anyone else. Elic, I would prefer to have you with us."

Elic nodded. He stepped to the side of the truck and climbed inside. "I'll get it started and turn it around."

Kathryn looked like a child behind the wheel of the truck. You could only see her head above the open window. It was a good thing because, before driving off, she sent her clothes floating to the ground. Alone and in the nude, she released the brake on the truck and started to backtrack.

"Weapons at the ready," Jake said.

Gwynn came to the front to lead them to the designated gate. Elic and Jake followed closely behind her. Raj was behind them, and Thomas delayed until they were well on their way so he could cover the rear.

Chapter Fifty-Eight

When the bird came over the horizon, Bannar felt his pulse quicken. A knot formed in his stomach when the bird continued to his position and took roost on the rock above them. Something had happened to prevent Lokins and his group from coming forward. From the corner of his eye, he saw Othan look first toward the bird and then at him. Othan's face was a mixture of concern and anticipation. Bannar thought he also detected a hint of satisfaction.

Bannar signaled the bird to go. He would lead them to where the wizard had either diverted his path or run into trouble. The bird took to the air and circled above their heads. The two soldiers began to trot.

Bannar knew he would either need to find the wizard or report his failure.

Chapter Fifty-Nine

Gwynn led the group onward at a quick pace. They covered the distance to the gate in a short time. She confirmed they were in the right place and could utilize the gate whenever they were ready.

"Let's set up a tight perimeter and wait for Kathryn."

They each took a position around Jake and faced the direction from which they had come, weapons at the ready. The run from the road to the gate and the heat from direct sunlight had combined to reduce their strength. Their clothes were soaked with sweat.

"Someone is tracking us," said Elic loud enough for them all to hear. "We're not in immediate danger, but I can feel them coming."

A breeze blew across them, giving temporary relief from the intense heat. As welcome as it was, it also served to remind them how exposed and vulnerable they were. There was only one band of trees between them and the road.

Kathryn burst through the tree line in feline form and at a full run. Everyone trained their weapons her way in case she was being pursued. She stopped just short of the perimeter.

"Do I have time to transition and dress?"

Jake looked toward Elic. "We have time," Elic said.

Gwynn handed Jake the posit and gave Kathryn her clothes then headed for the trees. It seemed to take forever for them to return but was in fact only a few minutes.

They all gathered, and Jake addressed the group. "The last time we did this we became separated with disastrous consequences. I don't want that to happen this time." Turning to Gwynn, he asked, "Is there any reason we can't be touching each other when we go through?"

"Becoming separated rarely happens, but I don't know of any reason to not be touching." She looked to the others, but none had comment.

"I would like for everyone to line up behind me and lay a hand upon the shoulder of the one nearest you, forming a chain."

They all did so. Jake could feel Elic's hand on one shoulder and Gwynn's on the other. As he brought the staff to a horizontal position at chest level, he was distracted by a sound from above. He looked to see the same bird circling overhead.

"We had better hurry," said Elic.

Jake turned and again looked to the sky. He brought the staff to shoulder level and lifted the tip skyward. He punched the tip forward and the bird was no more. He turned and felt the hands return to his shoulders. He reoriented the staff and brought it into his chest. Everything changed.

Chapter Sixty

Bannar and Othan cleared the trees just in time to see everyone disappear, including his Scoutwing. He hated losing the Scoutwing but the relief he felt at seeing the wizard and his party pass through the gate was palpable. He had dodged a very real bullet. He summoned the communiq and made some minor adjustments to several dials, which now became visible on the display. When the frequencies were set, he triggered the call button.

"Yes, Major," said the voice of the Determiner.

Although Bannar had expected a response, he didn't expect the Determiner to answer. He must have hesitated for a second too long because the voice came again. "Major, good news, I hope?"

"Yes, Lord Determiner, Lokins and his group just made a safe transition from this world, although not at the point we had anticipated."

"You saw the transition yourself?"

"Yes, sir. Captain Othan and I were watching from a short distance away. We plan to follow in a short while. We did, however, lose our Scoutwing. I believe Lokins saw it as a threat and eliminated it."

"That is unfortunate but not disastrous. Do you think he realized our involvement?"

"I don't know how he could. We were very careful not to be seen. The confrontation with the locals was the only time we were visible, and his group still had a good lead on the pursuers when we attacked."

"Very well. Continue to follow them and keep me informed. The parameters of your mission remain the same. You are to help if needed and remain anonymous otherwise."

"Yes, Lord Determiner," said Bannar, but the communication had already ended.

Turning to Othan, he said, "We'll give them a few minutes before we follow."

Othan didn't reply, but it was obvious this mission was just as distasteful to him as having to take orders from Bannar.

Chapter Sixty-One

Jamal entered the chambers just as the Lord Determiner was setting the communiq aside. It seemed to the Determiner that Jamal always knew when he was not wanted and chose that time to appear.

If he were not such a powerful sorcerer, I would have his head, the Determiner thought as he watched the painfully thin man approach. His snow-white hair stood in total contrast to his jet-black beard. Jamal took a position directly in front of the Determiner and bowed from the waist. He kept his head erect and stared into the Determiner's eyes. He was one of the few with the audacity to do so. Jamal's eyes, one blue and one green, were piercing, as if they looked through you instead of at you. The Determiner always found this disconcerting and felt the visceral urge to snap the man's neck.

"Is something amiss, my lord?"

"Just a minor annoyance. Nothing that you need to concern yourself with."

Jamal felt the lie before the Determiner's eyes gave it away. He thought this must have something to do with the Lokins boy. The Determiner may not be ready to share the specifics of the situation, but he would soon be able to find them out. He had not been sorcerer for all the years without developing a network of spies and informants. He also knew that he had to be selective in using them because if the Determiner caught a whiff of the deception, it would mean certain death to all involved. Still, he had a gut feeling that gaining this information would be worth the risk. It had to be important because the Determiner was keeping it all to himself.

"Is there any way in which I can be of service to you, my lord?"

"Not at this time, Jamal, although I may have use for one of your apprentices in the near future."

"Very well, my lord. I'll take my leave," said Jamal.

He bowed, took one step back, turned, and left the chamber. Now, he knew he must find out what was going on. Instead of returning to his chambers, he took a direct route to the lower levels of the keep.

At the bottom of the steps, instead of turning right toward the dungeon, he went left toward the armory. In addition to dispensing and keeping track of all weapons and equipment, Sergeant Cleraq, the armorer, knew the movements of all troops except the Supreme Protectors, who never left the vicinity of the Determiner. Jamal had noted early on how valuable such information could be. He made it a point to recruit the sergeant into his clandestine force. It amazed Jamal how easy it was to persuade someone to shift their loyalties. A little currency, a kind word, and the occasional favor of magic was all it took. Much more tangible reasons than political ideology.

Cleraq sat in deep concentration behind the barred entrance to the armory. He had not noticed Jamal's approach and was startled when he looked up to discover the sorcerer standing opposite him. He tried to hide his surprise. "Lord Jamal, so good to see you. To what do I owe the honor of your presence."

"I was thinking of you, Cleraq, and wanted to find out how the little spell we conjured up last month worked?"

The smile that came to Cleraq's face betrayed how well the spell had worked. Jamal felt sorry for the scullery maid. How maddening it must have been when the spell wore off to realize she had been bedded by one of the least desirable creatures in the kingdom. It was of no consequence to Jamal. He had only inquired to remind Cleraq of his indebtedness.

"Thank you, Lord Jamal," said the armorer.

"You are very welcome, my friend. Please let me know if I can be of further assistance in the future."

With that, Jamal turned as if he were about to walk away. After taking two steps, he turned back to the counter. Acting as if it were an afterthought, Jamal said, "I was just with the Lord High Determiner, and he seemed both concerned and irritated. I wonder what could have been the matter?"

"I wouldn't know, Lord Jamal, unless it has something to do with Major Bannar."

"Oh, yes, I should have guessed," said Jamal as if he were privy to everything.

"All weapons have been returned except those issued to Major Bannar and Captain Othan. The equipment was well used, and some weapons were speckled with blood."

"I will see you soon, my friend," said Jamal as he turned to leave.

Cleraq said something but Jamal paid no attention to it. The information he had learned was both good and bad. If Bannar was involved, then it was important to the Determiner. The only saving grace was that Othan was with Bannar, and Othan was loyal to Jamal. Now he only had to devise a way to communicate with Othan.

Chapter Sixty-Two

The first thing Jake wanted to determine was whether they had all transported together. Everyone was within sight of each other, but all had come through in a rough and tumble manner. Jake wondered if it would always be this way or if his inexperience was at fault. He and Thomas were standing, but everyone else was sprawled out on the ground, trying to gather themselves. He could only shrug his shoulders in dismay. Everyone smiled at him, which he took to mean "no harm done."

The second thing he noticed was how scantily clad they were. He and the other men wore little more than a loincloth. He could tell by his freedom of movement that the outfit did not provide any underwear. He and Elic looked somewhat normal in their dress, but Thomas and Raj had body types not completely conducive to their apparel. Gwynn and Kathryn wore loincloths and some type of crude halter with ties attached both around the neck and extending below to the loincloth. The top fit Gwynn well as she was tall and slender, but Kathryn filled her halter to overflowing. It was obvious the female attire did not include undergarments. Everything appeared to be made from some type of skin but upon closer inspection revealed itself to be tightly woven material. Whatever its composition, the fabric was well constructed and subtle to the touch. Nobody seemed self-conscious of uncomfortable in their outfits, so Jake did his best to not seem bothered. He hoped that one day he would be able to transition from world to world and take whatever was given him as comfortably as the others.

Looking around, he could only marvel at the beauty of their surroundings. They were in a grove of giant trees of a genus unrecognizable to him. The circumference of the trunks was so vast that it would take all of them with outstretched arms to reach around. The trunks towered to the sky where a thick canopy appeared to grow together from one tree to another. There was no way of judging their true height. Small openings at random intervals allowed light to come through. Jake was amazed at the brightness of the place considering the thickness of the canopy.

At ground level, the vegetation was lush but not overcrowded. Everything seemed to grow in harmony. Jake wondered if this pattern of growth was consistent throughout the land or if they would find more unruly growth deeper in the forest.

The colors were as vibrant and alive as something out of a coloring book. The paths running throughout the jungle were too narrow to allow for anything but foot traffic.

Movement overhead pulled Jake's attention to the canopy. He looked up and glimpsed a red bird resembling a parrot as it flew from one tree to another. Jake felt the bird was not what caught his eye, but he could discern nothing else. The sounds from their surroundings reminded Jake of old movies he had seen about jungle adventure. He wondered how primitive this land was. His allies were unusually quiet as they each evaluated this new world.

A breeze blew through the jungle. When it touched Jake's skin, he realized he was covered in sweat. He imagined this would be the norm in such a hot, humid environment. He was thankful for the light wind and hoped it would come often.

The other members of the team began to murmur, which Jake took as a sign they had completed their assessment of the place. They awaited his instructions. When he turned to address them, Jake noticed that each bore a simple weapon. Raj had a hatchet with one side sharpened and the other blunt. The head of the hatchet was lashed to the handle with strands of the same material as their clothes. Thomas held a longbow and had a quiver of arrows slung across his back. He was smiling at his good fortune. Elic carried a spear with a long shaft, and a sword-like weapon shaped like a scimitar hung from his side. Both Kathryn and Gwynn had a shorter sword sheathed on their sides. In addition, everyone, including him, had a dagger. Nobody seemed perplexed by the appearance of the weapons, so he took it as normal. Although he had his staff, he was pleased that everyone else was also armed.

"Well, we made the transition better this time than the last. At least we are all together and free. Let's move a little deeper into the jungle, continue to assess the situation, and determine how best to proceed," said Jake.

Without a word, they all formed a line and set out.

Chapter Sixty-Three

The book that lay before Jamal was an ancient text that had been passed from father to son, sorcerer to sorcerer, through his linage until it had become his time to take possession. With this and other volumes, he had taken his position as magician and sorcerer to the Lord High Determiner. His linage of sorcerers had always served that of the Determiner. Together, the two lines had shaped the land and controlled the kingdom. There had never been any question of loyalty until now. Jamal was not satisfied to blindly serve a man to whom he considered himself superior.

A single eye adorned the cover of this tome. No words were necessary. Throughout his youth, he had been taught to find answers to any question confronting him by just referencing the right volume. Each book was designated only by a symbol on its cover. He leafed from page to page, looking at a brief description on each one. He finally found what he was looking for. He knew there had to be a way of communicating with someone at a great distance without the use of a communiq. He read the details with great care and then set about gathering the needed items. Once everything was assembled, he locked his door and went to work.

Soon the cauldron was on the boil. He would need to let it cool to a simmer and hold it there before the final phases of the spell could be completed. While he watched the liquid go from a rolling boil to a slow bubble, he made himself ready.

After changing into his formal robes, Jamal went to the deepest recesses of his quarters. Here he kept the most potent components of his craft.

A row of crystal globes of varying sizes stood across the back wall. Although they all looked alike, each served a specific purpose. Choosing the one needed for his purpose, he returned to the cauldron. He carefully placed the ball onto the surface of the simmering brew. It immediately began circumnavigating the interior circumference of the pot. Jamal stayed in place with his hands stretched above the ball as it circled the surface of the liquid. After three rotations, the ball floated to the center of the cauldron and took a stationary position there. He stepped back, lowered his arms, and turned his body in a complete circle. He walked to a cabinet in the corner of the room. The temperature of the chamber became cooler with each step. It was protected by a spell of coldness to help preserve its contents. Inside the cabinet was a row of glass tubes. He ran his fingers along the tops of the tubes until he found the one with Othan's name on it. The tube held a sample of Othan's blood.

Now he was ready. He returned to the cauldron and took a position facing north. He uncapped the tube, reached it over the cauldron, and let four drops of Othan's blood fall at each point of the compass—first north then south followed by east and west. The liquid became perfectly still. He capped the tube, placed it beside the cauldron, and stretched his hands, palms down, over the floating ball. He then recited:

> *Lords of knowledge, it be our right.*
>
> *To search the darkness and bring to light.*
>
> *To see the one among them all.*
>
> *Through time and space thy searcher flies*
>
> *To see the world through blood's own eyes.*
>
> *To speak and hear without a sound*
>
> *And sharing all until unbound.*

When Jamal finished with his incantation, he stared into the cauldron. The surface remained calm, and the crystal remained in the center of the liquid. For an instant he thought he must have forgotten a key ingredient or that he misspoke the incantation. Just as he was about to turn away, the appearance of the liquid changed, taking on a mirror-like glaze that lasted only a few seconds and then returned to its liquid form, but now it was moving rapidly. A vapor appeared on the surface and continued to thicken until it obscured the entire cauldron. The vapor became stationary and hovered, neither rising nor falling. Jamal stared into it. Of their own volition, his arms rose to shoulder level, his hand perpendicular to the floor. The center of the vapor began to clear until he could see the crystal without obstruction. The inside of the crystal was milky and opaque. Jamal still had no control of his arms. Again, without any assistance, his left hand turned palm down.

The crystal cleared and Othan appeared before him. He was standing beside Major Bannar. Jamal's hand returned upright, and everything disappeared. His right hand turned palm down, and he found himself looking at the surroundings through Othan's eyes. Jamal was startled and made a gasp. From the twist of Othan's head, Jamal knew he must have heard, but Jamal didn't want to communicate further at this time. He felt a force let go of his arms. When he lowered them, the hole in the vapor closed. He feared he had inadvertently ended the spell. Almost in a panic, he realigned his arms and the portal returned. He tried each palm down in turn and was rewarded with the changing perspectives.

He lingered in overview mode and found himself gazing down on Bannar and Othan. Bannar took a step forward and disappeared, leaving Othan alone. Othan looked around in an attempt to locate the source of his unease. Not finding anything, he had no choice but to follow Bannar through the gate.

Jamal lost sight of both men and again felt alarmed. He changed the orientation of his hands and found himself looking at an altogether different world. Jamal surmised that they had just transitioned. He stepped away from the cauldron and watched as the vapor engulfed the surface of the liquid. He returned to the book and read that the spell would stay intact until he either removed the crystal from the cauldron, both he and Othan were in the same room, or until either of them died.

Smiling, he walked to his divan and took a seat. He must think of how to proceed.

Chapter Sixty-Four

Bannar had decided it would be best to let Lokins and his allies clear the area near the gate before he and Othan transitioned. The major also thought it would be better to follow before activating the communiq and speaking with the Determiner. Othan didn't venture an opinion one way or the other and didn't want to be on this mission. What they were charged with doing ran counter to everything he had ever learned or believed in.

He stood behind Bannar and waited for the major to make his move. He would do what was asked of him—no more or no less. The entire day had been a minor disaster as far as he was concerned.

By the time he had sent the men back and it was determined that he and Bannar would continue alone, he was fully stressed. He seethed as he stood behind Bannar. At that moment it came upon him. Suddenly, he did not feel completely in control of his mind or body. He questioned if this was the way a man felt at the time of his death. He had never feared death, although he had faced it many times in battle. In combat, he knew his strengths and was able to play away from his weaknesses. He trusted his instincts and training against any enemy. The strange feeling that came over him frightened him because he knew of no way to fight it. He was at its mercy. He felt his knees weaken as he watched Bannar step through the gate. He looked around and marveled at the thought of all he had faced. With head spinning and knees quaking, he too stepped through the gate.

Chapter Sixty-Five

J ake decided it would be prudent to walk through the woods rather than along the path. They could not let these idyllic surroundings lull them into complacency. Some of the most beautiful things were the deadliest. After traveling about a mile, he spotted a semi-clear space a little deeper into the jungle.

"Let's stop here and try to find out where we are," said Jake pointing to the clearing.

Thomas took a position in the thick growth, facing the path, his back against a tree. Following suit, Elic, Raj, and Kathryn moved to points around the clearing where they could observe the entire area. Jake had thought they all could rest but saw the wisdom in their actions. He also moved to the edge of the clearing and took a seat with his back to one of the towering trees. Gwynn came over and sat beside him. The heat and humidity were overbearing, so they both sweated profusely. Any breeze that was stirring was now blocked by the heavy vegetation surrounding them. Without a word, Gwynn wiped the back of her hand across her eyes and summoned the posit. Jake leaned in so he could look as well. The only thing on the screen was the pulsing amber of their position and a bright, blinking light that denoted the presence of a wizard. He saw no sign of a gate. Even the one through which they had transitioned seemed to have disappeared. When he shared his observation with Gwynn, she swiped her hand from left to right across the screen. Another totally blank screen came into view. Before Jake could comment, she adjusted the display from top to bottom, revealing a gate.

"It looks like that's our only option from here," she said.

"How far is that?"

She returned to the display, which showed their location, and created a grid overlay. When she moved back to the location of the gate, she said, "It's one hundred and six kilometers from here or approximately sixty-six of your miles."

"Is there any way of checking the terrain we will have to cross?"

"The posit will give us some topography but has no way of telling us what could grow in or inhabit the area. The only thing we can do is let Kathryn go ahead of us. She can tell us what to expect and Elic can let us know if any danger awaits."

After acknowledging everything she had told him, Jake went from ally to ally, sharing what they had discussed. When he got to Elic, he asked if he sensed any danger.

"I don't feel that we are in any danger right now. I did sense something soon after we transitioned, but it passed as quickly as it came and has not returned."

"Keep me informed," Jake said and moved on to Kathryn.

After explaining their situation to Kathryn, she stood and removed her garment, exhibiting no modesty whatsoever. He watched as the change took place. He didn't know what to expect as her feline form would take on the look and characteristics of the most predominate feline inhabitant of any given world. He found himself standing before a close facsimile of a black panther. Her coat was short and had an almost liquid sheen. Her eyes were a greenish yellow, and a tooth protruded from each side of her upper jaw, reaching to below her chin. The fangs looked much like those depicted of a saber-toothed tiger. She moved off into the jungle. Jake marveled at the grace and strength she exhibited.

Jake called the rest of the group together and again asked Elic for a threat assessment. After getting a favorable report, they decided it was safe enough to follow the cleared path, which would allow them to make much better time. Raj took the point and Thomas moved into position at the end of the procession. They were making good progress, but the heat and humidity soon overwhelmed them. They needed to rest.

Moving off the path, they took a position where they could monitor the path and still rest and catch the breeze. Jake's legs felt as if they each weighed a ton. He was thankful to sit for a short while. Thomas was the last to come in from the path. He walked from person to person and gave each one some berries.

"I saw these along the path," he said. "There were seeds strewn around the ground where something had been eating them. I decided to give them a try. They are delicious and I believe they make the heat more bearable. They appear to be plentiful."

Jake's first impulse was to be skeptical, but he was hungry and Thomas didn't seem to have any adverse effects from eating the berries. He popped two into his mouth and bit down. They were indeed delicious. The texture was much like that of a blueberry, but the skin was an orangish color. The pulp squeezed itself from the skin upon contact with his teeth and then the husk slowly dissolved. He ate the rest of them and, within a few minutes, began to feel better. Not only was he full but his legs felt fresh, and the heat seemed to have cooled by several degrees. The effect appeared to be the same for everyone. When he motioned for everyone to get ready to move out, they all did so with a little more enthusiasm. Once on the path, the pace quickened. Jake hoped the berries were a good source of nutrition and energy and not a time bomb ticking away in their stomachs.

Chapter Sixty-Six

Throughout the afternoon they walked along the path accompanied only by the sounds of the jungle. Their energy level remained high thanks to the berries, which were plentiful and easy to find. Shafts of light shone down through the canopy like beacons, leading them from one point to the next. As the day wore on, the light began to fade. Jake knew it was time to look for a place to pass the night.

As they crested a rise in the trail, Jake saw Kathryn standing a short distance from the path. At least he hoped it was Kathryn. He stopped and turned to face her. To his left he saw Thomas pull an arrow from the quiver and nock it onto the bowstring. Before he could pull the bow, Kathryn returned to human form. Jake stepped from the path and took her clothes, which he had carried for her. She didn't put them on.

"Follow me. I've found us a place to make camp for the night," she said and then fell back into feline form.

She took a few steps deeper into the jungle and then turned her head to see if the others were following. She led them into a clearing that was clean and dry. Visibility was good in all directions. Raj and Thomas left the clearing. When they returned, they were laden with dried fronds that would be perfect for making beds to keep their bodies from direct contact with the ground. Jake wondered at the wisdom of making a fire but decided it would be better not to have one as they did not know the nature of night in this world. Everything had been benign to this point, but he didn't want to become complacent and lead them into trouble.

Raj and Thomas continued to retrieve fronds until everyone had a platform to sleep on. While they all busied themselves in one way or another, Kathryn came into the clearing and took a position beside Jake.

"It's very strange out there. I have not seen a single person nor another animal other than birds, but I feel they are all around me. I'll retain this form and keep watch all night while you sleep. I can catch naps, but I sleep so lightly in this form that nothing will get past me."

"Maybe we'll come across a village tomorrow. I know this place must be inhabited, but by what?" asked Jake.

"There's a river just over the horizon. Maybe we can fashion a container to fetch some water," said Kathryn.

It was only then that Jake realized that none of them had taken any water since they transitioned. He could not remember being thirsty. The berries had not only provided nutrition but had kept their thirst at bay.

When darkness came, it was absolute. Jake lay awake listening to the sounds of the jungle. He had asked Elic if he sensed any danger, but he had not. One by one, he heard sounds of sleep from his allies. He still marveled at the way his life had turned. He was thinking about his mother and how she had struggled to keep things going. He had been proud when he was old enough to contribute and lessen her burden. He thought about his farm and all the work that he had done to make it productive. He wondered if he would see either of them again. These were his thoughts as he drifted off to sleep.

Chapter Sixty-Seven

Jake awoke surprisingly refreshed. Whatever the cause, it must have translated to the others as well because everyone seemed to have more spring in their step. Kathryn was nowhere to be seen, so he took for granted that she had gone on ahead. He remembered what she had told him about a river being close. He had an urge to see it.

"Kathryn says there is a river. I'd like to take a look."

"Sounds good, Boss," said Raj. "Can I tag along?"

"Sure. Does anyone else want to come along?"

"I'll watch your back," said Thomas.

"I think I'll check the posit for any changes," said Gwynn. "That way I'll be here if Kathryn comes back."

Elic only nodded his head and leaned back against a tree.

The further they walked from the camp the thicker the vegetation became until they had to pull their way through it.

"I don't know if it's worth it, Boss," said Raj as he struggled forward. The growth was over his head, and he was tunneling through it like a rabbit.

Jake was almost ready to agree when he heard running water. He wanted to fight his way through, but before he could Raj thrust his arm across Jake's legs. Once Jake stopped, he heard it too. The sound of a voice made its way across the water. Thomas came abreast of Jake and Raj, and together they crawled toward the sound. After creeping for another fifteen feet, they made it to the edge of the undergrowth. There was an open area leading to the river and more open space on the other side. Several large trees stood beyond the clearing. Growth did not seem as thick on the other side.

On the opposite bank stood a small child who appeared to be about four feet tall. His skin was the color of a latte. His legs and arms were thin and longer in a way that would be considered proportional in this world. Although the child was naked, Jake could not tell whether it was male or female. The youngster made a gesture, and another child came out of the forest's edge. They made a game of kicking at the water as it flowed by. They screamed and laughed like children would anywhere. Jake and his two allies remained still.

Under his right hand, Jake felt the staff emit a light vibration. This was the first time the staff had come to life since their transition. Jake thought he heard movement behind them and pivoted with the staff at the ready. He saw Gwynn and Elic crawling toward them. He signaled to tell them to approach quietly. The staff continued to vibrate. Before Elic and Gwynn could reach them, Raj pulled on Jake's arm and pointed down the river.

Two men stood at the edge of the trees, staring intently at the children. Their skin had a deep blue sheen. They too had elongated limbs but looked to be much hardier stock than what Jake imagined the adult version of the children would be. They each carried a long spear, and one appeared to have a net or bag draped across his arm. They began to methodically make their way along the tree line, always advancing toward the children.

Jake felt Elic squeeze his arm. Elic's eyes were wide and the pupils dilated. He motioned for Jake to stay down but didn't want to chance having a conversation. Jake dipped his chin to acknowledge that he understood the communication. Jake relayed the message to Raj and Thomas and then looked back to the far bank of the river. The two men had advanced until they were only a short distance away from the children who still seemed unaware of their presence. Jake feared for the children but was torn about what to do. He went to lift the staff, but Elic put a hand on top of his and shook his head. Jake didn't know if he could sit by when children were in danger.

The children appeared to tire of kicking the water. Together they walked toward the jungle. Jake looked toward the men and saw that it was a net that one of them carried. He now had it spread between his hands. There was no doubt about what he presumed to do with it. The capture was performed much faster than Jake could have imagined. The man with the net had used his long legs to leap from the jungle. While in mid-flight, he launched a weighted net that settled over both children. Both men descended on their captured prey. Their focus was entirely on securing the children.

Jake could not let this happen, but before he could react he saw movement behind the scenes of the capture. Long vines or ropes had fallen from the canopy of trees. Men were sliding down the vines. Their coloration matched that of the children. Before the captors realized their presence, the other men were upon them. Seven attackers with clubs and short swords fell on the blue-skins with a vengeance. In a matter of seconds, the would-be captors were dead, their bodies lying in the blood-drenched sand. The ferocity of the attack shocked Jake. He was happy that he had not made a move and exposed their presence. What happened next was both unexpected and sickening. While one of the men helped the children from the net another took a short knife from his loincloth and began to field dress the two dead men. When their organs and intestines had been removed, they were sorted. Some of the viscera was placed in a pouch and the rest thrown into the river. The surface of the water boiled with activity. The man who had freed the children from the net was congratulating them. The other men had retrieved long poles and had lashed each of the dead men to one of the shafts. The man with the children said something, and two men shouldered each pole. They carried the dead men into the jungle and disappeared into the interior.

Jake couldn't believe what he had just witnessed. The children had been no more than bait in a trap and had played their part well. The hunting party had been swift and sure and were now returning from whence they came with their prey. Jake thought of the way the dead men had been treated and the implications of what he had witnessed were deeply disturbing.

They each began to back away from their position. The staff had gone quiet and Elic had signaled that all was well, but all was *not* well. Jake's thoughts of an idyllic world had just been shattered. He contemplated the casual way they had traveled thus far and was overcome by thoughts of what could have been. He would never be so careless again. In his mind, the canopy above was now a sinister place from which death could rain down at any time.

Back at the clearing, it was obvious his allies had entertained some of the same thoughts because everyone was on guard. Kathryn came back into the circle in human form and with clothes.

"We are only twelve kilometers from a village. Everything appears to be very primitive. I think we should avoid contact if possible as there were some very interesting skins being hung out to dry. There doesn't appear to be any kind of mechanized transportation, so we will have to walk all the way to the gate."

"Were the natives of the village light skinned or dark blue?" asked Raj.

"They were very dark blue."

Jake took Kathryn aside and told her what they had witnessed.

To the whole group, Jake said, "We must assume we are in a very hostile environment and get to the gate as quickly as possible to transition from this world. What we saw in the river resembled a piranha attack. I think we will still be better to stick with the path as long as we can, but be ready to take cover. Watch the canopy and let me know if you see any movement."

They were a solemn group as they formed up and took to the path.

Chapter Sixty-Eight

Othan was both disturbed and relieved. Just before they had made the transition, he had been taken by a feeling of dizziness. It was not the kind that made you think you might fall but just a little unsteadiness. When they landed in this lush world, he had to rest before continuing. Bannar probably thought this was unusual because Othan had always been the one to press onward against all odds and caution. After a few minutes, his equilibrium had been restored, so they set off along the path. They hurried so as not to lose contact with the wizard and his allies. Once they were within range, their progress had been determined by that of the opposing group. Still, Othan felt as if something was not quite right. He was relieved when they stopped for the night.

As he sat, he took stock of the primitive trappings of this world. It was beautiful but he preferred some open spaces where he could feel assured that death did not lurk behind every tree.

When they retired for the night, what he had thought was a dream came again. He had been waiting for sleep to overtake him when he heard a voice in his head. He opened his eyes, but the voice persisted. Was he going mad?

"Othan, lie very still. It is I, Jamal. I have woven a spell which allows me to communicate with you. You will be able to hear me just as you hear me now. In turn, I will be able to hear you without words being spoken."

"Lord Jamal, how can I be of service to you?"

"You need not do anything but continue your mission. The Lord Determiner is concerned, so I took it upon myself to monitor your progress," said Jamal, the lie coming easily. "How is everything progressing?"

Othan didn't think it odd that Jamal chose to communicate through him and not Bannar. His ego told him that he was the most worthy and dependable. Bannar and Jamal had a mutual distrust of each other. Othan saw this turn of events as a way to further his own agenda while highlighting any shortcomings in Bannar's execution of the mission.

"We have already had to go into battle to protect the Lokins boy. I must tell you that we suffered some casualties as you must already know. The plan was not well conceived." He failed to mention that there had been no time for planning. "We have now transitioned to a different world and are within range of the boy and his group. I will keep you informed as we proceed."

"Very well," said Jamal. "Get some rest."

⁊   ⁊

Jamal ended the communication and stood, looking down into the cauldron. He was very pleased with himself. He had learned the nature of Bannar and Othan's mission and could monitor the situation. The thought came to him that he could also control the mission. He had seen no need to tell Othan the extent of the spell as it pertained to Jamal's ability to not only communicate but to observe from above and to see through Othan's eyes. Yes, he was very well pleased.

He moved away from the cauldron and took a seat at his desk. The book of spells still lay open.

Chapter Sixty-Nine

J ake and his allies decided that Kathryn would continue to recon the area in feline form. Not only would she scout what was before them, but she would also circumnavigate the group to assure that no attack was coming from the rear. Meanwhile, Raj and Thomas would travel parallel with the group a short distance off the trail to help look for anyone trying to flank them. They would also keep a watch on the canopy. After his morning observation, Jake did not feel safe from any direction. That left Jake, Gwynn, and Elic to traverse the path. Jake walked with the staff in both hands to be ready to wield it at a moment's notice. Gwynn and Elic also had weapons at the ready. They still found berries in abundance but would eat them while still moving forward. They all wanted to reach the far gate and escape without having to deal with the natives.

Kathryn would complete a round and, if there was nothing to report, make herself seen before repeating her actions. So it went until early afternoon.

As they moved forward, Kathryn stepped into the path and started toward them. Jake signaled everyone to halt and stepped forward to meet the large cat. Gwynn and Elic moved from the path and took up defensive positions in the vegetation.

"What is it, Kathryn?" Jake asked when he was close enough.

"I haven't spotted any emanate danger, but there are two men on the path behind us. They are moving at the same pace as we are. I don't know if that is a coincidence or not, but it was suspicious enough for me to report."

"Are they lighter skinned or dark blue?"

"That's what's strange, Jake. They don't appear to be from either tribe. They look just like us."

"Maybe there is a third tribe we haven't seen. Keep an eye on them, but try not to let them see you."

"It may be too late for that. I think one of them noticed me when I first came upon them. He was quick to pull his sword. I turned and ran."

Kathryn ran back into the jungle to continue her recon. Jake distributed the information Kathryn had given him. They continued but Elic replaced Thomas in his position so Thomas could take up a rear position. That left only Jake and Gwynn on the path.

Chapter Seventy

Bannar had become more and more troubled by the way this assignment was going. Since entering this world, things had become even more bizarre. Now, on the second day, he and Othan were walking down a path that was more like a stroll through the countryside than a military operation. Circumstances such as these caused Bannar to grow more watchful. His vigilance made the spotting of the big cat possible. The first time had not been alarming. He thought it would pass so as not to have to deal with humans. He had encountered all sorts of wildlife in his various crusades and found that most would rather avoid contact. The second time he saw it, he felt as if he were being stalked. Perhaps this was a more aggressive animal. He wondered if the cat's behavior was out of territorial possessiveness or hunger. In any case, he would be more careful as they moved deeper into the jungle.

The other thing that bothered him was Othan's behavior. When they transitioned from the sponge world, Othan had acted strangely—as if something had come over him. Bannar had seen such things when he had taken a new trooper on his first mission. This type of travel was unknown to the population at large, so when a new person made their first transition, it was not uncommon for them to experience some confusion and disorientation. Othan was a veteran of many such missions and should not be affected in any way.

"Continue on at this pace," said Bannar. "I'm going on ahead to see how far in front they are. I'll return shortly."

"I'll be happy to do that, Major, if you like."

"Thank you, but I think I would like the exercise."

Ordinarily it would have been Othan's place to do the extra reconnaissance, but Bannar didn't trust him to be stealthy enough in his present condition, although he seemed to be getting back to normal.

Bannar left the path and began moving forward at such a fast pace that he almost ran into the big man before recognizing his presence. Bannar saw him just in time to avoid detection. He dropped to all fours and angled his way back to the path. He proceeded slowly until he saw the wizard and the fae girl walking along the path ahead. He surmised that the others had taken up a more defensive position. Bannar stepped to the side of the path and concealed himself until he was sure that the big man had passed and then fell back to rejoin Othan.

Othan was still trying to make sense of what had transpired during the night. He wondered if it all could have been a dream but dismissed the notion. It had been real enough. His feeling of elation and self-importance returned. Even the thought of Bannar going on ahead pleased him. Soon, he may be the one dispatching Bannar to one duty or another.

He was so caught up in his imaginings that he failed to see the four men descend from the canopy of trees behind him. They were almost on him before he realized their presence. He drew his sword as they gained the path. He had little time to assess his attackers. They were deep blue in color and had elongated limbs. Othan reasoned that if there were only one attacker and he could get inside the long arms, he could use it to his advantage, but four such men were reason for concern. Without further thought, he went on the attack. His aggression took the men by surprise. The first could not react fast enough and fell victim to the sword. As he turned to engage the second one, he felt the sting of a spear as it pierced his left buttock. Pain came but adrenalin overpowered it. He advanced but felt another blade slip into the meaty tissue of his side. He still fought on. He scored his own blow as his sword sliced across the abdomen of the second man. A look of surprise came across the face of his foe as his bowels burst through the cut. Another spear tip found his right leg and felt like it continued through his thigh. He lost his footing and fell into the offal and blood of his second kill. In his present condition, he knew the end was near. He rolled to his back and raised his sword in hopes of taking at least one more with him. He was damning Bannar for his absence when the panther emerged from the jungle at a dead run. The cat was vicious in its attack. It was on the third man with such ferocity that he had little chance. The fourth man temporarily forgot about Othan and turned his attention to the cat. The cat had successfully dispatched his initial target and had turned to face the final native. Othan saw that the cat's paws and lower legs were covered in blood. Likewise, its maw was stained, and bits of flesh were entangled with the blood. Othan had little doubt how this was going to end. He decided that if he was to have any chance of survival, he had to get away. He sheathed his sword and pulled his way to the side of the path. He couldn't gain his feet but used his good leg to propel himself forward. He reached the undergrowth and continued onward. He knew he had little chance of survival but was determined not to be a passive victim to the cat or the fourth attacker, no matter which lived. His only hope was to get as far into the jungle as possible and pray the cat would be sated by four dead men. He crawled onward until he came to a small fissure in the ground only wide enough for him to fit into sideways. He rolled into it and began dragging the flora on either side of the ditch in atop him, hoping he could hide himself well enough to avoid detection. He was getting weaker but worked on. He thought about Bannar and what would befall him when he returned. He found that he really didn't care. He was having trouble getting enough air to breathe. His hand reached for one more pull of leaves, but as he did so his vision blurred and his world went black.

Chapter Seventy-One

Kathryn hated having to kill while in feline form. Although her feline form was the perfect killing machine, she found the actual act of slaughter somewhat sickening. That was not to say she would ever hesitate once the need was apparent. The blood and raw flesh she had ingested would have turned her human stomach but was a fact of feline life. The only thing that carried over from one form to the next was physical harm.

She didn't see any way to avoid joining the fight without sacrificing the life of the man being attacked. She knew nothing about him, but for some reason he seemed different. He was certainly an accomplished swordsman, but four against one were deadly odds.

During the attack, she had lost sight of him. When it was over, he was nowhere to be found. She made a cursory inspection of the surrounding area but failed to locate him. She thought it would be wiser to make Jake aware of what had taken place than to continue her search.

She presented quite a picture as she stepped onto the path in front of the others. Jake stopped cold. She came forward and started to explain before he could form a question. She could tell he was concerned on several levels.

For his part, seeing Kathryn covered in blood had at first scared him, then settled into concern and finally into curiosity. After she explained what had happened, he was more concerned than afraid. The thought of an attack taking place behind them without their knowledge tightened his awareness. Everyone heard and awaited his decision. He saw no alternative but to return to the scene of the attack. If the man had survived and they could find him, maybe they could get some answers.

"I thought you said there were two men behind us?"

"There were, but there was only one present when I came upon the fight. I don't know if the second man had moved away on his own or had already fallen in battle."

"I know we all want to get to the gate and out of this world," said Jake turning to the others. "We also have to know if we need to be concerned about being followed, whether by natives or these two men."

No one offered any input pro or con, so they reversed their course and set off.

₨   ⃃

Bannar had been on his way to rejoin Othan when he heard sounds of fighting. He drew his sword and set off at a run. By the time he reached the scene of the battle, everything was already settled. Four men lay dead on the ground. He didn't see Othan anywhere. He spoke Othan's name in a normal voice. He didn't want to shout. There was no reply. He checked the bodies of the fallen. Two were the victim of Othan's sword, one disemboweled, the other run through. The other two presented questions. It looked as if they had been mauled by an animal. He thought of the cat that had been tracking them. He worried that Othan had fallen victim to the beast and had been dragged away. With sword still in hand, he began a systematic search of the surrounding area. He stepped to one side of the path and searched along an invisible grid until he worked himself as deep into the jungle as he thought prudent. Finding nothing, he crossed the path and repeated his actions on the other side. When his search did not locate Othan, he faced a quandary. He didn't want to abandon Othan, but he could not lose touch with the wizard.

He need not have worried about the latter because when he returned to the path, Jake Lokins and four other people stood facing him. Slightly in front of the others, Lokins stood with his staff leveled at Bannar. Bannar didn't know which was more troubling, the staff or the black panther standing beside Lokins and covered in blood. Bannar slowly and carefully lay his sword on the path and raised his hands in submission.

Chapter Seventy-two

Jamal couldn't believe his eyes or rather he couldn't believe Othan's eyes. At the time of the attack, he had been watching from Othan's point of view rather than overhead. When Othan faced his attackers, it was as if Jamal himself was under attack. By reflex, Jamal retreated two steps from the cauldron. His mind cleared and, stepping back to the cauldron, he reached his arms out with his palms facing downward. He was rewarded with an overhead view. When Othan took the first man down, Jamal was hopeful. Othan was relentless but started taking some wounds. The second attacker fell in a bloody mess. It seemed to Jamal that Othan didn't have long to live. Nobody could take so many spear wounds and survive. Jamal was trying to think of some way he could intervene. He gave it up as hopeless just as the panther attacked. It was almost too brutal to watch. Movement away from the attack caught his eye. He looked just in time to see Othan crawl into the underbrush. He turned his palms perpendicular to the surface of the cauldron and watched as Othan found shelter and covered himself. Jamal knew that if he didn't to something fast, Othan's death would bring to nothing all his planning. He could not let that happen.

Jamal ran from his quarters and took the most direct route to the armory. Speed was more important than stealth. When he arrived at the armory, Cleraq was nowhere to be seen. Jamal took a moment to catch his breath before deciding not to wait for Cleraq's return. It would be better if no one knew he had been here. To his surprise, the gate opened when he tried it. Not believing his good fortune, he stepped inside. He almost hated to lose the leverage that finding the door unlocked would give him over the armorer. He looked up and down the aisles until he found the bin holding the communiq. He took one and hurried back up the steps.

Jamal understood the workings of the communiq although he had no personal experience with one. It would be a simple process to transition himself to Othan's location and then transition both back. That was the last thing he wanted to do. The idea began out of desperation and came full bloom out of fear. He took the communiq to the cauldron and placed it on the edge of his desk. He slid his hands, palm down, under the communiq and hooked his thumbs over the top of the devise. It was awkward but reasonably stable. He walked to the cauldron with his arms extended. The surface of the liquid was pitch black. Was Othan dead? His right thumb was against the activation control of the device. With almost no effort, he pressed it. As he did so, the communiq slipped from its precarious place and fell into the cauldron. The simmering liquid became calm, losing all of its power. What had he done? His chin fell until it rested on his chest. He silently chastised himself, Othan, the cauldron, and the situation that had triggered the whole mess.

He turned away from the cauldron. Othan lay on the floor behind him, unconscious and bleeding.

Chapter Seventy-Three

Jake watched as the man put down his weapon and assumed a posture of surrender. He was happy the man remained passive. Jake did not relish the thought of using the power of the staff against him but would not hesitate if it became necessary. Thomas had an arrow aimed at the man, so Jake lowered the staff. He called Elic forward.

"Do you sense any danger from this man or our immediate surroundings?"

"I do not," replied Elic.

"Traveler," Jake said. "You have nothing to fear from us."

"The arrow pointed at my heart and the blood covered beast say otherwise."

"They are simply precautions. As you can see by the carnage at your feet, there is danger about."

"It also appears that your beast was responsible for some of the danger and carnage."

"All in support of your traveling companion, sir."

Throughout the conversation, the two men had been staring into each other's eyes. Jake could see that the man was aware of his situation but could not detect any fear.

"Yes, but my companion seems to be missing. Do you know of his whereabouts?"

"We do not," said Jake. He had noticed a stiffening of the traveler's posture, although the question was posed without accusation.

"I was told that your companion was wounded. He must have sought cover. He can't be far from the path if he's still alive."

Jake again looked to Elic who still didn't sense danger.

"You may lower your arms and retrieve your weapon. We'll help you search for your companion. We should all remain vigilant as this is the second such attack I have witnessed today."

Still holding Jake's eye, Bannar lowered his hands and reached for his sword. "Thank you," he said as he returned the weapon to his belt.

They divided into two groups, and each searched an area beginning at the side of the path and proceeding deeper into the jungle. Neither group found the man, but Raj found a blood trail and followed it to a ditch with scattered leaves around it. From there, the blood trail disappeared. Both groups came together and scoured the area to no avail.

"I fear that your friend has been carried off by the local tribesmen," said Jake to the stranger. He then relayed what he had seen earlier.

"In what direction does their village lie?"

"There is a village ahead, but it is some distance away. That will be the first village we have seen thus far. If you wish to travel with us, we'll try to locate the village, although I have doubts about finding your companion alive."

"I must try," said Bannar.

They formed up on the path with Elic and Raj taking the flanks and Thomas bringing up the rear.

Bannar observed the formation, turned to Jake, and said, "I'll take the point."

This suited Jake because it solved the problem of how best to monitor the new man. It also gave some assurance of good intentions. Kathryn took to the jungle to resume circuitous reconnaissance.

They traveled in this manner all afternoon. Jake thought about the man who had joined them. He was curious where such a man would live in this world. They had seen no white-skinned people since arriving. In addition, this man's limbs were proportioned like Jake's own. Jake wanted to pose the question but had to find the correct way to frame it. Jake was not ready to reveal that he and his allies were alien to this land. He was concentrating on these and other questions so intently that when the man stopped he almost plowed into him.

Looking past the man, Jake saw Kathryn standing in the center of the path. He stepped past the point man and approached the cat. He saw she had cleaned herself of the filth from the earlier encounter. As he knelt in front of her, he could feel the eyes of the stranger on him. He bent to Kathryn.

"I've caught the scent of something cooking somewhere ahead. I didn't want to go any further until I spoke with you. I'm not sure how far ahead the village or camp lies, but I want you to see something before we continue along the path. It's just ahead."

"We'll need to find out what we are facing before we proceed. I'm afraid that task will fall on you, Kathryn."

Kathryn said nothing but began emitting a purring sound. Jake took that as an affirmative.

"Before anything else, you need to come with me," she said.

"Should we all follow?"

"Yes, that will save having to explain."

Jake signaled the group forward. "We need to follow Kathryn, but we need to do it quietly and with caution."

Everyone took their previous positions and moved with Kathryn's lead. As they walked, Jake came abreast of the stranger so he could watch Kathryn.

"Your cat seems to possess many talents," said Bannar. He knew Kathryn must be a shifter but chose not to reveal his awareness. He was at odds with himself at the strange turn of events which precipitated his joining the group. At the first opportunity, he would have to communicate with the Lord Determiner, but he had to be assured of his privacy before doing so.

Ahead, Kathryn stopped and turned to face them. When she was sure she had been seen, she left the path. Jake motioned to everyone before following. He went into a crouch and brought the staff to a position across his chest. If they encountered trouble, he wanted to be ready. The entire group brought weapons to the ready.

He had no way of knowing what Kathryn wanted to show him but was stopped in his tracks when they stepped into a clearing. What he saw was unsettling.

The field had been clear-cut in a rectangular shape. All stumps and vegetation had been removed. The layout reminded Jake of the way he had prepared his field, but no crop could be planted here. Instead of being furrowed, the rows were laid out with line upon line of bones. Most of the bones had been bleached by the sun, but some on the far side of the field appeared fresh.

"Set up a perimeter and keep a sharp eye," said Jake turning to the group. "I want to take a closer look at this."

"May I go along with you?" asked the stranger.

Jake knew the man was thinking of his companion, so he nodded.

Kathryn made a quick lap of the surrounding jungle. Seeing no danger, she returned, and the two men stepped into the clearing. They proceeded from row to row. Most of the bones were of a type belonging to the natives. They were stacked one atop another, so there was no way to ascertain a count. Jake estimated them at more than a thousand. Another thought of how bizarre his life had become flashed across his mind, but he brushed it aside.

Neither man spoke as they worked their way across the field. The last two rows of the field were fresh. The skeletons were all intact, and there were even bits of flesh still attached. Jake wished he could use the power of the staff to blast the contents of the field into oblivion.

"I don't see anything that could resemble Othan," said the man as they reached the end of the last row.

"No, most look local," replied Jake.

They started back across the field. The implications of what they had seen were not lost on either man nor on the others standing in the edge of the jungle.

Jake didn't know what to say when he reached the others. As he was trying to decide, the stranger tapped his shoulder and pointed to the trees across the field. Jake looked up in time to see movement among the lower branches of the canopy.

"Could you see if that was man or animal?"

"I couldn't but we should assume the worst."

Jake turned to Elic and the look on his face was unmistakable. Jake signaled for the group to retreat. They worked their way back to the path and formed around Jake.

"We have to assume we have been seen and that it's only a matter of time before we are attacked," Jake told the group.

What had appeared to be a tropical paradise had morphed into a lush nightmare fraught with danger. They were less than halfway to their intended destination and a village probably lay ahead. In addition, they had been joined by a man whose manner and appearance suggested he was as foreign to this place as Jake and his allies. It was time to review all the options.

Chapter Seventy-Four

Bannar was troubled by what he saw in the field. He too had been charmed by this land and its beauty. The attack, which had resulted in Othan's disappearance, had come as a total surprise. He chastised himself for being lulled by the docile appearance of things. He and Othan never should have separated.

He was further discomfited by the situation in which he now found himself. He had become a part of the group he had been charged to protect. He had never been this close to a member of the Society of Builders except in combat. The wizard had decided to backtrack in hopes of finding a safe place to pass the night. Bannar saw the wisdom of that decision. With Bannar on point, they had covered about two miles when the panther again stepped into the path. She led them to a secluded space. The trees were open enough for them to make camp but had enough vegetation to obscure the vision of anyone traversing the path. The wizard had excused himself and his companions to speak privately, leaving Bannar alone.

Bannar sat leaning against the trunk of one of the giant trees. His eyes scanned the canopy for movement. He was happy to have some time to analyze his situation. He needed to communicate with the Determiner in order to update him on the situation.

After the wizard returned, he said they would split into two groups. One would sleep while the other stood sentry. The first group would consist of the big man, the dwarf, and the one called Elic. Bannar, the fae, and the wizard made up the second. Bannar's group would rest first and relieve the others in what they approximated to be four hours. Nothing was said of the shifter. Bannar assumed she would continue to monitor the entire area.

After eating some berries, he and his group retired. His fatigue overpowered his mental agitation, and Bannar soon fell asleep. He was awakened by the fae. His group took up their positions. He took the place of the male fae, Elic, who assured him that nothing had been about. Bannar waited for what he felt like was sufficient time for everyone to settle down. He scanned the darkness and neither saw nor heard anything. Satisfied that he was both safe and secure from the others, he called forth the communiq. When the device came into being, it emitted a soft glow of light. He quickly extinguished it. Placing the communiq on the ground, he covered it with fallen foliage. His heart was pounding, and he realized he was holding his breath. He listened for anyone approaching and heard nothing. He was unsure if he would be able to hear the cat. In time, he uncovered the communiq and brought it to life sans the light. He reached into a concealed compartment, took out an earpiece, and fitted it into his ear. He took a deep breath and pressed the button to activate. With trepidation, he waited for the Determiner to answer.

Chapter Seventy-Five

The Determiner forced himself to remain calm as Bannar, talking in a whisper, relayed the status of the mission. As soon as the transmission ended, he could hold his anger no longer. He turned and slapped his hand on the table, making an explosive sound. The guards stationed outside the door burst in with weapons at the ready. He looked at them with a mixture of disgust and dismissiveness and waved his hand toward the door. They turned in retreat.

"Wait," he said before the last man could close the door. The soldier turned, came to attention, and clicked his heels. "Have Lord Jamal summoned to my quarters," said the Determiner. He turned away without waiting for a reply. None was needed nor attempted.

He took a seat at his desk and began thumping his fingers in no rhythm. Things had gone terribly wrong. He didn't know whether to blame Bannar or himself. The mission was meant to be as clandestined as possible due to its unusual nature. That no longer seemed possible. The only chance was if Bannar could conceal his true identity. He had to find a way to salvage what was left, and perhaps magic was the answer. He didn't trust the sorcerer but couldn't deny his abilities.

ഇ   ഇ

Jamal was awakened by the knocking at his door. He arose from his bed, pulled on his robe, and called out that he was coming. He looked to the back of the room and the cot with the still unconscious Othan on it. He paused to pull the curtain, which would conceal

Othan from prying eyes, and then opened the door. One of the supreme protectors stood facing him. They almost never left the side of the Determiner.

"Lord Jamal," the protector said with no other greeting. "The Lord Determiner would like to see you in his quarters as soon as possible."

Jamal felt a lump form in his throat. His mind was in turmoil, but he managed to say, "Tell the Lord Determiner that I will be there posthaste."

Without a word, the protector turned from the door and proceeded down the corridor.

Back in his quarters, Jamal contemplated the reason for his summons. Had the Determiner discovered his deceit? Would he be marching to his own beheading? He thought of dispatching Othan and using magic to dispose of the body. But if he was wrong and the summons was for any other reason, killing Othan would destroy his work to date. He managed a chuckle as he surmised that if his first thoughts were correct, Othan, dead or alive, would not matter. He donned his conical hat and left his quarters. He would either return or he would not.

Upon his approach to the Determiner's quarters, one of the supreme protectors opened the door and bade him enter.

The Determiner was seated slightly away from his desk. Another chair had been placed in front of him. He motioned Jamal to sit.

"How may I serve you, my lord?"

Without preamble, the Determiner launched into the story of Bannar's communication. Jamal felt the weight of what was being said. Since he had helped bring about the idea that had launched the mission, he feared he would be held responsible for the downturn. At the conclusion of his story, the Determiner rose and began to pace. Jamal started to get up but was motioned back to his seat. After moments of pacing, the Determiner stopped and placed his hands on the crown of the chair he had vacated.

"What I would like to know from you, Lord Jamal, is if you can use your powers to locate Captain Othan and get this mission back on track? I wish to extricate Major Bannar from the wizard's party in a way that allows him to continue his mission. Do you think that is possible?"

Jamal felt his heart settle back into its proper place and his bowels ceased to roll.

"I am your loyal subject, my lord. I will need to consult my tomes to ascertain the most efficient way to fulfill your wishes."

"Very well. I will wait to hear from you but, make no mistake, this is paramount, and time is of the essence."

Jamal rose, bowed, and back stepped to the door. The Determiner had already turned away.

Back in the corridor and out of sight of the protectors, Jamal shook his fist into the air. He could not believe his good fortune. The problem of Othan's presence was solved. Now he could be properly attended to. His concern about Othan's continued unconsciousness was also allayed. If he regained consciousness, he would not know he had been transitioned prior to the Determiner's request. If he didn't regain consciousness, Jamal still would have fulfilled his mission of retrieving him. All was well, he hoped.

Chapter Seventy-Six

The light began to filter through the canopy as Jake woke up. The jungle around him was quiet. He had been asleep for a couple of hours after his last turn on watch. He sat up and looked around. Gwynn and the stranger were still asleep. He would have to start thinking of the other man by his name, Bannar, rather than the stranger. He had given a great deal of thought to the implications of having Bannar along. Bannar could not transition with them if they were still together when they reached the gateway. He had not determined how he would handle the situation. Maybe they would find his companion, dead or alive, and he could go his own way. He heard some movement and reached for the staff as Kathryn stepped into the clearing.

"Shall I gather the others? I've detected no sign that anyone else is about."

"Yes, we had best get an early start. I'll gather some berries as you retrieve the others," he said as he removed the fronds that covered his legs.

After everyone was assembled and had eaten a few berries, they took to the path. It was easy to be lulled into complacency by the beauty of the jungle, but they all fought the impulse. Jake continued to check with Elic concerning any potential danger. Elic nor any of the others found any cause for concern, so it came as a surprise when they heard an injured cat coming from the jungle.

Without hesitation, Jake took off in a run, bringing the staff to bear as he did. The others followed suit. From that point, everything happened fast. The whimper he heard had changed to a series of growls, so Jake had no problem following the sound. As they ran, Jake looked at Elic, who just shrugged his shoulders. Jake took that to mean that Elic felt no danger. Ahead Jake could see a small clearing but proceeded at full speed. When he burst from the dense underbrush, he was shocked into a complete stop. Ahead Kathryn swung suspended from some type of snare. The rope had encircled her just in front of her hind legs and sprung her upward. She dangled, her head four feet from the ground. She was flailing about and trying to raise her head high enough to attack the ropes. Other than the manner of her capture, she didn't look any worse for wear. She saw the group and vigorously shook her head. Jake thought she was just redoubling her efforts to escape. He almost smiled as he began toward her with the others following closely behind.

"Wait," yelled Elic.

Then the big net fell. The net was large enough to capture the entire group and weighed enough to push them to the ground. Their weapons were useless although Bannar had been proceeding with sword in hand and now tried to use it to cut away the net. It did not seem to be going well. Jake could not use the staff because the tip had slipped through the mesh of the net. From his skewed angle, it appeared to be pointing directly at Kathryn.

They didn't have long to think about it as several ropes were dropped from the surrounding canopy and light-skinned natives descended. There were fourteen warriors as far as Jake could count and they surrounded the net. They showed little interest in Kathryn, probably thinking she could be collected after they handled those in the net. One stood directly in front of the protruding tip of the staff. Jake could blast him at any time but knew the others would retaliate. Kathryn had fallen silent.

The warriors appeared to gloat over their collective hunting prowess. They slapped each other on the back and pointed with the tips of their spears toward the captives. After a few minutes of celebration, they got down to business. They systematically worked their way from captive to captive with one or two warriors keeping their victim immobile while another reached through the netting and relieved them of their weapons, including the staff. These were placed on a tarpaulin, wrapped, tied, and then suspended from a rod to be carried by two men. One at a time, they were taken from the net, their hands and feet tied, and a rod slipped through the binding. A native shouldered each end of the rod. When two men tried to lift Thomas, his weight was so great they could not clear the ground. The warriors conferred. Jake was afraid they would eviscerate him to lessen his weight. Instead, they retied him in a way that would allow four men to carry him. This preserved their trophy but did not leave enough men to carry everyone without burdening the entire party. They considered the dilemma and decided they did not want to travel with everyone's hands encumbered. The leader of the hunting party looked from prisoner to prisoner and then cut the bindings from Gwynn's feet. They placed the captives in a queue, men ready to lift and carry upon orders to do so. One warrior stood at the front of the line and one at the rear. Kathryn still dangled from her snare. When the man at the front left the line and walked toward her, Jake feared the worst. She snarled upon his approach. When he was abreast of her, he stood just out of reach of her extended claws. He raised his spear but instead of running her through with it he changed his grip to resemble a baseball player at bat. He swung the spear, striking her across the top of her head. She fell limp and ceased all sound and movement. Jake feared she was dead. By the look of shock on her face, Jake could tell that Gwynn too feared the worst. The warrior returned to his point position and gave a command. All the captives were lifted and shouldered. They entered the trees and were carried along an alternate path. Jake could not see how this could end well.

Chapter Seventy-Seven

Traveling suspended from a pole gave Jake a unique perspective. He was forced to stare at the canopy. From time to time, he thought he saw movement, but it was so fast that he couldn't be sure. As they traveled along, he found his shoulders and neck beginning to ache. His feet were tied closer to the pole, shifting most of his body weight to his shoulders and wrists. He also felt the transference of blood to his head and upper body, causing his ankles and feet to become numb. He wondered if the others were as uncomfortable.

He tilted his head further back so he could see behind him. Thomas was directly behind him, and it was obvious he was in worse shape than Jake. He was suspended from two poles and the bearers were taking a wider track, causing Thomas's limbs to be spread further apart. He must have sensed Jake looking because he lifted his head, looked at Jake, and said, "Bloody hell. If we somehow survive this, I will take great pleasure in ripping these savages limb from limb."

"Not without my help," said Raj from further back. Both Bannar and Elic said something, but Jake could not discern the words. At least they were all alive.

As the procession made its way through the trees, Jake wondered at their destination. When they had first entered the jungle as captives, the men had turned sharply away from the field of bones. Since they had been traveling for quite a while, Jake surmised they had steered away from the village responsible for the bones. Be that as it may, he could not take comfort that their future would be any brighter or longer.

During these contemplations, Jake was dropped. He hit with a thud, and his breath left him. Struggling to regain his breathing, he had not noticed that all the bearers and their leader had abandoned them and run off into the jungle. He was surprised but not frightened until he saw Gwynn hovering in the air above them. Something had made her reveal her wings, thus giving up any pretense of belonging in this world. She looked down at him and he saw her lips move but could not hear what she was saying. She then flew away in the direction from which they came.

Jake tried to raise his head to see what had scared the natives off and caused Gwynn to fly away. He almost didn't see them at first as they blended into the area. They were humanoid in nature. Jake reasoned that they must be clad in camouflage. As they stepped toward the captives, their outfits morphed to take on the appearance of whatever they were near, much like a chameleon. He marveled at their ability to adapt so quickly. This must be highly advanced technology. He hoped he would live long enough to find out.

Chapter Seventy-Eight

Jamal let what he considered sufficient time pass before he was ready to go back to the Determiner. He didn't want it to appear to be an easy task. Finding the right spell, interpreting it for his use, and gathering any materials needed to cast it could be slow and painstaking work. Since he had to do none of that, he passed the time in an idle manner. His only concern was keeping Othan alive.

After his internal clock told him that enough time had passed, Jamal presented himself to the Determiner. He decided to play the situation to maximize his importance in solving the problem. He only told the Determiner that he had discovered a spell to not only find Othan but to transport him back. The Determiner had acted pleased but reiterated the need for immediate action.

Back in his quarters, Jamal checked that Othan was still alive. Afterwards he donned one of his used robes to make it look as if he had toiled under great pressure. Pleased with his guise, he returned to the Determiner to report his success in getting Othan back.

"Sadly, my lord, I must report that he has sustained quite a few wounds and is in dire condition."

"You will have all the resources of the keep at your disposal. I will send our best physicians. It is of paramount importance that we heal him and return him to the mission as soon as possible."

In what he deemed a stroke of genius, Jamal said, "My lord, I will endeavor to find a spell to hasten the captain's recovery."

Back in the corridor, Jamal was very pleased with himself. Circumstances had aligned to raise his esteem with the Lord Determiner. Now he was looked upon as a valued asset instead of being found out to be a conspirator, conniving to usurp the Determiner's power.

ॐ ॐ

Jamal had used magic in addition to all the resources of the palace healers. Othan's recovery had been swift and was now complete. Othan was profoundly grateful to Jamal for his rescue and recovery and pledged his allegiance to the sorcerer.

Jamal had considered Othan to be mostly loyal based on a shared dislike of Major Bannar. After this last ordeal, Jamal believed him to be a dedicated follower. Jamal had kept the Determiner apprised of Othan's progress for the most part. As Othan continued to convalesce, Jamal had ceased using the physicians. Before he told the Determiner of Othan's full recovery, Jamal wanted to devise a way to take full advantage of the captain's newfound zeal.

Chapter Seventy-Nine

Gwynn realized she was the only hope of a possible escape. Thomas's size was the only reason she too had not been strung to a pole. As she walked among her captors, she tried to conceive a way to free herself and then to rescue the others. Many scenarios crossed her mind, but none presented a clear path to her goal. She began to feel the pressure to act.

Her first indication that something was amiss came as a shimmer that caught her eye. It was just ahead and off the path. The leader of the procession must have seen it too because he stopped so abruptly that it startled those behind him. He yelled something that Gwynn could not decipher. Whatever he said caused a general panic among his compatriots. They dropped their captives and ran, each in a different direction.

Gwynn knew she had to act without hesitation. Giving up all pretense of belonging to this world, she scooped up one of the abandoned spears and took to the wing. She still didn't fully comprehend what was happening. She rose in a vertical line, gaining height as swiftly as possible. When she thought she was above any danger, she leveled out and hovered over Jake. She tried to tell him she would do what she could to protect them. Jake's expression showed that he didn't understand. She moved into the trees, far enough away to avoid danger but close enough to mount an attack if need be. What she saw as she turned back to the scene both confused and amazed her. A group of men emerged from the trees. At least, she thought they were men. Their basic shape was human, but their form and appearance changed with each step. What they had seen her do must have confused and amazed them as well. They had stopped in their tracks and were staring in the direction in which she had flown.

She looked back to her group. With the tension relieved on their bindings, each man was pulling and biting at their restraints, trying to free themselves. She wanted to swoop down to help them but felt it was better to let things develop a bit more.

Turning her attention to the chameleon men, she saw they were not acting aggressively but instead seemed amused. They made no move to advance on the still bound former captives. It was then that a white man appeared at the edge of the tree line. The chameleons parted, creating a path through. When he came front and center, he hesitated long enough to evaluate the situation, then walked to the group. He must have asked a question because Jake, who had one free hand, answered him. The white man knelt and helped Jake finish freeing himself. They each helped another captive until they all were free. The chameleon men had done nothing but look on. Gwynn felt sure that if anyone had made a move toward the white man, they would protect him. The aggressor probably wouldn't fare well. Jake tried to retrieve the bundle that held their weapons and his staff, but the man said something and Jake nodded. The man turned to his group and spoke in a language she could not understand. Gwynn found that to be strange since they could normally comprehend any language of the world in which they found themselves. She wondered if she should descend and take her place with Jake and the others but decided to check on Kathryn first.

Chapter Eighty

The blow that Kathryn had taken should have been at least debilitating if not deadly, but Gwynn couldn't accept that. The adage, "a cat has nine lives," came to mind, but Kathryn had passed that number years ago. The others didn't seem to be in any immediate danger, and she could use the posit to locate them at any time. She had to find out if Kathryn was alive.

She remained on the wing, turned, and started back toward the boneyard. Flying was only a mode of transportation for the fae. They didn't have the ocular acuity of a bird, so Gwynn had to proceed with a certain amount of caution. She would have liked to climb above the canopy and fly unrestricted to her destination but couldn't. The canopy was so thick that it would be easy to lose her way.

Flying so close to the canopy allowed her to observe that more was going on there than they could have suspected. She discovered paths cut through the trees where natives could travel from place to place without having to take to the surface. She saw structures built along these paths, some large enough to be dwellings. That these could not be seen from ground level suggested a level of sophistication she and her allies had failed to imagine.

That she could see the world concealed in the canopy meant they could also see her hovering just below it. She thought of returning to the ground and continuing on foot but rejected that thought as time was of the essence. Instead, she slowed to a hover and let her body settle into a vertical orientation, presenting a slenderer form. She moved from trunk to trunk in that manner, hoping that she wouldn't catch the eye of anyone above. It was slower than horizontal flight but faster than walking.

It felt like an eternity before she saw the clearing. She hovered, scanning the area for danger. Seeing none, she drifted to the ground, still holding the spear. It was not much but did give her a slight feeling of security.

Moving closer, she could see the mounds of bones. She paused at the edge of the trees, then stepped into the open. With trepidation, she looked to where Kathryn had been suspended in the snare. She no longer hung there. Forsaking safety, Gwynn took off at a full run. As she approached, she saw Kathryn in human form on the ground either unconscious or dead. Gwynn fell to her knees beside Kathryn's nude body. Acting without hesitation, she slid her arm under Kathryn's head and raised her upper body. When her arm emerged from under Kathryn's head, it was stained with a small amount of blood. She flicked her wrist and landed a light slap against Kathryn's cheek. She felt no response. She drew her arm back and, with all the force she possessed, slapped Kathryn's face.

Her friend's eyes flew open, and she said, "What the hell, Gwynn?"

Chapter Eighty-One

Jake was sure everything was lost. Their captors had abandoned them to flee from this tribe. After witnessing the brutality exhibited by the other two tribes, he could only wonder what the chameleons were capable of. Everyone was struggling to free themselves in hope of mounting a defense, but failure seemed assured. When the chameleons paused at the edge of the jungle, Jake wondered if they were playing a cruel cat-and-mouse game. Would the warriors look on until they had almost freed themselves just to descend on them with a brutal attack? In any case, they had to do what they could. At least Gwynn had escaped. Maybe she could make her way back to The Farm. He feared that without a wizard and the staff she wouldn't be able to access the gate between the worlds.

Jake stopped his efforts to loosen his bindings when he saw the white man. Good or bad, he felt that time had run out. He raised his head, determined to face his end with dignity.

In a quiet voice, the man issued a command, and the natives held their ground and relaxed their posture. Jake could not understand what was being said but felt a glimmer of hope.

The white man came to Jake's aid. He looked at Jake and said, "Looks like you found yourself in a bloody bit of trouble." There was a twinkle in his eye and a hint of a smile on his lips. Jake felt a sense of relief but couldn't see anything amusing about the situation. The man helped Jake finish freeing himself, and then the two of them worked to free the others. When everyone was free, Jake said, "Thank you. It's a good thing you happened along."

"Quite fortunate indeed! This would have been the last opportunity we would have to meet as you would not have survived the night. After watching the female of your party fly away, I look forward to the occasion of speaking with you."

"With your permission, I have some questions for you as well." Jake didn't want to be too assertive, but he also didn't want to seem timid or weak.

"Quite so. We will have time to speak at our leisure, but now we must leave this area before the Amok return with a large number of their brethren. I am Dak Thoren. Please come with me."

Jake was about to reply but Dak turned and walked through the trees. Dak gave an order and one of the chameleon men picked up the package of their weapons. Jake wondered if he could summon the staff to him but decided to let things play out. The natives parted so Jake could join Dak at the front. They only allowed the others to mingle among them. Two of the chameleons ran ahead, and each climbed one of the trees as easily as if they had been walking the path. They both disappeared into the canopy.

Dak hesitated as if waiting for some sign to proceed. Jake neither heard nor saw any such indication, but Dak turned ninety degrees from the direction in which they had been traveling and set out at a quick pace. They had traveled only a short time when something in the air changed. Jake had the distinct impression they were nearing a village. Then he could see it. There were only five structures arranged in a circle and fronting a large open area. As they approached, a female chameleon emerged from one of the smaller huts, carrying what appeared to be a group of plants. She looked toward the advancing party, increased her step, and disappeared into the largest of the structures. Smoke rose through a hole in the center of the roof. Jake surmised that this must be the cooking area and the other huts were used as storage. Jake thought the village itself was probably located just beyond this.

Noticing Jake's appraisal, Dak said, "This is our ground level. We live in the canopy and sleep among the trees."

Before Jake could reply, his attention was drawn to the trees behind him. Most of the chameleons in their party were scaling the trees. Only two and Dak remained at ground level. Two rope ladders were dropped.

"These are for you and your men. If you will come with me, we'll go where we can relax and talk."

"Thank you," said Jake as he stepped to the ladder and began his ascent.

As Jake climbed, he looked back to see the others following. There seemed to be no problem with the ladder bearing their weight. Dak came alongside Jake. He was riding in a lift much like a sophisticate bosun's chair. Two natives climbed behind Dak. Jake looked at the chameleons as they clung to the tree; the mystery of their climbing ability was revealed. Extending from each finger and toe was a talonlike nail. Jake had not noted this before and assumed they would extend and retract much like a cat's claws.

When they reached the first layer of canopy, Jake was amazed to discover a series of paths leading off in all directions. Several of the natives walked in the distance. They continued to climb. The final level was just below the treetops, allowing the sky to become visible and to provide light. Before them, a complete village had been constructed. Although there was shade above them, Jake could see that most of the trees had been pruned flat to accommodate structures and movement. At random, trees were allowed to grow to provide shade. There were trees as far as the eye could see. Just outside the boundaries of the village, growth resumed and reached higher. The blue of the sky reminded Jake of a clear day on the farm where he grew up, and the freshness of the air renewed his spirit.

"This is wondrous," Jake said to no one in particular. He looked to his allies and Bannar and discerned that they were also in awe.

"Quite beautiful indeed," said Dak. "It can also be deadly without the proper respect. Come. I'll take you to where you will stay while you are with us. I've arranged for you all to stay together." He led the way and motioned them to follow.

Jake didn't know what to think. He wanted to believe in what appeared to be a miraculous stroke of luck but, even in his short experience, he had seen so much. He determined not to let his guard down. At least they were alive and somewhat free.

Chapter Eighty-Two

Jamal had a plan formulating, but he had to find out if Major Bannar was still alive before he could propose it. If so, Jamal would need his location. With all this in mind, he requested an audience with the Determiner. He didn't have long to wait.

Upon his arrival at the Determiner's chambers, he was greeted in an enthusiastic manner. "Good day, Lord Jamal. I hope you bring good news."

"Yes, my lord. Captain Othan is fully recovered and eager to return to his mission."

"Good, good. I hope we haven't lost valuable time. No matter. It could not be avoided. Your help in this crisis has been most valuable."

Jamal was ecstatic at the praise but knew that with any stumble the pendulum could swing in the other direction. He had lived under that shadow for quite some time. That was the main reason he had decided to shift the power in his direction.

"If I might ask you, my lord, how do you plan to redeploy the captain?"

The Determiner leaned all his weight to the right, rested his elbow on the arm of the throne, and lowered his chin into the palm of his hand. His forefinger made a drumming motion along the side of his nose. He was in deep thought. Lowering his arm, he looked directly at Jamal. There was still a smile on his face, but his eyes betrayed a fierceness that sent a chill through the sorcerer.

"You have been of such great service throughout this ordeal that I think you should continue. You were able to find him and bring him here. I trust you can return him to action."

"Yes, my lord, it would be an honor. Do you have any further instruction for either Captain Othan or myself?"

"It is imperative that this mission not fail. Please impress that upon the good captain. Also, since the mission has shifted from a group operation to a two-man mission, I think it may be prudent to have a few more troopers accompany Captain Othan. Let me know when they have returned to the mission." With that, the Determiner looked away, and Jamal knew he had been dismissed.

"As you command, my lord."

Even though the task had been complicated by the addition of more troops, Jamal felt he could still pull it off. He would have Othan select the troops. He would impress upon Captain Othan that loyalty was just as important as fighting competence. He could indeed stack the cards in his favor. The success of the mission was not of primary importance. The only priority was avoiding any blame being attributed to him if the operation should fail. He would hate to lose his disciple, which Othan had become, but the goal was bigger than one man or group of men. He would mourn the loss but accept it.

Othan was waiting as Jamal came into his quarters.

Chapter Eighty-Three

Jake had not taken Dak literally when he said they slept among the trees. As they were led toward their quarters, he saw that it had been meant as a statement of fact. Trunks of trees had been hollowed to form sleeping pods. Individual pods were linked together by passageways built with fronds. In the center of each group of pods was a common area complete with walls, a roof, and a makeshift door to provide some privacy. They were shown to a group of pods of the number needed for each person to have his own area. The whole of the pod was furnished with items hewn from wood. Jake wondered if the natives had accommodations such as these. He could see that Dak had his hand in these designs. There was also a gravity fed water system; its source was a mystery.

"I hope you will find everything sufficient for your comfort. I'll give you a while to rest and then we'll talk," said Dak.

"Thank you for your hospitality," said Jake. The others also expressed their gratitude.

Jake accompanied Dak to the door. Dak stepped through, turned left, and walked away without looking back. As Jake turned to go inside, he noticed three chameleon natives standing in the corridor to his right. They were attired in heavier clothes than any Jake had seen since arriving in this world. Each wore an ornate bracelet that appeared to be made of metal. A collar of the same material girded their necks, rising from their shoulders and stopping just below the chin. In addition, they each had a rough-hewn sword hanging from one hip and a dagger on the other. They each carried a spear that matched their height in length. If they were aware of Jake, they made no indication.

Jake felt someone come up behind him. It was Bannar.

"What do you make of that?" Jake asked.

"It appears we are under the protection of some elite warriors. Probably more for our security than any concern."

Jake nodded and said, "Let's talk to the others."

They gathered and formed a tight circle to be able to communicate without having to speak above a whisper. The first thing Jake noticed was that Elic seemed extremely ill at ease.

"What do you think, Elic?"

"I can't pinpoint the source, but there is something amiss about this entire situation. I don't feel an imminent danger, but there is a menace lurking about that we can't afford to ignore."

"Yeah, boss," Raj said. "Our rescue was almost too timely to attribute to pure coincidence."

"It's also strange that there was no bloodshed between our captors and our rescuers," said Thomas. "From what we have observed of the other tribes, they are too fierce and ruthless to just give up and run."

"You may have a better grasp of our situation after meeting with Dak," said Bannar. "In the meantime, we need to figure a way to arm ourselves."

"You are all right," said Jake. "In any case, we can't afford to stay here long. We need to reunite with Gwynn if possible and continue to our destination."

Before anything else could be said, there was a knock at the door. They slid away from each other and tried to assume a nonchalant posture. Jake answered the door. It was one of the necklace clad warriors. He didn't say anything. He stepped back and motioned Jake to the left. Jake stepped through the door and, with the warrior by his side, walked down the hall. He assumed he was going to meet Dak.

ॐ　　ॐ

Kathrine had slipped back into a deep sleep. Gwynn could only hope that she would soon reawaken. She had tried to revive her with some light taps to no avail. She was hesitant to strike any harder since she knew Kathryn was alive. She didn't want to exacerbate any head injury from which Kathryn already may be suffering. In her internal dialogue, Gwynn cursed everything that had, may have, or possibly would happen. She was worried on two fronts. Kathryn, lying injured, should have commanded her full attention, but she couldn't help but torment herself for abandoning Jake and the others. *So much for the whimsical life of a fairy*, she thought. And with that thought, she couldn't help but chuckle. She surveyed her surroundings. This was not an area she wanted to spend a lot of time in. She rose and walked a short distance into the jungle, gathered some dried fronds from the ground, and carried them back to where Kathryn rested. She made two more trips and on the third took flight and rose to the lowest level of the canopy. She harvested tree leaves from the lowest branches. Returning to Kathryn, she formed a pillow from some of the dried fronds and placed them under her ally's head. With the rest of the dried material, she formed a blanket. She then used the green leaves as a combination weight to hold the others in place and makeshift camouflage. Secure in the knowledge she had done all she knew how to do, she picked up the spear, walked a short distance away, and took cover in a grove of smaller trees. There among the vegetation she waited.

Chapter Eighty-Four

Othan listened as the sorcerer recounted his conversation with the Lord Determiner. It would be easy to think that Jamal was embellishing some of the story in order to raise his own esteem, but it didn't matter to Othan. He was a pragmatic man and realized that without Jamal he would surely be dead now. If Jamal wanted to raise himself up, Othan was more than willing to provide the stool.

When Jamal came to the subject of Othan's redeployment, he hesitated.

"How do you feel about returning, Captain Othan?"

"I am a soldier, Lord Jamal. My rightful place is in the field of battle, doing my duty according to the orders given by those I serve. I want no more or no less."

"How very noble of you," Jamal said with a nod of his head.

"Being noble has little to do with it. I swore allegiance to the Lord Determiner and to my superior officers who serve him, but when I was dying only you came for me. Only you took it upon yourself to use your powers to restore me. Only you have asked my opinion of my returning to battle. Yes, I took an oath to fight and die if necessary for those whom I serve. Know this, Lord Jamal. From this day forth, I serve only you and, in so doing, await my orders." With that, Othan rose from his seat, snapped to attention, and raised a salute.

Jamal was ecstatic. He had felt that Othan's loyalties had shifted, but this swearing of fealty had come as somewhat of a surprise. If the captain remained true to this oath, then he, Jamal, could expand his ambitions and accelerate his time frame. All these considerations were tempered by thoughts that the zealousness of a new convert could wane as quickly as it waxed. There was only a moment of mental conflict before Jamal decided. It would be most advantageous if Captain Othan continued to honor his oath; they could accomplish much. Right now he needed him and right now he was available. If this plan of action failed, the chances of Othan living through it were extremely slim. If failure came, it would be better that he did not live long enough to testify to Jamal's subterfuge.

"Your words have moved me beyond all expectations," Jamal said. "Come. We must plan your return and discuss our goals for the continuation of the mission."

Chapter Eighty-Five

Jake was taken to a large enclosure. Guards dressed like the warrior leading him were posted on each corner with others above them. The warrior accompanying Jake stepped to the door, rapped once, and pushed it open. He moved aside so Jake could enter. Once he passed through the door, he heard it close behind him.

The compound was furnished like a more elaborate version of the pods given them. Dak had chosen not to use the furniture. He was sitting on a cushion of tree fronds. More fronds were woven together to form a table. There was another cushion opposite Dak. He rose and motioned Jake to join him. Jake took the other seat and faced Dak across the table. Vessels containing different dishes were laid out on the table. A large woven pitcher filled with liquid sat beside Dak's right hand. A woven cup was at each place. Without asking, Dak raised the pitcher, filled each cup, and raised his to Jake. Jake returned the gesture and took a swallow. The flavor was pungent but not unpleasant. Jake found himself liking it and allowed himself another sip before returning the cup to the table. Dak smiled.

"I see you enjoy our meadus. I hope you will join me in some nourishment. All you see before you is supplied by the jungle around us."

The bowls were filled with colorful bits of food, including the berries Jake and his allies had survived on since their arrival. Most of the food was served raw, but there were two dishes with steam rising from them. Jake was taken by the aromas but was hesitant after all they had witnessed.

Dak must have sensed his unease. He said, "These are all flavors taken from the vegetation. The Chroma people do not eat flesh."

Jake didn't comment but was relieved to have that knowledge. Dak picked up a flat leaf and dipped it into one of the steaming bowls. Jake followed suit and was amazed at the flavor and texture.

"This is wonderful," said Jake.

"Yes, the jungle is full of bounty. I have taken the liberty to see that the others of your group are offered the same meal with a full explanation of each dish."

Jake found himself conflicted. He was having a hard time reconciling the hospitable treatment with the incongruous circumstances of their rescue and relocation. They were under guard, and their belongings had not been returned. Jake decided not to volunteer any more information than he must. They ate in silence. After a short while, Dak made a show of wiping his mouth and hands with a woven cloth. He sat back on his cushion.

"Tell me, Dak, how did you come to live among this tribe?" Jake asked before Dak could speak.

"I thought I would be the one to pose the questions," said Dak with a laugh. "Your question, however, is fair and I will answer it truthfully. I hope you will be candid as well when I get to inquire of you."

"I will tell you everything I can," said Jake hoping he didn't sound too evasive.

"Before I answer your question, just let me say that with what I have observed, I don't believe you come from or belong in this land. I say that because I also am not of this land. Having said that, we can dispense of any ideas that either one of us may have of deceiving the other concerning that point."

Jake was somewhat disarmed by what Dak said but found that he was not uncomfortable with either the revelation or the implications as related to how honest he must be when his time was due. He settled back to listen.

Chapter Eighty-Six

Dak's Story

"When I was a child, I lived with my father in a country known as Denmark. It was freezing there, but there were also lots of activities for children, and I was happy. My mother died and I missed her, but my father made every effort to ensure my happiness and wellbeing.

"My father was a scientist and, although I was not aware at the time, he was a leader in theoretical physics. He was also an avid reader of fantastical tales. In retrospect, I believe it was his reading that informed his work and led indirectly to my being here. As a child, I marveled at his theories and hung on his every word. As I grew older, I became skeptical and eventually was embarrassed by some of the things my friends would hear him say. He did not let my skepticism bother him or dissuade his beliefs. As time moved forward, we each became so involved in our own struggles that we permitted some distance to come between us. That was when Mosta came into his life and work.

"Mosta was a strange individual who came into my father's life and by extension into mine. He was not a scientist and did not appear to work in anything technical, but he would talk to my father about all of his theories and had an uncanny understanding of my father's work. They would meet at our house and have discussions about unseen dimensions and hidden worlds. They would become so excited in their discussion that I was soon pulled from my lethargic attitude and found myself joining them. All I could do was listen because I had no basis to contribute. It did not seem to matter; they both acted happy that I was there, sharing their interest.

"It soon became clear to me that their discussions had moved beyond the theoretical. They spoke as if visiting these worlds was a real possibility. My father became more and more distracted from his normal work routines as he fell further under Mosta's spell. I began to worry. When Mosta was not with us, I tried to talk with my father about how distracted he was. He would only stare past me and speak of such travel as a foregone conclusion.

"It did not take long before my father and I had switched life roles. It was I who had to take care of him. Even in such simple tasks as hygiene, maintaining our home, and making sure he would eat, it was I who had to ensure the task was completed.

"I must admit that my interest was still piqued by what we talked about. Although interested, I felt I had to stay close to my father for his own safety and wellbeing. While I liked Mosta and found talking with him to be informative and exciting, my father's wellbeing was my central concern.

"One night, Mosta came to our house in great distress. He said he had been accosted by two men on his way. They had struggled, but he was able to escape with only a torn shirt. The material that covered his arms was ripped in several places. What I observed was very disorienting.

"After a short period of decompression from what had taken place, we moved on with each of us having several drinks of Akvavit. We had never had much to drink while together, but soon things became more relaxed, and we fell into our normal routine. As usual, my father and Mosta sat opposite of each other with a small table between them, and I took a chair perpendicular to both.

"As we talked, Mosta became more animated than usual, probably due to the stress of the night in combination with the Akvavit. I listened to them talk as I always did, but something drew my eye to Mosta's arm. As he moved about, the skin, which was visible through the tear in his shirt, appeared to shift. It moved like a liquid, changing colors with the different orientation of his arm. At first, I mistook it for a tattoo until I could see that it was fluid. I tried not to stare, but he must have felt my eyes on him. He turned to me and immediately knew what I was looking at. I felt as if I had been discovered as a voyeur. Instead of being angry, he settled back in his chair and a smile of relief came across his face. My father also smiled.

"'It would appear you have been found out,' said my father.

"'Apparently so,' replied Mosta.

"'Should we bring him completely up to date?' asked my father.

"Mosta nodded and said, 'Why don't you begin, Lars?'

"What followed was astounding," Dak said to Jake. "I don't think I will ever forget it. My father proceeded to tell me that everything we had been talking about was more than theory. He said that Mosta was living proof of the existence of other worlds and that moving between these worlds was possible and practiced by many.

"Mosta stood and opened his shirt. Under it, his skin was fluid but soon morphed into a color scheme to match his surroundings. There was no doubting what I had seen.

"Mosta closed his shirt, took a seat on the couch, and said, 'I do not want to offend you, but the world in which you live is one of the few places that still believes they are the only living beings in the universes. This is an arrogant attitude and one that is mainly responsible for this world's refusal to explore. It does not mean that your society is not as developed as others. There are many more primitive societies than this, but what they lack in learning, they make up for in shear faith. They accept the movement between worlds as either a sacred journey sanctioned by some deity or pure magic administered by some chosen individual or nature herself.'

"Mosta paused to let my brain assimilate what I was hearing. He continued, 'In each society there are forward thinkers, those who view the norm as a jumping off point. Your father is one of these individuals, and I believe you are too. That's why I contacted him. I was thrust into this world by a tragic mistake and found myself alone. I was lucky to be found by a couple who were somewhat knowledgeable about these things. I was nurtured, loved, and protected instead of probed, prodded, and treated like a lab specimen. They gave me an education and taught me how to move undetected through this society. The only thing I did not know was how to get back home. I don't remember much about my home world, but over time I have developed a burning desire to return. Now, with your father's help, I believe that to be possible.'

"My head was spinning, but I was deeply intrigued. How many nights had I spent with my head buried in some book that told fantastical stories about what we now discussed as fact?

"My father took up the conversation. 'I have always thought there was more happening in our universe than we had the native ability to perceive. My hypothesis has always been that our universe is made up of many dimensions, each independent from the other but connected by a series of passageways or doors if you will. Whether these doorways remain static or randomly manifest themselves according to either need or circumstance, I have not been able to determine. I believe that if we were able to identify one, we would be able to pass through it. Mosta and I are trying to find a way to identify the whereabouts of one of these doors.'

"They worked on this part of the problem for almost another year and developed an instrument that operated much like a spectroscope. They reasoned that, when available, these portals would have to create subtle differences in the property of light—differences not detectible by the human eye. These fluctuations, they hypothesized, were a result of a shifting of the electromagnetic field. They deduced that if a human body whose own magnetic field had been supercharged met a disruption of the earth's magnetic field, it could create a reaction that would allow the person to pass through into whatever existed on the other side. I am sure that vast scientific calculations were used, but this was the simplistic explanation I received. The invention would help them locate and identify potential doors.

"From there, we spent a lot of time in our vehicles, looking for potential sites. It took another three months to find one. We marked it and hoped it would remain viable.

"Our next problem was how to stimulate our own electromagnetic field to the level needed to interact with the door. Again, our walls were lined with complex formulas, but the end result, in the simplest of terms, was a portable, battery-operated microwave projector. Just as you would be impacted by standing too close to a microwave oven for an extended time, this invention would bathe you in the rays, supercharging your magnetic field. Of course, after a while you would begin to cook from the inside out," Dak said with a laugh. "I'm sorry this is taking so long in the telling. I will try to condense and move faster from this point on."

"Please tell it as you deem necessary," said Jake. "I find it fascinating."

"Very well, Jake. Once everything was in place, there was nothing to do but try it. My father decided we should try a quick over and back without Mosta. I would remain on this side while my father would step through the gate and, if he were successful, return. Without recounting all the details, suffice it to say it worked. My father was ecstatic, and I wanted a turn. Citing concerns about over exposure to the microwaves, my father would not allow it. He said he would test it a few more times and then we would pass through as a group.

"There was no way of knowing which world he had visited or even if it was the same place each time. My father didn't care. He had proof, at least to his own satisfaction, that he could go and come back. When he told Mosta, he was met with an attitude he had not suspected. Mosta seemed resentful that the attempts had been made without him. He did not voice his discontent but only went silent. When at last he asked my father about his transition, he became frustrated by the lack of detail."

"For all the time spent in theorizing about the possibility of dimensional travel, researching and fine tuning all the complex equations, and developing the equipment needed to make such a feat possible, in the end Mosta was just a lonely boy stranded in a strange place who wanted to go home. He wanted some type of assurance that we could make that happen, but, of course, there were no guarantees."

Jake thought of what Dak had just said. The administration of the Society of Builders certainly had a firm grasp on what it took to move between worlds with the posit to locate the doors and the wizard and staff to actuate the transition. Gwynn had even alluded to the fact that she knew which door would lead back to The Farm. If there were a certain procedure to reach a set location, that knowledge had not been passed on to him. There had to be a way. Certainly, they could not be expected to drift from world to world, hoping to stumble onto some Society business that needed handling.

"Mosta became so eager to transition that at times he was most irrational," Dak continued. "My father felt a sense of responsibility and a duty to help Mosta realize his dream. It was decided to suspend any more tests and transition as a group.

"Our plan was that we would all step through together, take a short while to evaluate our surroundings, and then come back through. From there we would plan increasingly longer forays.

"Jake, have you ever heard of Murphy's Law?"

"Anything that can go wrong will go wrong," Jake replied.

"Yes, that's it but it goes further. It also states that if there are two or more ways to do something and one of the ways can result in a catastrophe, someone will do it. In a nutshell, that is what took place.

"After we arrived at the site, Mosta became highly agitated. My father and I could neither understand the reason for his agitation nor could we calm him. Everything started to go wrong when we put on our backpacks containing the microwave projectors. As soon as we activated Mosta's projector, he took off at a run and disappeared through the door. My father had always allowed time for the projector to warm up and become fully functional. Even without that, it seemed to work in Mosta's case. Still, we took our time, hoping that Mosta would be waiting on the other side. When we finally approached the door, there was a boot lying at the base. It was Mosta's boot and his foot and ankle were still in it. My father panicked and stepped through. I followed. On the other side, strewn across the ground was the projector or at least what was left of it. There was a blood trail, leading away from the gate and into the jungle. My father said we had to find him, so without further discussion we moved away from the door and deeper into the unknown.

"My father was a good and kind man. He cared deeply for his fellow humans and was especially loving and faithful to those he considered his friends. Unfortunately, like so many who spent most of their waking hours dealing with theories and suppositions, he lacked a certain grasp of reality. I, on the other hand, was not burdened with any such vagueness of the human condition. As we moved forward, it became obvious to me that, judging by the blood trail we were following, Mosta was in real trouble. Still, we persevered."

"When we found Mosta, he was almost dead and totally delirious. He had torn his clothes off and lay among the vegetation. His skin had morphed to the color of his surroundings, and we would have missed him had it not been for the blood and the dullness of his colors as compared to those around him, which I attributed to his weakened condition. Following my father's example, I took off my backpack and began gathering any loose material we could use to make Mosta more comfortable. Before we could do much, his life force slipped away. My father was beside himself. I felt everything unravelling.

"I said that we should make for the gate posthaste. My father said we had to carry Mosta back with us. I argued that the reason we were in the shape we were in was because Mosta had acted irrationally while trying to get home. Now that he was home, we should leave his body. My father insisted we had no way of knowing if this was Mosta's home, so the rational thing would be to return him with us. I could see nothing rational in that proposition.

"The father is always the father, and the son is always the village idiot, so we bound Mosta's stump to prevent seepage, and I prepared to carry him.

"The second portent of disaster came when we went to retrieve our backpacks and found that one was missing. Donning the only functioning microwave projector, my father began following the blood trail in reverse while I trailed with the dead weight of Mosta's body draped across my shoulders in a fireman's carry.

"By the amount of blood on the trail, I could tell we were approaching the door. We quickened our pace, although I was almost at the point of exhaustion. My father was running ahead. He had initiated the microwave projector, and we were both hoping it could create enough energy to transition all three of us. I was lagging behind due to the weight of Mosta's corpse, but I struggled forward. When he paused at the door for me to catch up, it all went to hell."

"He looked back at me and, as our eyes met, an arrow slammed into his upper back between the backpack and his neck. Two more arrows struck the backpack. The force of the arrows sent him forward into the door. He disappeared through the door and I, with Mosta's corpse draped across my shoulders, was left behind.

"Can you see the irony of the situation, Jake?"

Jake wiped a hand through his hair, looked at Dak, shook his head, and said, "Yes, you were the most disinterested member of your entire party. You had less to do with the dream of interdimensional travel than either you father or Mosta. The theories, the calculations, the development of equipment, even the tests were the provenance of the others, yet only you were left at the successful culmination of it all."

"Yes, only I remained in the new world, although at that moment I neither grasped that fact nor had much hope of surviving much longer. I had seen my father struck by an arrow and the microwave projector pierced twice, so, even if my father was alive on the other side, he may not be able to come back for me. The one thing I was sure of was that if I did not live, nothing else would matter."

"What did you do?" asked Jake.

"I did the only thing I could think of. I placed Mosta's body on the ground at my feet, stood as tall as I could, and spread my arms as if I were presenting the fallen hero at court. I noticed three things immediately. First, the natives were of the same species as Mosta. Their skin was fluid and morphed into the same hues and patterns as their surroundings. Second, they looked from me to their fallen kinsman on the ground. Thirdly, the circle of natives went completely around Mosta's body and me, meaning that the door to the other side had either disappeared or did not figure into the reality of this place.

"A murmur began, somewhere in their ranks and spread to encompass the entire contingent. To my amazement, they all threw their weapons on the ground and knelt. As I looked on, another voice sounded, and each native prostrated themselves and lowered their faces to the ground. They remained in that position for quite some time. I did not know what to make of it. I noticed a few eyes raised to observe me. I became very uncomfortable. Finally, I decided to play it for what it was worth. I turned my palms up and raised my arms from beside my legs to shoulder height, saying, 'Rise' as I did it. Slowly they rose to their knees and, after several inquisitive looks, stood. Then, as a group, they surrounded me, not as an intruder but as someone they had long awaited. It appeared that for the time being I would survive. Two of the natives carried Mosta's body, and I was led deeper into the jungle. We finally arrived here, where I was housed and fed. Although I was being treated very well, all I could think of was my father and returning home.

"I did not know it then, but I was considered the fulfillment of prophesy. In the lore of this tribe, known as the Chroma, it was passed from generation to generation that a pale god would one day come to this world, returning a lost one to his family. This pale one would protect the Chroma and ensure their dominance of this land.

"There is so much more to the story, but suffice it to say that I adapted to the role I was meant to play, not just surviving but prospering. I found I had a knack for the type of thinking necessary to meet the expectations of the tribal elders. I have grown to love this land and these people, but I have never forgotten about Denmark. I never saw my father again and, if he lived through the arrow wounds, he never mounted another attempt to return for me. I like to think that he is alive and still searching for me and just not able to find the correct door. That is my story. Now I await yours."

Chapter Eighty-Seven

Jake didn't know how much he should reveal. His instincts told him that if he withheld too much or was deemed a liar, there would be dire consequences. He could put himself and all those who accompanied him in danger. He made the decision to tell the truth but with the omission of his being a wizard.

"I am in the service of a group known as the Society of Builders," said Jake. "Are you aware of this group?"

Dak answered in the negative without hesitation.

"The purpose of this group is to assure there are no outside influences brought to bear that would impede or accelerate the progressive development of different worlds and their inhabitants."

Dak's posture stiffened. He stared intently at Jake and then toward the door. Jake realized he had just described Dak's situation and that what he had said could be construed as a threat.

"That is not my reason for being here," Jake said quickly. "I am trying to locate and rescue my mother. She was forced to flee our home to avoid being kidnapped or worse."

Dak appeared to accept that and settled back to listen. Jake took his time in recounting the story. He was careful not to give away more than was necessary. At the completion of his tale, Dak seemed satisfied. He asked a few questions but none that required any more disclosure. He was most interested in their ability to move between worlds without a plethora of equipment. Jake didn't reveal that the staff was the vehicle with which they transitioned from one world to the other.

They had been together for several hours and Jake was tiring. He made no attempt to hide his fatigue. Dak took notice and suggested they retire for the night and continue their conversation tomorrow.

Dak opened the door and motioned to the guard. When the man stepped into the room, Dak must have told him in the language used earlier to escort Jake back to his quarters. Both the guard and Dak motioned for Jake to follow.

As he was leaving, acting as if it were an afterthought, Jake asked, "Would it be possible to retrieve my walking stick?"

"We can also discuss that tomorrow," said Dak as he closed the door.

Jake followed the man back to their rooms. Neither man spoke a word.

Chapter Eighty-Eight

Jamal let Othan choose those who would accompany him back to the jungle. Othan selected five soldiers. He would have liked a larger group, but for this mission loyalty was of more value than more bodies. Now he only had to wait for orders to mobilize. When he was called to Jamal's quarters, he thought the time was at hand.

Entering the sorcerer's chambers, he found Jamal staring into a boiling cauldron. Othan took up a position inside the door and waited to be acknowledged.

Jamal didn't want to reveal the cauldron to Othan but saw little alternative. He couldn't explain how the cauldron had continued to show the jungle after Othan's rescue without giving too much away. He didn't have a sample of Bannar's blood, so he couldn't form the same connection he had with Othan. While keeping one eye on the cauldron, he had scoured his tomes for an answer. He found a short passage in an old volume with only the word "Majick" on its cover. Following the instructions, he retrieved one of Bannar's gloves from the armory and dropped it into the boiling liquid. He was rewarded with a view of Bannar's whereabouts. The link with Othan had afforded him either an internal view. With Bannar, he could see the scene only from above. He had tried to communicate with Bannar but was pleased when he could not be heard. Neither could he hear Bannar. This was a simple tracking spell. When Jamal turned his attention to Othan, he was still agitated.

"Come in, Captain. I'm afraid this is much worse than I thought."

Othan didn't know how to respond, so he took a step forward and said, "How may I be of service, Lord Jamal?"

"Come; look at this."

As Othan approached, Jamal stretched his arms above the bubbling liquid. Othan looked into the cauldron. The liquid became still and mirrorlike. Instead of his own reflection, Bannar came into view. Othan took a sharp breath and stepped back.

"Don't be concerned, Captain. He can't see us and doesn't know he is being observed. This is how I found you."

Othan's heart was still racing, but he returned to the cauldron. Bannar was the focus but now more of the room was visible and others nearby came into view. Looking closer, Othan thought there was something familiar about them. A door opened and the wizard entered the room. Bannar didn't appear to be a captive. Othan looked to Jamal.

"It's not exactly like it appears," said Jamal as he stepped away from the cauldron. "Yes, Bannar is with the members of the Society. It was not entirely voluntary. He was found after you were attacked. He chose to join them instead of trying to survive on his own. The Lord High Determiner is aware of the situation and agrees with it. They are not aware that he is one of us or that Bannar is aware of the Society."

"How would you have me proceed, Lord Jamal?"

The time of truth was at hand. Jamal could not reveal his plan without exposing his treachery. If Othan was sincere in his sworn allegiance, then all would be well. If Othan still harbored any loyalties to the Determiner, by tomorrow Jamal would be in a dungeon cell or dead. The risk was great but there would never be a better time to make his move.

Jamal placed his hand on Othan's shoulder and said, "Come. Let's sit and discuss our options. I want you to help me formulate a plan."

Chapter Eighty-Nine

The temperature in the jungle can vary by as much as twenty degrees from day to night. While it felt cold only in contrast to the heat, Gwynn found herself chilled. To remedy this, she gathered fronds to make herself a cover. She kept an eye on Kathryn, who remained where Gwynn had found her and was still unconscious. She could only see the shadows, but nothing was moving. The sounds of the jungle were soothing, and against all intentions she fell asleep.

The sound of approaching footsteps startled her into semi-consciousness. She was in no position to either fight or flee, so she chose to feign sleep. She moved her hand to grip the spear, which she had placed at her side. She didn't know how she would wield it, but having it was assuring. She was relieved when she heard her name called just above a whisper. She opened her eyes to find Kathryn standing at her feet.

Kathryn must have been up for a while. She produced a handful of berries and offered Gwynn half. They moved to the edge of the clearing to take advantage of the new day's warmth. As they ate, Gwynn told Kathryn all that had taken place, including the rescue by the chameleon tribe. She related the existence of the white man among them.

"Jake and the others left with the white man and his tribe. It didn't look as if they were coerced."

Kathryn's memories were short. She recalled the trap and watching as the others were trussed and made ready to be carried off and then nothing until Gwynn had delivered the slap and nothing more until she had awakened this morning.

"What do you think we should do?" asked Kathryn.

"We need to pinpoint their whereabouts and assess the situation from there. We need to know if they are guests or if they exchanged one captor for another."

With that, Gwynn summoned the posit, and they both looked at the display. Jake's icon was flashing his location. Gwynn pointed out the whereabouts of a gate only a half day's walk from Jake and the others.

"If we can find a way to get them out and they are all healthy, we have a good chance of making the gate."

"We've got to be careful. We can't help anyone if we're captured," said Kathryn.

"It will be best if we travel separately. I'll go by air and you can travel in feline form."

By way of agreement, Kathryn transitioned into the black panther. Gwynn displaced the posit and rose to just under the canopy. They set off through the trees, separate but together.

The construct of Gwynn's gossamer wings made them easy to conceal and all but silent when in use. Unless someone saw her, she could fly undetected. As she flew under the canopy, she observed lots of activity above. The trees appeared to be the preferred method of travel. She surmised that the native inhabitants of this world would only descend to ground level to hunt or to accomplish tasks that could not be performed above. She wondered if the avoidance of ground travel was due to ease or to avoid some larger danger she and her companions were not aware of. She made a mental note to discuss this with Kathryn when they stopped for rest.

They had been traveling at a moderate pace for what felt like an hour when Kathryn came to an abrupt stop and slipped into the underbrush. Gwynn stopped her forward progress, went into a hover, and tightened her grip on the spear.

ↄ◦ↄ◦

Kathryn scented them before she heard the movement. She melted into the underbrush and settled down with her underside flat against the ground. Her rear legs were coiled under her and ready to spring. To make a low profile, she stretched her front legs out in front of her with her head resting between them. Only her eyes moved as she scanned the area ahead.

Three men came into view. They were advancing as if they didn't want to be seen. Gwynn could see that the men were not of the same tribe as those moving in the trees. She had a strange suspicion where she had seen these men before. That feeling was confirmed when she saw Kathryn change positions.

"No, Kathryn, no," Gwynn whispered with her eyes closed.

The sight of the men raised the hair on the neck of Kathryn's feline form. Her eyes darted from one to the other. She might have been able to let them pass but for her keen eyes and heightened sense of smell. First, she saw a pattern of spattered blood crusted on the man's loincloth. Perhaps she would have been able to control herself if her nose had not recognized the scent of it as her own blood. In her mind's eye, she could see this man approach her as she hung from the trap. His facial expression had shown great satisfaction at being able to stand before such a beast without showing fear. She had only been able to look on as he postured before drawing back the club. After the blow, as the light of her consciousness was fading to black, she saw him turn to the others and raise both arms in triumph.

The wisest course of action would be no action at all. Let them pass, proceed to Jake's location, take whatever actions necessary, and move on to the gate and out of this world. She knew she was not going to let them pass. She considered the next best alternative would be to kill them quickly and then revert to plan A. She could have lived with that if the smirk on her assailant's face and those outstretched arms were not continually playing in her head.

Gwynn hoped against hope she was mistaken in her assessment of Kathryn's intentions. She watched as the big cat coiled. The burst of speed with which she exploded from the underbrush would have been hard to follow at ground level, but Gwynn had the advantage of aerial perspective. Kathryn bypassed the man nearest her, moving past him before he realized what was happening. The second man, who appeared to be her prime focus, saw her coming and tried to step aside. For his efforts he received a powerful paw-slap across his knee. Gwynn saw the leg contort in an unnatural angle. She thought the leg had been severed but saw no blood as the man fell and writhed in agony. Kathryn made short work of the third man with claws across his throat. The first man had been carrying a spear but seemed more motivated to escape than to fight. Kathryn ignored him but Gwynn could not. Gwynn inverted herself, gripped her spear with both hands, folded her wings, and went into free fall. The man had made it to the edge of the trees before the blade of the spear entered his neck just above his shoulders. His spine was severed. His forward momentum would have carried him a few more steps if the spearhead had not emerged just above his pubic area and jammed into the ground. He stood like a scarecrow whose job it was to protect his surrounding area from winged creatures.

Without hope of freeing her spear, Gwynn exchanged it for the one carried by the dead man. She turned to see that Kathryn had not killed her prey. Instead, she circled him while he tried to gain some foothold with his ruined leg. She moved to his head. Instead of attacking, she fell to her stomach with her nose only inches from his face. The stench of ruined flesh was made worse as his bowels loosened. She rose, circled him once more, and opened her jaws. Gwynn watched as Kathryn's teeth sank into the fleshy area of his side. She lifted him and shook him like a rag doll. He cried out.

Gwynn called out her name, but Kathryn only raised her eyes and emitted a growl. Gwynn held her ground.

Kathryn stepped across the man and lowered her body, further pinning him to the ground. Next, she returned to his head, stared into his eyes, and pulled her maw away from her teeth. The man whimpered. Kathryn stood in silence until the man opened his eyes. When she was sure that he was looking at her, she raised herself to full height, balancing on her hind legs, and extended both of her front legs to full length. She held that pose for what seemed like a minute. Her claws became fully visible. It looked as if the man might lose consciousness, but before he did Kathryn fell on him and it was over.

Gwynn could not pretend to understand what had just happened. Kathryn had never been a loose cannon. She was intense, goal oriented, mischievous—sometimes to distraction—and had always been more than competent in battle. Gwynn had to have faith that Kathryn had acted with good reason. They could discuss that later. Now, Kathryn's actions had alerted anyone within hearing distance of their presence. All activity had ceased in the canopy. They had to put distance between themselves and the three mangled bodies.

Kathryn must have come out of what had overtaken her. She looked toward Gwynn and, although her paws and face were covered in blood, her posture was one of shame and submission. Gwynn, still on the ground, ran toward a heavily forested section of the jungle. As she passed Kathryn, she let her hand find the top the cat's head and tousled it. Kathryn raised her head and took a position at Gwynn's heels.

They ran for several minutes until Gwynn thought they had put enough distance between them and the attack. She stopped and took a seat with her back against a tree. Kathryn transitioned from her feline form, reached under the ground cover until she found some wet foliage, and cleaned herself. Gwynn looked on without a word.

"It was him," said Kathryn when she had finished cleaning and put on her clothes. "I'm sorry but I couldn't let him pass."

Gwynn nodded and smiled although she wondered if they would survive to get to Jake.

"I think we should travel at ground level and with as much stealth as possible. There was a lot going on in the canopy, and now they know we are here. With enough care, we can probably go on from here unnoticed."

Kathryn said nothing.

Chapter Ninety

Jake was finishing his morning meal when the knock sounded. He followed the warrior to Dak's quarters. As they came within sight of Dak's door, the warrior turned, motioned Jake forward, and left the hall. Jake saw that there were no warriors guarding the door. He knocked.

"Come in, Jake," came Dak's voice.

The first thing Jake saw when he entered was his staff standing in the corner of the room. Dak sat cross-legged on the floor. Two containers of steaming liquid sat on a table in front of him. Jake settled on the mat opposite Dak.

"Welcome. Please help yourself to some gah; it's much like the coffee we enjoy at home."

Jake was unsure but took a sip. He found it quite good and nodded his approval.

"Jake, I won't take a lot of your time. I know you and your companions are eager to continue your journey and I understand that. I will keep this as simple as I can. I want you to help me return to my home world."

Jake was taken aback. He hadn't expected this, but it was the logical conclusion to Dak's lengthy story. Jake sensed a hint of desperation in Dak's voice. He felt he didn't have long to respond, so he did.

"If that is what you want, I will do everything I can to help you."

Relief washed over Dak's face. Jake tried not to let the myriad reservations show in his face. Although he had answered in the affirmative, he felt a negative answer would have changed the tenure of their stay.

"Thank you," Dak said.

"How do you think the people of the village will take your leaving?"

"I don't have an answer to that. I think it would probably be best not to discuss it with them."

"How can you leave without them knowing?"

"I've thought of that and have a plan. Do you think you can be ready in three days?"

"I'm sure we can, but I'd like to know more of how we are going to be able to leave."

"I have already instructed my guard that, from today forward, you and your companions will be able to move about the village unencumbered. Have your people take full advantage of this freedom so that the villagers will get accustomed to seeing it. My hope is that after a couple of days you will become a part of the flow of activities and people will not be hyper-aware of your presence. If it takes longer, we will delay until this familiarity is affected. We will discuss the details after you have had some time to think about it. I welcome your input."

"I will need to discuss this with my companions."

"Yes, I understand the wisdom of doing so. We all have to be of one mind."

Jake smiled in what he hoped was a reassuring way. Dak returned it with a nod of his head. Jake picked up the gah, but it had gone cold.

Chapter Ninety-One

Othan had never understood the technology nor the magic behind moving from world to world although he had done it many times. He only followed orders. Now, he and his five soldiers stood at almost the same spot from which Jamal had summoned his wounded and unconscious body. He looked around but did not detect any activity. He signaled his troops deeper into the trees. He had not expected any presence at this location because he and Jamal had observed it remotely for the last three days. He knew Jamal was observing them at this very minute. Othan could not feel Jamal's presence but knew he possessed the ability to look through his eyes and see everything he saw. He found this deeply unsettling.

Many things in the last three days had troubled Othan. He had sworn allegiance to Jamal and felt it in his heart. He knew he would not be alive if it were not for the sorcerer. Not only did he owe Jamal his life but the sorcerer had confided in him in a way nobody ever had. Jamal had alluded to a future in which he would rule the land with Othan by his side. It was a heady discourse, but Othan still found himself conflicted.

He stood at a crossroad. Down one path was the familiar. He had been in the service of the Lord High Determiner since he was old enough to wield a weapon. He had sworn an oath. If he chose that path, he could continue in the comfort of his position. He had risen through the ranks but was at the place where the right person had to die for him to advance. One of those people was Bannar.

Down the other path, uncertainty awaited. There was also a sense of adventure. Above all, there was the chance of all he and Jamal had discussed coming to fruition. In Jamal's plan, all obstacles were removed. It was apparent to Othan that in the end either Jamal or the Determiner must die. If he chose to remain loyal to the Determiner, he could kill Jamal and reveal his deceit. If the Determiner believed him, he would be a hero. If he was not believed or if Jamal's death was in any way inconvenient, he could find himself without his head. As he considered these potential futures, he came to his truth. He couldn't take the life of the man to whom he owed his own life. He had transitioned with a steel intent.

His men knelt around him as he consulted the map he and Jamal had drawn. After confirming their path, he considered his troops. Sergeant Ronko and he had fought together many times, and he trusted the man with his life. Ronko also owed Jamal for many favors and potions. Corporals Smi and Lynn were not familiar to Othan, but Jamal had assured him they could be trusted. Privates Jessen and Sniky were both new troopers in service for just over a year, but Ronko vouched for both, which was good enough for Othan.

Othan gave the signal to move out and watched as each man checked his weapon and equipment. When everyone was ready, Smi led them single file with Jessen bringing up the rear.

Chapter Ninety-Two

After traveling several miles, Kathryn stopped and fell to the ground. Gwynn followed suit and immediately heard what had alarmed Kathryn. Something was coming through the jungle. They both waited. Six men dressed as soldiers moved through the trees, walking at a careful but steady pace. It was clear they were not of this world. They were heavily armed and moved in a disciplined manner. They were headed toward the village where Jake's beacon had shown on the posit.

One of the men looked familiar to Kathryn. He resembled the man she had rescued from the four natives. She had assumed that since she couldn't find him he was dead. He had not been a soldier, so she surmised it couldn't be him.

Gwynn watched as they moved away. All appeared to be seasoned soldiers except the two boys at the end of the column.

Gwynn and Kathryn held their positions until the men had time to move away. Gwynn motioned to Kathryn.

"I've got a bad feeling about that group," said Gwynn when Kathryn was by her side.

"It's strange," said Kathryn. "The second soldier in line reminded me of the man who was traveling with Bannar. I know it can't be him because he was so badly hurt. I'm almost sure he's dead."

Gwynn thought about what Kathryn had said before speaking. "It may be best if we fall behind them until we can learn their intent."

They followed the soldiers for the rest of the day. When the light began to fade, the soldiers found a secluded area and to camp for the night. They made no fires.

Gwynn and Kathryn also stopped and followed the same discipline as the soldiers.

"Do you think we can get close enough to see what they're doing?" asked Kathryn.

"I don't think we can take the chance of trying to get too close at ground level," said Gwynn. "I'll try to approach by air and hover."

"If you need me, yell. I'll be ready," said Kathryn and returned to black panther form.

"Try not to eat anyone while I'm gone," said Gwynn rising vertically.

Kathryn emitted a low growl and swatted her paw at the hovering fae.

Gwynn drifted up until she was under the first level of canopy. She looked above to be sure she was neither being observed nor in any danger. Trying to blend in as much as possible, she drifted into position above the encampment. She oriented her body to present the smallest profile. They seemed to be in a strategy session. When they broke up, one man left the group and walked toward the village. She hovered until the remaining soldiers began preparing to retire for the evening. She moved a safe distance away, changed her orientation, and returned to where she had left Kathryn.

Chapter Ninety-Three

Jake returned to their quarters and called everyone into the common area. As he spoke of his conversation with Dak, he was met with silence. He could feel there was more to be discussed but not in Bannar's presence. Luckily, Bannar seemed eager to exercise his new freedom of movement. He said he would like to survey their surroundings and was met with agreement all around. Everyone dispersed and seemed not to notice his leaving.

Once Bannar was gone, they all reassembled. None were privy to what type of surveillance was available, so they huddled closely and spoke just above a whisper.

"Boss, what the hell are we going to do?" said Raj. "You know we can't take all these people to The Farm."

"I know, Raj," said Jake. "Things are moving. I know the situation may seem out of hand. I don't know how we will work it out, but we will."

Thomas looked from face to face and scowled. "I'll handle it if need be," he said under his breath.

Jake sensed the unrest and understood it. He was aware of all the arguments. He also knew he was responsible for everyone's safety and getting them back to The Farm. The decisions he had made of bringing in Bannar and agreeing to help Dak were both what he felt he had to do. He didn't know if he was following his intuition or responding to the knowledge gained by his episode with Mr. Alphonse. He felt he could not trust his instincts in one instance and disregard them in another.

"We will cross each of these bridges as we come to it. Our first priority is to reunite with Gwynn and Kathryn."

"I fear Kathryn is lost to us," said Elic. "It was a vicious blow she took to the head."

"If she is dead, there is nothing we can do. If she lived, we can't leave her. We must know for certain."

The others nodded their heads in assent, each with his thoughts of Kathryn.

After a moment, Jake continued. "When I spoke to Dak, I had the distinct feeling that if I didn't agree to help him, our conditions would deteriorate along with our chances of continuing our journey. With that in mind, I figured to be agreeable, but I will impose some of the same parameters on him."

It concerned Jake that he could think of betraying Dak and Bannar, but his allies and the integrity of the mission were his first priority. He hoped he had allayed their uncertainties. If anyone harbored doubts, they kept it to themselves.

"I think we should all disperse and be seen around the village. What Dak said was true: the more we are seen, the less attention we will be paid. Keep an eye out for anything we can use to our advantage. Let's go in pairs this first time out."

Raj and Thomas left while Jake and Elic hung back.

↬   ↭

After leaving the quarters, Bannar walked about nonchalantly. He used his training to observe his surroundings without appearing to be overly interested. He was a curiosity and point of attention when he first began his walk. The longer he strolled, the less heed was paid to him. He may have appeared casual, but he remained vigilant.

He had been incommunicado for several days and needed to establish contact with the Determiner.

Continuing his walk, Bannar worked his way closer to the edge of the village. Once he determined that he had moved far enough, he looked for a way to ground level and soon found a rope ladder coiled beside a limb. He attached the ladder to the limb and descended. Once on the ground, he assumed a soldier's posture and scanned his surroundings. He was in a thick of trees, which suited his purpose. He moved deeper into the jungle until he came to a tree that was larger than the rest. He detected no movement in the canopy. He put the tree between himself and the village. After one more visual sweep of the area, he summoned the communiq.

Chapter Ninety-Four

Othan couldn't believe his luck. Once they made camp, he dispatched Corporal Lynn to reconnoiter the area. He later decided to have a look for himself and set off in the direction Lynn had taken. When he saw Lynn crouched and on high alert, Othan went into stealth mode. Lynn sensed his presence, turned to see him, and signaled him to advance. Upon drawing abreast of Lynn, Othan couldn't believe his eyes. Just ahead and with his back to them stood Major Bannar.

Othan had hypothesized about how he would go about finding Bannar. Of all the scenarios, this one never came to mind.

"He arrived a short while ago. It sounded like he was talking with someone, but I haven't seen anyone else," whispered Lynn.

Othan nodded in understanding. He knew he couldn't pass up this opportunity. There could never be another chance such as this. He reached into the equipment pouch that hung from his side and extracted the hood. He didn't know Bannar's mindset and couldn't risk a confrontation. He signaled Lynn and they both advanced. Moving from tree to tree, they proceeded to within a few yards of Bannar. When they were ready, Othan signaled Lynn and gathered himself. With the hood in his hand, he and Lynn burst from the trees. They were upon Bannar before he could turn. Othan put the hood over Bannar's head and cinched it with the ratcheted closure. At the same time, he clamped his hand over Bannar's mouth so he could not cry out. Lynn tackled the hooded man's legs and pulled them from under him. Once they had him under control, they started back toward their camp. Bannar was uncommonly passive.

Chapter Ninety-Five

Both Gwynn and Kathryn heard the commotion. In response, Gwynn took to the wing and Kathryn assumed feline form. Both moved toward the noise.

From above, Gwynn saw the two men walking toward the encampment. Suspended between them hung a third man. It was hard to tell if he was conscious or not. His head was covered by a hood, so it was easy to assume he had been abducted. When the men entered the campsite, they let the hooded man slip to his feet. The man who appeared to be in charge removed the hood. Each man looked to the other and burst out laughing and clasped hands. Gwynn could see that the third man was none other than Bannar. She found their familiarity troubling. As quietly as possible, she slipped away to rejoin Kathryn.

"What do you make of that?" Gwynn asked when they were back together and had moved out of hearing.

Kathryn hesitated before saying, "I saw who the man being carried was. I thought he had been captured, but it appears he was being rescued. The stranger thing is that one of the rescuers is the man I assumed was dead."

"If this is the man, he recovered quickly."

"Indeed, and now he is dressed as a soldier and leads a group of men."

"I felt they were not of this world when I saw the two of them on the road. Now I wonder if we were not too quick to take in Bannar?"

"We've got to let Jake know," said Gwynn.

"I can take care of that," said Kathryn.

Chapter Ninety-Six

Othan's moment of triumph was short-lived. After he removed the hood from Major Bannar's head, he was greeted with a smile and a clasp of the arm. Bannar expressed his joy at being reunited with his fellow countrymen. Othan was somewhat surprised by Bannar's reaction, especially considering the way they had transported him. Othan was pleased with himself.

"Captain, assign some men to the perimeter while we bring each other up to date. I don't want to take a chance of anyone seeing us," ordered Bannar taking command.

"Yes, Major," said Othan without much enthusiasm. He turned to give the order and saw the look on the faces of his troops. He had just been stripped of command and everyone knew it. He seethed but at the same time strived to remain nonchalant. He wanted to act as if everything was going according to plan.

Bannar summoned him and signaled him to the edge of the clearing. He listened patiently as Bannar recounted everything that had happened since they were separated, including the plans to escape this world, taking Dak with them. When Othan tried to tell his tale, Bannar cut him off.

"Yes, I've been in communication with the Lord Determiner, and he told me of your rescue and recovery," said Bannar as if it were routine and expected.

Othan's internal dialogue was vile and trite, but outwardly he remained calm. This was not the future he had seen for himself when he and Lord Jamal had last spoken.

"I think I should return to the village so I can stay up to date on the wizard's future plans," said Bannar. "We are allowed to move about freely, so I should be able to rendezvous with you almost daily. We should be making our move soon. You may assume command until that time comes."

"As you wish, Major," said Othan.

Othan watched Bannar's departure. "Yes, sir, Major, sir," Othan said under his breath. "Go back to the village and eat and sleep with our sworn enemies. Enjoy the last days of your life."

Chapter Ninety-Seven

Jake and Elic walked among the trees that surrounded the perimeter of the village. In stark contrast to the gentle breeze that always circulated above, the ground level was hot and humid. As they walked, they were aware they were a curiosity to the natives. Everyone glanced their way and some stared, but as time went on they seemed to be accepted as belonging to the village.

"I feel a sense of anxiety, almost a foreboding," said Elic. "I can't discern a specific cause of the feeling, but I thought I should mention it."

"I understand your feelings. I am apprehensive about what lies ahead, and I'm nowhere as intuitive as you. Let me know if the source becomes clear."

Elic nodded and they continued in silence. Suddenly, Elic stopped to survey the surroundings. Jake followed suit. His eyes were drawn to the thick vegetation to their right and deeper into the forest. A flash of black and the rustling of the leaves put them both on alert. As they watched, a panther moved into the clearing and settled itself into a flat posture on its stomach with legs stretched out front and back. Although Elic remained on guard, a smile broke across Jake's face as he recognized Kathryn. Slowly, she regained her feet and sauntered deeper into the forest, pausing to look back over her shoulder to see if Jake would follow.

"Wait here," Jake said to Elic. "Keep an eye out and alert me if anyone is approaching our position."

Elic acknowledged Jake's request and moved away from the trees as Jake turned and walked deeper into them. After a while Jake came to a place in the forest where there were scratch marks on the ground. There was a thicket to his left with a large rock beside it. Jake could see a shallow trough where the rock had been nudged from its original position to the point beside the thicket. Jake went to the rock and took a seat. He was rewarded by the sound of Kathryn's voice speaking softly from the foliage. She gave him a full account of what Gwynn had observed between Bannar and Othan.

While what she told him was troubling, he was elated to hear her voice. He had almost accepted that he would never hear or see her again. He told her he thought it would be prudent for her and Gwynn to stay separated from the others. They could keep an eye on the soldiers and Bannar's interaction with them. He promised to try to meet one or both daily so they would know when the group would move.

"I don't think it will be many more days," he said.

He heard her slip away through the thick vegetation. He gave her time to get away and then motioned for Elic to join him.

"Was that Kathryn?" he asked.

"Yes, and I think I have learned the source of your unrest."

Chapter Ninety-Eight

Raj and Thomas created quite a sensation around the village. While the others were mild curiosities, the giant and the dwarf were a show unto themselves. Some heads turned and never turned back. They found themselves being followed by an ever-increasing crowd. By the time Jake and Elic returned, it felt as if half the village was with them. Jake glanced their way, smiled, waved, and turned toward their quarters.

"Bloody hell," said Thomas, frustrated by the situation.

"Hold it together, big man," said Raj trying to allay some of his friend's annoyance. "We have to go through this if we're going to have any chance of slipping away. Each of us should have paired with someone else. Maybe the differences wouldn't be so stark."

A grunt was all that came in reply, but Raj felt an easing of the tension in Thomas. The huge man was strong, brave, and fierce. He was above all a warrior. He would leave diplomacy to diplomats. Thomas came to a stop and turned to face the crowd. Raj cringed as he too turned toward those gathered behind them. He felt a surge of relief when Thomas smiled and said, "Hello, my lovelies. I am so happy to be among you."

The natives murmured, some nodding their heads.

"Do you think they understood you?" Raj asked.

"I don't know. I don't want to get on the wrong side of them at this point."

The problem of language had been discussed since they arrived in this world. They had always been able to speak and understand the native language. That didn't seem to be the case here.

Raj and Thomas continued to smile, which they thought would communicate in any language. The natives and the two allies were doing well, each in their own tongue.

A different voice sounded, and the natives parted to make a path. Dak came to the front. His voice sounded authoritative but kind, almost as if talking to a child. When he finished speaking, the natives dispersed.

"I hope they didn't cause you any discomfort," Dak said when the final native had walked away.

Thomas stood silent, so Raj said, "No, not at all. We were just getting acquainted."

"You are being kind but thank you."

Dak left and the two men walked on.

"Why are we here?" asked Thomas, the edge back in his voice.

"We had to get out of that last place."

"I know that, little man," said Thomas. "I mean it seems as if we have been in a perpetual battle since we met Jake. I've fought necromancers, werewolves, tyrants, and manufactured soldiers, some of whom I was made to help manufacture. Now we have become burdened with Bannar and Dak. What next?"

Raj was also troubled but managed to keep it to himself. "Jake's doing well but he's still learning."

"I'm not worried about Jake. He's the wizard and has the knowledge. He will need to smooth some things out—like transitions," Thomas said with a little smile. "It's the other two that bother me."

"Both seem nice enough and well meaning."

Thomas turned toward Raj. Any mirth, whether real or faked, was gone.

"Yes, it will trouble me greatly when I slit their throats."

Chapter Ninety-Nine

Taking a circuitous route back to the village, Jake and Elic soon came to their tree and ascended into the canopy. Once there, they found Raj and Thomas surrounded by villagers. Jake was alarmed at first, but things seemed peaceful upon further observation, so they continued to their quarters. Jake was surprised to find his staff standing in a corner. He raised his hand, extended his palm, and summoned it. To his satisfaction, it rose and drifted into his hand. Elic came into the common area carrying a box composed of woven fronds. In it were all their weapons. Jake guessed this was a result of the pact he had made with Dak.

When Raj and Thomas returned, they were both in a somber mood. Jake filled them in about Kathryn's survival. This brought smiles all around. Next, he told them about what she had reported concerning Bannar.

"I never trusted that guy," Thomas growled.

Raj nodded his agreement.

Everyone was happy with the return of their weapons. Each man retrieved his personal gear and checked them for damage and balance.

"I don't think we should carry our weapons as we walk about the village," said Jake. Everyone agreed and went about storing the weapons with their other belongings. The only thing left in the box was the short sword belonging to Bannar. Jake was trying to decide if he should give it to either Gwynn or Kathryn when the door opened and Bannar entered.

"Ah, there you are," said Jake. "Dak returned our weapons." Jake held out the sword, trying to hide his surprise at Bannar's return. Bannar took the weapon, balanced it in his hand, and clipped it to his belt.

The others looked on in bewilderment. Thomas had a hard time concealing his contempt.

"I guess this means we'll be leaving soon," said Bannar as if having his sword returned was expected.

Jake saw that Thomas was staring at Bannar with a look of malevolence. He hoped Bannar wouldn't notice. Jake didn't want the man to suspect that he had been found out. Raj elbowed Thomas, diverting his attention. Jake was going to say more but there was a knock. Everyone dispersed to their personal spaces as Jake opened the door. It was one of the elite warriors. He motioned that Dak had requested his presence. Jake glanced over his shoulder at the staff but stepped through the door without it.

When Jake reached Dak's quarters, the door was open. Inside, Dak reclined on a mat. Beverage and some fruit and berries were set out on the table. Jake settled onto the mat that was in place opposite Dak.

Dak smiled and gestured to the goods on the table. Jake took some of the fare and ate, determined to let Dak start the conversation.

"I take it that things are all well," Dak said more as a statement than an inquiry.

"Yes, and thank you for returning our property."

"Please don't wear them openly. I don't want to alarm the villagers. The Chroma people are peace loving but also very protective."

"I've already advised everyone as such," said Jake trying to be as casual as possible. He returned to the food.

"I thought we would leave day after tomorrow," said Dak.

Jake's feigned casualness failed him. He stopped mid-chew, his head jerking erect and his eyes meeting Dak's. Dak smiled at Jake's astonishment.

"I didn't think we would try to leave so soon," said Jake after swallowing his food.

"I'm eager to finally return to my city and country. I had given up any hope of being able to return. Surely, you and your group must also wish for a speedy return?"

"We must have a solid plan before we begin," said Jake. "We must take into account that your people may not be as eager to let you go as you are to leave. There is also the real chance we could encounter one of the hostile tribes."

"Yes, I've been thinking of these things. Why don't you take the rest of the day to consider everything, and we'll get back together in the morning, share our thoughts, and finalize a plan."

Jake had more questions, but they would have to wait. He knew he had been dismissed. Dak remained seated as Jake left.

Once in the corridor, Jake struggled with his thoughts. Should he include Bannar when he briefed the others? Based on his demeanor, was Dak planning to take command of the escape? How would the group of soldiers Kathryn had apprised him of react when they moved away from the village? If there was an altercation with the soldiers, how would Bannar respond? What of the tribes below? All these concerns danced in Jake's head as he walked along. Any one of the complications could wreak havoc on the mission, but it was possible that they all could come to pass.

Chapter One Hundred

Hearing Jake talk of Dak's plan to leave in two days created an internal panic in Bannar. He forced himself to remain calm, but his mind raced. As soon as Jake's briefing was over, Bannar retired to his quarters.

What had he been thinking? He had allowed himself to get lulled by the situation. Believing Othan dead, he had convinced himself that joining the wizard's group would be the best way to fulfill his mandate. He had become comfortable in his situation. He had been taken in and treated well. While not welcomed as a trusted member of the group, no one had voiced opposition to his being there. He had known the day would come when he would have to separate himself, but that thought had slipped into the recesses of his mind.

Othan's reappearance had compelled Bannar to reassess his plans. This latest news had forced his hand. His first task was to bring Othan up to date. He wrapped and stored his sword and left his room. Finding the communal area empty, Bannar exited through the door and set out for Othan's camp.

ℰ ℰ

Kathryn had found a secluded space to hide under a hip-high shrub surrounded by thick vegetation. When she heard someone approaching the encampment, she eased herself forward. The man called Bannar entered the clearing. It was obvious he was the commanding officer. He and the other officer stepped away from the group, coming closer to her location. Some of what she overheard excited her while the other part was like an icy hand gripping her spine. Bannar had used the name of the Determiner. These were the troops of the sworn enemy of the Society of Builders, and Bannar was a high-ranking officer.

Without giving the other officer a chance to comment, Bannar dismissed him and left. It was apparent the other officer didn't appreciate how he was treated.

Kathryn was preparing to make her exit and share what she had heard with Gwynn. Before she could move, the officer stepped even closer to her location. There was no way she could leave without detection, so she settled to the ground and did everything she knew to control her breath.

₨ ₨

Moving out of sight and hearing of the others, Othan summoned the communiq. Lord Jamal came into focus.

"Did you see and hear what Bannar had to say?"

"Yes, Captain, I did. The next few days will go a long way toward determining our future, both yours and mine."

"Lord Jamal, what do you propose we do? Bannar is in direct communication with the Determiner and assumes that we will continue the mission as ordered."

"We cannot let it happen. We cannot allow Bannar to survive, and it is imperative that the wizard and his party not reach the gate and transition from this world."

"I understand," said Othan. "I will take great pleasure in personally killing Bannar."

"It must appear as if Bannar bungled his mission and was killed by the wizard. If possible, bring the Lokins boy back here. If that is not possible, make it look as if he and his group were overtaken by natives and killed."

"It will be done," said Othan ending his communication. He adjourned the communiq, turning to rejoin his troops.

ॐ   ॐ

Kathryn gave it a minute before slipping from under the shrub. Her feline instincts caused her to stretch her body before returning to Gwynn.

After giving Gwynn a summary of what she heard, they both decided to patrol the area for Jake. He needed these facts as soon as possible. Gwynn took to the air while Kathryn began a reconnoiter on the ground.

Chapter One Hundred One

The group decided they should go out as individuals into the village. Having always gone out alone, Bannar left first. Jake and the allies planned to reassemble in the wooded area of the jungle. Jake hoped Kathryn would join them.

As soon as they were back together, Elic professed a feeling of foreboding. Before leaving their quarters, Jake had summoned the staff and taken it with him. He hoped the Chroma people would not recognize it as a weapon. The staff had remained motionless during the walk, so Jake didn't feel any immediate danger. Before he could reply to Elic's sensitivity, Jake was startled when Gwynn descended and hovered behind the rest of the group. Seeing the surprise on Jake's face, Thomas turned to engage whatever foes he might encounter. Without any weapons, he assumed a crouched position with hands and arms at the ready. His semblance was not unlike that of a sumo wrestler. Recognizing Gwynn, he relaxed and turned back, almost kicking Kathryn in the process. He almost fell as he jumped to the side to avoid the big cat. Once everyone grasped the situation, all but Thomas chuckled in relief.

Jake perceived the danger of this meeting, especially if they were being spied upon. He ushered the group deeper into the jungle until he found a place where Gwynn and Kathryn could conceal their presence. Before taking cover, Gwynn ascended and flew in concentric circles. She felt sure they were alone and reported so to Jake.

Upon relaying the events she had observed and heard, Kathryn left the gathering along with Gwynn to resume their duties.

The allies looked from one to another and then back to Jake. Elic was clearly the most upset. His only other encounter with the forces of the Determiner had ended in disaster.

"I may kill that son of a dog myself," snarled Thomas taking some satisfaction in knowing that he had been right all along.

"Sounds like you have to get in line," prodded Raj.

"I'll be ahead of you in any line, little man," said Thomas and covered Raj's entire face with one of his massive hands.

Raj wrestled away. When free, he turned and spat into the trees as if he had been poisoned. Thomas laughed and slapped Raj gently on his back.

The mood lightened after the roughhousing. Even Elic's anxiety abated by a notch or two.

"It appears that we will face some challenges in the coming days," said Jake. "We do have the advantage of knowing who most of our adversaries are and something of their plans. What we don't know is the nature of Bannar's mission. We must assume that its intent is hostile toward us and the goals of the Society. The other wildcard is Dak. Are his only intentions the ones stated? How will another hostile force affect his plans? Finally, what of the other tribes of this world? We will surely pass through some of their territory on the way to the gate."

With so much to consider, they departed, each taking his own path. One thing puzzled and concerned Jake, but he was reluctant to verbalize it. The sorcerer Jamal could look through Othan's eyes and hear with Othan's ears. What kind of black magic might they be facing, and would he be strong enough to counter it? It was time for another talk with Dak. He didn't know how much he would share but felt that a more concise understanding of the escape plan would help him make some decisions. It could mean their survival.

Chapter One Hundred Two

Jake planned on taking some time to organize his thoughts before contacting Dak, but that was not to be. Once he was on the dwelling level of the canopy, he saw Dak and called to him. Dak turned and smiled.

"Just the man I'm looking for," said Dak. "I want to plan on leaving day after tomorrow in the early morning hours."

"We'll be ready," said Jake. "How do you plan to leave the village without being detected?"

"I thought you and your group could go ahead but wait for me along the path. If you have not been interfered with, I'll slip away before first light and join you. We'll proceed as fast as possible to our destination, and we will just disappear."

"And if we *are* interfered with?"

"If members of our tribe stop you, I'll appear not to be involved. I can favorably settle things once you are returned to the village. Then we will have to make another plan."

"What if we're accosted by another tribe?"

"If I am made aware of it, we will help. If I am not notified, I will see or hear it when I come to join you. I'll return to the village and bring help, but in all probability your fate will be sealed before I can get back."

"I understand," said Jake.

What he understood was that he and his allies were on their own. Dak had concocted a plan in which he couldn't lose. Jake knew he had to devise a plan of his own to level the playing field. Dak had said nothing about the soldiers Kathryn had described. Jake hoped he could find some way to use their presence in a favorable manner.

Without further comment, Dak turned and walked away. Jake would inform the others, and they would have some thinking to do.

Chapter One Hundred Three

Bannar made a decision. With a specific timeframe for their departure, he would need to separate himself from the wizard's group and resume his mandate. He knew he should tell Othan but was hesitant to do so. He planned to slip away late in the night before their departure, rouse Othan and the troops, and see the wizard safely to his destination. He would then return home and resume his normal duties.

₠₠

Jake was thinking of Bannar. Even with proof that he was an officer of an enemy force, Jake found it hard to feel any animosity toward him. It bothered him that Bannar would be betrayed by his second in command. Should he warn Bannar or just let the situation play out? He had to respect the anger displayed by his allies. He wished he knew more about this force and why they were so opposed to the goals of the Society. He was divided but in his heart Jake knew he could not let Bannar walk into a certain death.

Jake's opportunity came early in the afternoon. He was roaming the grounds in case Gwynn or Kathryn needed to speak with him. As he wandered into the jungle, he spotted Bannar sitting under a tree. Jake made enough noise to make Bannar aware of his presence. After Bannar looked his way, Jake approached the tree and took a seat. After some greetings, they both sat silently for a short while.

"Can we speak candidly to each other?" Jake asked.

"Of course," said Bannar without hesitation.

"First, let me say that I am aware of the small force camping a short distance from here," continued Jake. He felt Bannar stiffen and for an instant wished he had his staff. There was no option but to continue. "I also know something about where this force originated. I know of your status within the group. What I don't know is the prime purpose of the force and why you chose to come among us. I have felt neither danger nor animosity as a result of your presence." Jake paused.

Bannar turned so that he could make eye contact with Jake. "I am here to protect you."

It took only a few minutes for Bannar to reveal his assignment. As he did so, he felt he should be as truthful as his loyalty to the Determiner would allow.

"I don't fully understand the reasoning behind my being sent here, but as a soldier it is not my duty to question. My second in command is Othan, the man who now leads the troops you speak of. I assume he is here to assist me."

Jake observed Bannar for any signs of subterfuge. Finding none, he moved on.

"There is something else you should know," said Jake. Bannar looked on with interest. "Your man Othan is not here to assist you; he is here to kill you. Who is Jamal?"

Chapter One Hundred Four

Jake's asking about Jamal caused pieces to fall into place. Bannar was aware of rumors concerning Jamal's growing dissatisfaction with the rule of the Determiner. Until now, he had given the rumors only cursory thought. That anyone would challenge the authority of the Determiner was ludicrous. With what Jake had told him, he would have to reconsider the possibility that there was some truth to the stories. He also realized he would have to proceed in a new way.

As Bannar reflected on these matters, Jake waited patiently, neither inquiring nor offering anything further. Jake had been honest with him, and now it was his turn to return the favor. Bannar explained who Jamal was and shared the rumors of his subterfuge.

After Bannar finished his tale, Jake said, "That explains some things, but I don't see how I fit into any of this."

"That is also a mystery to me," said Bannar. "As a soldier I'm not asked to understand my orders, just to carry them out to the best of my abilities."

"What is your plan going forward?" asked Jake.

"I need to rejoin my troops. I can better control the situation if I am there. I don't know if I am meant to follow you from this world or return home after your transition. I would ask that I be able to retrieve my belongings."

"Of course, I'll get them now and return them here," said Jake as he turned to leave.

Bannar placed his hand on Jake's shoulder before he could walk away. "You have been very fair with me, and I would like to consider you a friend regardless of our differences. You will have nothing to fear from me. Have a safe transition, and I hope we will meet again."

Jake acknowledged what he had heard and agreed. Once Jake had disappeared into the jungle, Bannar called up his communiq and reached out to the Determiner. He relayed all that he had been told. He also had a new plan regarding how to proceed.

Bannar began his trek to the encampment where Othan and the others waited. He didn't notice the cat following him nor the flutter of wings overhead.

Nearing the encampment, Bannar took notice of the men securing the perimeter. Only then did he realize that the troops were made up of men whose first loyalty was probably to Othan and Jamal. Each man acknowledged him with a salute, but there was no respect behind it. He realized how far he had dropped his guard. When he entered the clearing, Othan was seated on the far side of the camp. Othan slowly stood and walked toward him. Bannar tried to appear casual. He was about to reach for Othan's hand when something hard connected with the side of his head and darkness engulfed him.

Chapter One Hundred Five

Jamal watched with satisfaction as Bannar was knocked unconscious and bound. He was pleased with the way Othan had handled his task from the picking of his troops to his being able to remain undetected since returning to the jungle world. Jamal had moved one of his chairs to the cauldron to be more comfortable as he watched his plan unfold. He could hardly wait for Bannar to regain consciousness. The look on his face when he realized he was no longer in charge would be priceless.

A knock came but he tried to ignore it. As it became more insistent, his anger increased. When he finally stood, he did so with such force that the chair almost overturned. He vowed to remember whoever was at his door so he could mete out the right punishment. When he opened the door, he found a lowly messenger facing him.

Jamal could not contain his anger. He backhanded the boy across his face, sending him to the floor.

"How dare you interrupt me, boy. I am in the middle of some serious business for the Lord Determiner."

The boy had risen to one knee. A thin stream of blood ran from his nose and already had begun to drip onto his shirt.

"Please, sir. It is the Lord High Determiner who wishes you presence." Having delivered his message, the boy rose and ran away before any more harm could befall him.

The boy was no more than eleven years of age. It was almost a shame, Jamal thought, that he would not live to see twelve.

Even though angered, Jamal knew not to keep the Determiner waiting. He took a quick look to ascertain that Bannar was still unconscious, donned his cap and robe, and started toward the Determiner's quarters.

He tried to quell his anger. He was not concerned that he had struck the messenger. After all, he was just a child and would probably not be returning to the Determiner's quarters. By the time he arrived at the Determiner's door, he had his emotions under control. Upon knocking, he was bidden to enter.

Stepping into the chambers, Jamal saw the Determiner sitting on his throne with a look of disgust on his face. Before he could wonder why, he was set upon by several of the guards. He felt something slip past his shoulders. It was immediately drawn tight, and his arms were clamped securely to his sides. He felt all his strength drain from him. As he slumped to the floor, he recognized his predicament. He had been secured with a leather noose at the end of a rope. The leather was lined with a thin band of silver and embossed with runes. Such a device had been used in earlier times to bind magicians and alchemists. The magic of the runes and silver together rendered him powerless. Jamal knew he was in dire jeopardy.

Chapter One Hundred Six

After Bannar was captured, Kathryn and Gwynn stayed long enough to be sure he was still alive. The fact that they bound and gagged him indicated that he was. They made their retreat.

"We need to let Jake know," said Kathryn.

"I'll fly overhead, find him, and get his attention. You are better able to remain concealed and watch."

Gwynn hovered, gained altitude, and was gone. Kathryn slipped into the underbrush. She watched Bannar being tied to a tree with his arms stretched behind him and his bound ankles staked to the ground. The soldiers milled about, talking and laughing, but Kathryn couldn't hear what they were saying.

Gwynn found Jake at the place where he and Bannar had last met. He had a satchel thrown over his shoulder. Seeing Gwynn, he placed the bag on the ground. The top fell open, revealing the hilt of a small sword. They moved further into the jungle where she talked about what they had observed.

"There is nothing we can do without jeopardizing our own objectives," said Jake. "He rejoined them knowing they meant him harm. Continue to watch them but do nothing to interfere. Once we move out of the village, you and Kathryn will rejoin us on the trail. If it looks as if the soldiers are going to move against us, let me know as soon as you can. I want to avoid any fighting if at all possible."

Gwynn resumed her surveillance, and Jake took some time to reflect. He knew that his decision was best for the continuance of their escape, but it was hard to abandon Bannar. He left the satchel and returned to the village.

If anyone noticed Bannar's absence, they made no comment. Since stealth would be so important, they reconfirmed the details of their escape plan. Nobody commented or posed any questions, so they adjourned, each one of them returning to his quarters to make final preparations. Jake was left alone in the common area.

Jake found himself getting restless. He paced the common area but couldn't shake a feeling of uncertainty. He decided to go back outside, try to find Gwynn, and check the posit.

The villagers had come to accept Jake as part of the ebb and flow of everyday life. Jake made his decent and moved into the jungle. He had the staff with him both for protection and reassurance. He returned to where he and Bannar had last spoken. The satchel was gone. He hoped against hope that Bannar had been able to retrieve it.

It didn't take Gwynn long to find him. She had not seen who removed the bag, but she assured Jake that it had not been Bannar.

Gwynn pulled up the posit, and together they checked the availability of the gate. They refigured the distance and confirmed that it would take two to three hours to reach. If things went right, they would be there just after first light.

Jake was startled when Gwynn suddenly took to the wing. She had taken the posit and was hovering above. Jake could hear someone or something approaching. He shifted the staff to a two-handed grip. If he had to use it, he would. It was too late in the plan to let an outside force interfere. After a tense moment, Kathryn came into the clearing. He relaxed the staff and Gwynn landed beside him.

"I just had to get out from under that bush," said Kathryn as she transitioned into human form. Jake still felt amazed by her ability to shapeshift. He also couldn't get over the fact that when she did she was totally nude. It didn't bother her, so he tried to conceal his unease. He must not have done a good job of hiding it because she had a mischievous smile on her face when she looked at him.

She solved the mystery of the satchel by telling them it had just been brought to the camp by a soldier who had stumbled upon it. She also had heard them speculate that departure must be soon since Bannar was packed for travel.

Jake was encouraged by the news that Bannar had not given up the timing of their departure. He hoped the man would not divulge that information to his captors.

The light was fading fast, so Gwynn and Kathryn resumed their duties and Jake returned to the canopy. He would be happy when all his allies were back together.

Chapter One Hundred Seven

S haddack Molen checked the contents of his rucksack. He had not used it in so long that he felt almost like a new recruit. His promotion to Minister of Arms had effectively taken him out of the field. Although his administrative duties kept him busy, he had refused to succumb to the siren song of ease and luxury. Every day he took time to maintain his fitness and keep his skills sharp. He felt satisfied that he was ready not only mentally but physically for his current assignment. He had to admit to a surge of excitement as he thought about the coming day.

After giving his weekly briefing, the Determiner had asked him to stay while the other ministers made their exit. The Determiner then dismissed the members of the Supreme Protectorate, leaving them alone. With its many turns, the story the Determiner related had both surprised and amazed him, but he was determined to keep a calm demeanor. That all of this could have taken place without his knowledge made him question the efficiency of his network of informants. He was given the specifics of his assignment and the package that he was meant to deliver and was dismissed. He had very little time to contemplate the assignment, so he set about his preparations. Within hours, he and the five Supreme Protectors he had chosen would be transported to some god-awful world with a specific task to accomplish. If all went well, he would be back home tomorrow night in time to sleep in his own bed.

Chapter One Hundred Eight

Bannar drifted in and out of consciousness but was trying not to let anyone know it until he could fully comprehend his predicament. It didn't work.

"Open your eyes, you old fool," said Othan. "Don't insult my intelligence by trying to maintain your ruse." To emphasize his words, he picked up a stone and threw it, striking Bannar on the shoulder.

Bannar opened his eyes and glared at Othan.

"Is this the way you display your honor as a soldier?"

"I am a soldier and a very capable one, just no longer under your command. Consider yourself an enemy combatant."

"Untie me, you cur, and I will consider letting you live."

"You are in no position to talk about letting me live, but since we are on that subject I will not consider letting you live. The question is how much you will have to endure before you die."

Bannar looked from man to man and then asked, "Are you all part of this mutiny?"

To answer, they all formed up behind Othan. Othan laughed and spit, the result landing on Bannar's leg.

"Not only are you a dead man but the wizard and all of his party will die as well. Your mission will end in total failure." Othan approached him and kicked him in the jaw. Once again his world faded to blackness.

Every time Bannar regained consciousness Othan would go into a rage. He would begin with more threats and then work himself into a fury by talking of every slight, both real and imagined. Finally, he would either strike or kick him again until Bannar passed out.

At first Bannar thought Jake might come to his rescue, but he finally had to admit the impossibility of that. Jake would not jeopardize his plan, nor should he. He had communicated with the Determiner, but the Determiner had no way of knowing of his capture. Soon he would have to accept his fate and reconcile himself to his own death, but not yet. If he could prolong things long enough, the group from the Society could make their escape. Although he would perish, his objective would be achieved. He only needed to last for one more day.

Chapter One Hundred Nine

Watching Bannar being beaten and tortured was painful for Kathryn. She had rarely seen a man filled with so much raw rage as Othan exhibited. She wished she could kill him but was under advisement to do nothing but observe. She vowed to herself that if a way presented itself after Jake and the others were well on their way, she would rip his throat out. A faint noise behind her brought her back into the moment. She froze and tried to make herself disappear into her surroundings. With her ears pricked, she soon recognized the flutter of wings and knew it was Gwynn. She carefully extracted herself and crept away from the encampment. She found Gwynn waiting.

"I talked to Jake this morning, and he wants me to check out the path between here and the gate ahead of tomorrow's departure. I should be back within the hour. I'll return here and get you so we can both bring him up to date when he meets with us. It will probably be the last time we have a chance to talk to him before tomorrow."

"Okay," said Kathryn. "By the way, you almost scared the shit out of me just now."

They shared a smile. Gwynn shrugged her shoulders, and they parted company.

∾   ∾

Minister Molen had been anxious before they transitioned but calmed down upon arrival. The feeling of adrenaline coursing through his body reminded him of the elation he had always felt with each new assignment. He would have to thank the Determiner for this opportunity when he got back. He had no time for further frivolous thoughts. He turned to check on his men and found all five Supreme Protectorate soldiers close by. He watched as they each checked their equipment. They had each been issued a sword, a long bow, and a quiver of arrows. In addition, they each had one of the new projectile throwers that was being developed by his armory strapped to their hip. He hoped they would not have to use them because the noise they made could alert others and complicate his mission. Everything being deemed ready, they set off single file on the short trek to their objective.

Kathryn settled back into the cover of the underbrush. She could not help but have pity for Bannar. She wondered how he could still be alive. One eye was completely closed, and the swelling threatened to do the same to the other eye. His face was a sick shade of purple and likewise swollen. His nose was broken in at least two places, and dried blood was crusted beneath it. He had no choice but to breathe through his mouth, which was a bloody mess. Blood covered his shirt front. His arms also had been beaten, but he probably couldn't feel it. His arms and legs had most likely lost all sensation long ago. He had taken most of the punishment without either crying out or begging for mercy. He should be dead, yet he lived.

The leader of his captors had given up using his fists after they started to swell. At first, he had ordered his men to take turns in the beating but finally had to resort to the shaft of a spear to continue. He had used the blade to score Bannar's skin in several places along his torso. They had tired during the night and took some time to rest. They now stood around the encampment, waiting to see if they were to continue or could finally put Bannar out of his misery. They talked and laughed, but Kathryn could not make out what was being said.

Kathryn's ears pricked up again as she thought she heard something from the other side of the camp, but none of the others seemed to have noticed. It was too soon for Gwynn to be back, so she drew herself further into cover just in case.

Kathryn had failed to look at Bannar after thinking she heard a noise. The movement of his head drew her attention. He appeared also to have heard something because he was trying to cry out, but his mouth would not cooperate. The leader of the soldiers also saw Bannar's movement. He rose, drew a short sword from his belt, and approached his captive.

"Well, Major, we've had about all the fun we have time for. Your time has finally arrived. We must go for the wizard now, so you must die. I wish I could say I'm sorry."

He had spoken so loudly that Kathryn heard every word. It sent a chill through her body. On some level, she knew her group would figure into their plans, but hearing it brought an immediacy to the situation. She alone would have to stop them. She knew she had the power and quickness to dispatch five humans, but could she do so unscathed? If she had to attack, she may as well do it now and perhaps avoid Bannar's death. She drew herself up and prepared to pounce. Bannar moved his head her way. She emitted a low growl as she was about to launch herself forward, but before she could leap, she heard a cry of pain.

℘   ℘

Molen had recognized the camp surroundings by the description the Determiner had elicited from Jamal. He halted his troops and crept forward to recon the site. What he saw made him sick and also infuriated him. He motioned to his troops, and they silently moved forward. When they were in position, he moved man to man, giving them their assignments. They each nocked an arrow and stood at the ready. When he gave the signal, they drew their bows taunt. At his next signal, they loosed their arrows, each finding his target. To a man, each of Othan's soldiers found themselves run through by an arrow with a twisted head. The spin of the arrows made sure no man could survive as it entered their chest and exited through their back, leaving a hole almost big enough to see through.

Othan turned to the noise made by the dying gasp of his troops. He saw five Supreme Protectors in full battle dress, each with an arrow pointed at his chest. Before he could speak, Minister of Arms Molen stepped into the clearing. He stared at Othan, turned his head toward Bannar, and then returned his gaze to Othan. Molen still had not spoken. He motioned to two of the protectors and indicated that they should free Bannar. As they removed Bannar's bindings, a third man joined them. He must have been a medic because he systematically began checking Bannar's condition.

"He is bruised and beaten, but he can travel," said the medic after his examination.

Othan knew his situation was dire. His only hope was that Jamal was watching this all unfold and would pull him from danger. This hope was soon dashed. The whole while Molen had been in the clearing, he had held a satchel by his side. Now, he opened it, changed his grip, and gave it a shake. Jamal's head hit the ground and rolled to a stop at Othan's feet. The bottom fell out of Othan's stomach. He was lost. He would probably spend the rest of his life in a dungeon. He was wrong. Minister Molen stepped closer. Still not having said a word to Othan, he drew his sword. Before Othan could flinch, Molen swung the blade in a high arc. Othan's head fell from his body and joined Jamal's on the ground.

"Get him ready to transport," he said to the three men still attending Bannar. They lifted him, each man supporting one side. Bannar raised his arm and brushed the medic's shoulder. When the medic turned, he pointed to a bag that leaned against a tree, his belongings. The medic retrieved the bag, and the whole group removed themselves from the encampment. Just at its edge, they all gathered. Minister Molen brought up his communiq, made some adjustments, and they all disappeared. The bodies and the heads remained in the clearing.

Chapter One Hundred Ten

The intensity of what she witnessed had frozen Kathryn in place. She had not seen the new group of soldiers arrive. Once she realized what was happening, she got as low to the ground as she could make herself. She felt as if she held her breath as she watched the whole scene. Something about the detachment of the man who had ordered everyone killed and then personally beheaded the leader, without a word, filled her with dread. Now, only six bodies and seven heads stood as testament to the transaction. She breathed an audible sigh of relief and slowly backed out of her cover. She had to find Jake—as soon as possible.

℥ Ω

One more day and then they could return to The Farm. That was his first thought as Jake came awake. He sat up on the side of his bed and smiled. He felt an overall sense of wellbeing. He dressed, retrieved the staff, and exited to the common area of their quarters. Raj, Elic, and Thomas were already there. On the table were a tray of berries and other fruits. A loaf of bread smelled as if it came fresh from the oven. A pot of what they used for butter and another one of puréed fruit stood on each side of the loaf. Jake could tell he was late to the party because only crumbs and a bit of crust remained from another loaf. Conversation was light, so Jake cut a generous portion of bread for himself as Elic put a cup in front of him and filled it with a hot beverage.

"Thank you," said Jake and took a healthy bite of his bread. It was delicious. He sipped from the steaming cup. He still didn't know what it was nor could he remember what Dak had called it, but it too was delicious. He was thinking that he would miss the taste of it when they left.

"Top of the morning to you, boss," said Raj. "I hope you are as optimistic as we are about tomorrow morning?"

"I was wondering if I was the only one feeling this way."

"We're all feeling it," said Thomas.

Jake looked at Elic. Although they were feeling good, Elic was the sensitive, and his opinion would carry the most weight.

"Everything seems to be good," said Elic. "Any reservations I had were gone this morning. I think we're ready."

They talked among themselves as they finished the meal.

"I had better go check with Gwynn and Kathryn and get our plan to rendezvous finalized," said Jake standing and reaching for the staff. "Finish packing and make sure your weapons are ready." They were all disbursing to their rooms as he walked outside.

The colors of his surroundings were vibrant. Each of the various shades of green of the leaves appeared to stand out. Through the canopy, he could see a cloudless azure sky. He knew that none of this had changed since they first arrived. He surmised his recognition of these things was an extension of his excitement and anticipation of leaving. As he walked to the point of descent, he decided not to over-analyze but to enjoy the feeling.

Chapter One Hundred Eleven

Dak stood at the edge of the encampment. He had been aware of the presence of these soldiers since they arrived but instructed his protectors to only observe. They had not maintained constant surveillance. Dak thought it was sufficient to check on them from the canopy several times a day. This morning his scout had found the carnage and reported to him. He had wanted to see it for himself. The arrows that had killed the soldiers were of a kind Dak had never seen. This led him to believe that another group of soldiers had come to this land intending to do this. Were they from this same group, another faction of Jake's group, or a different entity altogether? It also made him ask himself how many different entities processed the ability to move between worlds. The addition of an extra head led him to believe that either the attackers or the attacked has been a rogue faction from the same world. He ordered that any items still present be gathered and brought to him. He would return to the village and dispatch a group to clean up the bodies and take them to the boneyard.

Chapter One Hundred Twelve

Gwynn's feeling about tomorrow's plan was one of apprehension. She looked forward to returning to The Farm. On the other hand, there were a few complications. She had to trust Jake to make the right decisions. She pulled up the posit and rechecked the location of the gate.

She felt it was more important to move at a slow pace and be observant rather than fly flat out. That most tribes of this world lived in the canopy made stealth even more important.

She saw movement in the canopy only once, took evasive action, and left the path for the cover of the trees. She landed and traversed the next mile on foot, picking and eating some berries as she walked. After regaining the path, she took to the air. Nothing else out of the ordinary happened until she approached the location of the gate.

As she drew near the gate, she discovered a river. She had expected dense foliage. She landed, pulled up the posit, and confirmed her location. She was where she was supposed to be, but there was no sign of a body of water. By her calculations, the gate was situated on the other side a short distance into the jungle. She stood, making ready to approach the river when she heard voices coming from the other side.

She slipped behind a tree just in time to see a group of women and children emerge from the trees. The children never slowed down. They ran headlong into the water. The women stopped at the water's edge. They had brought some items to wash in the river. After taking care of their task, they too slipped into the water.

Gwynn continued to watch. There appeared to be a sharp drop off about a third of the way across.

Although she thought a village must be close by, she decided to check it out. She would have to follow the river until she felt she could cross without being observed.

Once she was a safe distance away, she took to the wing and flew across the water. On the other side, she landed and continued on foot. She took a diagonal path back toward where she had seen the women and children.

Through the trees, she saw structures. They were not as sophisticated as those in Dak's community, but they confirmed the presence of a village. She looked to the canopy but couldn't verify the existence of dwellings above. She thought it prudent to determine the size of the village and the nature of those living in it.

As she traversed the perimeter, she observed several groups of people, mostly women, involved in different tasks. About halfway around, she heard male voices coming from the forest. She ducked behind a tree to watch. There were fifteen young men in the group. Some were armed with bows and some carried spears. Each man had a long knife much like a machete hanging from the waist. This appeared to be a hunting party as they carried a boar-like animal suspended from a pole.

After they passed, she made her way around the rest of the village. It was smaller but very active. As she moved to return to the water's edge, she almost walked up on a sentry position manned by two warriors. They were the only two she had seen as she conducted her reconnaissance. They had been assigned to assure the safety of the women and children. That they needed guarding led her to believe this location was not as benign as it had first appeared. She moved away from the village.

When she was a safe distance away, she took to the air, flying along the course of the river. Soon, the mystery of the river was solved. These people were smart enough and industrious enough to dam and divert an entire waterway. The old riverbed had been planted in crops, and they had constructed a crude irrigation system.

She had seen plenty. Now it was time to get back and bring Jake up to date.

Chapter One Hundred Thirteen

Jake walked at a leisurely pace, admiring his surroundings. His feeling of euphoria had not diminished. As he entered the clearing, Kathryn was sitting on the benchlike log. She was in human form and dressed like the local women. Jake looked at her and thought what a beautiful human she was. It was hard to reconcile her present appearance with the total ruthlessness and violence she could manifest while in feline form. Neither his thoughts of Kathryn nor his euphoric state would last much longer.

The first indicator that something was amiss was that she failed to smile when she met his gaze. He had expected to see both Kathryn and Gwynn, so the first thing that crossed his mind was that something had happened to Gwynn.

"Is everything all right?" asked Jake. "Has something happened to Gwynn?"

"No, at least I don't know of anything. She should be back soon."

She motioned for him to take a seat beside her. After he complied, she told him in detail what she had witnessed. After she finished her report, he remained silent, thinking things over. He was relieved that Bannar had been rescued but troubled by the intense violence used to accomplish it. He wondered about the head in the satchel. What he thought about most was the rescuer's ability to transport and return without having to travel to a specific location.

"Take me to the encampment," said Jake. "I want to see what was left behind."

Kathryn stood, shed her clothes without a hint of modesty, and transitioned into feline form. Her nonchalance at being nude in his presence still startled Jake. It was almost harder to comprehend than seeing her change from human to cat. She started to walk away, paused, and looked back over her muscular shoulder. He stood and followed.

As they approached the encampment, Kathryn stopped short, waiting for Jake to come abreast. The site was a buzz of activity. Tribesmen were gathering the bodies of the soldiers. They carried them to the edge of the clearing where other warriors tied the dead onto long poles. When two bodies were ready to go, two men would hoist each pole to their shoulders and leave the camp. Each set of bodies was accompanied by four weapon-bearing warriors. Women of the tribe were gathering any belongings left behind. They were also turning the blood-soaked ground under.

Without thinking, Jake stepped into the clearing. He was recognized and a warrior moved into his path and held up his hands, palms forward.

"I don't think I would go any further," came Dak's voice from the canopy. Jake looked and saw him standing in the trees. Warriors stood on each side of him with arrows nocked.

"They take handling the dead seriously. No one outside the tribe is allowed. If you will come by my quarters later, I'll let you inspect the items that were salvaged."

"I'm sorry, Dak. I didn't realize I was intruding."

"Also, tell your cat and flying girl not to follow the processions."

"What do you make of the extra head?" Jake asked trying to hide his surprise.

"You'll be able to see both heads later. They will not be allowed in the boneyard. The heads must be burned. I will talk with you later."

Jake backed out of the clearing, only turning away from the warrior after he had rejoined Kathryn.

"That went well," Kathryn said. Jake only grunted.

His mind was racing. Dak knew of the presence of those soldiers all along. He also knew of Kathryn's survival and of her movements since rejoining the group. Gwynn had probably been under observation since they had been brought to the village. Jake realized he had grossly underestimated Dak's ability to stay abreast of what was happening in and around his village. Recent events and revelations had darkened his mood.

When they got back to the rendezvous point, Gwynn was waiting. She didn't have anything in the way of good news either. After she revealed what she had seen, the three of them sat in silence. Next, he brought Gwynn up to date concerning the happenings of the day and Dak's knowledge of her and Kathryn's status.

"Do you think we should join you and the others in the village?" asked Kathryn.

"No, I think it best if we remain separated until morning. With everything out in the open, Dak knows that I have not been completely honest with him. The best thing we have going for us is that he believes we are his only way back to his previous life."

Gwynn leaned into Jake and whispered, "Are we really going to take him with us?"

"I don't know. We may have to and deal with the fallout on the other side," he whispered his answer, being hyper-aware that they were probably under observation. "If anything changes, I'll try to let you know. Otherwise, follow the plan as we have laid it out."

He stood and without thinking looked to the canopy. "Watch each other's backs. I don't want any more complications."

As he walked back to the village, he replayed everything he had learned. He was not looking forward to telling the others. He also thought of the Determiner's soldiers being able to transport from any point without having to find a gate. That would come in handy now, considering Gwynn's discovery. Why couldn't things be simple just once?

Chapter One Hundred Fourteen

Upon his return from the encampment, Dak posted two guards at the door. He gave them instructions not to allow anyone past except for those bringing more the items from the site. One by one they came until all items were safely in his possession. There were five bundles. He then instructed the guards that if Jake came to have him wait. He wanted to cull the bundles before giving Jake a look. He opened the first and pulled one item at a time from it. There were mostly articles of clothing. He created a pile and haphazardly stacked the clothes to be burned later. The second was similar, but at the bottom were two daggers, each with a blade seven inches long. He sat those aside. He would take them with him. They may have some value on the other side. The next two bags contained nothing of value or significance. The final bundle must have belonged to the leader of the original expedition. There was writing on parchment like paper. None of the text was decipherable. He decided to set that aside in hopes Jake could read it. All the way at the bottom, he found what he was looking for. The device was surprisingly light and seemed to vibrate as he held it. It was a simple looking apparatus. There were no visible moving parts. He touched the screen, and it briefly came to life. There were symbols, again unreadable. He proceeded to touch each symbol with no results. He flipped it over but saw nothing useful on the back. When he rotated it back to its right side, one of the icons was blinking incessantly. When he touched it, it emitted a series of three shrill beeps followed by a longer whine and then went blank. He tried it again with no result. Frustrated, he banged his fist on the arm of the chair. After taking a few minutes to calm down, he went to his door.

"Go find the chief of the outsiders and bring him here," said Dak addressing two of his guards. Upon finding the device, he had thought of not sharing the knowledge of it with Jake. He had realized the probable use of the unit and thought that with it he could facilitate his own transport back to Denmark. Not being able to activate the device, now he hoped Jake would have some knowledge of how it worked. He could keep possession; after all, he was in charge. He settled back to wait for Jake.

"I believe you have something that belongs with me," came a voice from behind him.

Dak spun on his heels at the sound of a voice. It did not compute in his mind. There was no way in except to go past his guards. He was faced by an immense man. The intruder stood behind him as nonchalantly as if he had been invited. He towered over Dak and looked as solid as a tree. Judging by his dress, he was a soldier.

Since Dak had set the device aside, the man could not have seen it.

"What are you doing here?" Dak asked with all the bravado he could muster. "I'll have you thrown into captivity or feed you to another tribe."

The man's laugh was casual but could never be mistaken as affable. "Let's not dance about. The communiq has signaled its whereabouts, and I am here to retrieve it. I was hoping to do so with no problems."

Dak was not used to being on the short end of any transaction. He also did not like to feel like he was taking orders, but he was at a definite disadvantage. He reached down into his seat to retrieve the communiq. When he did so, his hand fell on one of the two daggers. The soldier was waiting, not having moved since he had first spoken. Dak slipped the dagger under the device, hoping that it was hidden from sight. He raised the device, relieved that the dagger could not be seen. Holding it with both hands, he made to move around the chair. Once he cleared the chair, he adjusted his hand to better grip the knife. He closed the distance between them. At what he thought was the optimum time, he let go of the communiq, took the knife in an underhand grip, and charged the soldier. Instead of dropping to the floor, the communiq stayed suspended in front of him. He bumped into it, giving the soldier enough time to draw a short sword. Dak realized his mistake, saw the sword move, and waited to feel the blade slip into his body. It never came. Instead, the soldier swung the sword and struck Dak on the side of his head with the flat side of the blade. Light burst in Dak's head, and he felt his legs giving way, but he was alive. He fell to the floor, stunned but not unconscious.

Shaddack Molen looked down at the man on the floor. He was moving. Molen was relieved. He was not opposed to killing, had done it hundreds of times, but saw no need for it here. He had already taken control of the communiq as the man approached him, so leaving it suspended had been an easy task. It may have saved his life; it certainly saved the other man's. He stepped forward and took the communiq in hand. It should have never been there. Othan or Jamal had taken it from the armory, but he, Molen, should have been more thorough and found it before returning home. All would be well when he returned with it. He held it with both hands, making ready to transport.

Dak was still on the floor but had gathered himself. The dagger had fallen beneath him. He felt it pressed between his body and the floor. The soldier was not paying any attention to him. He did not want to lose possession of the device. The soldier had returned his sword to its sheath and gripped the device with both hands. He was saying something, but Dak couldn't understand the words. He slipped his hand underneath his body and found the grip of the knife. He pulled his legs under him. He still had not been noticed. He took a deep breath and lunged, grabbing the soldier's legs. They both disappeared from the room.

Chapter One Hundred Fifteen

The events Jake reported to his allies had put a damper on everyone's mood. He could hardly remember the elation of the morning. As Jake finished bringing the others up to date, he was summoned to the door by an insistent knock. He was not surprised to be invited to Dak's quarters. He knew they would have to talk before morning. He just hoped their plans were still on go.

As he followed the guard, Jake replayed what Dak had said from the canopy, looking for clues as to how to respond if questioned. He decided to be as honest as he could without compromising Society protocol. Of course, he had hedged his bets by telling the others that if he did not return within a reasonable time frame, to leave the village and join with Kathryn and Gwynn. The staff, which he now took everywhere, gave him a feeling of security. He would use it if necessary, although that would mean having to take on the whole village.

He had been concentrating so hard that he almost ran him over the guard when they stopped at Dak's door. The guard knocked. On previous visits, Dak would bid him enter but no response came. Another knock still brought no response. Jake's escort turned to the other guards and asked something that Jake could not understand. They shook their heads from side to side. One more knock brought the same result. Their leader opened the door, which had not been locked, and stepped inside. Jake followed him with the rest of the contingent. The guards searched room to room and called to Dak while Jake waited in the main room. His eyes fell on a dagger in the seat normally occupied by Dak. He looked around and, finding himself still alone, picked it up and hid it in his clothing. A guard came back into the room and walked behind the sitting area. He bent, picked up a dagger just like the one Jake had concealed, and called to the others. They all concentrated their attention on the area where the dagger had been found. Jake walked around to see what they were looking at. One drop of blood was on the floor. They spoke excitingly and left the room. Jake thought that in their excitement they had forgotten he was there until he heard the lock engage on the door. He hoped he was being detained to contain the knowledge of Dak's disappearance. With the staff, he could escape any time he liked. He would not be hasty. He still had lots of time before his failsafe plan launched into action. He would see where all this went. He spotted the bundles of articles left behind from the encampment. He would go through those while he waited, but first he would use this opportunity to look around Dak's quarters.

He didn't want to disrupt things in the quarters just in case Dak had taken a walk about and would soon return. He moved from room to room, opening drawers and looking in closets, taking care not to disturb anything. The only thing he found of interest was a prepacked bag in one of the closets. Jake felt sure these were the items Dak planned to take with him tomorrow morning.

Chapter One Hundred Sixteen

Molen kicked the man who was clinging to his legs. The man rolled over onto his back and started to get up. Molen put a boot on his chest and pushed him back to the floor. How had this happened? In his entire career, he had never had a mishap during a transport, especially one where an unwanted human was involved. The time of the two coming together must have been perfect. What to do now? He instinctively drew his sword. The man cowered and held out his hands in the universal sign for halt. For some reason, Molen stopped.

Molen removed his boot and motioned for Dak to stand. They were standing in Jamal's quarters. Both men surveyed their surroundings. Molen motioned to a chair and Dak sat.

"Where are we?" Dak asked.

"I am home, and you are somewhere you should not be."

Dak was about to inquire further when the door to the chambers burst open. Two heavily armed guards entered the room followed by a man in splendid dress. Molen dropped to his knee but still pointed his sword in Dak's direction. Dak slipped from the chair and assumed a posture fashioned after Molen's.

The man stared intently at Dak before turning to Molen and asking, "Would you like to explain, Minister Molen?"

"I wish I could, my lord. I retrieved the communiq, and we had a brief struggle. When I was clear, I transported, and when I arrived he was clinging to my legs. I will take care of this problem immediately," said Molen brandishing the sword in Dak's direction.

Dak sensed that if he did not act his death was imminent. He stood and faced the man Molen had called my lord, fully expecting to be run through. He bowed from the waist and asked, "May I speak?"

The Determiner looked at the man. After a moment, he gave a signal to continue.

"My lord," he began. "I must beg your pardon in being here. I am the chief of my tribe on my world. I was transported there many years ago and stranded. Through providence, I survived and even prospered, but I have always wanted to return home. Just recently, I encountered a man also able to move from place to place. I planned to leave with him and his group tomorrow. The circumstances of the battle between Minister Molen's and the forces already in my home led me to believe that you also possessed the ability to move between worlds. After the battle, I found the device that Minister Molen was sent to retrieve. I thought I might be able to transport without depending on the man I mentioned earlier."

The Determiner turned and moved to the door. He turned to Molen and said, "Minister, thank you for taking care of two problems for me. I am grateful and you will be rewarded. We'll speak later." He opened the door and stepped aside so that Molen could exit. To two of the guards he said, "Bring this man to my quarters." With that, he left. The two guards moved to Dak. Each took an arm and led him through the door.

Dak looked around as he was walked through the corridors of the keep. Compared to the vibrant colors of the forest in which he lived, this place seemed bleak. He wondered if he would ever be able to step back into the forest.

Chapter One Hundred Seventeen

Jake estimated that he had been locked in Dak's quarters for approximately two hours. The time passed rather quickly as he explored the premises. He was careful not to disturb anything. He took a mental picture of how things were arranged and replaced everything to its previous position. He found no surprises. Dak appeared to live a rather simple existence given his position in the tribe. He found no evidence to indicate a deception on Dak's part. Back in the seating area, he started looking through the salvage from the encampment.

As he worked through the bundles, he began to plan his escape. He would have to make a move soon or his contingent plan would kick into action. It had seemed to be a good plan when he made it, but now he worried the natives would assume his allies were responsible for Dak's disappearance if they left the village. The chaos and bloodshed that might follow was not something he wished on his group or the villagers. These people had rescued his group and treated them with respect. He wished them no harm. If he had to blast the door to gain his freedom, confrontation would be immediate and full on.

As he considered his options, he gripped the staff and rolled it about in his fingers. When the sound of something falling on the floor behind him came, he jumped to his feet, turned his body toward the noise, and brought the staff to bear, ready to fire.

Dak rose from the floor, brushed himself off, and said, "You, my friend, are a very important person."

Chapter One Hundred Eighteen

Jake was more surprised than elated to see Dak. He wanted to ask what happened to him but had to curb his questions.

"We have to let your people know you are here. They've been searching for quite a while. They've kept me locked in here since my arrival. I don't know if my people are involved in the search or locked in their quarters. Could we check before talking further?"

Without speaking, Dak opened the door and called to the guards. The guards stood in open mouthed surprise. Dak said something to the guards, and they dispersed, probably to call off the search. They had neither asked for nor received any explanation.

Dak turned to Jake and said, "Come. I'll walk with you to your rooms."

Together, they walked down the corridor to Jake's quarters. The people of the tribe stopped what they were doing but nobody spoke. Once they were clear, the people of the village fell in behind them and followed at a distance. At the end of the corridor, Jake looked down through the trees. He saw that the ground was filled with tribesmen and women. Even with those numbers, it was eerily quiet. Dak was also aware of the phenomenon. Before reaching Jake's quarters, they stopped, and Dak addressed the people. Although Jake could not comprehend what was said, he understood that Dak was telling them that all was well. The crowd sent up a cheer and began to disburse. Jake was relieved and doubly so when he opened the door and found Elic, Thomas, and Raj waiting.

"We may as well all speak," said Dak. "I think you will agree that what I have to tell affects everyone."

The allies looked to Jake.

Addressing Dak, Jake said, "I've already brought them up to date concerning everything up to your disappearance."

Without preamble, Dak asked, "What do you know of the Determiner and the realm in which he lives?"

Elic slipped forward on his seat and, out of reflex, formed a fist. He felt his nails dig into his hand, and he broke into a cold sweat. Jake looked from man to man and had no doubt that all were aware of the sworn enemy of the Society of Builders.

As Dak recounted the events of the last few hours, no one appeared to relax. Jake had to admit that he was as perplexed by what he was hearing as anyone in the room. That Dak had been transported to and from the realm of the Determiner was amazing. After what Elic had described of his experience against the forces of the Determiner and the ruthlessness with which the soldiers of the encampment had been dispatched, Dak's survival seemed miraculous.

"He told me it was imperative that you, Jake, and the others be returned to your world unhurt," Dak continued. "I was allowed to return here because he thought I could facilitate that. If you are successful, I will also be returned to my original home, but if anything happens to you…" Dak paused. "If anything happens to you, he guaranteed that I and all of my tribe would not live to see another day."

When he finished, Dak took a seat. He sat as if a weight had pulled him onto the cushion. Most of his confidence and composure had abandoned him.

Jake looked from man to man and saw the same expression on each of their faces. No one, including himself, believed that this village would survive regardless of the success of them safely leaving.

Dak stood to leave. Jake followed him through the door. Once outside, Jake stopped and moved to the railing. "There is one more problem," Jake said when Dak joined him. There was no reason to hold back. "Our device is not like that used by the Determiner's people. We cannot transport from anywhere. There are a series of gates between the worlds, and we have to access one of those. The problem is that a tribe of people have moved their village around the gate we must use. It may complicate our leaving. If we are successful, we will not be returned to the world you and I are from. We will transition to the world where my group is stationed. I will try to get you home from there. You may be better off with the Determiner's device if you can trust them."

"It appears we have some things to work out before we can even try to leave," said Dak. "I don't believe we can handle all of those things before morning. We will have to delay."

Jake nodded in agreement.

Chapter One Hundred Nineteen

Jake saw the wisdom in delaying but hated to tell everyone. They were all disappointed but felt that the extra time was prudent.

Next, he had to tell Gwynn and Kathryn. They too were disappointed but took it as "the way it was."

"How does Dak propose to help with the gate obstruction?" asked Gwynn.

"We haven't discussed it yet, but I don't see any other way than visiting the village. I hope we will finalize a plan tonight. In the meantime, if you want to come to our village, it may be easier. I don't think there is any danger from the villagers or the Determiner, but their ability to transport to specific locations troubles me. I think I would feel better if we were all together."

After they followed Jake back to the village, everyone was happy to be reunited. Kathryn and Gwynn would share the room that had been occupied by Bannar. They complained in a joking way and then went to set up their chamber.

For the first time since their rescue, they all gathered to enjoy a meal together. There was a lot of banter, and everyone laughed at any joke made whether it was really funny or not. The relief everyone felt at being back together was palpable.

Jake expected to be summoned to Dak's quarters, but the invitation was never issued. As the time for retiring for the evening approached, Jake called everyone together.

"I thought I would be in on the planning regarding how to handle the situation with the gate. I may still be, but I can't be sure. The only thing I am sure of is that it is time to go. I propose that we don't wait for Dak to solve the problem. We will give it one more day, and if nothing has been settled, we will leave. We will have to trust that we can transition safely."

Gwynn spoke up, "I believe we can do it under the cover of darkness. We don't know what we will face if we try to gain cooperation with the other village. In the best case, we would have to make them aware of our portal and the ability to use it."

"The more people who know, the more opportunity for mishap or mischief," said Elic.

"There's a chance it could go badly. I would rather try to sneak out than fight our way out," added Thomas.

Neither Raj nor Kathryn had anything to add, but it was obvious by their demeanor they concurred with the wisdom of stealth over possible confrontation.

"Let's get some rest," said Jake. "I may want to see the location of the gate for myself tomorrow."

With that, they all retired.

Chapter One Hundred Twenty

The Determiner paced back and forth across his quarters. He was waiting for Bannar to join him. Upon Bannar's arrival, the Determiner was taken aback by his appearance. His face was a patchwork of black and blue. If they were not already dead, he would have personally killed all those responsible.

"My God, man, they told me you had been beaten, but I had no idea how badly."

"Thank you for coming for me. I am healing well. I am ready whenever you need me."

"That would be now, Major. This situation with Jamal and his traitorous cohorts has served to remind me what can happen if I am not vigilant and keep all loose ends tidied up. I feel that we have left too many loose ends behind."

"I am sorry, my lord," said Bannar wondering where this was going.

"I want you to return to that world, rejoin the Lokins boy, and resume your mission. I will send Minister Molen and some men back to tie up loose ends. See that nothing happens to the boy."

Bannar had never seen the Determiner like this. His attitude toward members of the Society of Builders had always been to eliminate them to the man. There was something happening here, but Bannar thought it imprudent to question.

"I will have everything sent to your quarters," continued the Determiner. "I want you to leave as soon as possible. It is imperative that you rejoin the wizard before they attempt to transition."

"Yes, my Lord," said Bannar bowing before his exit. As he was leaving, he passed Minister Molen in the corridor. They acknowledged each other in passing, each wanting to speak to the other but deciding against it.

Molen entered the Determiner's quarters and found him sitting at one end of a long table. He was motioned to take the seat to the left of the Determiner.

Without preamble, the Determiner said, "I want you to take some men, return to the jungle, and clean up the mess. There are too many people who think they know too much of our business. I want them gone. The wizard and his group are not to be harmed, but everyone and everything else is expendable. You will leave tonight. Major Bannar will be there also, but he is not part of your mission. Do you understand what I'm saying?"

"Yes, my lord," said Molen, and he did. They were to scorch the ground under anyone who either posed a danger to the larger mission or got in the way.

Chapter One Hundred Twenty-One

As he awoke, Jake knew it was early. The morning light never quite penetrated the thick canopy, but now it was not even evident. His sleep had been fitful, and he had a feeling of dread. Everything was out of control. Sometime during the night, he made the decision to reconnoiter the village at the gate.

He fixed himself a hot beverage and let some time pass. There were no sounds of activity from any of the living quarters. Growing impatient, he knocked at Gwynn and Kathryn's door. When it opened, Kathryn stood there with only a flimsy garment to cover her.

Trying not to stare, Jake asked, "Is Gwynn available?"

"I'll ask her," said Kathryn with a mischievous smile. Kathryn's nakedness always made him feel like a schoolboy seeing his first flash of female flesh.

He returned to the common area and used the time to make some notes for the others. Gwynn took several minutes before joining him. She was fully clothed when she walked into the common area and took the seat opposite him.

"I would like for us to go to the gate so I can see it for myself."

Gwynn asked, "When would you like to leave?"

"As soon as we can be ready."

"Give me a few minutes to get prepared."

Jake agreed and retrieved the staff while he waited. Kathryn entered the room wearing a robe.

"I overheard your conversation," she said. "Would you like me to go also?"

"I think it would be better if you stayed here," he said and handed her his note. "I want you to be sure everyone sees this and understands. It may also be a good idea for you to keep a watch outside."

Before he could say any more, Gwynn came back into the room. She was dressed to be able to fly. When Jake looked back at Kathryn, she had shifted into her feline form.

"I'll take a look around before you leave," said Kathryn and slipped out the door.

Jake and Gwynn waited a few minutes. Outside, everything was quiet. Jake knew there were sentries, but they were predominately posted along the perimeter of the village.

When they reached ground level, Kathryn slipped from the underbrush and gave them an "all clear."

Gwynn took flight and hovered overhead, waiting to lead Jake out of the village. As they moved away from the village, Gwynn would indicate the path that would lead Jake away without having to encounter any of the sentries. Once clear, they made good time. Almost at their destination, Gwynn landed just ahead of Jake.

"Something's wrong," she said without preamble. "I went to the river's edge and could detect no movement. Every other time I've been here there have been people at the river and guards posted close by. There is also a foul smell."

They both raced forward on foot. Gwynn led Jake to a place where they could ford the river. Once they reached the other side their anxiety increased. The foul odor they had smelled at the river became worse and soon revealed itself as the smell of death. Gwynn drew her short sword and took to the wing. Jake readied his staff. He stepped into the village. The scene was both horrifying and mesmerizing. Bodies were strewn everywhere. It was a massacre. Someone had made a thorough job of killing everyone in the village without regard for gender or age. Gwynn landed beside him.

"I don't detect any movement in or around the village."

"We need to do a hut-by-hut search just in case," Jake said with an obvious edge to his voice.

"What is it?" Gwynn asked.

"Dak told me he would handle the situation with this village, and we would have no trouble accessing the gate. I wonder if this is his work. If so, I will deal with him when we get back to the village."

Gwynn made no reply as it seemed none was needed. Together they started their search. Most huts were empty, but a few held bodies, most of the aged and infirm. In one hut, he found a group of bodies, maybe five, that had been stacked atop each other. When he turned to leave, he heard a faint cry and stopped to listen. He heard it again. He moved to the stack of bodies while Gwynn stood guard against any threat. What he found was the last thing Jake could have imagined: Michael McAfee, badly wounded and dying. Jake could not understand how he was still alive. Jake wanted to question him about what had happened and how they came to be in this village, but the question that was paramount was where was his mother?

"She transported without being harmed," Michael said before Jake could ask the question.

There was so much Jake wanted and needed to know, but time was short. By the extent of Michael's wounds, Jake knew he couldn't last much longer. There was nothing Jake could do for him.

"What happened here?"

"We came looking for you. Your mother never stopped trying to find you. Just after we got here, we were taken captive. Even with that, she held out hope that we could somehow attract your attention. We came through the gate that she knew you would most likely be using to escape this world."

A cough wracked Michael. Jake could see the blood in his mouth and a drop ran from each nostril.

Michael rolled his head to the side and spat. Blood was coming faster now. He tried to continue.

"They came this morning. I tried to transport both of us, but the assault was too heavy. I had to fight so she could escape."

"I can try to get you out of here," Jake said.

"We both know I will never make it back." He looked at Jake and then his eyes shifted. Jake had not sensed Gwynn come up behind him. Jake looked at her and saw an expression of both sorrow and resolve.

"Give me the honor of death without further suffering."

Michael closed his eyes as Jake lowered his head to the floor of the hut. Jake stood, backed away to the door, and with Gwynn looking on raised his staff and pointed the end at Michael. Jake could not tell if he was alive or already dead. He pushed the tip of the shaft forward and lightning erupted, blasting Michael into oblivion.

"Nah moam arthic. Neh joam articam. Mehhan shoa Michael McAfee, mehan shoa abot."

"Mehan shoa abot," repeated Gwynn.

Jake let out a roar that was almost deafening. It startled Gwynn so much that she jumped away from him and brandished her sword.

"I'll kill that son of a bitch," Jake yelled. He brushed past Gwynn and stood in front of the hut. He started walking, bringing his staff to bear as he passed the carnage. Without a word, he blasted every hut and every dead body he passed. By the time they reached the river, there was nothing behind them but barren ground.

Chapter One Hundred Twenty-Two

Minister Molen was the first to transport. His men would follow, transporting to the site that had been used by Othan. There they would rendezvous with Molen and complete their mission. He was being deployed with twenty of the best troops available. Only the Determiner's personal guards were better.

Molen arrived in Dak's quarters to find them vacant. He did a quick reconnaissance to be certain he was alone. Once satisfied, he took up a position out of the line of sight of the door. He didn't have long to wait.

Dak came in accompanied by the two guards who had been on watch outside. Once inside, they did a visual scan of the immediate area before resuming their position outside.

Dak poured himself a drink, took a sip, and turned back to the room. Molen was standing an arms-length away. In his alarm, Dak inhaled sharply, causing the liquid to be sucked down his throat, choking him. He went into a coughing fit, dropped the cup, staggered to his left, and stumbled into a table. Everything on it crashed to the floor. Despite still coughing and falling, he let out a yell.

Molen had held hope that his business could be completed without complications, but that was not going to be possible. He heard the guards and knew it would not be long before they were in the room. Still choked and coughing, Dak he did not see Molen draw his sword. With practiced deftness, he sent the blade of his sword through Dak's neck and upward into his brain, causing instant death. He was still in the act of retrieving his blade when the door exploded inward. The guards' eyes fell on Dak, then quickly turned to Molen. They fanned out. Both were armed with a spear. The shafts were approximately six and a half feet long. The spearheads were wider than most, double edged, and looked razor sharp. Molen noticed the braided material that adorned each one at the midway point. He thought it to be ornamental until he saw each man snap the shaft of the spear at about four feet, lace the braid around the following wrist, and pull it tight. Molen was not overly concerned when he originally thought of the warriors wielding the long spears in the tight quarters, but now it was a different matter. These were well-trained men, experts in tactics and the use of their weapons. That the weapons could be adapted to the conditions in which they were being used spoke of intelligence and experience in their development. All these thoughts came to him instantly. Molen also knew that if he were to survive, he would have to do something out of the ordinary.

During his earlier search, he had observed a lantern-like light fixture. He crouched, grabbed Dak's body, and backed toward the wall. This would keep the action in front of him. The warriors continued to advance but at a slower pace. Molen's sword was at the ready. When he sensed the wall behind him, he lowered his sword. The warriors were almost within the range of their weapons. He saw a look pass between them and knew that attack was imminent. He would have to take a chance that would either provide an opportunity to even the odds or signal his death. He exploded out of the crouch with a deafening roar. Next, he swept his sword from left to right. At the end of the sword's arc, he feigned a stumble, turned, and grabbed the lantern. His hand was instantly singed, but he did not lose his grip. All his movement had taken him closer to the man approaching from his right. He tossed the lantern and swept his sword to the left. As he hoped, his blade smashed into the globe and shattered it, showering Dak's body with accelerant. The body and the area around it burst into flames. The eyes of the man on the right went to the burning body; that was his undoing. Molen's blade swept across the man's midsection, easily penetrating his thin garment and tearing into his abdominal cavity. The man hardly had time to recognize his predicament before Molen reversed the direction of his blade and took the man under his chin. The warrior's blood and viscera pooled across the floor as his body dropped.

Molen moved quickly into the hallway. With Dak's burning body and the eviscerated warrior between him and the other warrior, he bought some time. He thought the tighter quarters of the hallway would limit the scope of the spear turned battle-axe. The warrior grasped the limitations of the situation. He probably also thought of the consequences of overseeing Dak's safety and failing miserably. In any case, he hesitated at the entrance of the hallway, pulled the spear against his chest, and charged ahead. He came with such fury that Molen hardly had time to react. The man was on him before he could ready his sword. The best he could do was try to turn away from the blade. As he did so, he felt the blade slice between his upper arm and the side of his chest. He was knocked off balance and fell to the floor. The warrior's forward momentum took his upper body onward while his feet slammed into Molen and stopped. The man fell face first to the floor and lay still. Every ounce of energy drained from Molen, and he just lay there, immobile and breathing heavily but at least alive. He could hear chaos coming from outside. He didn't know if the commotion was being caused by his soldiers or if someone had noticed the smoke. He raised his head, saw that the fire was growing, and knew he had to get out. He pushed the legs of the dead warrior to the side of him. He blessed his good luck as he saw the tip of the spear sticking out of the man's back. So many battles are won by the fortune of the moment.

He crawled along the floor, hoping to reach the door before the smoke could do what two elite warriors could not. His right arm was useless, and he felt the steady flow of blood running from both wounds. He did not believe the wound to be life threatening if he did not bleed out. He had to rejoin his men.

Chapter One Hundred Twenty-Three

Bannar transported himself to the edge of the village close to where he had last seen Jake. He was not surprised to find it empty. He thought it best to speak with Jake alone, to make his intentions clear. He found a place where he could observe their quarters without being detected. After a few hours, he still hadn't seen any of the group. He began to wonder if they had already left. The smell of smoke did not alarm him until the sound of voices increased in volume, and in panic he moved to investigate.

The smell of smoke became more prevalent. Trying to stay concealed, he moved toward the source. Even before he could see, he knew that the fire was in Dak's quarters. The level of noise foretold of the chaos. He knew he could not afford to be seen. He dropped into a crouch with the intention of going deeper into the trees and waiting for things to settle. He moved diagonally, dividing his attention between the village and his path to escape.

The moan was faint, but Bannar heard it. He tried to ignore it but it came again. He decided to find the source.

Molen was lying on his side, bleeding from two wounds that appeared to have been delivered by a single thrust. He must have lost a lot of blood and had become too weak to continue. Casting caution to the wind, Bannar ran to Molen and pulled him into the forest. Molen's eyes came open. He recognized his rescuer. Being the good soldier, he did not utter a sound although the pain of his rescue must have been intense. Once he was in a safe enough area, Bannar stopped to examine Molen's wounds. Molen had passed out but when Bannar touched the shoulder he came awake with a start.

"I'm going to have to transport you from here. I don't think we'll make it back to camp," said Bannar.

Molen nodded his ascent. "Major, you will have to combine your mission with mine. The threat to our security has been eliminated."

Molen's eyes started to drift. He was losing consciousness. Without any further delay, Bannar called up the communiq and transported Molen. He couldn't say if the minister was dead or alive.

The next order of business would be to assume command of the contingent of soldiers that had accompanied Molen. He would need to hurry as he did not want to miss Jake.

Chapter One Hundred Twenty-Four

After crossing the river, Jake took off at a run. He was hell bent on getting back to the village. On a visceral level, he wanted to blast Dak and anyone who got in his way into oblivion. After running for about a half mile, reason returned to him. He pulled up. Gwynn landed by his side. Jake placed his hands on his knees and spat onto the ground. She gave him a minute to gather himself.

"Jake, at least you know that your mother got away. Maybe she'll be waiting when we get back to The Farm."

"I just want to make some sense of all this. People keep dying, and I'm not sure if I should even be here or not."

"After what we've been through, I think you know you are where you were destined to be. I...we have faith in you. We had to wait until the time came for you to join us. We knew about you a long time before you knew about us. You were always meant to lead us."

Hands still on his knees, Jake turned to look at Gwynn. How could she be so calm? She was always by his side when he needed her. He tried to muster a smile. He straightened, returned the staff to a vertical position, and started down the path. Gwynn rose to resume her flight.

They had traveled about a mile when Jake heard a crashing through the jungle to his right. He turned and pointed the tip of the staff toward the commotion. Gwynn called his name from above just as he readied to fire. A large black feline burst from the undergrowth. From the look of her coat, Kathryn had run at top speed for an extended period.

Chapter One Hundred Twenty-Five

Bannar knew that time was of the essence. He needed to rendezvous with Molen's troops. He also knew that danger was ever present. The going was slow. There were tribesmen everywhere. The entire village must be aware of what had transpired in Dak's quarters. Now they found themselves not only fighting fire to save their homes but looking for the murderer of their leader. The implications of the general panic were clear: anyone caught would be assumed guilty and killed immediately.

The closer he got to the encampment, the greater his sense of doom. His worst fears were realized when the encampment appeared to be overrun by angry tribesmen. He dared not get any closer. The chance of survivors was almost nil. Once again, he was alone in this hostile world.

With no panic at all but with a sense of urgency, Bannar retreated. He moved deeper into the forest and angled toward the path. He did not have a definite plan but knew he had to apprise the Determiner of the situation and find Jake. He still had his mission and would not abandon it until he was either successful or dead.

℥ ℣

Thomas, Raj, and Elic were also in hiding. This time Elic's ability to sense danger had been spot on. He had called to the other two and told them about his feeling of impending trouble. They did not question him. They made ready and left their quarters. By the time the sound of alarm and the smell of smoke came, they were already out of the village. They thought it wise to avoid the path. They didn't know what had happened but felt certain they would be blamed if they were discovered leaving the village. They had left with just the essentials, including their weapons.

The smoke they smelled was now making its presence known as it billowed from the village. From the look of things, fire was spreading through the canopy and onto the ground.

There seemed to be movement all around them. Animals fled the fire and men moved through the area. Both could be dangerous. All the allies assessed the situation and came to the same conclusion: speed was more important than stealth. They broke cover and ran in the direction of the river and the gate. Raj brought up the rear, allowing Thomas and Elic, with their longer legs, to move on ahead. As they forged a path forward, he would guard the rear. If danger approached, he would sound an alarm.

⅘ ⅙

When he felt he was far enough from the village to stop, Bannar summoned the communiq and immediately connected to the Determiner. Bannar could see the anger in the Determiner's eyes and knew to proceed with care.

"Did Minister Molen arrive in time?" asked the Determiner.

"Molen is dead," Bannar said.

"What is the status of your mission?"

"All of Molen's men are also dead. The village chief, Dak, is dead. The village is on fire, and I am not in communication with the wizard."

"Do you think you can accomplish your mission in light of everything that has happened?"

Bannar knew there was only one answer to that question. "Yes, I'm trying to make contact with the wizard now."

"Do you need further assistance?"

"No, my lord. Time is of the essence now. We have a small window of time before success will become impossible."

"Make it happen, Major. I need you back here as soon as possible."

With that, the screen went black. Bannar resumed his search for Jake with the realization that this could be the last day of his life.

Chapter One Hundred Twenty-Six

"Did the others get out of the village?" asked Jake after Kathryn told him what she knew.

"I'm not sure," she said.

Jake could see she felt as if she had failed by not having an answer. Jake reached out and put his hand on her head, giving it a bit of a shake.

"We have to assume they have escaped. Gwynn, why don't you fly back toward the village? If you spot them, you can lead them to the gate. Kathryn, work your way back through the jungle. If you find them, let Gwynn know. We will all rendezvous at the gate. If they are still in the village, we will have to get them out."

Gwynn took flight and Kathryn moved off into the undergrowth. Jake watched them go. He had instructed Kathryn and Gwynn but was not sure what he should do. His hand began to cramp. He realized he was squeezing the staff with a death grip. Loosening his grip on the staff triggered a relaxing of his mind and body. Gwynn's statement of trust came back to him. He resolved to get them all back to The Farm. He heard something to the left of the path. He squared in that direction and leveled his staff. He thought maybe Kathryn was returning, but he would take no chances. He would not hesitate if he needed to use lethal force. He heard his name.

"Jake, don't shoot. It's Bannar."

Jake relaxed his grip but just slightly. Bannar stepped into sight with his hands in the air. His sword was sheathed, but there was blood on his hands.

Jake raised the tip of the staff to point toward Bannar's hands. "Do you want to tell me whose blood that is?"

Bannar relayed everything he knew of the situation. As he talked, Jake felt his hand tighten on the staff and his anger rise.

"Jake, if you are going to leave this place, it has to be soon. With Dak's death, our fate is sealed. We won't survive another day here."

"Did you see the others?"

"No, but I did see your quarters raided by angry tribesmen. No one was there."

Even as dire as the situation was, Jake felt relief wash over him. Maybe there was a chance for everyone.

Chapter One Hundred Twenty-Seven

Gwynn was trying to balance the urgency of getting to the village with trying to find her allies. As she neared the village, she could see and smell the smoke of still burning or smoldering fires. The noise level was intense and angry. She saw movement to her left. The trio was unmistakable. Thomas was a giant of a man. Raj was short and rotund but with an unmistakable look of power. Elic brought up the rear. He was tall, slight, and his head was disproportionally large for the rest of his body. They were moving at a brisk pace. She felt a moment of relief, but it didn't last long.

From her vantage point, she could see a group of tribesmen advancing along the path. They were dangerously close. The dense growth of the jungle was all that separated the two groups. She rose higher until she was just under the canopy. She would be harder to see. She drifted to the side, using as much stealth as she could. Fortunately, the tribesmen were so intent on finding their prey that they never looked up. Once she was out of the tribesmen's view, she flew until she overtook the fleeing allies. She had to warn them of the pursuit and direct them toward the gate. She swooped down to intercept them.

Kathryn had watched Gwynn stop in mid-air and hover. The action made Kathryn aware of the two groups. She knew Gwynn could warn the allies and take them to Jake must faster than she could. She would be of the most value trying to slow the pursuit of the tribesmen.

Kathryn broke away without letting her presence be known to the allies. She worked herself into a position in front of the tribesmen.

When they came into view, she let out what she hoped was a blood-curdling roar. It had the desired effect. The pursuit stopped. They assumed a defensive posture, looking about to find the danger. Having slipped away, Kathryn crossed to the other side of the path. After a pause, they began to slowly creep forward. When they came near her new position, she repeated the roar. Hearing the roar from their other side, the group again stopped. This time, the man in charge called two archers forward and had them prepare to let loose their arrows at the next roar. He also posted two at the back of the group. Each tribesman was on alert with spears ready. Again they resumed the hunt.

Kathryn tried to calculate how much time she had bought the group. One more attempt to stop them should be sufficient. She moved forward. It was time to be seen. She roared but this time followed by running into the path. She turned to face the group. They came to a halt but, just as she continued across the path, an arrow barely missed her from above. She retreated and turned to run but was stopped by another near miss.

She heard a flutter from the canopy above. The first archer crashed to the ground, falling at the feet of the leader. Before they could sort out what had happened, a second archer crashed into the center of the group, knocking several tribesmen, including the leader, to the forest floor. Gwynn flew toward the gate. Kathryn didn't stay to see how fast the villagers would recover. She set out at a full run.

Chapter One Hundred Twenty-Eight

Bannar heard the commotion before Jake. He drew his sword and turned to face the thicker part of the jungle. It was good that he turned away because Jake was bringing the staff to bear. If Bannar had remained facing Jake with sword in hand, he may have been blasted from existence. Jake now heard the noise and turned to target the direction of the disturbance.

Thomas was first to be seen followed closely by Raj and Elic. They saw Bannar first, and each man reached for his weapon. Jake's voice defused the situation.

"Stand down; we've got a short distance to cover to reach the gate."

He was about to inquire about Gwynn and Kathryn when Gwynn came in just under the trees. She drifted down and hovered just above their heads.

"They are right behind us. Kathryn bought us some time, but we have to hurry if we're going to make it."

She rose to lead the way just as Kathryn burst through the undergrowth. Her black coat was glistening from a combination of her expended efforts and running through the underbrush. Jake thought he saw a few drops of blood standing atop her fur but couldn't be sure. She remained in feline form as they turned to go. Gwynn was leading them back to the path. Kathryn and Bannar brought up the rear. With his staff at the ready, Jake fell in behind Gwynn. He only had to look at Elic to know how dire the situation was.

They reached the river. Jake thought they were close to the point where it was safe to ford. They all leapt into the river. The depth of the water was high but still manageable. Raj was having the hardest time because of his height and girth. He regained his feet and, with his chin just above water, started forward. They all made for the far side. The riverbed was deep sand, which slowed their advance. When they reached the other bank, Bannar and Thomas pulled Raj out. They ran the short distance to the gate. Kathryn, who had crossed the river in human form to avoid the feline disdain for water, was the last to join them. Gwynn stood at the gate.

They all gathered there. Jake came to the front, oriented the staff vertically, and made ready to transport. Bannar stepped to the side. Jake invited him to transport, but he said he couldn't. Movement caught everyone's eyes. The tribesmen were on the other side of the river. Archers lined the far bank. Thomas and Elic stepped in front of Jake just as the arrows were loosed. Many fell short but Jake saw one hit Elic in the shoulder. Thomas must have been hit too because he staggered to the side. Jake shifted the position of his staff to be used as a weapon against the attack.

"No, Jake. Go now," Bannar yelled as he turned to charge the oncoming warriors. He took a line that put him directly in front of Jake and the others. Raj had stepped forward and pulled Thomas back into the group. It was now or never. Jake pulled the staff to his chest.

ﻼ　　ﻼ

Bannar ran toward the hostile warriors. He had no plan. He knew he was about to die, but at least his mission would be successful. He waved his sword above his head, determined that he would go out with dignity and honor. He reached the river without being hit. Arrows were pointed at him like accusing fingers. He was ready.

His chance came when the others disappeared. Not knowing anything of teleportation, the tribesmen must have thought the disappearance to be magic. They were confused and mesmerized enough to hesitate in their attack. Being a soldier, Bannar's first reaction was to use their confusion to charge his enemy. Being a human and wanting to live, he took those moments to summon the communiq. The eyes of the warriors returned to Bannar just in time to see him too disappear.

കൂ ൽ

Jake could not be sure where they were. He hoped they were back in the land of The Farm. He looked around for his allies. They had all made it. Gwynn and Kathryn stood over Thomas, who had two arrows protruding from his chest. Jake could not tell if he was dead or alive. Elic was upright but wounded. Elic and Raj ran toward him. He rolled over to get up and was struck by the most severe pain he had ever experienced. He looked at his legs and saw the shaft of an arrow sticking out of his thigh. His pants were soaked in blood. Everything went black.

Chapter One Hundred Twenty-Nine

The old sorcerer stood leaning on his cane. He had been lost in thought for a few minutes. The Determiner tried to be patient, but it was becoming more difficult.

"Lord Locklan, were you able to find the spell we spoke of yesterday?"

"Oh, yes, I was able to invoke it. I first cast the spell of temporal stasis some fifty years ago. It was one of your father's favorites."

The Determiner was going to ask if there had been any problem since Jamal's untimely death, but Locklan had drifted into one of his absent states of being.

Instead of trying to pursue this rather one-sided conversation, The Determiner said, "Thank you, Lord Locklan. I will let you get back to your other work."

The old man's eyes focused, and it looked as if he were really trying to remember what they had been talking about.

"With your permission, Lord High Determiner, I'll get back to my quarters. I have some other work to do."

With great effort, the Determiner fought back his anger. He sat in silence. The old sorcerer took the silence to be permission to leave. He hobbled to the door and was gone.

The Determiner summoned his Supreme Protectors. He had to look in on the two Lokins wizards himself. If the old sorcerer's magic was still viable, they would be asleep. If not, they would be dead. He didn't know which situation would be the better outcome for him. He had spent a lot of time considering the situation. Major Bannar had successfully completed his mission and made it back unscathed. Jamal had been the one to persuade him to save the Lokins boy rather than kill him. Now Jamal was dead.

He left the protectors at the dungeon level and proceeded to the vaults alone.

Although Jamal's plan was that of a traitor, he had tried to use the details of it to save his head. The plan held merit if the Determiner could bring it to fruition. Gaining power by robbing the Society of Builders and the three Lokins wizards of their powers would be a poetic coup. If the Lokins wizards had survived Jamal's death, he would act. As soon as Jake Lokins left The Farm, he would mobilize Major Bannar. His mission going forth would be to deliver Jake Lokins and his mother or to kill Jake Lokins.

Standing in front of the two vaults, he felt both excitement and a sense of dread. He pulled the vaults open. The two bodies looked as if they had shifted. They had definitely started to regain consciousness. The Determiner moved in for a closer look. Although they may have partially regained consciousness, they now rested in a deep sleep. They were very much alive. The senile old sorcerer had done it.

Chapter One Hundred Thirty

Jake awoke in stages. First, the scent of bacon frying in a cast iron skillet worked its way into his consciousness. Next, he heard his mother's voice. Many mornings, she would let him sleep until breakfast was ready. She would sometimes sing or talk on the phone while she cooked. The cover was pulled up under his chin, and he felt as if he were in his own bed in the house he and his mother had shared. He wouldn't want to be called. As he rolled to get out of bed, the pain he felt brought him completely awake. Raised railings blocked the sides of the bed. He had an IV tube running from his right arm. He was in a hospital somewhere. The feeling of emptiness and despair he felt was worse than the physical pain. For a brief time, things had seemed normal, and he was back home. To find that it was only an illusion was heartbreaking.

"Good morning, Jake. Welcome to the land of the living."

He lifted his head and saw Kathryn sitting in the corner chair. She was tastefully dressed and beautiful. Her smile was breathtaking. This was the first time Jake acknowledged such a thought, although he knew he must have noticed before.

"How long have I been here?"

"This is the third day. You lost a lot of blood and were very weak by the time we got you here."

"How are the others?"

Before she could answer, the door opened and his mother entered the room followed by a giant being. Her companion and the nature of her dress confirmed Jake's certainty of not being home. She rushed to his bedside, bent, and pulled him to her.

"I'm so glad to see you," said Jake as she kissed first his forehead and then his cheek. He felt tears forming and threatening to flow. This was probably not part of the accepted behavior of a society wizard, but he didn't care.

"I'm happy and thankful to see you too, son. We had no idea that things would escalate so fast when you left for The Farm."

Jake thought that an odd thing to say, but when he tried to ask her she sidestepped the question. She said she needed to leave but would be back soon. With that, she disappeared through the door, followed by her mysterious and yet to be introduced companion. He decided not to dwell on it.

Turning back to Kathryn, Jake asked, "How are the others?"

She stepped to the side of his bed. "Raj, Gwynn, and I are fine. Maybe a few bruises but nothing much. Elic is recovering and should be fine soon, but his return to The Farm was not received well by everyone. Thomas got the worst of it. He is still in critical condition but is expected to recover. We thought for a while we might lose the both of you."

"What do you mean that Elic was not received well?"

"It's rare for someone to leave the Society. Elic was granted permission by Randolph Meekins. It was understood that he would neither reveal his association with the Society nor try to return. He has violated both. The four of us spoke for him, talking about his part in helping us return home. The issue is being considered, but I think it's you they want to hear from."

"My decision was made before we left the world of the fae."

Katheryn left it at that.

"Who was that with my mother?"

"That is Metach. He is Senagon. They are fierce and live but to serve. Their traditional role within the Society is the protection of our elders and members of the governing bodies. Most of the time, you don't see them, but they are always present. Suffice it to say that your mother is well protected now that she has taken her place here."

"What is her place here?"

"She sits on the Council of Elders and takes responsibility for the assignment of allies to wizards. It was she who chose us to be a team when we were young."

"Did you know it was her?"

"No, we were only told that when we got back."

"I still don't understand why we were not always here?"

"I'm not the one who can or should answer that. We only knew that you and she were allowed to live away from The Farm until it was deemed appropriate for you to take your place."

"Is it common for families to live away from The Farm?"

"You are the only one of the 'true born' children that I know of having left The Farm."

"True born children?"

Kathryn had gotten in over her head but continued, "Babies who are born who are in the lineage of originals. You are a third-generation wizard. You are very powerful. All of us knew that we were waiting for our wizard to come but none of us knew you would be true born."

It was clear to Jake that Kathryn was uncomfortable with some of his questions. His queries were curtailed when a nurse came into his room. She took his vital signs and then introduced something from a syringe into his IV. He was asleep before she left the room.

Chapter One Hundred Thirty-One

Jake was awakened by something striking the door of his room. Too groggy to be startled, he turned his head toward the door. Gwynn came into his room, pushing what he could only equate to a wheelchair. A nurse followed. She came to his bed and started removing his IV and monitors. She was a solidly built woman with a face that betrayed no emotion. She readied the chair and lowered the rail on his bed. Before he could make a move, she swept him up like a child and deposited him into the chair. Without a word, she turned and left.

"I thought you might like to get out of the room. Thomas is conscious now, so maybe you'd like to see him," Gwynn said.

"I'd like that."

"Mr. Meekins wants to see all of us within the hour," she said, almost as an afterthought.

Jake had not looked in a mirror, so he had no idea of his appearance, but when he went into Thomas's room he was shocked. Thomas seemed to have lost at least a third of his bulk. Jake knew that was not possible in such a short time, but the difference was dramatic. Thomas was propped up on several pillows. He made a gallant effort to smile when he saw Jake, but it looked more like a grimace. Jake could sympathize.

"It's good to see you," Thomas said with a rasp. "I didn't know if we would make it or not."

"I wouldn't have made it if you hadn't stepped in front of those arrows."

"You don't look like you came out unscathed."

They both had a laugh. Rather than compare wounds, they talked about how happy they were to be back at The Farm. After a few more minutes, Gwynn stood and reminded Jake of the meeting. Each man said their goodbyes and promised to talk again soon.

Gwynn wheeled Jake to what he remembered was the conference room. Although they were expected, Gwynn stopped at the door and knocked. After they were acknowledged and told to enter, she pushed the door open and rolled him through.

Randolph Meekins was seated at the end of the table. Mr. Alphonse sat to his right and Jake's mother was on the left. Next on the right were Elic, Raj, and Kathryn. A space for his wheelchair and a seat for Gwynn remained open on the left. After everyone was seated, Mr. Meekins stood. Over his clothes, he wore a long scarlet robe with large flowing sleeves. Mr. Alphonse had on a similar garment in blue. Jake's mother wore a red robe. Jake found himself a bit uncomfortable at what looked and felt like a formal conference.

"Jake, after each mission, we gather to discuss the assignment and the outcome of that endeavor. You were not given a mission but managed to find one for yourself."

Jake was not sure if Meekins' words were intended as a simple statement or a rebuke. He chose to remain silent.

"When we were last in this room, I expected you to take a few days at home and return to The Farm. Once back, you were to be assessed and either given more training or sent on basic assignments. Instead, you have been gone for several months and have had quite an adventure."

Jake looked from Mr. Meekins to Mr. Alphonse and finally to his mother. All of them wore a somber facial expression. He wished he were back in his hospital bed.

"Mr. Meekins, if I did anything wrong, I apologize. I didn't have a lot of experience, but I felt circumstances called for my decisions and the actions of our team," Jake said. "I had to find my mother."

"Yes, we are happy to have both of you here, where you have always belonged. What happened was unfortunate. In any case, it seems you handled yourself well. You had some protection from a very unlikely source."

"I don't understand that myself. I was fortunate to have Elic to warn me about the Determiner. I had no idea of any of it. After the death of Seamus, Elic presented himself and offered his help. Without him, our outcome could have been very different."

Meekins took his time, looking from one of the allies to the next. His eyes fell on Elic.

"Elic, you asked to be relieved from your duties to this Society. This is not a matter to be taken lightly. Contrary to my better judgment, I granted you your wish. I thought we would never have the occasion to speak again, yet here we are."

Elic said nothing but his gaze fell to the tabletop.

Jake stood and said, "Mr. Meekins, I don't know about your history with Elic, but I do know about my history with him. I have and will trust him with my life. I guess I received help from two unlikely sources, Elic and Bannar. I don't know why either came to be available, but I am thankful. In the end, Bannar helped us get home, probably at the expense of his life."

"It has come to my attention that Bannar survived and has been made Minister of Arms. We can talk of all that later. As to Elic, he will become your permanent and lifelong ally."

Jake settled back into his wheelchair. He was exhausted and weak, but he was also elated. He couldn't help but notice the smile on the face of each of his allies. Jake had questions but knew that now was not the time to ask them. Neither Mr. Alphonse nor his mother had spoken.

Mr. Meekins almost smiled. He said, "I am told that you will be well enough for duty within the month. At that time, I have a mission for you."

With that, Mr. Meekins stood, motioned to Mr. Alphonse, and they left the room. Jake's mother stood and dismissed the allies. Only she and Jake remained.

"I know you must have a lot of questions," she said. "Our history as a family is very complex. You deserve to hear it at some point, but now your only concern should be your own recovery. You will need to be strong."

Before he could say anything, she stood and walked to his side. She bent, hugged him, and placed a kiss on his cheek.

"Thank you for coming after me. You were very brave."

"Mom, I…"

"Shhh," she said as she kissed him again. "I will tell you everything—soon."

He didn't know how to feel. His mother appeared to be a different person. She had always tried to make him understand anything he had questions about, but now she seemed stronger and more driven. She stepped behind his chair, helped him around, and started back toward his room.

The nurse was waiting outside his room. His mother stopped short of the door. She knelt beside his chair, rubbed his hair with a gentle hand, and whispered, "I love you, son."

"I love you too, Mom."

She motioned to the nurse, turned, and walked in the direction from which they came.

EPILOGUE

The road was almost a part of Jake's DNA. He had traveled it to and from his home for his entire life. He looked to his left as he passed the field where he and Randolph Meekins had first transitioned to the world of The Farm. He wondered if the gate was still active. He would check the posit when he got back to their headquarters.

Jake had visited the site several times since being assigned to this world. He drove past the house, looking for any activity or movement, human or otherwise. He had yet to see any signs of movement. The most troubling thing was that he had seen no signs of habitation anywhere along the road. This time of year, there should be activity in the fields and gardens of each homestead. He had not even seen any livestock.

He had not gone inside his or any of the other houses. He needed to get back to their residence in rural Orange County soon, so he knew that again today he would not go inside. He had been told by Mr. Alphonse, Mr. Meekins, and his mother that it was not safe to go into the house he had grown up in or even to be spotted near it. Despite the warnings, he had to see it for himself.

❧　☙

As time passed in the hospital, he had healed and grown stronger. He was given a physical therapy program, which grew in intensity as he progressed. Finally, he was called back into the conference room.

As before, Randolph Meekins, Mr. Alphonse, and his mother were there. He had expected that the team of allies would be present, but they were not. There was only one open chair at the table, so he took it.

"Jake, up until now, all of your actions and decisions have been a result of impulse and circumstance," said Randolph Meekins. "There will always be the need to think on your feet and to adapt to changing circumstances. Be that as it may, having a specific assignment with guidelines and parameters is not only more effective but it is safer for your team and any civilians around you. With that in mind, are you ready to accept your next assignment?"

"Yes, Mr. Meekins, I am. If I have done anything wrong in the past, I apologize."

"You did well—under the circumstances."

Before anything else could be said, Meekins and Jake's mother stood and left the room.

Mr. Alphonse motioned for Jake to take the seat beside him.

"Jake, you and your team will be going back to your home world. On that world, there has always been a veil that kept the people from having to deal with a lot of the creatures they have only known in their nightmares. That veil has been breached. There is a lot of paranormal activity taking place, and the authorities are having a difficult time understanding and explaining it away. Right now, a lot of it is centralized around the cities near your old house. We believe the attack on you during your leave marked the beginning of their activities.

Your assignment will be to curtail any of the activities you encounter and to eliminate the perpetrators—all as discreetly as possible. You will need and be provided modern weapons and transportation. Gwynn will have the use of a more modern posit. Ultimately, we want you to find the core of their operation and report back to us.

"Jake, we think your old house and others near it are being used by these forces. Therefore, you cannot go back to your house. Right now, the element of surprise is on your side. Try to keep it that way. You have been set up in a rural area of the county adjoining yours. You will operate from there. One word of warning. We don't know yet if these activities are in any way to be attributed to the Determiner. If you see Minister Bannar or any other troops that might be dispatched by the Determiner, do not be taken in."

ജ ൽ

Jake could not dismiss a feeling of nostalgia. He pulled his car into the edge of a driveway, backed out to turn around, and headed back to Orange County. A plan of action was forming, and he was eager to share it with the others.

He had not noticed the parting of the curtains nor the yellow eyes marking his presence.

ജ ൽ

To Be Continued in Book 2